The Oracle of Malcontent

Athenaeum of Assierium series
Book 1

Jason Wylie

BLACK LABEL BOOKS

The Continent of Azarth

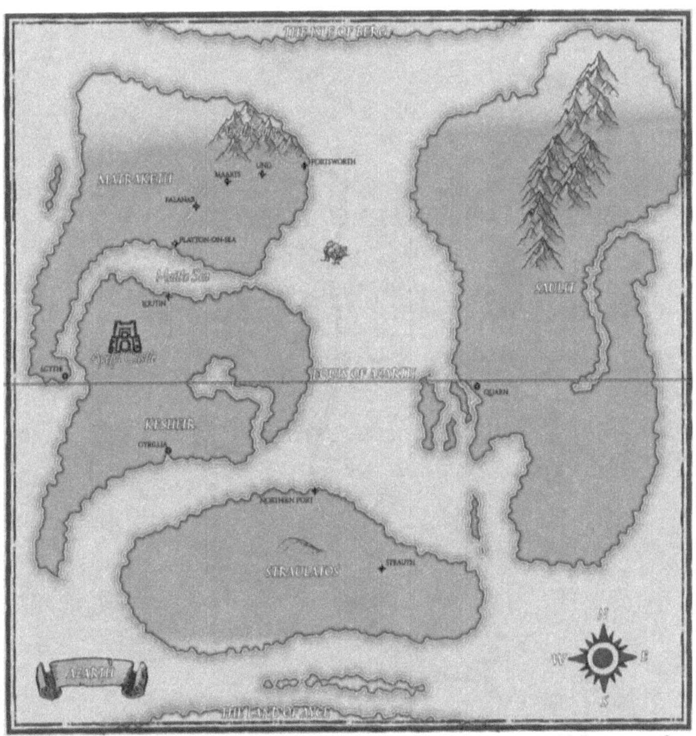

Map Drawn and Annotated by Death-Elect nee Pthorn of Strauth throughout his travels in his second turn following Initiation.

Notes: The Land of Ayce and The Isle of Berg is yet uncharted and are only approximate based on maps found in the Archive.

Other books by Jason Wylie

ATHENAEUM OF ASSIERIUM SERIES (Adult Fiction)
1. The Oracle of Malcontent
2. The Oracle of Beauty (Coming Soon)
3. The Oracle of Prevail (Coming Soon)
4. The Oracle of Anew (Coming Soon)

THE ROYAL CHATTELS SERIES (Middle Grade)
1. The Serpent Crown (Coming Soon)
2. The Songbox of Creativity (Coming Soon)
3. The Sabre of Combat (Coming Soon)
4. The Sceptre of Life (Coming Soon)

The Royal Chattels series is set in the same world as the Athenaeum of Assierium series

Black Label Books
ABN: 19 631 806 202
www.blacklabelbooks.com

First published in 2023 by Black Label Books
Revision 1, 2023 – Minor typographical corrections
Text, cover illustrations, and graphics copyright © 2023, Jason Wylie
Cover smoke graphic - Robert Zunikoff (rzunikoff) used under free Unsplash licence
Cover illustrations by Jason Wylie
Graphics by Jason Wylie

National Library of Australia and State Library of Queensland Cataloguing-in-Publication entry
Wylie, Jason, 1991–
    The Oracle of Malcontent.
    Paperback – ISBN 978-1-922990-00-6
    Hardcover – ISBN 978-1-922990-01-3
    Ebook – ISBN 978-1-922990-02-0
    I. Title. (Series: Wylie, Jason, 1991– Athenaeum of Assierium; 1)

Typeset in Calibri
Printed by IngramSpark

Firstly, this book is dedicated to family, both found and blood. Dedicated to the parents and grandparents who raised me, the friends who have stuck by me, my wife who has always supported me, and the kids who give me every joy in the world.

Secondly, this book is dedicated to those who inspired me to write. Amongst many others, Eoin Colfer as a kid and Brandon Sanderson as an adult.

Author's Note

Welcome to my debut novel, The Oracle of Malcontent!

I can assure you that this has been quite the journey. It all started when I was barely old enough to understand the concept of a publisher; ironically, I thought that an author and a publisher were the same entity, and here I am today, being just that. At the mature age of ten, I had my own publishing house, "Jason Press Publishing," or JPP, as I affectionately referred to it. I would write such short novellas as "The dinosaur who went puff" (refer to my Instagram for this gem), and many others simply lost to time.

Over the years, I tried my hand at writing many things, and unsurprisingly, they all failed. I would write a few chapters and then simply give up when the creative juices became less juicy and more crispy. Most of my previous attempts had been contemporary fiction rather than fantasy, but I realised that wasn't even my genre of choice for reading, let alone writing.

"So! How did you get here?" I hear you ask.

Well, since you asked, I finally stumbled on a great idea in the form of a meme that I thought was funny. While I cannot remember nor find the meme again, one sentence gave me the inspiration I needed to create a story. My daughter, Aria, was about a week old, and I was sleep deprived. I was up at all hours of the night and needed a way to keep my mind awake... so I started writing my story.

The first chapter I wrote was the first interlude. I immediately realised how much I enjoyed Tom's character but found that he wouldn't be the right person to tell the story. I quickly realised that the obvious choice for a protagonist was Pthorn, and thus, Athenaeum of Assierium was born.

I do have two favours to ask of you.

Firstly, I have made every attempt possible to be grammatically consistent and avoid continuity errors; however, I am but one person with a laptop. If you find any errors, please feel free to reach out to me via email, socials or village messenger for any corrections; please don't report via Amazon.

Secondly, if you bought a hard copy of this book and think, "I probably won't read this again," please donate it to someone else who may. A state library or local book nook might appreciate something new to share.

I now leave you in the hands of Pthorn's personal narrator... enjoy!

Contents

Prologue

The last time he had walked through the door, he had done so as a boy.

He had been utterly naïve to the world and the horrors that lurked outside of the house he had grown up in.

This time he entered as a man. A god. Where he went, death was never far away.

He did not know what he expected upon his return, but it certainly was not this.

He felt numb and confused.

Thoughts began to come slowly, and time seemed to pass in waves.

The house was empty.

The austere furniture he had grown up with was still in place, but it was devoid of life, save the orbite webs, and a thick layer of dust had begun to take hold of the room.

The house felt cold, and he felt a shiver pass through his body.

What has happened here? Where are they?

The young man made his way towards the rear of the house, and as he peered into the first room, he found a mirror; his drawn face reflected right back at him.

He had spent hours of his youth staring into it for entertainment, pretending he could see his future or some sort of hidden secret within its silvery reflection.

Today he saw exactly that. Within the face that stared back at him, he saw two people; the man he was and the man he would become.

The second face was one he had already met without realising he had been staring at his future.

The mirror shattered into a million pieces before his eyes as his balled fist returned to his side. Bright red droplets crashed to the floor.

Betrayal.

Loss.

Anger.

Hate.

The young man's reflection was replaced by the water-stained wood that had formed the mirror's backing.

He moved to the second room, and within, he found a letter carefully placed in the centre of the bed. The yellowed letter was neatly folded, and he knew the author at once.

He looked closer and found it was addressed to him and sealed using a sticky gum; they had been too poor to be able to afford stamping wax.

The man broke the seal and unfolded the letter, hoping to find any clue as to why the house was empty.

A ring fell to the floor. It bounced on the edge of the sleeping pallet as it made its journey downwards.

His blood smeared the rough, cheap paper.

A single tear welled in the corner of his eye as he read it line by line.

There was no closure in his mother's words, only empty goodbyes and more questions. Things he already knew, or at very least suspected, were confirmed.

A father's shame, a mother's love, and the loss of his family.

He let the note fall to the hardwood floor; it swooped silently as it fell, then came to rest.

He moved back into the common area and exited the house through the kitchen.

Outside he found everything his mother and father had worked for gone to seed or rotted.

The crops were dead.

The grass was dead.

Everything from the life he had once known was dead.

He walked back into the house he had once called home, picked up the ring, and held it close to his chest. He knew there was only one remaining path for him.

Revenge.

War.

Death.

Part 1

1.
Life on the Farm

hile I firmly believe that if there was a competition for lazy gits sitting in fields, you would be the winning candidate, what I really need from you right now is for you to get up off your arse and plough some dirt!"

Pthorn's father always had a way with his words when he bothered to use them.

It was the middle of summer, and it was sweltering. Sweat beads glistened on the young man's head, and he could feel them as they slowly coalesced and cascaded down his spine. His duty for today was to plough an overgrown, grassy field in the northeastern corner of his parent's farm to begin preparations for fertilising the soil. His father had recently expanded the crop farming business after a steep decline in the demand for high-quality meats. The local priests had said something about a disease that had scared a lot of the wealthy meat consumers off.

By contrast, crops were bland; nothing was interesting about planting and irrigating a field. At least with animals, you could tend to them and prepare them for slaughter when the time came. They never did that part themselves on the farm; a nomadic caravan would collect the livestock and transfer them for the kill.

Pthorn continued to reminisce but made himself get up off the tree stump he had sat upon, gave his father a weak smile, and then remounted the wooden plough behind the giant mant. The beast was a large, shelled creature that could pull its own weight fifty times over. The hard shell was a slick, glossy black, and each piece overlapped the next to cover most of the soft body parts. The mant had a longish neck with a bulbous-shelled head and eyes that protruded from the end of black stalks; unless you looked closely, it was hard to see where the stalk finished and the eyeball commenced. Its six long spindly legs protruded from its carapace-covered body and back down to the ground like an oversized insect.

To control such a beast, a harness was attached to the neck, right at the base where it jutted from the main body shell. It was here that the mant had its weakness. A weakness of softer skin, which, with the aid of a few sharp spurs, could be manipulated to get the beast to do heavy, and menial work. While mants were gigantic and slow, if one decided that it was no longer under the control of a master, it could become extremely dangerous. Trampling-related deaths were not uncommon during the harnessing or de-harnessing processes, or so he had been led to believe by his father.

Pthorn's father, simply known to him as Father, returned his smile with a scowl of disgust before he mounted his own mant-plough and gave the harness a harsh tug. The spiteful man ambled off in the direction of the homestead. Somehow Pthorn had never quite lived up to the expectations that Father set.

After settling himself into the ploughman's seat, Pthorn pulled a lever to drop the tynes and gave his reins a sharp tug. Slowly his beast lowered its head and body, lifted a leg and started to move forward. The plough assigned to him by his father was the oldest piece of machinery that Pthorn believed existed in the entire continent of Straulatos. The linkages had finger-width clearances and rattled furiously as the tynes furrowed through the ground. Often, the mechanism which held the tynes in place would jump out of position and result in a sharp forward movement by the mant. Pthorn had been thrown from the plough several times, all of which were away from the mant and moving plough, "Thank Assier!"

Pthorn's mind was on the holiday celebration happening the next day; Assierium. Assierium was not only the name of the religion of Azarth, but it was also the name of a day in which they celebrated their God and all of creation. It had become a tradition in the local village of Strauth to have an Assierium Festival. The local priests oversaw the event to ensure the day was observed in a holy fashion. During one of his few visits to the village, Pthorn witnessed that most families hung decorations and torches around their houses, often making the shape of the four-pointed star of Aiel, the prophet of Assier. For many, though, he had heard it was just an excuse to drink large quantities of liquor or partake in the consumption of other substances to change one's consciousness and become wildly rowdy. The clergy and his father severely frowned upon anything of the sort.

Celebrations were mild in his family home, ruled over by his tyrannical father. His kind-hearted mother would weave a star from dried crops grown in their field and lay it on the mantle with four candles placed in front of it to symbolise the four faces of Assier. Every year, in pure indulgence, Father procured a single smoked leg of wild-caught onk to accompany the nightly meal of thin broth, though he ensured that he saved the choicest cut for himself. It was both this meat and the single gift he would be given that gave Pthorn any hope this time each year.

Every year Mother sang to the family softly; she had a beautiful voice. As he had grown up, she had always sung lullabies to him before bed, and she had even tried to teach him some one day. Father had overheard his attempt, and he was told instantly that singing did not become a man and that he should "shut his maw and go quietly".

Last year he had received the traditional gift for a young man of eight-and-ten turns; a golden ring with a single gem inset into the band. Usually, this would be an extravagance; however, the gift is not given to the man himself. At the age of eight-and-ten, a boy becomes a man and is expected to soon find a woman with whom he will spend the rest of his life. The Nameday Ring is given as a gift to the man's wife during their nuptials as a sign of blessing from the man's parents and shows that a man is willing to give up one of his more valuable possessions. His ring had pride-of-place atop the dresser in his room; it still sat lightly within the softly padded box it had come in.

This turn, Pthorn did not know what to expect. His father's increasing displeasure at the sight of his son didn't instil much hope in Pthorn that he would receive much in the way of a gift.

The sun had just touched the horizon to the west when Pthorn pulled left on the reins. He raised the tynes on the plough and started the journey back towards the homestead. Father had already left him to finish up for the day by himself. The mant slowly ambled along the hard-clay thoroughfare between crop fields; the sun was almost entirely extinguished when he reached his destination. There was a stable to the rear of the homestead, which housed the two mants owned by his father.

Pthorn uncoupled the mant from the plough and led the beast into a stall; he topped up the slops tray with a bucket of mash. Next, he picked up a cloth and a bucket of shell polish and began to clean and buff his beast to a high gleam. His father had constantly reinforced that this helped keep the mant's shell clean and prevent the build-up of scale; plus, it was the last remaining nod to the livestock that he had previously tended with his father. When he finished, he locked up the stables and made his way into the homestead proper through the back door.

Mother stood in the old country kitchen, slaving over the range. Pthorn noted the large pot of the night's broth was already on to boil.

Pthorn looked over to his mother as he entered. She was a frail, thin woman, aged and weather-worn from the time spent at work around the farm and the home; there was beauty in her hard-earned lines and kind eyes, which were almost always there to meet him as he entered a room. He couldn't see them today, though.

"There are some of Assier's men here; they are waiting in the lounge," Mother announced as she heard him enter the room. She didn't turn, she chose instead to hide those eyes from him, but Pthorn swore he heard a sniff as though she had been crying. Pthorn had come to learn this wasn't uncommon, but she always waited for moments of solitude before she released her emotions, lest she encumbered Pthorn with the burdens of her life.

He made his way past the kitchen through to the lounge room. He tried not to feel the weight of her emotion, not let her see that he knew.

The lounge room was simple; no paper or decoration adorned the walls. An old potbellied stove sat in the centre of the room; it was used sparingly for warmth during the colder times of the year. Only one chair sat in the room, an old armchair rescued from a wealthier family in the local village a long time ago. When the family spent time together, Father sat in the chair while Mother and Pthorn sat on the threadbare rug in the centre of the room.

The chair was exactly where he found his father this evening; the man looked even more stern than usual.

What wasn't usual were the two men who stood across the room from him. They looked serious and uninviting. Father looked far from impressed at the presence of their visitors; his eyes were piercing and unkind.

"Sit, boy!" said the first priest. "Do you know what tomorrow is?"

"Yes," Pthorn responded. "Tomorrow is Assierium."

"While correct, that is not what I am referring to. Tomorrow is forty turns since the last Choosing. That means that the High Priest of Straulatos will attend a village as seen in a vision from Assier and hold a Choosing ceremony. Every boy or girl between eight-and-ten and twenty turns within three leagues of that village will have to attend the ceremony."

The first priest paused to let the news sink in, and the second continued, "Pthorn. The High Priest has given word that this village was foreseen as having one of the next Chosen Four. You will attend the ceremony tomorrow; your parents can accompany you to the village, but once there, you will stand alone with your peers."

The first priest started again, "If you are Chosen as one of the Four, you will have the greatest honour of a generation. You will leave your current life and join Assier as one of his Most Devout. Do you have any questions?"

Pthorn considered for a few moments, "What do you mean by 'leave your current life and join Assier?'

It sounds like you are going to lead me away to be killed! And what exactly is a 'Most Devout' anyway?"

"Well, um, no, of course not, and a 'Most Devout' is someone who has the greatest honour of being one of the high servants of Assier," the first priest said, as he stumbled slightly over his words, not sounding very convincing.

Given his lack of direct answer, Pthorn suspected that the priest had no idea what would become of him should he be Chosen but thought he would try again, "yes, but what do they do?"

"They, um, well…" the priest attempted to answer before Father's patience finally ran out.

"I think that is enough questions, young man." He announced before he dismissed the pair of clergymen.

They both made to leave through the door before one turned for a final blessing, "may the Almighty Assier look fondly upon you and shower you with his blessings. In the name of the Singular, his true form Assier and the prophet Aiel."

Pthorn had always known his father to follow the traditions of the Assierian religion unfailingly but had never shown any signs of belief. In fact, he had always shown a high level of contempt for the faithful.

After the two men had left, Father turned back to Pthorn from his chair.

"Now is the time for you to act like a man, and while I don't believe for a second that any self-respecting God would choose someone as pitiful as you to join him as one of his 'Most Devout'."

He enunciated the title with the same level of contempt that he always set aside for the clergy.

"You must not embarrass our family at the ceremony."

Pthorn could tell that his father was far more concerned with his family's honour than his son's future. He couldn't help but feel hurt, but he was used to feeling that way around his father.

"I will do us proud, Father; I will speak only when spoken to and act as you would," Pthorn responded as his father would expect.

"Now go back and help your mother bring my dinner in; I'm starving."

Dinner was consumed in relative silence, like typical family meals at home. Father was the only one allowed to break the silence when he wanted to announce updates to the family about the state of crop and beast farming in the region. After dinner, Mother moved to the kitchen to scrub the dishes while Pthorn left his father and made his way to his room. His room was very small, just large enough to house a small, child-sized sleeping pallet. The pallet had been his bed for as long as he could remember; Father had never seen fit to upgrade the size of the furniture as he had grown. The sheets were threadbare linen, and the padding was straw which had been replaced every few weeks to prevent mould.

Pthorn removed his soiled work clothes and placed them in a pile at the foot of the sleeping pallet. His mother would wash the clothes the next day and return them to his room. It was not as though there would be much to clean; his clothes more closely resembled a dress than formal work wear. No small clothes and just a simple brown robe with a rope cinched around the waist. Mother always made the clothes he wore, hand sewn in broad stitches. Linen and thread were considered to be an expensive staple to the family, so clothes were always worn until they could no longer be patched or no longer could be modified to fit.

Completely naked except for the last few days of soil from the farm, Pthorn made his way to the bed, pulled back the single sheet, and crawled in. He closed his eyes to sleep.

He opened his eyes.

Assier's hairy arse crack! Why can I not sleep? Pthorn thought to himself. *There is no chance I could be the only person on Straulatos to be chosen to be... whatever the Most Devout is; not even the farmin' priests could answer my question about that!*

His eyes tried to focus on the bare wooden roof above his head as he counted the thin, silky webs from the ten-legged orbites which spun their homes from the rafters above. Twelve silvery nets were cast across the joists without a single orbite to be seen. Not that he would see much in the middle of the night, all light after dark was man-made; with no sun to light the world, torches and reflected light was all they had. He had heard stories of far-off lands that had light throughout the night; his only thought on this night was that it certainly wouldn't help his current sleep-related predicament.

Sleep continued to be evasive. Pthorn removed himself from the bed and made his way through the house towards the back door. Naked as his Nameday, he continued out into the night. There was no need to cover up as there wasn't another soul, except his parents, within a thousand paces of the homestead. It was also very dark. Neither of the two moons shone more than a sliver of light at the best of times, and tonight was no exception. Like a pair of squinting eyes, Ariathea and Noahadrian just peered through the darkness. A single torch mounted in the centre of the yard, the only source of light by which to navigate.

Animal fat was used as the fuel source and was one of the few luxuries allowed by his father in the event that emergency lighting was ever needed during the night; he used to exchange it with the livestock caravan at minimal cost, but since the disappearance of the meat trade locally it had become harder, and more expensive, to source. In recent times his father would light it later, and get up earlier, to extinguish it.

The light cast from the torch lit up a surprising distance, contrasted primarily by just how dark it was outside. This single torch had enough light to allow the family to find their way through the house and stables without walking into every wall. The open roofline and windows on the eastern end of the building allowed light to filter in almost entirely unobstructed.

Pthorn crept across the yard until he got to the stable. He reached up to a ladder and climbed into the hay-keep on the mezzanine. This was his quiet spot within his corner of Azarth, where he could sit and stare at the blackness above uninterrupted. The gable of the stable roof had a small round port window that faced the northern fields. He walked across the mezzanine, sat on a bale facing the window, and stared into the distance.

The village was southwest of the homestead; Pthorn recognised the dull glow in the distance from various fires used for lighting. The light was easy to see in the pitch black of the night. He hadn't spent much time in the village and barely left the farm except when he ran various errands for the family. His father believed that his time was far better spent tilling the soil, planting crops, and feeding beasts around the farm rather than spending time in the village with other locals his age. Formal education was entirely out of the question, but his saint of a mother had taught him all that she knew to teach. His education was the bare minimum required to survive as a farmer. That said, Mother made sure that Pthorn was well articulated with his language. She always said it would serve him well to act as a professional businessman in the future, just like his father, although Pthorn wasn't entirely sure that his father could read that well himself.

His future would be simple. His parents would soon find him a woman, he would be married, and he would live with his new wife in a currently vacant homestead on the farm. It had been a tradition for generations that the two homesteads would become the marital home in an alternating fashion for the family's firstborn son. If the previous generation still survived, the younger generation would assist them until they passed. Pthorn's grandparents were long dead, and the homestead stood in disrepair; he would be required to make repairs before making it his own.

Pthorn could barely make out the vague silhouetted form of the other homestead off to the west. While similar in size to his parent's house, it was of a different building style; his parent's house was of all wooden construction, and the other homestead was made of a clay-clad thatch. It had a chimney on one end, and from previous exploration, he knew it had an earthen floor. He hoped he could make some changes to make it more comfortable. Although any extravagant renovations or modifications would undoubtedly be frowned upon by the family.

He looked out towards the distant landmarks and dark sky. He found that this took his mind off the Choosing ceremony the next day. Thinking of the future made him more confident that life would continue according to his father's plan and family's tradition. He pictured what his future wife might look like; she would likely have the same tanned skin as him, just as all the locals in his village did. He pictured a relatively plain girl with wavy dishevelled hair, big blue eyes, thin pink lips, and...

"Oh, Assier, really!" he exclaimed.

Even the mental image of an imaginary girl was enough. He knew he couldn't go back to the house yet; what if he walked in and found himself face-to-face with his mother or father? What made matters worse is that he knew his only knowledge of the female form came from the sight of his own mother washing. He dared not consider the thought.

At that moment, he heard a noise, a sort of scoff, like stifled laughter. His arousal disappeared as quickly as it had arrived. The noise came from behind some of the stacks of hay. Pthorn, initially frozen with fear, slowly thawed and turned. The noise was followed by the scuffing of feet. He made his way over to the pile and gradually allowed himself to peer around the corner.

As he looked around, he caught a glimpse of a dark form before it quickly disappeared. The scuffing turned to swiftly pounding footsteps upon the wooden floor and then silence. Pthorn ran to the ladder at the edge of the mezzanine and found the figure running away from the lower level, heading back toward the village.

Pthorn ran back to his window, wondering who could have been hiding in his hay keep. He was relatively sure that the running figure had been a girl. A poor-fitting, loose sheet tied over her shoulder was all she had for modesty. With no footwear, she seemed to be of a similar class to himself. Pthorn deduced that she likely lived on one of the local farms in Strauth.

She turned her head back towards him when she was almost fifty paces away. Although unfamiliar, her face was not dissimilar from the one he imagined. About the right age, wild hair which looked like it hadn't seen the love of a brush in many years. He thought he saw her smile in the dim light.

He felt himself stir again.

"Maybe I'll wait a few more moments before heading back," he said quietly to himself.

2.

Hydrofluor

The next day Pthorn awoke from his restless night of sleep to the sound of his father's booming voice.

"Get up, ya lazy arse, and get dressed into your best cloth! I don't need you being an embarrassment to me today."

Pthorn slowly rose from his slumber and made his way over to a small shelf with his modest collection of brown robes. He looked through the small pile and found the least worn out and stained and made to pull it around himself when his mother walked in.

"Now, let's get you scrubbed first, I think. Yes, you are filthy; off to the tub with you, boy."

His mother had always been the loving and caring parent in his life. She had always been there whenever his father belittled or made him feel small. She had a way of lifting him back up and reminding him that he was worth something.

Mother had already put a pot of water on the range to boil; it was her habit to boil water first thing in the morning. "You just never know what you need boiling water for until you need it", she would announce regularly. His father would sneer at the waste of good firewood, but she never let it stop her.

Pthorn carried the boiling-hot water to the fired-clay tub outside and poured it in before he turned to fetch a few pots of cold water from the small rainwater reservoir. He climbed in and scrubbed himself with a small linen cloth. By the time he was done, not even an onk would drink the water of that colour. He climbed out, bucketed the water out of the tub onto the few plants surrounding the homestead and walked back inside. He was almost dry by the time he made it back to his room.

He donned the cleanest of robes and walked back into the common room to receive his breakfast from his mother. It was commonly known as clag, a thick porridge made from one of the cheaper crops grown on the farm. It was the kind of meal used by the more affluent farmers as animal food, but it did a good enough job of killing off hunger pains. The clag was served bland and half cold. Had luck been on his side, and the harvest was recently sold, dried sweetroot could have been powdered and stirred in to make it more bearable.

Pthorn quietly took the bowl from his mother and walked outside to eat in the morning's early glow. The sun had just begun to move beyond the horizon and rise into the vast, cloudless azure sky. The warmth of the sun in the cool morning was refreshing, particularly considering the dark sleeplessness of the night. He settled down upon the small patch of grass cultivated by Mother to enjoy the morning. Grass was not plentiful around these parts, at least not a nice soft lawn. Most of the grasses in Straulatos were spikey, short tufts, eaten only by mants and other shelled creatures. His mother had saved up some coins and bought a small seed pouch from a travelling merchant. Good soil was already plentiful on the farm, but exotic grass seeds were hard to come by. Father had dismissed it as a passing fancy, but she had taken it seriously. The patch had been off-limits to Pthorn until it had become well-established. Eventually, it had become a place where the two of them could sit and enjoy each other's company away from Father's arrogance.

This morning the grass had only a light remnant of dew and was a warm, welcome place to ponder the world. Pthorn thought again of the day ahead. Not so much of the potential to be Chosen, more of the long uncomfortable journey into the village. This would be followed by him trying his best to uphold his family's social standing, albeit not exceptionally too high to begin with. The clag was almost entirely set by the time he took his last spoonful. His spoon scraped at the clay bowl. At this point, there was virtually no telling food from the bowl.

The trip into the village was not to be made by mant. Father needed the beasts to be fresh for the farm the next day; truthfully, they would have been slower and more uncomfortable than just walking. Pthorn loaded up a large burlap kerchief with some hard biscuits and a waterskin before he tied it to a stick to make it easier to hold. The bindle, as it was called, was usually a symbol of a traveller who moved between villages regularly and needed to carry the bare essentials for the road. The irony was not lost on Pthorn as one of the least travelled people in Azarth; their journey was also hardly one of great distance.

Pthorn walked through the doorway and followed his father. He turned to wrap his arms around his mother.

"I love you, my boy; you be good and make us proud today!" she called to him as he walked away.

Pthorn just nodded as he turned to follow his father, who was already several paces ahead.

The trip started in silence and continued much the same way. The road to the village wound its way to the west for half a league before it turned south. The roadway was dirt and well compacted by mant-pulled wains. Washouts were a common occurrence and, if one was not focused on their footing, could easily result in a rolled or broken ankle. This was compounded by bare feet and long distances between neighbouring farms.

Much like the surrounding area, the roadway was reasonably sparse with vegetation. It wasn't that the soil itself was free of nutrients; the environment was harsh, and plant species were limited to native, drought-resistant bushes. Water runoff from the road pooled in the rudimentary drainage by the wayside, resulting in a greater-than-average number of saltbush plants. Beyond two paces from the lines of wild vegetation, the dirt returned to barren and lifeless.

As they passed one such saltbush, a small frilled-neck reptile poked its head out from between two small boulders. Father ushered Pthorn to stop abruptly and silently. Pthorn moved to question the sudden stop but was quick to keep his question to himself after he was met with Father's severe glare. Pthorn tried to get a better look at the small beast but dared not move any closer. It was not much larger than a man's forearm from snout to thorny tail. Like most wildlife around the area, it had a tough exterior but had more of a rugged leather hide than a shell. The plates of its skin were tessellated with softer-looking parts allowing movement. Two almost invisible wings protruded from just behind its front legs, tucked snuggly to its side. The texture of the wings was practically identical to its body which made them blend in. Pthorn's investigation determined two apparent facts. Firstly, this thing looked straight at Father with determination, and secondly, it was not happy about being disturbed.

Father whispered under his breath, "I am assuming you are aware of the stories of fire-breathing dragons and the ill-fated knights tasked with destroying them before being seared and consumed?"

Pthorn nodded his response.

"Well, forget that moogshit because they are just stories. These are worse. Dragon fire may burn with the heat of ten thousand lanterns, but these little bastards spray acid. The acid won't just burn your skin; it soaks through to your bones and dissolves you from the inside out. Hydrofluors are also excellent runners, and if you haven't already noticed, they are very capable of flying. Don't let the size of this one deceive you; they also have a serious appetite."

At that, Father began a slow movement to back away from the hydrofluor. Its deathly glare remained unchanged as it continued to stand as still as a corpse. Pthorn and his father slowly edged farther and farther away from the angered reptile until at least fifty paces stood between them.

"This way!" instructed Father as he pointed across a neighbouring field, "from what I understand, they are almost always alone; we shouldn't stumble across any more along the way."

The detour across the field almost made up any time they had lost during their faceoff with the hydrofluor. Although this was offset by the rough terrain, which made hard work of the two men's bare feet. Pthorn's feet were well accustomed to the plough fields back home, but they were less used to the untilled field in which they walked. Sharp thistles and roots were just a hair's breadth below the sandy soil and proved to make short work of the hard skin on the soles of his feet.

No complaint was voiced by either Pthorn or Father. Sympathy was going to be hard to come by, particularly when the other was also experiencing the same hardship.

The shortcut across the field soon emptied onto the southbound road towards the village. The route had missed the crossroads between the family's farm, the village, and other way-off towns. Once back on the road, the walk continued in an abundance of monotony and silence. Pthorn almost wished for another thorny-tailed menace to make the journey more interesting....

Maybe I could get it to eat Father... he thought to himself. Pthorn allowed a slight grin to escape and paint the edge of his lips.

The pair's arrival in the village was by the main entry road. Given the magnitude of the day's events, the local village's government had seen fit to spend more than their regular Assierium Festival budget on adornment and fanfare. Large timber structures had been erected to form a square arch across the road. The cheap lumber was nailed into a truss structure and covered with a thin hay thatching. Bright red, interwoven with shining golden ribbon and altogether too expensive-looking material, was wrapped around the columns of the arch in a double helix. The material flowed down from the oversized figure's robes which sat upon the pinnacle. The God Assier was depicted in the throes of war and rode upon a chariot of lightning. Clearly, the town had run out of money or at least creative talent. The chariot was undrawn; it seemed that beasts were too expensive to recreate as part of the sculpture. Assier himself more closely resembled a scarecrow having a bad day. Below the figure of Assier was the four-pointed star of Aiel. Pthorn had always wondered why their prophet was never depicted as a figure.

Pthorn and his father passed beneath the arch and continued their journey into the centre of the village; Pthorn looked at the small shops lining the main road. The shops all had mant-stays in the street for locals to tie up their beasts so that they could go in to purchase whatever they needed. Most shops had a veranda in the front, which acted as a mud room for when the rains did arrive. Customers could knock off their boots on the rough-hewn wooden porch before they migrated inside. On quiet days you might see the store clerks sitting on a chair, watching the world pass by, waiting for customers. Today was not one of those days. The shops were all closed and shuttered, with small festive shrines displayed for the viewing pleasure of passers-by.

Music slowly began to flow like a gentle river down the street; it got increasingly louder as they approached. Toward the centre of the village, a square opened up as part of a crossroads. On each corner was hotel accommodation for passing travellers, each with only a few beds, but all owned by very different proprietors. While Pthorn himself had not spent enough time in town to witness the publicans' antics, rumours and tales told tall always made their way around such a village.

The first hotel on the left was called the Two Moons inn. Its owner Carrth was known for his foreign workers. It was said that his staff were almost exclusively Saulit women looking for adventure in Straulatos. With their jet black skin, bright white eyes, and tall, lean, muscled bodies, they were Azarth-famous for being the world's warriors; here they were young ladies of only twenty turns, backpacking their way across the vast continent. They were also rumoured to be more than just the barkeep; more like helping locals and travellers seeking adventure beneath an inn's starched linen sheets. Pthorn had never met anyone from Saulit, but their reputations preceded them, both good and bad.

To the other side of the road on the right of him, Pthorn could see The Onk. This was more of the pub than home-away-from-home accommodation. The owner, known only as The Club, was a giant of a man known to throw good patrons out the door and keep the trouble-makers. For all the things they broke, they were usually the better drinkers. It was rumoured that anyone who passed out from intoxication was dragged into the onk sty out the back and left to sober up. They would then be hit with a bill for his finest accommodation upon their return to sobriety.

The final two inns were owned by brothers; Naas and Siam Haerk. Two men with a searing hatred for each other; the origin of the tension was long discussed as a rumour. Most stories centred on a love triangle gone wrong, with some far more outlandish than others. These two inns were known as Left and Right to the locals; their actual names had long since peeled off the timber signboards hung on the landings. Ironically, the inns were named in the opposite direction to the main village entrance from the north, the legacy of a long-forgotten southern trade route.

The crossroad between these four inns, usually a barren dirt road, was today centred by a raised dais that featured a golden pulpit. The same red material, inlaid with gold, was draped across the stage to create a sort of grandeur. For Pthorn, it did precisely that. He had never witnessed such a display of wealth and colour. Only for the High Priest of Straulatos would they go to such an extent to decorate a stage. To the right-hand side, in front of Left, was another raised stage with far less lavish decoration. A travelling string band performed to a disinterested audience. Given the lack of time spent appreciating the arts, Pthorn was taken in by the sound of it.

The centre of town bustled with people. Men and women stood around the dais and talked in hushed tones of anticipation. The position of the sun overhead suggested it was nearly midday, and the High Priest of Straulatos should arrive momentarily.

Moments passed, and Pthorn was so mesmerised by the band he didn't notice the mood change as the High Priest entered. He made his way from the closed doors of the Two Moons and across to the stage. The band received their cue and, without decrescendo, ceased to play immediately.

Silence crashed over the square, and the High Priest let it hang.

Long moments passed while Pthorn studied the man. He wore long white robes, plain with just a sheer fall of linen and no pockets. The robes were covered with red and golden material that hung across his shoulders like a scarf. His head was topped with a cardinal hat. Jewels shone from the leading edge as if to reinforce his position of great power. The man himself was well into his twilight years. His beard was well-kept but white as snow, with a dash of pepper in the corners of his mouth.

"Forty turns!" he exclaimed, again with the flair for leaving his voice to hang with a few moments of silence.

"Forty turns since we have had a Choosing. Our Lord God, The Singular, came to me in a dream in the form of Assier and spoke a name. He spoke just one name and showed me a face. The name he spoke was of this land. The village in which we stand. 'Strauth! Strauth' he called! and I was there to hear it."

Pthorn noticed the polarising effect this man had upon the crowd. Those devout looked upon the High Priest with adoration and unmoving belief. Others seemed to wear a look of scepticism. Almost audible eye rolls from those further back who were just there for the show. The vagueness of the fate of the Chosen seemed not to be lost on them. They looked hopeful that they were about to witness some sort of human sacrifice to a God.

"Now! Who amongst us is of the age of Choosing? You must not fear, for your path will bring you to the side of the great and only Assier! Death is not what awaits you, only life and power. Come! Join me in front of the Almighty Singular!"

That sounds less than reassuring, thought Pthorn, *given the concept of everlasting life in death.*

At first, no one moved. People wanted neither to be first on stage nor push their children into what sounded ominously like some sort of ritualistic death at the hands of a priest.

A surprising calm befell Pthorn, an almost acceptance of fate. Either today was not the day to be stabbed through the heart in a blatant act of human sacrifice, or it was and his time as a poor farmer's boy with a disapproving father was at its end.

Pthorn dropped his bindle beside his father and moved away without so much as a turn. He made his way through the thick crowd, which happily dispersed to form a corridor to the steps of the dais. He stood momentarily at the platform's base and breathed in and then out. After a brief moment, he climbed onto the stage in front of the eager crowd.

3.

The Choosing

Pthorn stepped onto the stage, hands by his side, and gave the High Priest a slight bow. The High Priest returned the gesture with a vague nod as he walked across the stage away from the steps to allow others to join him.

Pthorn's eyes then made their way around the crowd. They were young and old. Everything from swaddled babes in their mothers' arms to elderly men who stood with the assistance of younger family members. A sobering thought crossed Pthorn's mind, *how many people here are actually of age for the Choosing?*

He quickly realised that it was far less than he had initially assumed.

A small number of others began their journey to the stage.

The first was a young man whom Pthorn suspected he had previously met in passing. It seemed to him that he was likely a store clerk's son who spent their days working around the shop as an apprentice or shop hand. Compared to Pthorn's brown rags, his more stately attire suggested considerably more wealth than a farmer's life.

Next on the stage was another man, slightly younger and significantly shorter. 'Man' may have been too generous a word as the boy looked sickly and small. His face was pockmarked from either disease or severe acne. He looked on the verge of tears as he made his way onto the stage. He made a slight bow, much the same as Pthorn had, and joined them.

The fourth and final figure definitely looked more familiar. The girl was about Pthorn's height and wore farmer's rags with nothing else to protect her from the elements. The clothing was no cleaner nor any less stained than his own. Her feet were uncovered, dusty and hard-worn from a life with no shoes. She wore no head scarf, as was standard attire for ladies heading to the village for supplies. The girl turned to look at Pthorn with more than a hint of recognition in her fiery brown eyes. She flicked her wild mane of brown-red hair as she made her way to the stage.

Pthorn could feel the heat as it rose within his cheeks. If he wasn't nervous enough about the outcome of today's Choosing ceremony, last night's visitor joining him on the dais certainly didn't help. As she made her way to the stage, he saw that she had a simple beauty about her. She had a heart-shaped face that was well-tanned by the southern sun. He turned his attention away to stop himself from staring; instead, he chose to look back towards the Two Moons. Anything was better than being caught staring or having to make eye contact with Father throughout the ceremony.

After a long while, it became clear to Pthorn that there would be no more than four people. That was it. Just four. The odds did not seem to be in anyone's favour.

"When the Lord God Assier spoke to me the name of this land, he showed me a face. The face of his Chosen One. The Lord High Servant of Assier.

"The face he showed me is here today; I am absolutely certain of it. I have never been so sure of it in my life."

The High Priest turned to the sickly boy to his right. "You boy! What is your name?"

The young man almost passed out on the spot. His knees weakened, and he became a smaller version of himself.

"Ah...ahh... Ahndo, Mr Sir High Ppppriest Sir" He stammered.

"Pitiful!" sighed the High Priest under his breath before he continued to address the crowd, "do not worry yourself, young Ahndo. Assier has not seen fit today to bestow upon you this blessing. Go be with your family."

Ahndo turned and scampered off the stage. Tears of relief streamed down his face.

"What about you then, boy? What do they call you?" the High Priest asked the well-dressed boy.

"Donalt, Son of Dunrald, Proprietor of the Apothecary and Mayor of Strauth," the young man replied matter-of-factly.

"I don't need your title, even if it was yours!" said the High Priest, once again under his breath rather than address the crowd but still loud enough for Pthorn to hear clearly.

"Donalt, neither you nor your father's title has been Chosen by the Assier today. You are free to return to your family."

The young man seemed more than a little disappointed. Pthorn suspected that Donalt had believed that his father's well-held title within the village would somehow buy him the prestige required to ascend to the role of Assier's top servant.

This left two final people atop the dais; they stood alongside the High Priest. Both were equally as scraggly and worn. Pthorn snuck a look at the girl who stood to his right, on the other side of the High Priest; her previously confident face had faded and been replaced by one of terror. Similarly, Pthorn's moment of calm was also teetering, at risk of falling away like a canvas curtain held in the corner by a single pin.

"One of these two who stand before me have been chosen by the Lord God Assier." He paused to let it sink in; Pthorn just wished he would stop repeating himself and get the suspense over and done with.

"The image supplied to me was vivid but fleeting. It showed neither man nor woman, rather a hard-working farm hand. This leaves us with the question of 'whom?'. For I am confident that he has chosen one of these two. I must confer in prayer to understand more the will of Assier."

And with that, he marched from the stage and back into the Two Moons.

As if directed by some unseen hand, everyone split into four separate groups, and the crowd immediately started to move away from the central stage. A low hum slowly turned to a rumble of discussion as everyone made their way to their choice of liquor provider. Everyone except Father, who instead ambled back the way they entered the town and found a timber bench to set himself upon. The two youths stood by themselves upon the dais in silent solitude.

The band behind them began to play again, even though there was no crowd to entertain. The music would carry throughout the square and become background music for the drinking patrons.

It was the young lady who first broke the conversational silence.

"Found something to hide ya bits then, didja?" she said with a half smirk as she nodded in the direction of Pthorn's clothing. "Well, that wasn't the ceremony I was 'specting. Thought there would be a bit more choosin' goin' on!"

Her speech was far more typical of the local farmers who surrounded the village. Had not it been for his parents' insistence on being taught how to speak well, Pthorn was sure he would also sound the same.

"Firstly!" Pthorn responded hotly, "what were you doing in my hay keep in the middle of the night?"

"There a secondly there somewhere, aye?"

"How about we start with the firstly and go from there!" he stammered.

"Well, if ya must know, I was hidin' from ma pappy. He got ta drinkin' last night, an' when he gets ta drinkin', he gets ta beltin'. I don't mind a bitta slap an' tickle if ya get ma drift, but not the sort that ole bastard hands out," she replied, followed by another cheeky smile, "Plus, up there, I got to see a little cutie take his tackle out for a whirl in the torchlight. Now, how about that secondly?"

"What in the name of the droopy ballsack of the Assier happened today? I swear by Aiel if we are stuck here until nightfall and I have to sneak for a league past a hydrofluor with Father again..." he trailed off as he reached the end of his rant without being able to think of a consequence.

"Nah idea, aye, my guess is that the old fella's eyesight has packed up and left 'im if 'e ain't able to tell the two of us apart. Shoulda got us to lift up these rags; that should do the trick, aye, I've seen what ya hidin'," she replied, cackling at her own joke.

Pthorn wondered what sort of cruel practical joke Assier was playing on him.

"Just leave my dick out of this, will ya! Aiel!" he swore.

"An' how good was the hydrofluor! Bet ya farmin' packed yasself!"

Her laughter had reached a whole new level, "run like a little bitch didja?"

It slowly dawned on Pthorn. The small acid-breathing dragon was not there by accident; it had been placed by the side of the road as a cruel joke by the scraggly-haired farm girl in front of him.

"You?" he spat like venom, "you? But how?"

"Ya juss gotta know how ta catch 'em. I bet it was farmin' pissed off by the time you two tripped over it." She clutched at her knees to keep herself upright from laughter. "I gave it a farmin' good sore head with the lumpa wood I bonked it with. Stuck it under the rock to wake up meaner than a... well, meaner than a hydrofluor with a sore head."

Her laughter had started to die down, "what's ya name anyway, kid?"

"What do you mean, kid? We are both clearly the same age!" Pthorn considered not engaging further, but he had started to see the funny side of the practical joke and began to calm down. "Pthorn, my name is Pthorn. What about you?"

"Darn!"

"What? Is my name not good enough? Something else to tease?" Pthorn started to see red again.

"Nah ya farmin' half-wit, ma name is Darn. Short for Darnalla."

"Oh, sorry," he said as he gave her his best apologetic face, "so, what about our competition for human sacrifice?"

Pthorn was unsure how Darn would take the light-hearted conversation about their potential near-future ill-fate. Thankfully he was rewarded.

"Well, spotty damn near shit 'imself. Pretty sure I heard 'im fart and smelled the piss as 'e left... and it was worth watchin' Mister Ma-Dad-Is-A-Politician get knocked down a few pegs."

Pthorn moved towards the front edge of the stage and sat down with his legs dangling. Darn moved over to join him. Her legs swung forwards and backwards as she sat. That was the end of the conversation. They both sat in silence. Pthorn could not think of anything else that he could make conversation with. The best he could come up with was farm talk, like "hey, isn't it funny when your mant takes a dump when you are ploughing" or meaningless small talk like "hey, did you see the moons last night?"

He knew that if he asked the second, he would get another snide comment about her private viewing session of his body. He instead decided silence was the safer option.

He looked up to see his father was still just sitting on the bench without so much as a glance at his son.

Sometime later, the cue was given to the band to cease playing, and silence returned to the square. The bustling movement of bodies started in the Two Moons, where the High Priest had gone to 'pray'. The High Priest's advisors had begun to march people back outside. The message was soon relayed to the other inns around the square; the people slowly began to reform a crowd that encircled the stage. Only once everyone had finished shuffling into place did Father bother to uproot himself from his throne of untreated timber to stand amongst the crowd.

Once again, the High Priest of Straulatos entered the square from the doors of the Two Moons, although he looked a little flushed this time.

"Must have been some solid prayer," Pthorn noted to Darn under his breath. She returned with a light chortle before she returned to a deadpan stare.

Darn and Pthorn returned to their previous positions and stood on either side of the pulpit, so they were both back on show for the village.

The High Priest continued through the crowd and slowly ascended the stairs to resume his position at the pulpit.

"People of Strauth in the nation of Straulatos. Your God has once again spoken to me and shown me his path more clearly than ever. He has shown me the one who will join him as one of his Chosen Four. He came to me in a moment of pure ecstasy to show me the...."

Darn released another one of her subtly hidden chortles while Pthorn maintained a stoic face. He distracted himself as he focused on his father and bit his lip. Pthorn watched his father's reactions as the High Priest spoke his rhetoric; his father actively avoided eye contact with his son. The High Priest was momentarily distracted by Darn's subtle outburst and stammered. "... ah the way. His way!"

The High Priest grunted his dislike at having been interrupted.

"Young lady, what do they call you?" he asked as he addressed Darn. He was presumably almost at the end of his speech and had begun to make more of a show by gesticulating as he spoke.

"Well, I don' think you would approve of what ma Pappa calls me, but if you an' the fat farmin' loser upstairs wanna holla at me, you can call me Lady Darnalla."

You could have knocked the High Priest over with a light breath. Silence permeated the square like the smell of a dead and well-rotten beast. A look of disgust crept into the face of the High Priest before he cried, "Get off this stage! You dare commit such heresy in front of your family and friends! Go or be smote by celestial lightning right here and now!"

The High Priest had gone from red to purple. The veins in his neck bulged like they were just begging to burst forth from his jowls.

Darn gave Pthorn a wink, left the stage, and headed straight for The Onk. Pthorn had to admit that he liked her style, even if it did come at his expense.

After he watched her walk away, a realisation dawned on Pthorn. He stood alone upon the dais with the High Priest. There were no others to be chosen from. It was him! He turned away from his father to face his fate as it was delivered to him.

The High Priest had slowly calmed himself down and returned to a far more healthy hue of red before he continued.

"Your name?!"

"Pthorn."

"Pthorn! My Son, you have pleased the Almighty, the Singular, and his true form Assier. You have been chosen. You will go henceforth and join him in the rank of his highest servant."

Once the High Priest finished, he turned to face Pthorn and placed his two hands on his forehead. The High Priest's fingers formed the four-pointed star of Aiel and delivered a silent blessing.

"From this moment forth, you are no longer a farm boy, nor do you retain any claim to your family title. As of today, you begin a new life. A life of servitude to the Most Holy. You will travel to a faraway land where you can serve as the Singular intends."

Pthorn turned to face the crowd.

Father was off into the distance, halfway back toward the entry to the village and the decorated archway; his back turned, head down, and he did not look back.

4.

Preparation

art of the crowd dispersed back towards the inns while others stood around and waited for the rest of the Assierium Festival to commence. The storeowners returned to their shops to gather the things they needed to set up their festival stalls in the square; the stalls didn't sell their regular wares.

The butcher would typically set up a stall selling aged sausages that had been sitting in the cellar since the previous year's festival. He also set up games that used cheap un-aged links, which involved throwing foot-long meats at various targets. Winners would get bags of roasted nuts or some other goodie that was generally difficult to come by during the rest of the year.

The barber always set up a stall for the children and young at heart. He put his artistic talent on show to decorate children's faces with cheap lead paints in the shape of their favourite beast or fantasy creature. Pthorn had visited the Assierium Festival once as a small child and had begged his mother to get a black web across his face with a sizeable red-bellied orbite positioned on his nose. His mother had given in to his request, but it was quickly removed once in his father's company.

The blacksmith had a ring toss game, the tannery had a crafts table, Left had wine tasting, and Right had whiskey tasting. The Onk hosted wrestling competitions under the watchful eye of the clergy, who disapproved of violence, particularly on the day they celebrated their God.

Stalls had barely begun to be erected as the High Priest led Pthorn from the square to a back alley at the rear of Right. The carriage was fronted by two magnificent equestra mares, jet black in fur and tackle. The carriage resembled a larger form of the High Priest; it was primarily white with red inlaid in the door cards and gold, which corded its way around every edge. The entire vehicle was the height of elegance, power and position. Equesta, particularly those as prestigious as the ones chained to the carriage, were highly uncommon in Straulatos and only native to the other inhabited continents of Azarth; Matraketh, Saulit and Kesheir. There were stories of Saulitan warriors riding into battle on the back of mighty equestra and romantic tales of chivalry involving Kesheirian men with long, black, flowing hair riding silver equestra stallions to save beautiful women from the clutches of beasts.

Pthorn's imagination ran as wild as those fabled equestra at the sight of the black beauties; he had never actually seen an equestra, only heard the description from stories told by his mother. She had told him of their large muscled forms, long thick necks trimmed with manes that flowed like sweetroot syrup, long pointed snouts, and massive wings which protruded majestically from their flanks. These had their wings tucked neatly to their sides and waited patiently. Mother had said they couldn't actually fly and just used the wings for show.

As Pthorn approached the carriage, a white-gloved guardsman who wore a well-fitted felt tunic stepped around from behind and opened the door. The guard maintained a thousand-yard stare behind Pthorn, a sign of respect for those he worked for. Pthorn was ushered wordlessly into the carriage by the High Priest, who waved his hand toward the door. He obliged and hoisted himself into the red velvet interior. On the bench seat to his right was a pile of neatly-pressed material.

"Get changed; I'll be back momentarily!" the man barked before he closed the door.

The carriage had blackout window coverings cinched into place, which would have normally plunged the space into total darkness. Instead, four dim lights hung from each corner of the carriage and cast a dull glow. Pthorn had never seen such a thing. He reached out to feel them. A fire with almost no heat, smoke or odour. He studied the curious light for several more moments before stripping off the farmer's rags and inspecting the pile beside him.

Atop the pile was a pair of small clothes; again, this was a curious wonder to him. Small clothes had always been seen as a waste of material and more clothing for Mother to wash. He had heard of their existence but never actually worn them. He tried putting them on several ways before discovering what seemed to be the most likely orientation based on comfort level and the number of limbs in each hole.

Next was a white robe similar to that worn by the High Priest. Given the style of the robe, there was little concern for sizing, and it fitted surprisingly well, albeit a little loose. Very plain and simply impossible to get wrong. He quickly threw the robe over his head and pulled it down.

The final piece of clothing was a red vest, once again inlaid with gold thread. It was not nearly as richly adorned as the High Priest's vestment but much more than he was accustomed to.

By the time the High Priest returned, he had already begun to itch with the new fabric. The High Priest climbed into the carriage, grabbed his old clothing, tossed them out the door, and then sat down across from Pthorn. The guardsman closed the door before two thumps were heard from the rear of the carriage, presumably by the guardsman riding on the back, and then the carriage started moving slowly.

Immediately after the carriage left the land behind Right, it turned right to head north through the middle of the square. The sound of locals formed a cacophony as they passed between the crowd. The din was a mixture of cheers, prayer and general conversation overlayed with the continued sound of the band playing. The carriage weaved around the stage in the centre before it headed towards the exit of the village.

Pthorn moved to pull open the curtain, attempting to get one final look at the village that he had never had much time to see. The High Priest swiftly batted his hand away.

"No! It is tradition. Those you have lived amongst and knew you must never again see you as you are now. From now on, you will forever be a symbol of one arising from a mere mortal villager to one of Assier's Chosen Four."

Pthorn retracted his arm from the window and seated himself back into the chair. The seat was luxurious and comfortable. Overstuffed velvet with the softest filling he had ever felt, a far cry from the straw-stuffed pallet of his home bed. Pthorn sat with his hands at his side, slowly changing the velvet pile from flush to proud and back again.

The High Priest made no attempt to start a conversation and sat motionless as he looked past Pthorn at the front wall of the carriage.

After several minutes of staring at the floor, curiosity outweighed Pthorn's fear.

"So, what happens now? Where are you taking me?" said pthorn without looking up.

"There is much you will learn, but it is not for me to teach you. We are heading north to the ports and will be on the road for a span. From there, you will leave me and set sail for Matraketh. The journey will be a couple of months on a trader's vessel. Don't think you will get any special treatment on your sea journey. Anyone who sails pulls their weight, and a young man like you will be up and down rigging all day long."

Pthorn raised his head to look at the High Priest. "Matraketh? What is in Matraketh?"

"Truthfully? I do not know."

The High Priest almost looked like he cared for Pthorn's welfare or pitied him.

"There is a holy site in the mountains that only we High Priests know of. This is where you will serve Assier. I have been given written instructions in a sealed envelope to guide you to your destination. As to where it is or what you will find there, I cannot tell you."

The High Priest's earnest reply did nothing to calm Pthorn's nerves but raised serious questions about the validity of some aspects of the religion.

The highest religious authority in Straulatos, and not even he knows where his boss works. So what? Does he just get sent instructions from overseas with details of when to send a kid his way? Pthorn thought to himself.

Pthorn realised that it was probably best not to question this man on a theological basis. Instead, he just nodded and averted his gaze to the floor to avoid staring at the High Priest.

Several hours later, the carriage pulled to a stop. The High Priest made no move to exit the carriage; instead, he just continued to sit in silence. After several long moments, the door opened, and the guardsman peered in.

"A room is prepared, Sirs; please follow me."

Pthorn followed the High Priest from the carriage into the cool evening air. Somehow the air inside the carriage had remained at a steady, comfortable temperature without becoming stuffy or cooling down with the outside. They had pulled up in front of a respectable-looking inn, not the sort of place you would expect to find ruffians and outlaws. The building was a large square block with two floors; the upper flow had a balcony around its entire perimeter with rooms that looked out over the road and surrounding landscape. The lower floor was more of a public bar and bistro with just one set of swinging doors and several large sash windows.

About five-and-ten patrons had been ousted from their places in the bar. They now lined the path between the carriage and the inn. It was clear that the guardsman had been busy during the few minutes before they had disembarked from the carriage. A man who wore a well-worn off-white apron, presumably the publican, stood at the front of the crowd. They all stood bowed in respect, with their eyes averted from Pthorn and the High Priest.

As the pair passed and made their way through the front doors, each person returned to their normal upright position. The guardsman guided them to a private booth in the corner of the inn, and they took their place at the table.

The other patrons filtered back in and resumed their previous places with a new air of conversations surrounding the recent arrivals.

The publican soon attended their table and bent into a respectful half-bow.

"What can I offer to please you, Your Holiness's?" he offered.

"Save your pot for the regulars. Meat, roasted vegetables and your finest wine will do nicely."

"Right away, Your Holiness. We slaughtered a fat Moog just yesterday, and the best cuts still remain. I have wine in my private collection, which has come all the way from Kesheir. It would be an honour to present it to you."

"That will suffice!" the High Priest retorted without bothering to look up.

Once again, long conversational silence was the topic of the night. This allowed Pthorn to eavesdrop on some of the room's gossip.

"Must be travelling from The Choosing. Poor sod probably has no idea what is gonna happen to him...."

"Those equestra, 'ey, they would make travel on the road faster; I bet they cost a pretty coin or two...."

"He swore it on his Pappy's grave; she had three tits and was hornier than an onk on heat...."

That particular conversation was clearly not being distracted by once-in-a-lifetime religious happenings.

So much for no ruffians, thought Pthorn to himself.

The publican returned to the table with the promised food and a side of soft buttered bread. Pthorn had never seen such extravagance and wasn't sure he would ever get used to it. The roast moog was seared on the outside and was deep, burgundy red, and almost bloody on the inside.

The meat simply melted in his mouth. The vegetables were crunchy on the outside and soft on the inside. Food had never been fancy at home, and while his mother was a good cook, she could never have produced such a well-cooked meal.

The meal was accompanied by the promised bottle of Kesheirian purple. The wine had a deep hue and almost metallic swirl as it poured from the bottle into their cups. Pthorn had never tasted alcohol, let alone the wine from a private collection. His mouth went on a journey. It started sharp, and he could feel the burn from the alcohol on his tongue; this was followed by a full body of flavour, fruity without sweetness, tart without sourness. Once he had swallowed his first mouthful, he was left with a lasting subtle flavour that he failed to describe to himself. Pthorn took the wine in sips; he had heard stories of people who became drunk and obscene and did not want to lose control. After the first few sips, he could already feel the effects and decided slowly was the key.

The rest of the night was uneventful. Pthorn ate his fill of food and drank enough wine that his head started to feel light before they were led up to their sleeping quarters for the night. They had a room each, and Pthorn's was a simple accommodation with a clean pallet, a small wooden chair in the corner and a set of bare shelves for clothing. Once inside, Pthorn simply removed his robes and slipped into bed. His head had barely touched the pillow before he was thrust into the darkness of sleep, a stark contrast to the night before.

The next day, and those that followed, were much the same monotony. A silent carriage ride that stopped only to water the equestra, followed by a night of fine food and expensive wine. The fare changed each day as they moved north. The meat started as moog and onk before it changed to various game poultry and finally seared ghoti or other food-of-the-sea as they approached the ports. Lunch was usually the same as the previous night's dinner, stuffed inside small loaves of bread. One thing had improved now that they were away from his home village; he was allowed to have the window uncovered to look at the ever-changing countryside as it passed. The arid farms transformed into greener and greener fields by the day. Different crops suited to the coastal rainfall patterns also made for different dinner sides; gone were the starchy root vegetables, and in their stead were vine-ripened delicacies that increased in sweetness every day.

Finally, after an entire span on the road, they arrived at the port. The port was the busiest place Pthorn had ever seen. A town had grown radially outward from the docks to cater to local and transient workers alike. As they entered, housing density increased steadily until near the centre, where people lived in two-storey units with no land to speak of.

Beyond the accommodation was the central business district of the port. Here stalls were set up with vendors who cried their daily catches and specials. Ladies in revealing bodices stood on several corners and talked to men in trench coats; Pthorn didn't need to use much of his imagination to know their line of business.

People made their way in unruly chaos, walking every which way, going about their business. The carriage made its way through the jumble of people and across to the waterfront. Several large wooden ships sat docked with gangways that led from the jutting piers to their cargo holds.

Here they stopped for the final time. The High Priest turned to Pthorn, produced a letter from his robe lining, and spoke simply, "may Assier be with you always," as he handed it to him.

Then the door opened, and Pthorn stepped out into the salty sea air one last time.

5.

The Captain

Pthorn walked away from the bustling town along the old wooden pier with nothing but the clothes on his back for possessions. The pier went a fair distance out to sea, presumably to reach deeper open water for the large ships to dock at. He looked about as out of place as you can get in his robes in a world of rugged ghotimen, sea travellers and vendors.

The ship itself was imposing; the words 'Sea's Fury' was written in large, bold letters across the front. On the deck stood two great masts, each with three furled sails. Another two sails were strung across the front, and a final sail at the back. Pthorn saw some crew members scurrying around to prepare the ship for their voyage to Matraketh. Pthorn had seen a crude map of Azarth before but had no concept of scale or the distance they would cover. The magnitude of the ship, the number of crew members running around the deck, and the fact the High Priest had told him it was a couple of months' worth of a journey gave him reason to believe this would be an arduous trip.

When Pthorn reached the end of the pier, he turned and walked up the gangway. As he reached the top, his path was blocked by another imposing figure, this time in the form of a sun-and-salt-worn man. His face was as hard as boiled leather with what looked more like cracks than wrinkles in his skin. His naval uniform spoke of authority; a white linen shirt, stockings covered with dark blue breeches and a dress coat that flowed down to his knees at the rear but cut short in the front. The coat was crisp and adorned with a plethora of bright, brass buttons up the centre in two columns; it was clear the man took great pride in his uniform.

The man's unexpected appearance startled Pthorn, who tripped over his own feet, almost stumbling over the unprotected side of the gangway.

"Papers!" the man growled.

Pthorn pulled out the letter given to him by the High Priest. The message, 'To be opened by The Chosen only, contains travel papers,' was written across the envelope.

Well, that was lucky, he thought cynically to himself.

Pthorn turned over the envelope and broke the red wax seal, which formed the shape of the Star of Aiel. Inside were two pieces of paper. The first was the documentation he was looking for. For obvious reasons, the paperwork did not state his name but authorised the bearer's travel without hindrance. The second piece of paper was sealed with a second wax seal. This seal was not the same, although it did have a striking resemblance.

Where the Star of Aiel was an acutely pointed four-sided star, this one had a more obtuse angle. It was plain to see that it was still a four-pointed star, but it was modified for some reason. Pthorn decided that this letter could wait until he was in the privacy of his own company.

Pthorn handed over the travel papers for inspection.

The man looked them over before he returned them to Pthorn.

"First thing you need to understand on this brig is that I am The Captain; my word is not only final but also legally binding law. I am the judge, jury and executioner. No one will question me."

Pthorn nodded, although he suspected that if anything happened to him along the way, the instigator would be met with severe implications given his recent elevation within Azarth's only religious body; that said, he didn't want to challenge that suspicion.

"Second thing you need to understand is that you are not just cargo. You are crew; you will work for the berth you sleep in and the food you eat. If you don't work, you don't live on this ship. Are these conditions understood?"

Pthorn nodded his reply and added, "Yes, sir."

"And you are to refer to me as Captain. Every instruction I give shall be met with a 'Yes, Captain'. Do you understand?"

"Yes, Captain."

"Right now, boy, have you ever sailed on a ship before?"

"No, Captain," said Pthorn shaking his head.

"You will get to know all the words of a ship but some things you must know. 'Fore' and 'aft' are front and back, the same as 'bow' and 'stern'. 'Port' is left, and 'Starboard' is right, looking at the bow from the stern. You got that?"

"Yes, Captain." Although Pthorn was not entirely sure that he would remember it after this conversation.

"The Sea's Fury has ten crew, including you plus me. There is almost fifty paces worth of ship to run. Go down below and find the First Mate. He will get you set up and changed out of those. It's best you don't spend too much time hanging around this ship wearing that shit."

"Yes, Captain."

The Captain moved to the side and directed Pthorn to an open hatch in the ship's centre.

Pthorn moved past the Captain before he stopped to survey the deck. To the fore of the ship was a raised deck that serviced the front sails; a staircase led from the main deck to this fore deck on both sides. He moved towards it to get a closer look. Two crew members worked with the rigging attached to the sails. Another sailor was perched on the bow, his nether regions exposed to the fresh air below. A thought suddenly dawned on Pthorn, *taking a shit may not be quite as private as back on the farm.* The man eyed Pthorn, who quickly averted his eyes and made his way away from the front of the main deck.

Pthorn continued to look around. The rear was almost the same as the front, except a large iron-banded wooden wheel stood in the centre. No crew seemed to be walking around this deck.

Pthorn moved to the hatch and found a ladder that reached down into the depths below. He turned and climbed down. Once inside the ship's hull, Pthorn expected to see cargo; instead, he found lines of hammocks and two large trestle tables with bench seats on either side. At the far end of the room was a map table attended by a man in a similar uniform to the Captain, just without the dress coat. The man was at least ten turns younger than the Captain but was almost as weathered.

As Pthorn approached, the man looked up, eyeing his robes.

"Right! First things first, they call me Lun. Strip that shit off, and let's get you into some proper clothes."

He pointed to a hammock stuffed with grey clothing.

"That is where you will sleep and live until we get to Matraketh. Make yourself at home."

Pthorn made his way over to the hammock and surveyed the room for any indication of privacy. Once again, his realisation was that privacy was a thing of the past, at least for this journey. He removed the robe but decided to keep the small clothes on. He only had one set, so he would need to find some way of regularly laundering them, although he suspected that would involve seawater. Pthorn had no experience with the sea but knew enough that the water was not drinkable and contained a large amount of salt. Captain's skin was a living testament to the long-term contact with seawater; from that, Pthorn inferred that the salt content probably didn't increase its cleaning abilities, nor the comfort of the clothing following its use.

Pthorn got dressed into the grey crew clothing that was provided. He had already seen the uniform on the crew working on the deck. It was far plainer than the Captain and First Mate but still had an air of fashionable style. White breaches and undershirt with a long grey overcoat topped off with a grey flat cap. It seemed shoes were in limited supply and the crew not deemed worthy of them; Pthorn was happy with this. He had never owned a pair of shoes and didn't fancy having to wear them either.

Once changed, he stashed his recently acquired religious garb in his hammock and returned to the First Mate for further instructions.

"Almighty Assier! That is an improvement," the First Mate exclaimed, "now, you will be joining your crew team on shift tonight as dusk falls. The current team will get us moving very soon; you would have already seen them on deck. You don't need to worry about setting the rigging yet; you will soon learn. We have three teams of three crew to man the ship, plus the Captain and me. Caln will be your team leader; what he says goes unless I tell you to do something else. Ness is also on your team; she is saltier than the ocean below us about having a greenskin on her crew and won't be happy when she finds out you are some religious freak."

"I'm not, though!" Pthorn almost shouted. Lun gave him an inquisitive look, and Pthorn continued, "I'm not some religious freak; I was chosen by the High Priest for this. I don't know the first farmin' thing about Assier and Aiel besides what my parents told me. I swear it on the sweaty taint of Assier!"

"Just keep that attitude about yourself, and you might just win her over, maybe," he replied, "now, your team is downstairs stacking kegs and taking inventory. You'd best scurry down and make yourself busy helping them, or you will be put on scud for the whole trip. The morning crew are on shore leave and due back any time now with lighter pockets and balls."

Pthorn didn't need the definition of scud explained to him; clearly, there were tasks given to those who didn't pull their weight enough, and they weren't likely to be very pleasant. He also didn't question the actions of the third crew.

Pthorn left the First Mate at his station and went down another hatch. This one was located towards the aft. The room was poorly lit, with candles only used in the first half of the hold. Pthorn suspected this may have to do with the types of materials stored at the far end and the likely outcome if an open flame were to become involved with the cargo.

As expected, there were two crew members in the cargo hold. The first Pthorn quickly identified as Caln, a big brute of a man. He was almost as wide as he was tall, which said a lot for his shoulders, given his height. Caln was bald with ears that would have made good wings if that were their purpose. He wore the sort of scowl that Pthorn had become well used to seeing on his father's face, but it was nothing compared to the visual contempt painted across the face of Ness.

Ness was as far from your typical farmer's wife or village woman as possible. She was well muscled and, by her look, had been well seasoned at sea for a long time. If Pthorn wasn't already aware of her sex, he might have mistaken her for a slightly less ugly man.

"Look at the floatin' state of this kid. I bet he can't even lift a rope, let alone tie a floatin' knot. At least we are going to have clean floors 'ey Caln."

Pthorn wasn't sure this was a good time for an argumentative response; instead, he said, "just let me know what I can do to help. I'm here for the trip and am working to pay my way."

"Just don't get in my way!" she retorted before she pushed past and made her way up the ladder back into the accommodation deck.

"Don't mind her son. Just do your best; she might come around by the time we make port in Matraketh. Now, how about you help me with this inventory, hey? You count, I write... You can count, can't you?"

"Of course!" Pthorn responded; he sounded sincerely offended at the thought.

Caln motioned towards a stack of wooden crates in the middle of the hold, not entirely flooded with light but not completely in the dark either. The boxes were sturdy and seemed to be built to be reused. They looked square, with hand holds cut into each side and a plank aligned on the bottom to stop each box from sliding on the box below. Heavy rope netting was slung from the roof to the floor to keep the crates from toppling in rough seas.

"Twillerite Sloe Fuse," read Pthorn from the black stamp on the front of the front crate, "... nine, ten, one-and-ten, two-and-ten. There are two-and-ten boxes here. Are all the boxes back the same?"

"Should be, unless those witless fools from the last shift messed up again."

Caln checked his ledger and nodded in agreement.

"Yep, two-and-ten it is. What's next?"

Upright tall crates marked with 'Textile Bolts', square containers marked 'Rhodella Parchment', and barrels with dark black writing which stated 'Arture's High Proof Liquor'. After he had counted all of the crates and barrels of items with increasing flammability, the two finally reached a large stack of boxes. Stacked six wide by six deep and all the way to the ceiling. Even in the blackness of the back of the hold, Pthorn could see that these boxes were painted with what was once bright red paint, well weathered and worn by age but easily identifiable as dangerous. Within the diagonal stamp was the large lettering of the warning label, 'High Explosive – Do Not Drop'.

Pthorn eyed the boxes suspiciously and kept a cautious distance.

"I wouldn't worry yourself about that one boy. Either it doesn't blow, and you keep the red stuff inside your body, or she goes up, and you won't have a body, or a ship, to worry about ever again."

Pthorn couldn't entirely tell if he was joking. Caln's remark was accompanied by a smirk with just a hint of fear behind his eyes, suggesting he was also not feeling entirely secure with the cargo.

"How many have we got, son?"

Pthorn recomposed himself and went back to counting, "ah, six by six by four, that is um... one hundred and four-and-forty … I think."

You could have knocked Caln over with the fart of an onk, thought Pthorn.

The bald man looked up at Pthorn with a stunned look and then back down at the ledger before slowly nodding.

"Um, yes. That's right. I swear by the bloody four-pointed star, I thought you would be sitting here for the next turn counting those boxes."

Caln shook his head to shake the look of bewilderment from his face.

"On the plus side, Ness owes me her drink ration tonight. She bet me you would have given up after the second row."

Pthorn felt a rush of pride fall over him. Finally, the seemingly useless education his mother had bestowed upon him had started to pay off. He was neither used to being appreciated nor having his knowledge validated. He was usually belittled by his father and made to feel like he wasn't good enough. He tried not to let the smugness he felt make its way to his face, but it was too late.

"Good job, son! You are going to make a fine ship's hand. Just keep your nose to the gunwale and out of Ness' way, and you will do just fine. Come on, it must be just about time to get some dinner and let the night crew get us sailing."

6.

Lice and Calm

Eight span and a day had passed since he had boarded the Sea's Fury if Pthorn's count was correct. It had been a whole span before he could walk on deck without feeling greensick. He had spent most of his time with his face over the gunwale of the poop deck, dry heaving or sitting down in the centre of the cargo hold where the ship's movement could be felt the least. After he came to terms with the ship's movement and managed to keep his breakfast down, he could finally start assisting the crew with their daily tasks. Some days they threw out some drag nets to catch the food for the next few days; other days, he would scrub the deck under the Captain's watchful eye and hateful gaze of Ness. Caln had started to teach him some knots; by now, he knew all the main knots required to secure or join ropes.

If the journey had gone to plan, they would almost be at their destination, and land would have been in sight within days. That would have been the case had the wind not suddenly ceased two span prior. Without warning, their steady journey across the ocean had come to a halt of eerie silence. The only sound was the gentle lapping of water on the side of the great brig, the dull creaking of timber, and the light thump of bare feet moving on the deck.

The Captain was immediately cautious and quartered the rations. They had already been nearing the end of the food supply. The store of salt meat had been eaten with only the long-life non-perishables remaining. Without the ship moving, ghoti nets proved ineffective in catching anything more nutritious than sea lice.

Breakfast consisted of hard weevil-infested biscuits, with lunch and dinner not offering much more by way of variety. Water was also rationed. Caln had, on multiple occasions, reminded him that even though they were surrounded by water, drinking the water of the sea was a slow and painful way to die of thirst.

The only thing not on a diminished ration was the liquor allowance. Everyone was allocated a share of the barrel stock on board, but once it was exhausted, there would be no more.

The First Mate had been sure to inform Pthorn that "Drinking your allowance too soon would only be to your own detriment, both by a hangover and lack of future supply."

This journey aboard the Sea's Fury was Pthorn's first introduction to hard liquor. He hadn't dared try any in his first couple of span on board, given his stomach uneasiness. On the first day of the third span he poured himself a swallow at the end of his shift as he sat in the mess deck with Caln.

Not knowing what to expect, Pthorn took a small sip from his metal pannikin and immediately felt the burn from the tip of his tongue down to the back of his throat. Once the immediate alcohol burn subsided, he could taste the strong, smoky taste of the wooden barrel it had been aged in. It tasted like the smell of the cook fire back home when they burned the good hardwood. Finally, the booze had an after-taste that could only best be described as almost grassy, not that he had ever partaken in the consumption of grass. After a few more sips, he could feel the effect on his consciousness. His senses dulled, his speech slowed, and a calm fell over him. He sat back in his hammock and stared at the ship's ceiling as it gently rocked through the waves. Like back home in his tiny room, he counted the orbite webs strung across most of the joist supports for the upper deck. Unlike the webs back home, orbites were far more active in their inhabitation of the ship. In the centre of most of the larger webs was a tiny body with an enormous abdomen with ten legs poking out. On each side, two pointed forward, two pointed back, and one out to the side. Long pincers protruded from the front of the body between the legs. It was rumoured that the pincers could inject venom so potent it could rot the flesh of a fully grown man in a matter of days, or so his father had told him. He also said that the operating mountebanks often had to risk removing limbs to save lives before the greenrot set in.

Several span, and more than a few more cups of liquor, later, he could drink more than just two sips before he zoned out. With his remaining liquor ration far greater than those around him, he felt no need to limit himself. On this night, he sat around the table with Ness, who was slowly coming around to the idea of him being in their team, and Caln. They played a tile game, a common pastime for sailors during their downtime. 'Scupper', Caln had called it. Supposedly, depending on the mood, it could be played friendly, gambled upon or turned into a drinking game. Tonight, given the dwindling supply for Caln and Ness, and with Pthorn being new to the game, it was played for mere entertainment.

There were eight-and-forty types of tiles, each denoted by one, two, three or four dots and two-and-ten different nautical symbols. The aim of the game was to bluff other players and trade tiles to get a group of two-and-ten tiles with the same number of dots. You could also lose points if you had too many of another type of tile; for example, if you had a complete set of tiles with four dots, two tiles with three dots, eight tiles with two dots and two tiles with one dot, then you would lose eight points from your winning total of two-and-ten. It was better to have a complete set plus three sets of four tiles. In the event of a tie, certain tiles are worth more than others. If you got the perfect hand of low tiles, it was called a 'Captain's Daughter', and a dead-even hand was called 'The First Mate's Fist'.

"You play like my grandmother, and she had no wits about her when I knew her. Even she could get better than a five-tile hand."

Ness was one for trash talk, and it only increased with a little bit of liquor inside her.

"Any worse, you would have yourself a 'Fist' every round. You're lucky we ain't gamblin' or drinkin', or else you would have pissed yourself poor."

Pthorn had, admittedly, not picked up the game very quickly and was yet to win a hand but enjoyed the comradery of the game, even if it came in the form of insults from Ness and gentle coaching from Caln.

The night finally ended once Ness realised she was using up her liquor ration too quickly, and no gambling was happening to allow her to win anymore. She bid her farewell to the table in a slur of words before she slumped into her hammock. Caln was soon to follow.

"Night, my boy; I think you might be improving a little there. Don't let Ness worry you; she plays better than she fights."

He left with a chuckle, more to himself than anyone else. Pthorn made his way across the deck, crawled into his hammock at the end of the mess deck and went to sleep to the dulcet tones of Ness' snoring.

The next day the calm persisted. With jobs onboard limited and Ness feeling less than amiable to work, Caln decided to attempt to teach Pthorn how to catch ghoti the old-fashioned way. Pthorn sat beside Caln and observed him as he unwound a thick and heavy rope to remove only a thin cord. He severed the cord with his knife before he fixed the heavy rope to prevent it from fraying.

Caln gripped the thin cord tightly with one hand before he dragged the back of his knife along it, causing it to make a low, squeaky noise. Pthorn soon noticed that the cord had become straighter. Soon he had finished straightening about thirty paces and coiled it up at his feet.

Next, he sliced off a small piece of the coil, tied a small knot in the centre, and teased the end of the cord to fray. He set aside the tiny tuft of fibres and picked up a small broken piece of wood from one of the downstairs crates. It was the same dark, weathered timber.

He used his knife to whittle a hook, about the size of half a hand span, from the piece of wood. It started with a large round section before extending into a loop and finishing as a sharp point. Pthorn was amazed at the workmanship of the hook.

Finally, Caln threaded his teased cord onto the hook, referring to it as a lure, before he tied it to one end of the coiled cord and secured the other end to the gunwale.

Caln hoiked the hook and lure over the gunwale; it landed with a splash in the becalmed sea below them. The pair watched as the cord uncoiled and the hooked end sank into the depths.

For a long while, nothing happened. The two men just sat with their backs to the stern while Pthorn attempted to fabricate his own hook. After what seemed like an eternity, Pthorn had whittled what resembled a very rough attempt at a hook, except there was no way of attaching the cord. Each attempt to make the rounded section on the top just resulted in more and more wood being removed until there was nothing to carve. Pthorn handed the hook to Caln and set to work on a second hook.

Caln had just started inspecting the recently completed hook, looking moderately impressed, when they noticed a tug on the cord. At first, it was just once and then silence.

"Stay still, my boy; if we move it now, we lose it. If we wait, the ghoti will try to pull away and catch itself."

They both sat there and waited silently.

Tug.

"Hold it."

Tug tug.

"Hold it."

Tug, tug, tug, tug, tug.

"Give us a hand, my boy!" shouted Caln as he scrambled to his feet.

They both leapt up and grabbed the rope, pulling it up from the ocean's depths. As the rope was retracted, Pthorn could slowly see a dark shape as it formed beneath the ocean's glassy surface.

Finally, it breached, thrashing about and knocking the ship's side.

"Pull, pull, pull!"

They heaved until the great black ghoti was left flapping about on the deck.

"Ah, we've got ourselves a speckled helleck. That should be good eating for a few days. Come on, I'll show you how to gut and salt it while it is fresh."

Without another moment of hesitation, Caln had his knife back in his hand, grasped it with both hands and stabbed the ghoti straight between the eyes. It quickly stopped thrashing and stared off into the distance with its dense black pupils.

Caln led Pthorn to the ship's galley, a small room off the side of the main mess deck, where the crew took turns preparing meals. The room had two wash tubs, a bench around the perimeter, and an island bench in the centre. Cooking pots here stacked under the bench, along with a few remaining dried vegetables, which could be added to soups or stews and several crates filled with salt.

It took both of them to carry the large ghoti into the room and lift it onto the island bench. Caln felt around the gut area of the ghoti until he found what he was looking for. He inserted his knife into the belly of the speckled helleck and sawed from head to tail. He removed the head and placed it in an empty iron-banded wooden container off to the side. Pthorn peered in to get a closer look at the slopping entrails; he was curious about how that wet, tangled mess of organs could keep the ghoti alive and wondered for a brief moment whether it was similar for people.

He was shaken from his morbid thoughts by Caln as he announced, "that will make a fine soup for dinner tonight. We should be able to mix a bit of seawater in with the fresh to make a salty broth. Maybe even ask the Captain if we can throw one of those dried roots in to keep the scorbutus away."

Pthorn gave him an inquisitive look; he was unfamiliar with the term, and Caln realised immediately.

"Sailing fever! They say that eating things grown from the ground prevents you from catching it. Ole mother's tale if you ask me."

Pthorn nodded his reply.

Next, he moved on to scraping the furry skin from the pink flesh of the ghoti. He put the skin aside, presumably not for eating. The fur had a waterproof effect, like a good oilskin cloak that Pthorn had seen travellers wear as they passed the farm; the water just beaded off it. This was all entirely new for Pthorn, who had only tried food-of-the-sea for the first time on the carriage ride to the port.

"Skin makes for some good winter gloves if you know the right man to craft them for you."

He then moved on to cutting off sides of flesh from head to tail and slicing it into chunks before tossing the pieces into one of the crates of salt from below the bench.

"That should keep the crew happy for at least another couple of days!" he said happily before he cleaned his knife in the pail of seawater, "now, how about you go back up to the deck and throw these bones back into the sea? We don't need them stinking up the place."

That night only one crew member, the nimble and aptly named Munkley after the tree-swinging animal, remained above deck on look-out duty in the cawsnest; the remaining nine crew and the Captain sat below in the mess deck to enjoy the day's catch.

The Captain stood up to make an announcement to the crew.

"Even though the wind be still and the ocean be calm, I feel our luck turning. I may not be a Godly man any other day of the turn, but today I say this. Assier has chosen to send this black beast our way. Soon the wind will return to our sails, and we will make for land with the haste of a thousand men. Mark my words men... and lady...."

The Captain gestured at Ness playfully, which was returned with a somewhat insubordinate hand gesture herself. The Captain just smiled.

"Mark these words today; tomorrow, we sail again for Matraketh!"

"Bukkah!" The ship's crew cried in response, "Bukkah!"

Pthorn wasn't familiar with the term, but it sounded like an exclamation of excitement. Almost as an echo, he joined in, "Bukkah!"

7.

Deep Mysteries

ython had also never been the deeply religious type. Still, after the Captain's proclamation and the events that followed, you could almost make a devout believer out of him, which was probably for the best given his recent career change into the clergy.

The Captain's prediction that the winds would return the next day was met with the unexpected response of north-westerly winds. Just past the hour of the caw, in the dead darkness of the night, the sails flapped into life. At first, the wind started as the fuel they needed to begin making for land again; they still had two span worth of solid travel to complete.

Then the rain came.

It rained for almost a complete span. The sun didn't so much as make an appearance the entire time. The wind was steady, and the rain was cold. The deck of the ship was slick and made for uneasy walking.

The rain and the cold were bad, but then it took a turn for the worse. Pthorn had been working the rigging under the careful instruction of Caln when the call rang out from the cawsnest.

"Clip the main sail! Clip the foresail! Lower the trysail! Stow the jib!"

The cries continued as the entire crew, on shift and off shift, made their way onto the deck. An unimaginably black cloud rolled in across the dark grey sky. It reached as far and across as the eye could see. The cloud had a storm front of blue and red lightning. The bolts jumped from left to right before the storm built into a crescendo.

Every man, and woman, on-board scrambled for their place at the rigging. The Captain and First Mate convened at the ship's wheel on the rear deck. They worked frantically to keep the ship from listing when the storm hit. The rain began to come down in sheets; it lashed at the deck and those who stood upon it.

Caln ushered Pthorn to the front deck to help with the foresail. Before he started on the sail, Caln lashed a rope around himself and secured it to both Pthorn and the fore sail mast.

"This should stop us from being swept overboard when the waves hit us hard! Now, grab that rope and get the sail up as high as you can. Munkley will scramble up the ratline to lash the sails to the boom."

Pthorn immediately got to work. Hand over hand, he pulled the rope into a messy pile on the floor. Typically rope would be coiled as it was drawn to prevent knots, but today all would be forgiven if the sails were saved and the ship stayed upright. Munkley made his way up each mast to secure the sails, wrapping short lengths of rope around the booms and raised sails. In the time it had taken for Pthorn to get his sail up, Caln had raised the other two sails on the foremast.

"Let's all get below deck and ride this out!" called Caln across the short distance between them. The wind howled and stole the words almost as soon as they left his mouth.

Caln untied the rope from the foremast but kept the two of them lashed together as they made their way across the main deck. Pthorn glanced up at the aft deck and saw the captain hitching the ship's wheel to the deck rail. Caln guided Pthorn into the hatch and down the access ladder, only untying them after they completed their descent into the mess deck. The wind continued to wail above, and slowly the remaining crew filtered back down through the hatch. Munkley was the last one through, along with the Captain and First Mate. They closed the storm cover behind them, muting the sound of the ferocious storm.

The sound may have been dulled, but the rocking of the ship only continued to intensify. Pthorn decided to move a little farther toward the ship's centreline and migrated through the lower hatch into the cargo hold. The crates would be well-restrained by the webbing rope, and the ship's movement would be significantly less than up higher.

Pthorn let himself down the ladder and found himself in complete darkness. At that moment, it occurred to Pthorn that the candles would have only been lit while crew members were inside the cargo hold. He fumbled around a pile of coiled rope at the ladder's base and located a small tinder box with a flint stone. He sparked a flame and ignited the first few candles that lined the ship's hull to provide some level of light before he set himself down with his back towards the boxes of Twillerite Sloe Fuses that he had counted all those weeks ago. He closed his eyes and listened to the thumping of the waves outside the tar-lined timber hull of the ship. The boxes surrounding him creaked with the movement of the rolling ocean. He closed his eyes and tried to pretend he was on dry land in Matraketh, ready to start his unknown future.

Bang!

The sound and force of the strike on the ship shook him from his unexpected slumber. He opened his eyes a crack, only half awake. The cargo hold was still dimly lit by candlelight, and the ship continued to list and sway. Crates sat tight against the rope nets. Pthorn was thankful for the diligent stacking work the crew had done; it had so far protected him from being crushed by a tumbling crate.

Bang! Crrrack!

The sound of timber as it exploded on the deck did more than raise him from his sleep. He leapt to his feet and scrambled up the ladder to the mess deck.

"What was that?" Pthorn asked as he entered the mess deck.

Caln and the rest of the crew were wide-eyed and scared.

"Monster from the deep, that is, come to take us down to its watery lair below the waves," replied Caln.

What happened next was a combination of an explosion of sound and a splintering of wood. A tentacle, as thick as the masts, was thrust through the roof of the mess deck. Ness was forced to jump and tumble for her life as the disgusting limb narrowly missed her. The tentacle was grey in the candlelight and had large eight-sided discs attached to the underside. The discs puckered in the corners like an onk's arsehole and dripped seawater. A foul smell accompanied the sea limb, like rotting ghoti flesh. The puckering tentacle thrashed violently from port to starboard and back again as it tried to attach itself to anyone in its path before it retracted. The howling wind and sheeting rain from outside made their way back below deck, the damp floor slick below Pthorn's feet.

As the beast removed its tentacle, the ship listed violently to the side. The creature rocked the brig in a concerted effort to destroy it, planning to take the souls on board for its own.

In all of the chaos, no one had noticed the wisps of smoke beginning to fill the mess deck. Slowly at first, like the gentle haze of a cookfire, before it became choking. Cognicence soon set in for Pthorn and those closest to the centre of the mess deck. No one knew where it came from, and everyone looked around for the source.

The realisation suddenly hit Pthorn like a runaway mant.

"The cargo hold!" he yelled to everyone and no one in particular, "the cargo hold is on fire!"

The room turned from terror to panic. The monster continued to thrash at the ship causing the ship to list from port to starboard and back again.

Pthorn thought quickly about how he had put out fires back home. He knew that water could be used to douse the flames. Pthorn looked around but could see no more than a couple of barrels of drinking water; that was needed to survive, and wasting it on fire would be problematic long term with thirst set in.

The only seawater within reach had blown in through the gaping hole in the roof. Thinking back to his cooking lessons with Mother, Pthorn remembered that a fire could also be smothered. He sprinted to the galley and ferreted around each crate stacked on the under-bench shelves. Most crates were empty, and some contained ghoti. Eventually, he found a container of salt not packed with the remaining ghoti from the last span's catch and brought it to the top of the hatch ladder for the cargo hold. He looked down through the hatch to find the pile of rope which once held the tinder box was well alight; presumably, the crash from the sea monster had loosened a candle, and it had fallen in the untidy heap. Pthorn leaned through the opening and poured the salt over the fire, covering the larger flames until they died down. Clean burning flame with a bit of smoke soon turned to thick billowing smoke as the now-smouldering rope slowly burned at the tar lining the hold. The bulk of the flame petered out. Once they could see the fire had been subdued, a few crew members climbed down the ladder into the hold to stamp out the remaining embers.

"Oi, Munkley, you are on fire duty. Grab a pail of water and douse any flare-ups," called the First Mate, "the rest of you back up into the mess."

With the fire out, the crew climbed back up the ladder but kept a sizeable distance away from the enormous hole in the main deck floor. Everyone congregated near the galley, where there were more things to hold on to. The rest of the crew had earned their sea legs, but Pthorn was not the only one who struggled to stay upright.

With everyone huddled in the corner, Ness chose this time to voice her concerns about their latest crew member.

"All of this shit started when Assier Almighty over here joined our Aiel-forsaken crew! Smooth sailing for turns, and now this. I say we give the sea what she wants and throw priesty-boy overboard."

Pthorn looked stunned. He didn't know what to say. A few other members of the crew joined in.

"Yeah, give him to the ghoti gods!"

"He is a good one for the plank if I've ever seen one!"

Even the Captain joined in, shouting, "FLOAT HIM!"

Over the cacophony of the crew, it was Caln who came to his defence.

"You all know this has nothing to do with Pthorn; you just want someone to blame!"

Crash!

Another tentacle crashed through the floor of the main deck; this time, it struck Lenk, one of the ship's crewmembers from another shift. The tentacle caught hold of him with one of the giant suckers and plucked him straight through the floor with a sickening crunch.

The room looked on in stunned silence for several heartbeats.

"Who's with me?!" Ness cried.

The resounding response of "Yeah" was not what Pthorn had hoped for. He was swiftly relieved of the use of his legs as he was swept up by the crew. They collectively braved the beast above and swung open the storm hatch. Above him, Pthorn got his first look at the beast, which had set an attack on the Sea's Fury. The beast was a kraken, and it towered over the aft mast. It had one eye and an enormous slimy, black, bulbous head. Its mouth was nowhere to be seen, but Pthorn guessed he would soon find out about its location. The monster had at least eight tentacles that Pthorn could count above the water, although in the jostling to get him to the side of the ship, he could have missed a few. The kraken had wrapped itself around the masts, and some of its tentacle suckers were caught in the rigging. Its struggles made the ship rock with each tug.

The crew crossed the slick deck and toward the starboard side. Pthorn had been taught by Caln that it was good luck to return scraps to the sea from the starboard side, so he guessed that a human sacrifice was probably the same deal.

As they moved towards the gunwale, it finally occurred to Pthorn that the destiny he had suspected back home was coming true; he had become a sacrifice to appease some unseen God.

"One!"

They swung Pthorn back and then forwards again.

"Two!"

Again a little higher.

Silence.

The storm just broke in an instant, and the rain stopped.

The beast untangled itself from the rigging and slinked back towards the depths, leaving a trail of destruction and flotsam behind.

Pthorn was still held onto by the feet and arms of a stunned-looking crew. They all looked to the sky, which had quickly returned to a bright blue. The cleared sky was joined by a gentle breeze, perfect for smooth and fast sailing. The storm had made the day a turmoil of night, and no one could have guessed that the sun was hiding behind it all.

Thump.

Pthorn found himself laid out in a heap on the ship's deck. He was drenched from head to toe but still very much alive and uneaten by the kraken. He outlined the four-pointed star of Aiel on his chest and looked to the sky in silent, unspoken prayer.

"I reckon that proves it! The sooner we get the little floater off this ship, the better… and they say women are bad luck. Pwah!"

Ness spat before she turned away and left Pthorn on the floor.

Even Caln seemed more than slightly suspicious but still offered an arm up. His actions spoke of trust, but his eyes betrayed him and spoke of superstition.

This was a stark reminder that beliefs could get you killed.

The rest of the journey passed much like the start, only with much less vomiting over the poop deck gunwale. The day after the kraken attack, the entire ship's crew had a total shift rotation of quiet and mourning for their lost crew member. Lenk had been one of the lower-ranked crew members, probably the equivalent of Pthorn, but with a few journeys across the sea under his belt.

That night the Captain proposed a toast to the young man's soul and issued a free-for-all on the liquor. Surprisingly very few took him up on the offer beyond a single swallow; however, Lenk's shift's crew drank well into the night before finishing up on the main deck singing sea shanties and passing out in the chilly winter's air beneath the sky.

The next day, work started back on board in earnest. They unfurled their sails, and the Captain used the ship's wheel to guide them in the direction of Matraketh with the assistance of the First Mate and his orienteering devices.

Pthorn was tasked to fetch and measure wooden planks to temporarily board up the main deck. The ship would need a proper shipwright to repair and seal it, but at least the crew could keep the outside from getting inside. Extra planks were stowed in the cargo hold behind the access ladder. The fire had burned directly beside them and had scorched a few but not beyond use.

Pthorn dragged them up the two ladders and marked them out with lumps of char before Ness cut them up with a sharp axe. Caln secured them to the deck using wooden pegs hammered into place before he layered the repair with pitch.

Within days they came within sight of land. As they approached, the crew became more and more relaxed in the presence of Pthorn. They clearly could not wait to get him off the ship and be rid of him.

Finally, the ship pulled into the dock on the shores of Matraketh. The port was similar to that in Straulatos, except without the dry heat. Behind the docks were the same types of vendors selling their wares, ladies of the night braving the day for a few extra coins to warm their bed, and what looked to be inns and pubs by the plenty. Beyond the small town stood the most remarkable difference between this port and the last. A mountain range towered over the port, extending into the distance and beyond the cloud line.

Pthorn disembarked from the ship before he turned toward Caln. They nodded to each other, and Pthorn made his way into the bustling market.

8.

Portsworth

Pthorn made his way from the ship through the throngs of vendors towards the outlying town, hoping to find somewhere to sit down and gather his thoughts. He quickly found a bar that didn't look too grubby and sat down in a booth, and piled his small supply of belongings beside him.

The barman, a tall man with a well-receding hairline and thick wiry moustache, made his way across to him.

"What will it be?" he asked.

"I've got nothing to pay with; I have just arrived from Straulatos."

"Then out with you, go on, get going," the barman said, flapping his arms dismissively.

Not a moment later, Pthorn remembered the sealed envelope that accompanied his travel papers.

"Hold on, there might be something here."

The barman did not look impressed. Pthorn suspected that he expected some sort of urchin scam.

Pthorn fingered through his clothing and found the letter sealed with the strange symbol, like a deformed four-pointed star of Aiel.

The barman caught sight of it and eyed it curiously but without comment.

Pthorn broke the wax seal and found a letter and a stack of pale purple notes. Pthorn had never seen any foreign currency, but the barman seemed to know its worth.

"Be still and seek the glory of the Assier; that is a lot of cash for someone who has no money!" he exclaimed. "Only the best food will do. Will you also be needing a room? We have good long-term rates."

"Yes to the food and room, but only for tonight."

"Well, if you find yourself in need of more time, just let old Gillium here know, and the finest room is yours, for the right price, of course."

The barman slipped away into the kitchens, and Pthorn unfolded the letter, which had been sealed within the envelope.

Dear Chosen One,

I hope you read this letter upon embarkation onto the Sea's Fury. There is a particular part of the sea that can be a little tricky at this time of year. You may wish to offer the Captain some advice to avoid the direct route to Matraketh; instead, turn east and follow due north for a few weeks before heading directly west. I am reasonably sure he will ignore this request, so good luck.

Pthorn stopped reading for a moment to be briefly annoyed at himself for not opening the letter sooner and to internally question how the author might have predicted their predicament at sea.

When you finally land on the continent of Matraketh, you should find your way into the Arrats. They are the prominent mountains you see in the distance. You can't miss them.

I might suggest using some of the enclosed money to stock up on some supplies while you are in Portsworth, such as food and very warm clothing. Don't pay any more than four broan and a scroat for anything.

I have enclosed a detailed map of the route to get you to your destination. Do not, under any circumstances, lose this map or show it to anyone. Not even to ask for directions, nor to a passing scuriat.

Yours Sincerely, Tom.

P.S. I hope you like the cold.

P.P.S. The map is encoded to keep it secure, although simple in its genius. Where you see a mountain drawn is actually Portsworth. Where you see a port drawn is actually the Arrat Range. What did I tell you? Genius, now burn this letter but keep the map.

Pthorn was not entirely sure what a scuriat was, let alone why he shouldn't show a map to one. The barman soon returned with a thick broth that smelled of roasted moog and a side of soft white bread. Pthorn had stowed his papers and money back inside his clothes bundle when he saw him leave the kitchen in his direction.

"If there is anything else I can assist with, sir, please let me know."

Pthorn nodded his response, and the barman turned away.

Once out of direct eyesight, Pthorn returned the envelope. Behind the letter from Tom was a hand-drawn map. 'Detailed' was certainly not the term he would have given the map; it was closer to a drawing that a child might draw in the dirt and proudly show their parent.

Indeed the map did show a mountain and a port. It also showed lines webbing across the page from various villages, lakes, and, curiously, what seemed to be some exotic animals.

To any passer-by, the paper was just filled with the mindless sketches of a child, but to Pthorn, it was the directions to his destiny.

What that destiny was had yet to be explained to him in any level of detail that made a modicum of sense.

Pthorn folded the map, the letter, and the cash before he stuffed them back into the envelope. He would burn the note later in his room.

His attention returned to the cold and congealed broth in front of him. He dipped the bread and enjoyed the first fresh mouthful of food he had eaten in many span.

Once finished, the barman led Pthorn from the booth and up the staircase to the accommodation. The hall was wood panelled with doors lining each side. Cheap art adorned the walls in the form of various sea animals.

Fitting for a port-side inn, he mused to himself.

There were all shapes and sizes of ghoti as well as more menacing creatures like the kraken that had set upon their ship. Pthorn let out a slight shudder as he passed its likeness and continued to follow the barman.

He was led to the last room at the end of the hall. The barman unlocked the door and handed him the key. The heavy wooden door creaked as it opened, and he was presented with an oversized estate room. In the centre was an ornate sleeping pallet with upright posts and curtains hung around it. A mirrored desk sat off to the side of the right-hand side of the room, with clothing storage and a large hearth to the left. Two large picture windows were positioned on either side of the pallet, each with a window seat inset for reclining. Above the bed was a large round window that sat inside the vaulted ceiling.

The room was the definition of opulence, and Pthorn had a passing suspicion that the barman would charge him more than his money's worth.

"Your room awaits, sir. Please do not hesitate to ask for anything; the kitchen is never completely closed, if you understand me."

Pthorn nodded his reply and closed the door behind him. He walked farther into the room so that he could take in more of the finer details. Unlike the artwork just outside his door, the room did not look like it fit in as part of a portside inn. The wooden structure of the sleeping pallet was carved with flowing vines, or perhaps seaweed, and the curtains were made of a light, delicate and perfectly white material; gossamer he believed Caln had called it when he'd enquired about the various bolts aboard the ship. The table was seemingly made by the same craftsman and included flush drawers, which proved to be lined with padded velvet on closer inspection. The craftsman and materials for it would have been readily available by the port but would have been worth a year's wage to most working-class people.

Even the floor, which for the most part was stained timber hardwood, had seen the hand of an artisan. In the centre of the room, a woven rug, which measured at least five paces, spread out from below the sleeping pallet in each direction. Pthorn could feel the softness of the pile beneath his feet and between his toes.

He laid out his religious clothing on the bed. It was almost ditched when he disembarked, but he thought better of it. If his receiving party, presumably someone named Tom, was expecting a priest rather than a ship's crewmate, he could end up in a bit of trouble.

Pthorn quickly decided that neither his current garb nor the religious one would keep him warm enough, given the warning in the letter. He placed the map, letter and a few notes of currency in his pocket and made himself a mental note to ask about the value to someone who wasn't trying to sell him something.

After he had descended the stairs, the barman scurried over to provide assistance.

"Is there anything I can do for you, sir?"

"Actually, yes, could you please point me in the direction of a place to buy warm clothing? I find myself in need of some heavy winter gear."

"Absolutely! You won't find any better than Arnult's. Out the door, and you will find him about fifty paces to the right. Best tailor in all of Matraketh he is. Is there anything else?"

Pthorn thought again of his letter.

"Yes, while I am gone, could you please get a fire stoked up in my room? I am not used to the chill of the north quite yet."

"As you say, it will be done."

Pthorn turned and left through the doors of the inn. He immediately turned right in the direction of Arnult's. Looking around, he noted some other key differences from the port back in Straulatos. The road seemed to be a dark colour, without the dirt and dust of a regular road. It had been sealed with some sort of clean material that stuck together but was not sticky like it looked.

Pthorn looked around as he walked down the roadway and found that, unlike back home, the transport was provided by equestra rather than mant.

They must be pretty common this side of the sea, he mused to himself.

He knew they were native to other continents but had not expected them to be everywhere.

Not far down the road, and just as described, Pthorn arrived at a small boutique with a sign hung from the eve.

'Arnult's Attire for Distinguished Gentlemen', the sign read.

Pthorn wasn't sure that was him but decided it was worth investigating further.

As he entered the shop, a young boy, several turns his junior, scampered out the door and back the way Pthorn had come.

"Good morning, young man; how may Arnult be of assistance to you today?" said a voice, old but spritely, from the rear of the shop.

A man who was north of sixty turns made his way towards Pthorn. Khani tells me you require some winter gear. Not to worry, my friend, I have just the thing.

Pthorn was unsure of how to take the man's familiarity with his situation before it dawned on him that the barman must have sent the boy as a runner ahead of him.

It seems that news travels fast when you flash some cash around in these parts.

"The boy is right, I am not used to the chill of these parts, and I may find myself needing some very warm clothing."

"Yes, yes, yes, I see, I see. Well, come now, my boy, let's get you sized up and don't you worry, you will get a good deal for someone of your... well, you know."

Pthorn wasn't quite sure that he did know but nodded anyway.

He was made to stand up on a raised platform while the tailor started to measure him.

Whilst he had intended to find out more about the value of the local currency before ending up in precisely this situation, he decided that he may as well broach the topic; the tailor seemed an honest enough man.

"Do you mind if I ask you some questions?" Pthorn started.

"Go ahead, my boy; my mind is yours."

"Could you please explain a little about money in these parts? Back in Straulatos, we used coin, but there are printed notes of different values here?"

The tailor finished measuring his arms and moved to start gauging the size of his waist and hips.

"Ah yes, well, the notes are called broan. One broan will buy you a loaf of bread and maybe a small piece of ghoti but not much else. Five broan will get you a comfortable meal and somewhere to lay your head, and ten broan will get you pretty much anything you want in a town like this."

The tailor continued to work his way down, measuring his leg.

"Then what about a scroat?"

The tailor looked up from measuring his inside leg with a look of horror. It quickly dawned on Pthorn that he had been pranked by his letter's author at the most inopportune time.

"Oh, Assier, I'm sorry I realise I must have misunderstood some advice I was given."

Pthorn made a mental note to throttle whoever this Tom guy was when he finally got to meet him. First, he predicts the storm and attack then he sets him up for embarrassment. The tailor replied with a "humph" and moved on from his previous location.

After he had completed his measurements, the tailor moved back to his counter at the rear of the shop to do some calculations while Pthorn looked around.

The walls were lined with what Pthorn assumed to be the latest clothing styles. Sharp suits with long tails and contrasting breeches. Lines of tall black and brown hats and fine scarves in all sorts of colours.

None of these would be suitable for any sort of cold journey, he thought to himself

Arnult seemed to understand Pthorn's thought process.

"You are in luck, my boy; there is no need for a custom suit with your sizes. Especially with heavy winter clothing. What do you think about a nice heavy baahti wool cloak and long breeches? I may even have some nice soft leather gloves and boots to match?"

Pthorn had grown up in the hot, arid fields of Strauth, so there was no need, nor money for, warm tailored cloaks and clothing.

The tailor took his silence as a cue to return to the back store to find the clothing. He materialised a matter of moments later with an arm full of clothing before he handed them over and pointed Pthorn toward a changing screen.

Pthorn ducked behind the screen and stripped off his deckhand clothing.

"Do you mind fetching a few more sets of small clothes for me as well? These could do with a burning," he called across the thin barricade.

"Certainly!" came the response, far closer to the screen than he was expecting. Pthorn nearly jumped out of his skin.

Pthorn donned the new breeches and cloak, followed by the boots and gloves. They felt soft and too warm for the room, but he was sure they would do the job when he ventured into the mountains.

Pthorn stepped out from behind the screen and moved towards the counter.

"A perfect fit! How does it feel?"

"I think it is just what I need. How much for these and the small clothes?" Pthorn question, not sure what to expect, even given their previous discussion about currency.

"For you, six broan will do nicely... and keep the scroat."

He gave Pthorn a cheeky smile. The elderly clerk had clearly come to terms with the joke and probably suspected someone was having Pthorn on.

Arnult packaged the small clothes in a couple of small paper packages and tied them off with a thin piece of string.

"Is there anything else I can assist with?"

"I will be travelling a long distance. I will need a bag and something to keep warm by night."

Without another word, the store clerk turned on his heel and disappeared back into the back store. He produced a large leather knapsack with a rolled bag attached to the base.

"It's all yours. Some young traveller used it as payment for some boots last summer, and I find myself with no use for it."

Pthorn thanked Arnult for his generosity as he silently wondered how he seemingly got a fair price for high-quality clothing and a free set of camping gear. He then left the store in high spirits and returned to the inn for a good night's sleep in his fancy room.

9.

Journey's End

Pthorn awoke in the morning and felt the freshest he had ever felt. The sheets had been clean and soft. There had been no movement of a ship beneath him. The room was still warm from the burned-down fire in the hearth, which slowly smouldered behind the grate; the letter from Tom had long since burned to a cinder during the night.

He swung his legs out and placed them on the rug before stretching in the rising sun's early morning glow. Light filtered in through the picture windows. He moved to look out at the vista dominated by the mountain range. Once again, the peaks were not visible from ground level, and a vast forest spread out below the foot of the mountains like foam from an over-boiled pot.

Pthorn packed his various sets of clothes into his new leather knapsack and donned his new warm-weather clothing, albeit without the gloves he had tucked into the front pocket. After securing the straps on the knapsack, he made his way down the hall and into the dining area.

It was too early for any public patrons to be in the bar, but he was quickly met by the barman who offered a hot breakfast, an offer Pthorn was not about to let slide.

He settled in the same booth as the previous day and was soon presented with a couple of rashers of onk bacon and porridge far superior to the horrible clag he had been served back home.

Once he was done, he settled his bill at just two broan. It was well below the going rate for a room, let alone the experience he had been presented with. His initial assumption that money had driven the barman to provide superior service had been a misconception. The only explanation was that he had recognised the deformed star of Aiel and felt it was his duty to provide for anyone who carried that seal, whatever it meant.

Pthorn threw in an extra broan by way of a tip and asked for some hard food for the road. The barman quickly returned with some cheese, sausage and bread. Enough to last a couple of weeks on the road if rationed well. He also threw in a water skin, which Pthorn was very grateful for, given that his previous plan had been to source fresh water daily.

The barman bid Pthorn farewell as he walked out of the bar and into the street.

Once he had travelled a couple of hundred paces down the road, Pthorn consulted his map, mentally rearranged the mountains and Portsworth into their correct locations, and started at the wrong end of the route. The track seemed to follow the road for about a day's walk before it took a sharp turn north towards the range. It looked like there would be a three-way crossroads, and he was to take the non-existent path off the sealed track.

Pthorn folded the letter and again set off with his knapsack hitched over his shoulders, all his worldly possessions on his back.

The road continued to be sealed with the strange dark material. The sun was high in the sky before the road transitioned to the traditional wagon-compacted dirt he had been accustomed to. Pthorn had also noticed the change in plant life. To the right of him remained unchanged, rows upon rows of tall needle-like trees with broad, sparse foliage. They looked to have been planted in an almost intentional pattern. The other side of the road to the south was a completely different story. That side of the road had been buildings and side roads before it quickly became dense, deep green brush. This brush slowly thinned as he progressed before it gave way to vast open fields of lush green grass like nothing Pthorn had ever seen back home in Straulatos. Wildflowers of every possible colour grew in the meadows; purples, blues, yellows and oranges with dots of bright red throughout. Distant animals frolicked in the grass but were too far away or too exotic for Pthorn to identify by species.

Soon Pthorn's amazement turned to boredom, and he began to hum to himself one of the songs his mother used to sing to him. Thinking of her gave him a little bit of comfort, and he was surprised to discover that he felt almost a little homesick.

Eventually, late in the afternoon, Pthorn came to the crossroad. He turned north, away from the comfort of the road and into the dense grove of trees. The green canopy immediately began to blot out the remaining warmth and light provided by the sun, which had started to set overhead. He decided that there was not much good that could come from travelling in the dark, and once he had travelled a few hundred paces from the road, he set up camp for the night. He would have no light or fire for warmth after dark, so he made sure to set up his bedroll early enough that any complexities could be sorted out in the light of the day.

This turned out to be a good decision. The bedroll was not just a simple sleeping bag; instead, it had a collection of rods that were used to prop it up, allowing for space to move. Pthorn had never assembled anything like it in his life. Night had begun to fall deeply across the land by the time Pthorn crawled into his accommodation for the night.

With nothing else to do, he put his head down, covered himself with the blankets and fell asleep, far less comfortable than his slumber from the previous night.

Pthorn awoke the following day to a symphony of squawks and shrill chirps. Outside the tent was a flurry of flapping wings. It sounded like a flock of some species of luftun fought over food or played in the treetops. He unclasped the flap on the side of the propped-up bedroll and peered around the end, trying not to scare them away. The luftun were brightly coloured and about the size of a grown man's forearm. Their colourful plumage extended into a long, fanned tail which moved into discrete up-and-down positions as they squawked at each other. The fur which covered their bodies was thick and became thin as it covered their delicate wings. Two young luftun, whose colours had barely come in, fought over a golden tree nut even though thousands more were ripe for the taking.

Pthorn sat there for a while, enjoying some 'quiet' nature-watching time. Back home, luftun were a rarity. Most were black, very large, and only interested in pecking at the remains of dead animals. These were a thing of beauty. When they spread their wings and fanned their tails, their skin became semi-transparent, and the light shone through, making the colours even more vibrant.

Pthorn soon decided that breakfast was in order and that he should probably make a move sooner rather than later. Judging by the map, he still had a long way to go before arriving at his curious destination. He was getting anxious to meet up with this Tom, but he wasn't sure in what way.

To settle his nerves and take his mind off the task, he broke off a piece of sausage and a bit of cheese and began to eat. The luftun must have had some unique sense of smell as they immediately left the berries to rot and flew down towards his cover. Pthorn fell backwards into the bedroll with a start, dropping the cheese but kept a hold of the sausage by some minor miracle. He quickly sealed the opening and waited until the hungry flock gave up their pursuit of more food. With his lesson learned, he broke off another tiny bit of cheese, finished breaking his fast and packed away the rest of his food for later.

The bedroll was far simpler to erect than it was to pack away. After countless failed attempts to get it back to its initial dimensions, Pthorn finally managed to get it rolled up and fastened with the leather straps. With his last night's bedroom mounted securely back onto the knapsack, Pthorn started his hike for the day. He consulted the map, which, more or less, just directed him towards the centre of the range. There looked to be a few days of straight walking to the toe of the mountain before the climb began.

The following day and night passed without issue. Pthorn sighted a few more exotic birds and several small burrowing animals, but that was about it. As predicted, just after the morning of the third day, Pthorn reached the toe of the mountain. The terrain became more steep and barren of plant life. Rocks, or more accurately, small boulders, covered several hundred paces worth of ground and made the final approach to the mountain a risk to his ankles if he misstepped. Pthorn completed the slow journey across the rocky outcrop and arrived at a sheer wall. It was as it had appeared from a distance, and he desperately hoped that there was a more clearly delineated path to be shown up close. Upon his first inspection, no such luck was to be had.

Pthorn had few options except to try to look around the base. He looked first towards the left, the boulders pressed all the way to the toe as far as he could see, and the face of the mountain remained sheer. He looked to the right, and it seemed much the same except that it curved around, making it impossible to see much further than thirty paces. He decided to check out the right-hand path and had just turned when he heard a light, airy voice call out.

"We were starting to get worried you had lost your way, Master Pthorn."

The voice almost caused Pthorn to jump out of his skin. He turned back to find a man in a plain white robe standing not five paces from him. He had only just looked that way and determined there was no clear path. One thing was for sure; he was confident that there had not been a robed priest standing there.

The startled look of confusion was evident on his face as the priest continued, "I am Gular, the Holy Advisor to the Oracles; please follow me."

The priest turned toward the mountain and disappeared into the rock through what seemed to be nothing more than a fault line. Pthorn moved to investigate the apparent gateway and stretched out his arm to feel the stone. His hand brushed solid rock to the side of the fissure. As his hand slid across, an arm shot out, grabbed and pulled him through.

Pthorn was utterly puzzled. He had somehow just travelled through solid stone and now stood in a dark tunnel, lit only by another one of the strange light sources he had witnessed in the High Priest's carriage back in Straulatos. The walls and roof were carved from stone, something he didn't even know was possible.

"How did we? I mean, we are standing inside a mountain...."

"All will be explained in more detail soon, for now just accept that, yes, we are inside one of the mountains that form the Arrats. We still have a long, and sometimes uncomfortable, travel ahead of us."

Pthorn had hoped for more of an explanation but settled for being told later. The Holy Advisor plucked the light source from its sconce, and they started their journey into the mountain. Pthorn quickly found that the heavy baahti wool cloak was too warm. Not wanting to seem out of place he stopped, shrugged off the cloak, and dressed into the white robe that he had been supplied with back in Strauth.

The climb through the mountain was challenging but, overall, not too taxing on him. The priest, however, was well into his senior years and struggled with the endless climb. Most of the tunnel had a sloped floor, but steeper sections had rectangular blocks cut into the slope to act as steps. These sections made for a very slow climb for the pair.

When they stopped to make camp each night, Pthorn did not bother to erect his bedroll; instead, he just unrolled it and laid it flat to provide some barrier between himself and the hard rock.

Another three days passed since they had entered the mountain, and Pthorn noticed a change in the air. It had become colder and felt wetter. They soon found themselves standing just inside the mouth of an exit from the mountain. Pthorn first thought was that they had made it to their destination, but if that was the case, he figured that the expensive warm clothing wouldn't have been required. He quickly realised that there was to be an outdoor trek and changed back into his cold weather gear, including the gloves and boots, but left his robes beneath.

Pthorn walked out of the comfort of the tunnel and into a world of wind. He pulled the cloak's hood tight and followed the priest into what lay beyond. The air cut like an ice-cold knife as it whipped around. The air seemed to carry tiny swirling shards of ice that beat at what showed of his face.

A two-pace wide path wound its way around the outside of the mountain with what looked to be a sheer drop to the side. They slowly edged their way along. Pthorn made sure not to look too long into the swirling abyss below; he knew it would be death for him if he wandered too close to the edge.

After a few hundred paces, the path turned and led away from the mountain. Visibility was not far, and the course's destination was unclear. It seemed to head into the unknown rather than keeping to the known. The priest led the way across and away from the safety of the mountain. As they followed the path across the pass, the wind only increased and seemed to grow colder. Pthorn pulled the cloak tight to his body and followed the priest closely.

They walked for what seemed an eternity before they reached another mountain. It looked just as the first had to Pthorn.

Pthorn let out a triumphant "Whoop!" and immediately regretted it. The priest threw him a deep look of concern, his eyes alight with fear.

The holy man grabbed Pthorn and, with more force than Pthorn would have thought possible for an elderly man, pulled him tight to the sheer face of the mountain. Not even a few heartbeats later, a shower of small rocks rained down like tiny knives. The rocks shattered as they impacted the path in front of them, and the two travellers narrowly avoided being speared.

They stood still with their backs firmly pressed against the stone for a while until they were confident that no more rocks would shower them. Finally, the pair began to move and continued to walk along a new path.

The path was only a few hundred paces, similar to the one on the first mountain, and once again, Pthorn was led through seemingly solid stone into another tunnel. This tunnel had permanent light fixtures, which gave Pthorn hope that they were approaching their final destination.

The priest continued through a series of interconnecting tunnels with antechambers until they reached a sizeable carved-out room.

"Welcome to the Sanctum of the Sect," said the Holy Advisor, "I hope you are ready for your first lesson."

10.
Interlude: The Oracle of Malcontent

The Oracle of Malcontent | The Sect

Grey sky, grey rock, grey robes.

The colour of washout had come to rule the world of the middle-aged mage, the Order-Master of Death. He stood high above the cloud on a rocky plateau, watching the horizon from atop one of the three major peaks of the Arrat range. Nothing grew at this altitude, and very little life survived; the weather was frigidly cold after dark, even during the warmer months as it was currently. It was the middle of the day, and the mountain air was crisp. The breeze brought tiny shards of ice, needles of frozen water, that felt like they were trying to pierce the skin and sap the warmth from within. The

Oracle of Malcontent knew that down below in the valley, the weather would be warm, the sun providing the light required to turn the fields into a sea of green dotted with colourful wildflowers of violet, yellow and pink.

Unfortunately for the mage, the perfect vista of autumn, come summer, was a distant memory, still vividly remembered from the time long past when he was free to roam. He thought back to a time, long ago, before he spent twenty-two turns training, much of the time in almost complete silence, to become inducted into The Sect.

The swirling grey, icy wind blocked all colour from the world; the clouds below him looked almost solid enough to walk out on. He could see no more than fifty paces into the distance. When he relaxed his vision, he swore that he could see forms in the flurries, his eyes merely playing tricks on him after turns of isolation. The mage understood enough about the mysteries of death to know that the forms must be a figment of his imagination.

The mage reached into one of his pockets, retrieved a small yellow ball, split it in half, and began slowly massaging them between his gloved fingers. Once shaped into two small cones, he renewed his focus on the unseen world beyond, closed his eyes and placed the small pieces of wax into his ears to block out the remaining small amount of local stimulus. He had to become completely isolated from the area immediately within his vicinity and become one with the world. He drew in a long deep breath and began to hum. The vibrations reverberated through his skull. He lifted his arms perpendicular to his body, straight forward in front of him; his palms faced outwards in a pushing motion.

Time was of no object while completing the Push. The mage stayed in this position, unmoving until the grey world became almost black. Muffled by stone, a deep, long 'DONG' rang in the frigid air. The mage could not hear it, at least not with his ears. He could feel it, though. His connection to everything around him allowed him to simply know the gong had been rung. His head dropped low in defeat.

Another day of 'work' completed, he thought to himself.

His thoughts focused on the knowledge that this would be his life for yet another forty turns... and his time was only just beginning.

Weary and sore, the mage turned his back on the grey void. He walked the thirty paces back towards a small gap in the mountainside, a gash like an axe wound cut into the face of a sheer wall. To any intrepid mountaineer who might stumble upon it, the entrance would simply look like a continuation of the wall face; there was much that could only be seen by the Initiated. He began his stride, giving a small hard-shelled creature a swift boot as he walked. The burnt orange scuriat gave a high-pitched shriek as it was launched across the plateau; it struggled to stay on solid ground before it skidded off the edge and plummeted into the abyss. The mage almost thought he recognised the look of horror in the black, stalk-mounted eyes as it realised that death awaited it within moments.

"Vale, I hope you have better luck in the next life," muttered Death.

Somehow, he had hoped the shattering of the innocent creature would pick up his spirits. It didn't. Being the Order-Master of Death gave the mage more insight than any other into life's final moments, and it didn't provide him with a single shred of solace.

Once inside, he passed through the void, and the mage found himself back within the shelter of solid stone. The passageway turned twice to keep the weather out, preventing too much of the warmth of the cave from escaping. The antechamber where he now stood was one of the hundreds of rooms within the mountain connected by tunnels and stairs. The mountain had been systematically hollowed out, crushed and placed around the base of the mountain range to discourage the likes of explorers. Thousands of turns ago, one of the first Creativity Oracles had made it her life's work to provide a sanctuary for the Sect and allow their order to live, research and train far away from the rest of the world.

It was during the mountain's excavation that much of the mechanical technology now used for construction was developed. Leverage and pulley theory was discovered, studied, developed and slowly disseminated to the world. The ongoing study of this technology was a joint effort between Creativity and Combat, the latter providing much of the insight and study into the strategy and manpower requirements.

The Oracle of Malcontent slowly made his way across the empty room and into a narrow, damp-light-lit tunnel. Damp-light was another invention of The Order of Creativity, a product of very slow combustion which required very little fuel and produced very little smoke.

Damp-light could be used to illuminate deep within the cave network without removing the atmospheric life force that provided breath. Men and mages alike had been known to stop breathing where fires had burned in confined areas; the exact reason remained a mystery. The Order of Life maintained that an invisible life force was present and flowed into any breathing creature to keep it alive; this was one of the interests of the current Order-Master, The Oracle of Anew. The previous Order-Master and the now Oracle of Anew, known then simply as Life-Elect, had dedicated several decades to understanding, measuring and quantifying this life force in the study of what they referred to as Atmospherics. Ducting had been included in the design of the caves at the request of an ancient Life Order-Master. This allowed for smoke displacement and ensured a light breeze was always present.

The Order-Master of Death continued through the tunnel network for several hundred paces until he found himself within the Sanctum Sacellum. In this holy chamber, the masters and apprentices of the four orders must spend part of the evening every day bowed in solemn silence, meditating and reflecting. Holy was probably a bit of a stretch, as The Sect was less about being believers and more about being believed in. Theologically speaking, they were closer to being gods than priests. It was a firm belief of the order that for progress and research to be most effective, a portion of the day must be spent without further stimulus.

A thin man, well beyond the eightieth turn since his birth, was giving a lecture to a single young man, not quite old enough to grow facial hair.

"The four orders are known to be descended from a single being, The Singular. This being was not made of flesh and bone but rather a singular sentient life force that had way too long to consider itself. It is believed, from the knowledge handed down through the generations of The Sect, that this being finally posed itself with a choice; remain the disembodiment of power itself or be power made physical."

The holy man looked up at the mage as he entered the room before continuing his lecture to the young man.

"The Singular finally decided, based on the infinite amount of knowledge it had amassed over its existence, that it was to transform itself into a physical manifestation. It created Azarth, including all that inhabits it and all that surrounds it. In becoming power-made-physical, The Singular was destroyed almost entirely, but not before leaving behind a few traces of knowledge. Four mages, representing Life, Death, Combat and Creativity, were created to maintain the knowledge and order of the new world. Much of the knowledge of The Creation was lost, but the philosophy of research and order was established, and The Sect was conceived. That will conclude your first lesson, my son; it is time for reflection."

The holy man turned his back on the young student and placed his brow upon a threadbare floor mat, his legs together, and arms pushed forward. The other Order-Masters and Order-Elects soon filed into the room with their bodies covered head to toe in grey robes, taking their places and bowing in silence.

The Oracle of Malcontent watched from the floor as the young man looked around the room, unsure of what he should be doing. The Order-Master gave a few silent hand signals to suggest that the young man should join in. After a few moments of studying the other room's occupants, he lowered his head to the ground and bowed in silence.

The bell tolled once more, sounding much louder than earlier but still somehow seemingly distant. One-by-one, everyone slowly arose and filed out, with the exception of Death and the new recruit.

"So," the Order-Master started, "you must be my new apprentice. How did you come about the misfortune of being in this dim shit-hole?"

The young man was not quite sure how to react to the question; it had been preached that it was an honour of the highest level to be selected to join the Gods.

"I was hand-picked, sir, by the High Priest of Straulatos, sir; he told me I had pleased Assier and that I was going to join him as his highest servant... sir."

Death chuckled, probably a little too insensitively.

"The Singular's Almighty dingleberries, save me. Are they still preaching that drivel across Azarth? And save me the 'sir's, we are going to be working together for a long time, and I can't stand being called sir. My name is The

Oracle of Malcontent but please, for the love of The Singularity, call me Tom."

The young man nodded but chose to stand in silence.

"You, however, shall be known for the next two-and-twenty turns as Death-Elect to everyone in this Singular-Damned mountain, as is the tradition going back to the beginning. Is that all good with you, Del?"

Del managed a slightly confused nod; the contradictory name took several moments to sink in.

"Unfortunately for you, you have drawn the short straw when it comes to the four orders. You were unlikely to have been inducted into Life or Creativity as your cock would likely get in the way of you being a woman, but at least combat would have been much less dull. More strategy and less decomposition; you were simply born on the wrong continent. Any questions so far?"

Del looked as though he had a million questions but perhaps considered very few of them to be appropriate. "What exactly do you, I mean we, do here?" he posed.

"As I am sure the holy man will explain to you in excruciating detail, there are four orders here in The Sect; each one compliments and opposes the other. Life and Creativity are closely paired, as are Death and Combat. Without creativity, there would be no originality in combat strategy, and without life, there would be no death. We deal with the knowledge and power of death and all that it entails. We have the power to enact death or prevent death, to deliver disaster or ensure old age."

"Does nature not already do this for us? Why do they need me?" the boy questioned.

"Balance," replied the mage, "we are meant to provide balance... and just what do you think nature is?"

He left the rhetorical question hanging in the air for a few moments.

"We in the Sect are nature, yes, life continues when we aren't looking or focusing on it, but we are the guiding force. We exist so that the world doesn't simply become a complete disaster. Think about it: the population would become uncontrollable if everyone had prolific crops without the occasional hopper plague or lived without an epidemic disease or two. Life would cover every square pace of Azarth without the hope of control. As the bringers of death to Azarth, we have the shitty job of undoing the work done by the other three Orders in the name of balance."

"As you will learn, small and simple changes are usually the most effective. Every change in the world has a flow-on effect. Did you know that there is a small creature that lives only one day?"

The young man shook his head, still trying to take everything in.

"It is known as a barg; once it hatches from its birthing shell, the creature latches on to the nearest living creature and starts draining it. It uses the life of its meal to create the next generation of its own. Two offspring are produced at the end of the day, which lay in wait, growing over the next turn, feeding on the life given by its parent.

Can you imagine the effect of changing one variable? Maybe changing the gestation from one turn to half a turn or decreasing the likelihood that the unborn creature is not trampled, thereby doubling the rate of reproduction and the rate of decline of its food source, which by way of mention, is also your food source. Hunted meat sources like the small, slow, brown onk and the large, prancing, grey keil. Do you understand?"

"I think so; it is our job to make small changes to the world to ensure it is sustainable. Like, not too big or too small?"

"Exactly, now come with me. I'm getting a headache."

Part 2

11.
Welcome to the Sect

om led Del to his new living quarters. He pulled the heavy door sheet of tanned leather aside and found the room strangely lavish in a dull sort of way, even though the room was lit by pale blue damp-light. The space had presumably been occupied by generations of young men who had come before him. Carvings of grossly oversized phalluses and nude women adorned most surfaces in the room. There was a strange, stale but familiar scent of body odour, a staple of every teenage boy's bedroom; it reminded him of his own room back home.

The room was approximately eight paces in each direction, with a large sleeping pallet in the centre and small carved wooden bedside tables on either side. A matching scribe's desk was beside the door with a few blank parchment scrolls and an ink pot. In addition to the crude additions to the room, there were intricate carvings on all of the wooden furniture in the form of creatures, just like those in fae tales told to children at bedtime. The detail was far more intricate than Del had ever seen, whirls of scrolls between the faces of evil-looking pixies, bright red stones inlaid where the eyes of the creatures would be, and the dark staining that furniture gets after hundreds of turns of use. Del assumed that this was the work of the Order of Creativity, probably homework set for an Order-Elect one afternoon.

"The privy is through that door to your right, and, as you may have guessed, we are a little short on washerwomen and pages here in the Arrats. You and the other three Order-Elects will be required to heat the water for washing every evening. The water supply to the room will run cold for drinking at all other times. Continuously melting mountain snow supplies us with running water all turn."

"Thank you," Del replied, "I'll try to make myself home."

Tom gave a reassuring glance and nodded before making to leave the room.

"What did you say your proper name was earlier, Tom?" asked Del.

"When the Order-Master of any order undergoes The Changing, the Order-Elect becomes the new Order-Master. About the time you were born, my mentor of two-and-twenty turns became the latest in the long line of Oracles to complete The Changing and leave me to take his place."

Del looked confused and somewhat annoyed that Tom had not answered his question.

"When I completed my transition to Order-Master at the ceremony eight-and-ten turns ago, I was given a name been chosen by my fellow Oracles. They decided, by popular vote, on a name that they deemed most appropriate for my station and my personality. They chose Malcontent because, as it turns out, I have never been entirely content with my position as the bringer of death and destruction."

"So, where does Tom come from then?" Del asked, "why not Mal?"

"Do you know your letters, my dear boy?" he replied.

"Yes, Mother made sure that she taught me how to read and write properly, sir, um, sorry, Tom, for when the time came for me to take over the farm and run the business."

This made him think of his family back home. *How were they moving on without me there? What would my mother and father do without a succession plan?*

He decided that thoughts of back home would probably end in an emotional display, so he pushed it down and shook his head.

If Tom noticed Del's internal thought process, he paid it no mind.

"Tom is an acronym of The Oracle of Malcontent, and by that, I mean that each letter of the name represents the first letter of my title. Now, you had best get some rest; you will have noticed the full room of other Order-Elects who have beaten you here by several span and have already commenced their duties and training. We start on the basics tomorrow."

With that, Tom turned and left the room, leaving the leather 'door' swaying in his wake.

Del turned to continue surveying his room; a small square hole was visible in the centre of the ceiling. He moved closer and noticed a light draft pulling towards the hole. After closer inspection, he deduced that this was some form of wind generation device which led to the outside of the mountain.

Del continued through the door to the privy, and he found himself wishing that he had asked for more clarification on how to use the facilities. A large stone tub sat to the left of him in the small room. A single, iron-banded, wooden pipe came down from the ceiling. Below that were a further three half-pipes; one angled and passing through the stone wall with water running through it, one pointing into the large stone tub and the third pointing towards a strange seat with a hole in it. Deciding to investigate further, there seemed to be an iron mechanism that could divert the water between the three half-pipes. Del pulled the mechanism across, first allowing the water to pass into the tub, then, further along, allowing the water to flow into the chair. Water sprayed up from the bottom in an arc, presumably allowing the running water to clean one's nether regions after evacuating the bowels.

"Good Assier, have these people never heard of leaves!" he exclaimed a little too loudly.

It soon dawned on Del that leaves were probably hard to come by at this altitude. He re-diverted the water to the tub and tested the water for temperature. His hand had barely become immersed in the water before he suddenly pulled it away; the water was deathly cold.

Del ambled back towards the sleeping pallet and laid down, thinking over the last day's events.

How did I go from being nothing more than a farmer's boy, tending to crops and livestock, to being the apprentice of a God?

"I don't have any special powers! Why was I chosen? How can I possibly be chosen?" he exclaimed, verbalising the last of his thoughts aloud.

The walls seemed to answer for him as though they embodied some higher power.

"For the love of Assier's arse, shut up!"

Nope, it was just his friendly neighbour letting him know that, while the stone walls may be soundproof, the leather 'door' was just that; leather. The voice was feminine and sounded like she might be of a similar age. He decided that, given her somewhat less-than-friendly response, he might wait for at least another day before investigating further.

He stripped off naked, settled into the pallet, and pulled up the quilted linen blanket to sleep. Sleep welcomed him after a long, confusing day. He was grateful to have somewhere to lay his head that he didn't need to unpack or pack up the next day.

At least there can be no surprises in sleep, he thought to himself.

Del awoke to the sound of chanting; it was not a language he understood. He spoke only the common tongue of Azarth. While there were nuances around the globe, all of the people of Azarth kept a common language. There was one exception, High Elder, which was spoken exclusively by the clergymen and religious scholars. It was believed that High Elder was the language of the gods and that to communicate with them, the most pious must worship in the odd, strange tongue.

Del deduced that the language must be High Elder and opened his eyes to see what fate had befallen him in his sleep. Too late, he realised his mistake in removing his clothing before falling asleep. While the hooded figures who surrounded him had managed to remove him from his room, they had not taken the time to prepare anything for his modesty. He found himself laid upon a padded stone plinth in the centre of a large chamber, not one that he had seen during his day of orientation.

Del looked around the room. He could see curious damp-light torches. They were positioned within ornate iron sconces on the walls and threw dull red light around the room. The room was shaped like a massive dome. It was a perfect hemisphere, with the arc starting from the centre of the ceiling and finishing at the floor; a white orb hung glowing in the centre. Del considered if it was just his eyes adjusting or playing tricks on him, but the sphere seemed to be starting to increase in brightness.

The chanting also increased in volume and speed. He looked around the room to see what was happening. He looked down and saw the first figure, a grey-cloaked figure with a red, knotted rope tied around its waist. To his left, he saw the same but with a green rope, and to his right, gold. Tilting his head back as far as he could go, he could see a figure with a black rope.

The chanting stopped suddenly as the orb above him reached a crescendo of brightness. All four figures dropped their cloaks simultaneously. The red and green figures turned out to be middle-aged women; looking around, he found the gold and black to be similarly aged men. Two things struck him at that moment; he knew the man in black to be The Oracle of Malcontent or Tom as he introduced himself, and the second was that they were all as naked as their name-day.

Del's regrets about bed clothing choices were amplified once more by the further realisation that he had never seen a naked woman besides his own mother. Almost instantaneous humiliation occurred, which was surprisingly ignored by the four figures.

The figure who had worn the red rope spoke first, now in the common tongue of Azarth, "Pthorn of Straulatos, you have been chosen by your High Priest as a sacrifice to The Singular. I, through your mother, gifted you with life and breath; however, I provide you with no further gifts. I am the Order-Master of Life, The Oracle of Anew."

Her golden skin almost glowed in the bright white light of the overhead orb. Her skin tone, and deep brown almond eyes, clearly marked her as being of Kesheir origin, a continent of women known throughout Azarth for their beauty.

She was followed by the man to Del's right, who had been wearing the golden rope. He had the body of a warrior, with a body rippling with a muscled tone. His skin was the deepest black he had ever seen. Del had never seen such a man but had heard the tales from wandering storytellers who would drop by his village speaking of the giants of Saulit or the bar staff at the two moons.

The man introduced himself, "I am the Order-Master of Combat, The Oracle of Prevail. I have not seen fit to grant you the skills or physique of a warrior. Your talents are otherwise allocated."

To his left, the remaining woman, who had been wearing the green rope, began to speak, "I am the Order-Master of Creativity, The Oracle of Beauty. I, too, have not seen fit to grant you the skills of a craftsman nor that of an artist."

Pthorn took in the features of the wide-eyed third figure. Her complexion was washed out in the light, almost like she had never seen a moment of sunlight. Her pale skin and bright blue eyes marked her as being from this continent, Matraketh. Of all the Order-Masters, she showed her years most visibly on her skin, with aging lines adorning her brow.

Finally, the fourth member of the order spoke up. "Pthorn of Straulatos, I am the Order-Master of Death, the Oracle of Malcontent. I am yet to present you with a gift, for until now, this would have required you to relinquish the gift provided to you from The Oracle of Anew. Today I present you with a unique gift, a gift of power born from the death of The Singular. Today you become a god-in-training, an apprentice to myself. Indentured servitude and training for two-and-twenty turns, followed by forty turns of mastery of your craft. You will be the balance to

Life, the bringer of difficult times to those who require strengthening, the final word in relieving the world of the pain of life and failure."

The chanting commenced once again for several moments before the orb overhead flashed like lightning in an explosion of white light. Warmth flowed from the orb and struck Pthorn in the chest. It flowed through him, down through his arms to his fingertips, before making its way through his legs, toes, and head.

Then, blackness.

12.
Beginning the Routine

el awoke the following day, unsure of what to believe.

His mind told him that he had been part of some form of initiation ceremony, but presently he wasn't quite sure whether to trust the stories his head was telling him.

Too much had happened in the last few days, too many ceremonies, too much chanting, and way too much nudity.

Del's eyes had barely opened before another young man entered his room. Much like the golden rope-adorned man from last night, this man was tall and very dark-skinned. He held his left arm up and raised his middle finger in a friendly gesture of welcome.

"Good morning, you must be the last new Elect. I am the Combat-Elect, although you might have already guessed that. My name was Ka, but I suppose that doesn't really matter anymore."

Del returned the hand gesture without making much effort to sit up in his pallet before he rolled onto his side and replied, "Death-Elect, or as Tom calls me, Del. My name was Pthorn back in Straulatos but, as you said, that probably doesn't mean much anymore."

After finally becoming more lucid and remembering that he still had not redressed himself, Del sat up in the pallet and covered his body more thoroughly with the quilt.

"How long have you been here?" he asked.

"I arrived about seven days ago; the other two Elects have been here much longer. I had to travel almost the same distance as you, coming from Saulit. Terrible weather, though. As much as I would love to chat, we need to get moving. I'm not sure how much your Order-Master has told you, but nothing much happens around here without an Elect pulling a lever or turning a wheel. It turns out that they have been looking forward to having us do all their work for them for quite a few turns. I have some robes for you to wear today; get dressed and meet me outside."

Combat-Elect threw the grey robes at Del and left the room.

Del crawled out of bed, grabbed the robes and made his way into the privy room.

After setting the robes down, he sat on the cold stone chair to complete his morning routine. After a few moments, he suddenly realised that he had made a very significant error. He thought back to the previous day, and two fundamental concepts came to mind; firstly, there are no leaves with which to wipe oneself after one's business has been conducted, and secondly, the water is only heated once a day, in the evening, by the Elects. It seemed highly unlikely that the water flowing through the pipes was heated because it was first thing in the morning.

Del was left with two choices, both almost as unpleasant as each other; use the fresh white linen towel to wipe himself with or utilise the water system, which was almost undoubtedly icy cold.

Given that the first option wasn't really viable without a very awkward explanation, he steeled himself against the cold. He reached up and pulled on the iron mechanism allowing water to flow into the tub and then once more to divert the water to his bottom.

Very few words could describe the sensation that followed nor the scene caused by his reaction. The water quickly did its job but also made Del remove himself from his seated position in what can only be described as a springing leap across the room, accompanied by a shrill squeal of surprise. Being only a small room, his head made contact with the hard, cold stone wall on the other side. Del lay on the floor for what seemed like an eternity before picking himself up and drying off. Once he had removed all traces of the icy water, he re-diverted the water supply and donned his robe, noting the black colouring of the rope as he cinched it around his waist. His hand went to his brow. A large egg was beginning to form above his right eye, along with the makings of a headache. He made a mental note to find some dullingroot for the pain.

Del left the privy, walked through his room and found three people standing together, all doubled over in laughter. Clearly, his misadventure had been heard, and they had all understood his error in judgement. The lump on his head continued growing as he massaged his brow.

Del mustered up the only response he could think of, "shut the farmin' hell up!"

Unfortunately for him, this only increased the laughter tenfold.

Once the laughter had died down to a rolling chuckle, they all set off through the network of damp-light-lit tunnels and soon found themselves standing in a large kitchen. To the far end of the room, Del noted a heavy sheet of leather, much like the door in his own room, and small clouds of cold air emitted from the doorway as white, wispy tendrils.

Even though he had only been there for a span, Combat-Elect had been given the responsibility of providing Del with a tour of the facilities.

"That there is the cold store," he said to Del, "I have been told that we do supply runs every few months to keep it full, especially through the winter."

To one side and in the centre of the room were two heavy stone benches, presumably for food preparation. The bench on Del's left had a tub mounted in it with a constant flow of ice-cold water passing through a pipe into it, similar to the pipework in his privy. A shudder passed through him, and Del moved to massage his new head egg.

To the right side of the room was a large hearth; a pot hung above the wood, and an iron plate was mounted beside it. The entire room screamed of cold hard stone, particularly with the burned-out ashes which sat dormant inside the hearth. Del felt a physical shiver just thinking about the room; the stone seemed to leach the warmth from his body right through the air.

"Alright, you guys know the drill by now; let's get this moving. Del, build us a fire, would you?" called Combat-Elect, "the wood is stacked in the airing room behind us."

He pointed to another curtained doorway.

Del made his way into the airing room and found what can only be described as half a forest turned lumber. After many years of setting the hearth for his mother, Del knew to select a range of sizes of wood, from fibrous kindling to logs. It took three trips to move a small stockpile of dried hardwood over to the empty hearth, setting the wood to the side.

Del knelt down and created a small pyramid of medium-sized, chopped wood with a centre of kindling before realising he had an, albeit slightly distanced, audience. It very quickly dawned on him what they were curious about.

What was my plan for turning the sticks into fire? I couldn't very well just ask it to become fire, could I?

"Alright, what's the joke? Where's the flint box?" he asked.

This was returned with sniggers confirming his suspicion that something was definitely amiss. He had to think. You can't light anything from damp-light; the slow burn meant there was no way to get the wood hot enough to start a fire.

Think, think, think. TREES!

That was it; trees were once alive and now dead. Burning the wood further transforms the wood from life to death.

He knew that this was to be an impossible challenge.

"Hilarious guys, you know I can't do shit yet! Where is Tom?!"

"Well, you worked that out faster than Shit-for-Brains Combat-Elect over here last week," laughed his female neighbour.

Judging by her taupe skin and stark alikeness to the Order-Master of Life from last night, she had to be the Life-Elect.

"Hey! I really thought I could get it going by rubbing the sticks together," he retorted.

"Come on, where will I find him? I'm freezing my balls off here."

Surprisingly it was Life-Elect who eagerly came to his aid, "alright, let's go find you a deathly Oracle. I'm sure he is already awake and raring to start his day."

Tom was not ready to start his day.

If Tom had been cranky when he had already been awake for half the day, it was nothing compared to when he was woken up by anything other than his internal body-dial.

The throwing of his pillow was easily anticipated; however, the immediate follow-up of a far more solid stone bowl was not. Del's quick reflexes prevented the castellated dish from becoming millions of pieces of shattered soapstone.

Upon closer inspection, the bowl was darkened with soot and had an acrid, burned odour. Tom had pitched his personal ashtray at Del's head. His instinct of self-preservation was soon lost once he realised there were no more objects which could be easily thrown his way.

"I, and by I, I mean we, need fire, Tom. No fire, no breakfast!"

"Urgh, fine," he grunted as he rolled out of bed.

Not one to be bothered with decency, he threw back the covers and walked stark naked across the room to fit himself into his all-black outfit.

"Come on, lesson one; Combustion!"

Del watching on in anticipation from in front of the hearth with the rest of the Elects.

"The first thing you need to know is this, and you may have already guessed it. Last night was more than just a light show. The power of the Singular was transferred to you, giving you the potential for the same abilities as me. You just don't know how to summon the power and harness or control it yet. We will have plenty of lessons to come on life and death, but right now, a good simple lesson in matter Manipulation should set us in good stead."

Tom clicked his fingers, and the hearth burst into flames.

The others didn't seem surprised, but Del was shocked. He had just witnessed something only possible in the fae tales parents tell their children.

"Now, while that heats up the water, it is your turn to try. Set up some nice dry kindling over in the corner there."

Del did just that. He set it up the same way as he had for the hearth but without the large wooden blocks. His best chance of getting fire was light kindling with lots of shaggy bark.

"There are a couple of fundamental concepts you need to understand to complete any Manipulation. Firstly, belief; you have to be able to believe that the thing you are trying to achieve will happen. This seems simple in theory, but it is not just the belief that the wood *can* catch on fire; it is that it *will* catch on fire. Secondly, it must be within the boundaries of your order. In our case, that is death, decay and disorder. When we create fire, we fulfil this by converting the wood to smoke, ash and heat, breaking apart those elements in such a way that they can never be reassembled."

This all made sense in theory to Del but still didn't answer the question of 'how?' so he continued to look curiously at Tom.

"Give it a try," directed Tom.

Del turned his focus on the wood pile, picturing it in his mind's eye, a spark catching on the strands and starting to burn with a tall crackling flame.

Click. Nothing.

Click. Nothing.

Click. Still nothing. The kindling remained just as cold as before.

Tom laughed.

"The click was for show. Forget the click, but I do recommend using your hands. Hold your hands out towards the fire and use them to focus your thoughts and energy on the wood. Remember, you have to believe."

Del continued to try, and eventually, a tiny wisp of smoke, forming a snaking tendril, rose into the air.

"Well done, now keep trying that. We will have you running the killing field in the next war in no time."

With the fire now going and Del occupied by his newfound, albeit weak, powers, Tom shuffled off towards his quarters, mumbling something about getting more sleep.

Del continued to practice for a short time, still not producing much more than a low smoulder. He still considered it progress but still had trouble believing this was real. After a short time, the Death-Elect realised his continuous disbelief was likely the reason for his lack of good progress. Soon he found himself whisked away by the other Elects to help with the daily tasks. They had already prepared and delivered breakfast for the Oracles and the curious old priest while he practised.

Next, they led him to another room not far from the kitchen, which held several large tubs, each filled with washboards. It seemed that no matter where you went in life, across the width and breadth of Azarth, laundry would always be there waiting for the lowest of those in the pack order.

Del was allocated a large basket of robes, bed linen and other articles of clothing to scrub in the warm flowing water of the tub. A mixture made from a white powder and the warm water produced suds which helped bring out the dirt.

The other Elects had their own jobs in the laundry. Life-Elect took the cleaned clothes from Del and rinsed them in the flowing water of the next tub. Combat-Elect passed the clothes through a series of rotating cylinders which squeezed the water from them. Creativity-Elect hung everything on a line directly below one of the air ducts cut into the ceiling.

"So," started Del, "what have your masters got you doing? I'm assuming not starting fires?"

Creativity-Elect responded first, "not much so far. It has mainly been the theory and history of crafting. She made me learn the name of each different technique and which Oracle invented it. Who would have thought magic could be so boring!"

"It can't be that bad, can it?"

Life-Elect interjected, "not for me; Anew has already shown me how to grow a flower in my hand from nothing. Watch!"

With that, she held out the palm of her hand and concentrated. Her tongue poked out of the side of her mouth as she focused all of her energy. They all stopped working as she continued to try to manifest a flower. Then, very slowly, a green seed appeared from nowhere, slowly germinating and growing before their eyes. In a matter of moments, a green stalk was standing from the centre of her palm."

"Farmin' hell, you're good!" Del announced, and she lost her attention.

The unfurling green tendril went limp and died as quickly as it had thrived. Life-Elect snorted in derision; Del was unsure whether she was mad at either herself for losing focus or at him for interrupting.

"Anyway, I managed to grow a full-headed flower in class just yesterday. I should be onto animals in no time," she said matter-of-factly.

The group made for a very efficient team, and after their brief interlude of what could only be described as magic, they had finished the whole job in almost no time.

13.
Death Class

After the morning chores had been completed, the Elects all made their way through the dimly lit tunnels into the Sanctum Sacellum. From there, they each followed their respective Oracle off into another room.

Tom led Del down a tunnel before entering a huge room set up as a classroom with just two desks. One for the master and one for the student.

"Sit!" Tom instructed him, "let's go back over what we were discussing this morning and see if we can make some more progress."

Del made his way from the stone doorway and into the yawning void of the room before he plonked himself into the wooden pupil's chair at the desk in the centre. Set into the desk was an ink well and quill with a stack of paper set off to the side. The table itself was rough with decades of carvings. Anything from names to images of animals to weird symbols he had never seen before. It made him think about the strange four-pointed star he had seen on the envelope seal.

"Before we start, Tom, do you mind if I ask you a question?"

Tom rolled his eyes, "well, I guess we only have another one-and-twenty turns to get through this; why not?"

"Well, when I was at Portsworth, I opened the letter you sent me while sitting in the inn's bar. At first, I thought the barman treated me differently because of all the money, but I later realised it had something to do with the wax seal on the envelope. What does it mean?"

"You haven't worked it out yet?" he asked mockingly, "Assierium is a farce. Neither Assier nor his prophet has ever existed. We Oracles, together, are the four faces of Assier and the four points of Aiel. One day you will replace me as an Oracle. Very few commoners suspect, and even less know, that those of us living here in the Arrats are the foundation of that religion. Generations of us ago, we adopted the symbol of the four-pointed star. Over time the common religion developed based on an abstraction of our relation to the Singular, and they adopted our symbol as a sign of their belief. Their symbol has evolved over time, whereas we keep the ancient symbol as a form of respect for those who have come before us. I suspect that barman is one of the few who knows enough to respect us. I am assuming you were treated well above your means?"

Del nodded, "yes, he gave me the best room in the inn. Fit for a god it was."

"Yes, well, don't come to expect that and don't go flashing that symbol around. There are those who would try to burn you as a heretic. Uncomfortable burnings are, I'm particularly not fond of them. But enough about that particular sideline. Onto your first proper lesson in Death Lore."

Del busied himself by cleaning his quill on a clean piece of linen before dipping the tip into the inkwell and shaking off the drips.

"Now, we have already touched on this before, but as Death, you will be responsible for the balance of life in Azarth. You will be the black to Life's white. Life will try to create irresponsibly. She will always find a way. A drop of lust in the ear of a youthful couple on a warm summer's eve or the hint of a backrub for a loving wife after a long day. The result is the same, screaming new life entering the world almost a turn later. Our job is to ensure the population evens itself out fast enough that they aren't overwhelmed with too many mouths and not enough food. Do you understand?"

Del nodded that he understood the concept but didn't understand how this was his job. In fact, the idea of killing people to manage a population caused a very uneasy knot in the pits of his stomach.

"What happens if we don't keep up and it gets out of hand? What do we do? And isn't Life red, not white?"

"On the final point, shut up! On the other points, that's when we work together with our friendly Combat Oracle. He is always itching for a battle every ten turns or so. Sometimes I take some time off in a few regions just to give him something to look forward to," he said with a chuckle.

"General death management is just part of my daily routine. Have you ever wondered why they call it the dead of the night or why most people just happen to pass away in their sleep? Well, now you know. But that isn't what you will be doing for the foreseeable future. You get to learn about the Manipulation of death and everything that comes with it. How to recognise the signs of a man on the brink of artery collapse, turn wood into heat and ash, and use the universe's disorder to the advantage of our order."

During this time, Del attempted to take notes but quickly gave up. Instead, he gave Tom his full attention and tried to mentally retain everything.

Tom continued his lecture, "Azarth is naturally trying to get to a state of disorder. If you pick up a handful of sand and let it drain through your fingers, does it fall and land in a neat column? No, it falls randomly and disperses over the ground. Have you ever seen an abandoned building that has succumbed to neglect? Even things that aren't truly living can still die through disorder and decay. That is the world's way, and it is up to us to ensure that balance continues. It takes the Oracle of Anew a magnitude more power and concentration to create life than it does for us to destroy it because what we do is natural."

"So if what we do is just nature, why are we needed at all?" Del questioned his master.

"Good question; I'm glad you asked it. If Lady Life out there didn't keep getting carried away, we probably wouldn't be needed, but as you will find out soon enough, both she and her latest protégé are, shall we say, strong-willed."

Del had to agree with him on that one. He hadn't had the chance to spend any time with the Oracle of Anew, but her Elect certainly seemed to be studious and strong-minded.

"So, how did your fire go this morning? Any more progress?" Tom asked curiously.

"No, not really. I think I am still just struggling with believing that this is all happening. Do you have any advice?"

"Do you believe you can walk?" Tom asked, more seriously than Del expected.

"Of course."

"Could you always walk?"

"No."

"Then when did you believe you could walk?"

Del thought this seemed a dumb question to ask but responded anyway, "probably when I pulled myself up and walked."

"So, when you made the wood smoulder this morning, what did you believe? Do you not trust your eyes? When has your sight ever deceived you?"

The man made some excellent points, although Del wasn't sure if it would help him summon his power.

"For the sake of not causing a fire in this room, how about we start with something a little more alive?" The Oracle walked out from behind his desk and left the room. There was some noise and raised voices from another room before Tom walked back, holding a flower by its stem. It was white and delicate, with its petals closed in a tight formation.

Tom and the flower were quickly followed by a heated student making demands that were being ignored.

"I finally manage to make a flower that survives longer than a few moments, and you just waltz into our classroom and steal it. Give me back my flower!" cried the distressed Life-Elect.

Tom continued to make his way to the front of the classroom as a fourth person slowly entered the room. The Oracle of Anew stood in the doorway and cleared her voice.

"Death, just for once, can you just not be a dick? Come Elect, you need to learn your place. Dick or not, he is an Oracle."

The two Life orders left the room, and Tom placed the flower stem into a small pot so that it stood tall and proud.

"Right now, this flower is full of life and, given its lack of consciousness, is blissfully unaware and seeming unaffected by its absence of a continued life supply through a root system. The flower is in a state of being alive but not living. When the flower dies, the very being of the flower breaks down into its smaller components. This is what you have power over. Take the flower to your desk."

Del did just that, taking the flower pot and placing it in the centre of his workstation.

"Now, focus on it, understand the flower, understand that it sucks water from the roots into the petals and is fed from the sun's warmth. Do you understand these things?"

Del nodded his head without turning his attention away from the flower.

"Now, remind the flower of that. Remind the flower that without the sun and the water, it shrivels. The pure white petals turn brown, and the leaves fall away from the stem."

As Tom talked, Del could feel a Connection forming between himself and the flower. The more he understood the flower, the stronger the Connection grew. The longer he focused, the more he believed that he could influence the life of the flower.

Slowly but surely, a brown vein began forming on the snow-white petals. It grew, radiating from the outside edge of the petal towards the stem. The stem began to droop as the brown grew and the pure white faded. After several long moments, a brown husk of a flower lay crumpled in the bottom of the pot.

Without a word, Tom picked up the flower and went back outside the room. He soon returned, grinning with a handful of more flowers. He seemed delighted in annoying his fellow Oracles and their students.

Del stood up each flower in turn, focused his power on it, forced himself to understand the flower's life, and systematically destroyed it. Near the end of the lesson, and approximately twenty shrivelled flowers later, Tom produced a living potted plant.

"This is a special plant not created today by your feisty counterpart. This plant needs almost no sunlight, warmth, or water more than a few times a turn. Your goal for this span is to kill it."

Del thought about it for a long time. His current methodology for killing the flower would, in all likelihood, not work as the soil contained all the nutrients required, and it needed minimal sun. Del thought that it might have been a trick challenge. He accepted the potted plant from Tom and placed it down at his workstation.

Immediately he set to work focusing on the strange plant. It was small and green with long white needles pointing out from the stalk in every direction. A peculiar white hair was strung between the spines forming a web of protection over it.

To start, he tried the same method that had proven successful on the flowers. The resilient plant remained as stoic as ever and continued to live just as green as it was when he had placed it down.

Del went back to studying it, trying to determine its weakness. Tom had obviously thought this challenge was beyond his capability, given that he had told Del that he had a whole span to try to kill it.

The rest of the lesson proved to be futile. Eventually, night set in, and the Elects left to prepare dinner in the kitchens following their evening meditation.

After three days of trying to kill the death-resistant plant, Del lay awake in his sleeping pallet. The challenge had worn him down and had started to cause insomnia. He decided to get up for a drink and made his way into the privy room. He cupped his hands under the icy cold flowing water and drank deeply.

It was then the thought occurred to him. He had been thinking about it the wrong way. How do you kill a plant that doesn't want water? Give it water.

Del pulled on his grey robe and tied his rope around his waist before he snuck out of his room through the tunnels. He made his way into the Death classroom, sat in front of the strong-willed plant and began to focus.

He thought of the established root system deep within the soil beneath the plant. He willed the plant to do as he had done, drink deeply and suck the water from the ground into itself. The water filled every void within the plant. He watched the plant swell from a thumb width to the size of his fist. The soil became grey and arid as the plant swelled.

Pop!

The top of the small plant burst open like a flower in full sun, sending water and plant goo all over the desk. A large glob of the goo landed on Del's face before he wiped it free with his sleeve.

A feeling of satisfaction swelled over the young man as he returned to his quarters.

Once back in his pallet, he pulled the covers up and settled in for a well-deserved rest before immediately falling asleep.

14.
Dead Scuriat

The following weeks slipped by in much the same way: menial chores in between lessons about understanding and controlling his power. Most of Tom's classes were given as a challenge whereby Del needed to find the solution by himself while Tom sat in the corner taking the occasional puff of his tobacco pipe that he had stuffed into his robes.

After various stolen articles from the Life-Elect consisting primarily of plants and flowers, they eventually moved on to more complex creatures. Today's lesson featured a scuriat, trapped during one of Tom's daily outings before the evening mediation. It was entombed inside a glass dome on top of his master's desk. With its dark stalked eyes looking every which way for an escape route, it scurried from one side of its prison to the other. The tiny beast had some weight behind it; each time it ran into the glass, it made a loud thump and moved the lid one way or the other. Tom had readjusted it several times to prevent an escape.

"Scuriats are resilient little guys. We will open him up when you work out how to kill this one, and I will show you why. For now, it is your job to work out how to end its poor, miserable life."

While most of the practical examples had been flora, Tom had started to teach him about the human body and what was contained beneath the skin. He had begun to learn about the brain and the cardiovascular system. He now knew that removing blood flow from the body would cause almost certain death; that went for humans and animals alike. Until now, it had just been theory and drawings on a slate. Now it was time to apply what he knew, but somehow he also knew there was a hidden trick here. Del knew how to Manipulate living things now; knowing what to Manipulate was often the challenge.

Del stared at the little orange creature and extended his arms to focus his concentration and energy. He could sense a beating rhythm within the beast and a pulsating flow. Recalling what he knew about blood flow and the brain, he applied pressure to the source of the beating. The rhythm quickened briefly before falling away slowly. The creature began to stumble. Every second leg twitched while the other legs turned to panic and made an effort to escape. One of the scuriat's long eyes drooped and fell backwards.

Del felt the beating cease, but still, the creature moved. He looked up at his master. He had already known that it was simply too easy.

With Del's focus gone, the creature went still for a few moments before returning to life. All limbs and eyes were back, hard at work, as it redoubled its escape efforts.

"Well, what did you learn?" called Tom from his cosy corner of the room, looking very unsurprised that the creature was still alive.

"That the little bastard really doesn't want to die today!" Del called back, slightly irritated.

"Come on, what else? What did you notice? I am assuming you stopped its heart?"

"Yes. Its heart completely stopped, but the creature only slowed down. It was still moving, even without any blood flowing. That goes against everything you have taught me."

"Yes and no," came the response, "you stopped one heart from beating, and half of his body essentially died, but as you will see very soon, it takes two stopped hearts to kill a scuriat. They are able to start their own heart using the other half of their body, assuming they aren't both stopped simultaneously."

That made much more sense to Del, given that only half of the scuriat had seemed to shut down. The creature had put itself into life-supporting mode and brought itself back to life.

"Now, try again. This time you will need to divert your attention into two parts; one for each heart."

Del returned to his previous 'concentration' pose with his arms outstretched and extended his mind to feel his way through the creature. He had found the first heart easily enough the first time but to look and concentrate on two was a challenge. After several failed attempts, Del found that if he focused on the first and brought it to a stop, it allowed him to easily isolate the second heart. Once he had control of the second, it was just a matter of time. The scuriat went from its panicked motion to slowly come to a stop, as still as the table upon which it sat. Finally, the poor creature's eye stalks dropped for one final time, and it fell completely still.

Dead.

Del felt sort of sorry for the innocent creature. He knew by now that this was just going to be part of his life and that killing a small scuriat was nothing compared to what he would face in the future. That didn't stop the feeling in the pit of his stomach.

"Well done, you have now managed to kill a small insect!" said Tom sarcastically, interrupting his thoughts, "now, let's open him up and look at what we are working with here. Go grab that dissection kit from the cupboard over there."

Del made his way over to a large glass-faced cabinet filled with all kinds of curiosities. Various reptiles and ghoti in glass jars filled with translucent yellow goo stared back at him with dead eyes, and boards with curious creatures pinned to them hung on the back. A large iron-banded, blackened-wood chest sat on the lower shelf, and more than twenty hefty leather tomes sat on the shelf above it. A surgical tool roll on the cabinet's middle shelf lay unfurled to display various sharp silver implements. Del opened the doors, making sure not to touch anything he wasn't meant to, and rolled up the dissection kit.

He returned to the Order-Master's table and unrolled the kit.

"Now, scuriats have a tough shell on the top and bottom of their bodies, but that doesn't mean you can't get through it to see what they are hiding inside," Tom said as he removed the glass lid and picked it up. He gestured to the front of the shell, "here you can see the legs protrude from the side, and there is no shell protecting it. If you get a small saw, you can cut around the front of it, starting at the legs. Then do the same with the back."

Tom handed the small orange corpse back to Del, who inspected it further. He could see what Tom referred to and selected a small file with a fine, serrated edge, setting to work on the poor creature. It took an age to finally separate the shell, and Del's hands were on fire by the time he finished. Finally, Tom took it from him and selected a flat tool that he used to separate the top half of the shell from the bottom.

Inside was a delicately laid-out organ machine. Fleshy tubes linked each organ with a labyrinth of viscera held together by some sort of white membrane. The curious part was that the left half was a perfect mirror image of the right. Tom continued to move parts of the demised creature out of the way, explaining what each entrail was in turn. He explained how the veins connected the hearts to each of the limbs, brains and organs. The stomach was connected to its mouth and continued through the intestines and out the other end. The stomach and intestines were the one system that wasn't duplicated on the scuriat, and it ran straight down the centre as if trying to maintain symmetry.

Once they had finished, Tom directed him back to the cabinet, "fetch me an empty jar and bring that flask of balm."

Del moved back to the cabinet, located the items, and returned to the desk.

"The balm fluid will keep whatever you put in there preserved. It will stop the rot from setting in. Now, place the body of our little friend there into the jar, then fill it to the brim with the fluid."

Del did just that, stopping the jar with a glass lid and adding a steel band to secure it. He then picked it up to place it alongside the rest of Tom's collection.

"Tom?" he questioned, "what is in the box at the bottom?"

"That is of no consequence to you for the next twenty-one turns, young man. If I even see you try to get your way into that box before the choosing in your fortieth turn, I will make sure to make your life a living nightmare until you become me!"

Tom's tone was severe, and Del was inclined to believe him. It only fuelled his curiosity, and he wondered if there was anything else he may be able to learn from him.

"What about the books, anything worth me reading when I get bored of staring at my ceiling at night?"

"Here, read this one. It has lots of pictures," Tom said as he selected one of the larger tomes from the shelf and dropped it heavily into Del's arms, "now, back to your desk; you aren't finished for the day. I want a full write-up of today's autopsy, including annotated diagrams."

Tom walked over to another shelf with far less interesting items on display. He selected an old, but good condition, book from the shelf and placed it on the desk in front of Del. He opened it, flicked through the first half of the pages and found it empty.

"I want you to start keeping your own records for the future. This is where you will record future practical lessons. Those books on that shelf are mine; one day, you will have your own collection of knowledge written by your own hand."

Tom turned and left the room to complete whatever his afternoon duties entailed as the Order-Master of Death.

Del left the first-page blank, hoping that the Creativity-Elect might lend him a hand with a design of illuminations and a nice border. On the next page, he began to draw a detailed diagram of the scuriat. First alive and then a cross-section from within, making sure to label the name and function of each tiny body part. Below he included a detailed description of how each component worked and interacted, but most importantly, how he could Manipulate that component.

Del continued filling in the details of the scuriat until he heard the evening bell toll and made his way to the Sanctum Sacellum. It finally occurred to him that he didn't know who, if anyone, actually rang the bell. He made a mental note to ask someone.

The meditation time passed in complete, deafening silence before they were released at the second toll of the bell. The four Elects met to discuss their daily lessons as they always did. They had become close friends over the last four span, and nicknames had quickly replaced their formal Elect names. Since their old names were forbidden, they each took on a variation of their Elect name. Combat-Elect became Batter, Life-Elect became Ellie, and Creativity-Elect became Crea.

Crea continued to complain about being forced to learn about the history of ancient architecture. While none of the Elects had ever seen them, ruins were known to exist across the various continents from ancient civilisations that had come to an end through war or famine. At the suggestion of these events, they all gave Del a knowing look as though he had some part in it through history.

Ellie was bursting to show everyone her latest skills. As the group turned the corner, they disturbed a mass of brightly coloured winged insects. They seemed to appear and disappear back into thin air. She was beaming and altogether too proud of herself for her achievement, given the short time she had been practising.

Batter remained his usual stoic self, happy to talk about other people's days but slow to bring his achievements or work into the conversation. Batter had become the closest of the three to Del, and he would often join him back in his room for a chat.

Del also preferred not to share his daily achievements. His world was the destruction to their creation and skill. He chose not to discuss the murder of various plants and animals. Instead, he thought he might ask the others about his earlier question.

"So, I've been wondering. Who is it that rings the bell? We are always all in the same room?"

Batter and Ellie looked at him like he had made a very sound point, but Crea just chuckled.

"Wouldn't you like to know?"

"Yes, as a matter of fact, I would. Do we have a hermit hiding in these mountains just to ring it or something?"

"No, silly, it is run by a clock. It is a mechanical device that keeps time. At the same time every day, the device will pull a lever which causes a series of hammers to strike the bell. The Oracle of Beauty makes me climb up, wind the mechanism daily, and reset the hammers."

That made more sense to Del, although he was curious about how this clock device worked. He had only ever told the time by looking at the sun in the sky. He knew there was a dial-stone in Strauth, which had a shadow that also indicated the time.

The group walked along silently for a few moments before Ellie made for more conversation.

"You won't guess what I overheard Life talking about to the Order-Masters this morning?"

The group stared at her blankly, not willing to try to guess.

"She was joking about one of us having a sea monster set upon us on the way here. I am assuming that could only have been Batter or Del. Which one of you did they release the beast on?"

Suddenly the storm and the kraken made sense. The letter from Tom had hinted that he should avoid a particular part of the sea.

"Why, for all that is farmin' good in Azarth, would they do that?"

"Practical joke, I guess; I am also guessing it was you. The Order-Master's got you good then, did they?" Ellie sneered.

"Yeah, farmin' near killed me. The crew was going to throw me over the side until the storm broke, and the kraken slithered away back into the depths. When I see that woman, I am going to cave her farmin' nose in!"

The hollow, empty threat brought on laughter from the others. Eventually, Del joined in.

What was I going to do? Punch a god?

"You know they were all in on it, right?" Ellie noted.

Del retorted by poking out his tongue and screwing up his face.

15.

Hunting

Dawn, or whatever passed for dawn, inside of a hollowed-out mountain, broke the next day with an unexpected visit in the kitchen from The Oracle of Beauty. The four Elects were summoned to the Sanctum Sacellum for some sort of briefing.

"Even Death has rolled out of his pallet for this, so make haste!" the Order-Master of Creativity noted.

The four Elects stopped their morning chores. At least Del had managed to get a fire going in the hearth so there would be hot water in the system by the time they returned. They followed Crea's master through the damp-light-lit tunnel network until they arrived in the large holy room.

The Oracle of Beauty ambled to the front of the room and stood alongside the other mages.

"We have collectively decided," The Oracle of Anew started, "that your individual lessons have come far enough that it is time for you all to start working together. Today will be a challenge, one which can only be achieved if all four parts of the team complete their job individually with the group's common interest in mind."

The Oracle of Prevail spoke in his deep booming voice, "we will only tell you the final goal; it will be up to you to work out why and how you need to work together to achieve it."

The Oracle of Beauty stepped forward and flourished her arm in a dramatic wave, "it will be your challenge to return with a writing quill made from the tusk of a mountain rarn."

Next, it was Tom's turn to add to the challenge brief, "one tiny, little thing we may or may not have forgotten to mention after your Initiation into the Sect. As an Elect, you are, in essence... immortal."

A stir went up amongst the Elects but was swiftly interrupted.

"But, that is not to say that getting a limb removed by a rarn does not hurt nor leave you minus a limb. It just means it will hurt for turns, not moments. You will have noticed stubbing a toe still hurts like a bitch. One final word of caution, they are faster than a keil hit with a cane. Now off with you; go finish making my breakfast and get to packing. You leave as soon as you are ready and return to the Sect only after completing the task."

The group of Elects made their way back to the kitchen while discussing their recently discovered lack of mortality.

"I 'spose it kinda makes sense, doesn't it? We couldn't have been the Chosen ones to live in a cave until our eightieth turn if there wasn't some way of making sure we don't die before the next Choosing," said Batter.

The group agreed. Del did wonder, not for the first time, what happened after eighty turns, but he wasn't left long to think about it.

As they entered the kitchen, Crea started to strategise, "so where do you think we start? Clearly, making a quill from a tusk is part of my job unless we stumble upon a shop in Portsworth that sells oddities. Do you think we have to kill it?"

"You mean, will Del have to kill it?" Del interjected, feeling somewhat judged for his part in the task, "yes, I am going to assume I have to kill a large beast intent on killing us before it has a good hard crack at it."

"I should be able to track it," said Batter, "warrior's intuition and all. What about you, El? What do you think they have in store for you?"

"I guess we will just have to find out now, won't we?" she replied.

They all broke away and returned to the jobs they were doing before they had been called into the meeting. Batter cleaned dishes as the girls continued cooking. Del tended to the hearth by adding more hardwood before sweeping the ashes and loose bark from the stone floor.

After all the chores had been completed, Del packed the bag he had acquired in Portsworth with everything he could think of needing on the trip. He had no idea of how long this journey would take them, but he suspected they were unlikely to be back by suppertime tonight.

He placed bread, cheese and salt-meat into wrappings before tucking them into a pocket. He stuffed the heavy coat, gloves and boots into the main compartment of the bag, alongside the two books he had been given by Tom; one for reading and one for writing. He quickly stopped in Tom's classroom to locate a few quills and a stoppered jar of ink, which he hoped would make the journey without leaking.

By the time he returned to his quarters, all of the other elects were standing in the tunnel.

"Come on, let's go," said Batter.

As the tracker of the rarn, he was clearly asserting himself as the leader, and Del was only too happy to leave that responsibility to anyone but himself.

They walked through the tunnels, retracing the steps he had taken only four or five span ago. At least, he assumed they were retracing those steps. Besides remembering his way through the tunnel network, Del had never found a meaningful way to interpret the web of pathways and navigate his way around. He made a mental note to find out before exploring any further through the mountainous labyrinth that he called his home. Moments later, it dawned on him that he could simply ask the person currently navigating.

"Hey, Batter, how the farmin' hell do you know your way around these tunnels? I'd be lost like a mant down a mine!"

Batter was at the front, and Del was taking up the rear, but the tunnel's acoustics meant that it was pretty easy to have a conversation spanning quite some distance.

"You have to read the stone. As you near the centre of the mountain, the stone becomes denser, harder and darker. The stone closer to the surface is lighter."

"Okay, but how do you know you aren't heading in completely the wrong direction but towards the surface?"

Batter stopped and gestured towards the wall.

"Take a good look, and tell me what you see when you read the stone."

At first, Del tried to apply his magic and feel the stone, but all he felt was cold. It was lifeless, and it told no story. Soon he realised that it wasn't what Batter meant, and he refocused his eyes rather than his energy and began to see more than he had initially noticed.

"There seems to be more than one colour of rock, like the veins in a body they spread out over the rock."

"Exactly, that is exactly what they are; veins. Different areas of the mountain have different veins in the rock. Once you take notice of the veins throughout the mountain, you get a good idea of where you are; however, that won't help if you are new to the mountain."

"So you have spent a fair bit of time in this part of the mountain, then?" Del enquired.

"Nope," replied Batter smugly.

"Then remind me again, how do you know we are going the right way?!"

"These tunnels were created thousands of turns ago; that means that hundreds of Elects and Order-Masters have walked these tunnels and felt these walls. Follow me."

They continued to walk for a short while before coming to a halt again.

"Now, do you see anything different?"

Del had another look. First, at the rock, which looked exactly the same, then at the roof, then at the floor. They stood at a wye junction in the road. There on the floor was a smoothly carved but subtle hollow veering to the left.

"Ah, got it; you follow the worn floor. Well done! I would never have seen it," Del exclaimed.

"While that is true, you are still wrong," said Batter pointing to the other side of the wye junction, "there is no damp-light down there, so it is doubtful that it leads to the exit of the tunnel."

The group had a good laugh at his expense. Even though he had managed to humiliate himself with a very obvious overlooking, he had still learned a lot about his new home mountain. The rock veins and worn floor should help him navigate other areas.

As their journey progressed, Del became surer that they were not retracing his steps from Portsworth but were instead going in a completely different direction. They must have ventured deeper into the mountain and headed for the other side. Much like the first mountain he had entered with Gular, the permanent damp-light fixtures soon finished, and they were forced to carry their own light. Each Elect removed a damp-light torch from a sconce and continued penetrating the darkness ahead. It was hard to tell without some external reference, but the tunnel floor seemed to be steadily heading in a downward direction. Del hoped that this meant they would be exiting somewhere far below the unstable snowcaps and swirling clouds filled with icy knives that had almost killed him on his entrance into the mountain. They walked for many long hours before he finally got his wish; they exited at the mountain's base through a yawning void in the rock. It occurred to Del that to the casual passer-by that they probably didn't see what he could now see but what gave the mountain its protections, he could not be sure.

"I think this is as good a place to make camp as any," stated Batter, "we have a long trip ahead of us; we may as well take it easy now while we still can."

"I'll get the fire going," called Del to everyone and no one in particular.

"Conjured greens or forage?" asked Ellie.

Del hadn't given that any thought before. While packing, he only thought they could eat what they could carry.

"Go on, make us something sweet and tangy, El!" called Crea, "I'll see what we can find as well, just in case. Oooh, can you make dessert fruit?"

"I'll see what I can do," she replied with a smile.

Crea finally returned with black and red berries foraged from some sort of bush while Ellie had been working on Creating a fantastic designer fruit for each of them. The mystery fruit had brown skin and was about the size of Del's fist. Ellie split one in half and handed it to Del. It felt solid and dense in his hand; Ellie had made it come to life and stay alive without it immediately wilting and dying. Del dug his fingers into the dark brown flesh and scooped it into his mouth.

The taste was so sweet he almost choked.

"Assier Almighty El! Go easy on the farmin' sweetroot next time, aye!" said Del, spluttering.

Ellie began to look offended before Crea tossed over a few berries.

"Mix a few of these in with it first; they are really tart and should go well with the sweet fruit."

Del tried as Crea suggested, and she was right. The tart berries and the sweet fruit combined to form the perfect meal.

"You should Create more often, El; all we eat up there is hard and bland. Why can't you be on dinner duty every night making us things like this!?"

"Firstly, what am I? Your slave or mother? And secondly, that is not how Creating life works. I still need to get the nutrients from somewhere. All those flowers you killed took cultivated soil and time to Create!"

El removed herself from the warmth of the fire to sit alone at the edge of the clearing.

"Nice going, arse-wipe," said Crea with a smirk.

Batter was still setting up the camp and hadn't stopped to eat dinner yet.

"How was I supposed to know?" Del replied.

"You were a farmer, weren't you; you swear by it often enough? How could you not know what it takes to grow things?"

"I don't know, I just assumed that, whatever it is that we do, took care of things like that. I don't need anything special to... well, you know, do what I do."

"Nothing special? What do you mean? You need life first!"

Del hadn't considered that. Their powers were what the common folk would consider magic, but ultimately, it all boiled down to one thing, Manipulation of matter. The matter had to exist first to Manipulate it. In his case, it had to be living or organised before he could do anything with it. Ellie just needed the basic building blocks of Life to create it. Del assumed the same thing went for Creativity and Combat. Creativity would need a physical medium with which to work. Combat, well, that was more abstract. Combat was more about understanding people and what drives them or has power over them.

Eventually, Batter finished setting up the camp and returned with Ellie, whose mood seemed slightly better and less mopey.

"Does anyone know any good campfire stories?" asked Crea, "I do love a good story."

After a few moments of silence, Batter cleared his throat and sat down directly beside Crea.

"Stories are how knowledge is passed through the generations of my people. Stories of great warriors in times of war and peacekeepers in times of peace told beneath the great shining moon of Tha'Abbi."

The Elects all moved forward in anticipation, and Batter threw a handful of green grass on the fire, causing a plume of smoke to start rising from the flames.

"There is a story about an ancient Saulit warrior who went by the name of Badar. It is said he had a special connection to Assier, which made him invincible in war, but it was not always the way.

Badar was born in a small nameless village in the east and grew up like many other boys, helping their mothers work the land, harvesting tropical fruits and playing when their backs were turned. While the women and children toiled, the men were off training or warring somewhere across the great land. Back when Badar was a boy, there were no ships to sail across the ocean; there was only Saulit."

Batter gestured with his hand, causing the smoke to swirl.

"This was the way until the Agumne came. The Agumne was the organised crime syndicate of ancient Saulit, armed with knives as long as your arm or longer. Badar watched as every soul in his village, including his mother, was slaughtered in cold blood before he was stolen away. He was raised as a slave to the Agumne, at the mercy of whatever wants and desires they had; sometimes, he was merely a servant required to fetch water, the unwilling victim of vicious sparing, or much worse with unspeakable acts made against him.

"Badar could have been beaten down by this abuse, but instead, he let it make him stronger. Every day he woke up and believed that he could somehow leave this life and be a great warrior, like in the stories his parents had told him.

"This is where most of the stories differ. Some say Aiel himself appeared in the centre of the Agumne encampment and struck every last man down. Others say he escaped to a faraway land, and some have even suggested that the Agumne just let him go after he had served ten turns of service. What the legends can agree on is that Badar spent the rest of his life in pursuit of greatness. There is no record of him for many years; most believe he found himself an apprentice to a great master before working his way quickly through the ranks of one of the great militant tribes."

He blew on the coals and fanned the flames, so a great ball of smoke erupted.

"Finally, after many turns of servitude, he became their leader. People flocked to join his ranks after word spread of his greatness. He was not known for blood thirst but rather for his careful strategy. He is believed to be the longest-reigning leader of a militia before he vanished in the dead of night. By this time, he was old but surprisingly agile and sharp of mind. Again, people have offered theories as to what happened to him that night. Some say he was quietly assassinated by a usurper, others suggest he left to enjoy a quiet life back in another nameless village, but more likely, he simply died, and his people refused to believe that he was mortal.

"By the time he passed, it was generally peacetime. Badar had never gone looking for a war; rather, he showed a force of might to quash uprisings of presumptuous dictators who thought they could rule over the land of Saulit by waging war. The strong had chosen to follow him, not as a dictator but as a fair leader. His strength was his integrity and determination."

Batter finished his story by marking himself by habit in the shape of the four-pointed star of Aiel.

"Is anyone else thinking what I'm thinking?" Del asked the group of Elects.

He was met with a circle of blank stares.

"Badar was obviously one of us. He was the Combat-Elect and then Order-Master. He must have had some way of getting to Matraketh, or there was another Sanctum over there."

"Actually, you know what, that makes a lot of sense. Huh..." said Batter, now deep in thought, presumably wondering how many other stories of his ancestors related to chosen Elects, "so, who's next?"

16.

One Tough Tusk

el arose the next morning to find it was nowhere near as cold as he was expecting. He was so used to living up inside the top of the mountain, knowing it was blisteringly cold outside. The valley floor was crisp and cool but not freezing. When he poked his head out of his propped-up bedroll, he found the other Elects already awake and sitting around the cold fire. Del slowly unfolded himself from his warm blanket and made his way to the pit. After stacking some small pieces of wood, he performed Combustion and got a small fire lit to warm them and cook their morning meal. He saved his hard travelling food for later and joined the others in eating fried greens on bread.

Once they had finished breaking their fast, they broke camp and put out the fire. Crea unstopped a small glass vial and coaxed some wet ashes into it. She didn't stop to give any reasoning, and Del didn't feel like questioning her.

Thick vegetation surrounded them as they moved away from the clearing; it was a stark contrast to the barren, grey stone that had entombed them for the past six span. The trees formed a tall green canopy that let in mottled light, and the forest floor was covered in thick decaying vegetation with small undergrowth stifled by the dimness. That was one thing Del knew from his time as Pthorn the farm boy: crops were slow to grow if the weather was poor and there was insufficient sunlight. The crops would grow uncontrollably when sunlight was plentiful, particularly following a big wet.

The forest was unlike the road he had followed when he left Portsworth; it was far denser with no beaten track, nor were there any obvious signs that anyone or anything had ever been through here. Whatever Batter was tracking was invisible to someone like Del, but given the fiasco of the damp-light in the tunnels, he thought it was best not to ask further tracking questions.

The group walked for what seemed to Del like half a day; the sun was trying its best to seep past the heavy canopy and sat high in the sky. They entered a small clearing that was still shady and found a water hole with a river flowing in and out of it; the Elects heard the water before they saw it.

"This is a perfect place for animals like rarns and keil to come and drink. There is scat and prints all around. We should stop here and think of a plan."

Once again, Del had been oblivious to the obvious signs of the animal they were tracking. When he looked again, he saw precisely what Batter was talking about. There were hundreds of different tracks in the dry mud surrounding the water hole. Batter investigated one set of tracks that seemed to interest him.

"It was definitely a rarn that made these, and there could be more than one. Rarns hunt in packs but send out scouts; we will want to try to capture a scout. We do not want to be trying to take down one in the middle of a pack."

Del could not have agreed more as it was on him to subdue the creature. He had to kill it before it made lunch out of the team of Elects.

The group all sat down by the stream. Ellie and Crea took off their shoes to let their feet dangle in the stream's flowing water. Coming from the hot climate of Straulatos, Del thought better of joining them as the water was likely recently melted from the snowcaps and way too cold for his comfort. He suspected that Batter was thinking the same thing. Instead, they sat on a log beside the stream.

Crea was the first to speak up, "I think we need a trap. Something that the rarn will walk into to keep it where we want it while Del... you know, does his thing."

It seemed that everyone was uncomfortable discussing Del's newly given powers.

"We should dig a pit, I brought some tools from the store that we can use to move the dirt, but we will need something to cover it. Even a rarn is smart enough not to just fall into a hole in the middle of the jungle."

"I might have a solution for that," said Ellie, "I have been working on growing continuous vines rather than just one single plant. I think I can make a ground-cover vine. Crea, do you think you could weave some sticks or branches into a structure for me to grow the plants over?"

"Sure thing, let me get started!"

Del sat on a fallen tree, feeling useless. The others had practical tasks they could do; he was just there to kill a rarn and make everyone feel uncomfortable about it. There had to be more he could do as a mage-in-training than just kill things every day.

The two girls got to work on their weaving and growing while Batter started digging a hole. Del pushed down his feelings of inadequacy, instead offering to assist Batter. As they excavated the clay ground, they placed the spoil a few paces away. The ever-strategic Combat-Elect suggested that they put it there so they could hide behind it as the rarn approached. He also indicated that it would be easier to backfill once they were done if they didn't move it too far.

The digging took most of the rest of the day, and concerningly, they spotted almost no wildlife during that time. A few small animals had scurried in for a quick drink before disappearing into the undergrowth.

By the end of the day, Crea and Ellie had finished their masterpiece. They placed the screen over the hole, and everyone sat down behind the mullock hill to wait. It looked like a patch of living undergrowth to the casual observer. A green vine was entwined in the branches and was covered in tiny, delicate white petal flowers.

They collectively decided not to set a fire that night as it may drive the wildlife away. Instead, Del distributed his hard bread, cheese and salt-meats before they all went to bed early.

In the dead of night, the camp erupted in a cacophony of yowling. Del's eyes slammed open, immediately awoken from his slumber, and he scrambled from his bedroll. The other three Elects followed suit, and they adjourned behind the pile of dirt which had been dug from the hole.

The night was black as pitch; even without the tree cover, the hour of the dead was always dark. For a brief moment, Del wondered what it was like back in Batter's homeland of Saulit under the ever-light of Tha'Abbi from his story.

Batter brought out the damp-light torch from the tunnels and ignited it, the torch slowly sputtering into a low light before growing to bathe the area.

The animal changed from a shrill yowl to a low growl of displeasure.

Del crept forwards to inspect the hole. There was no guarantee that they had dug deep enough that the beast could not climb out. He slowly edged closer until he could peer inside the pit.

"Batter, come here. I can't see; I need some more light."

Batter joined him at his side, and they both looked over the edge.

Down in the bottom of the pit was a small, slender beast pacing around the floor. Two tusks as big as its face protruded sharply from its maw. The beast was an entire arm span long and half an arm span tall. A pattern of black lines crisscrossed its bright orange body, ending in a long whipping tail.

Del had never seen a rarn but knew the description of what he was meant to be trying to hunt. This was definitely their quarry, and it looked to be a young one at that.

Remembering what Batter had told him before, he looked around to ensure there was no pack in the vicinity trying to encircle and trap them. He could discern no shining eyes in the forest's darkness, just a void where the light failed to reach.

"What is it?" called Ellie from behind the mullock, "is it a rarn?"

"Yep, and he is none too happy about being down there," replied Del.

"Well, you wouldn't be if someone dug a hole and made you fall in it, would you?" came the sarcastic reply from his Life counterpart.

"Well, what are you waiting for? Just get it over and done with, will you!" cried Crea.

Del looked down at the creature pacing below him.

Such a waste of a beautiful creature, he thought to himself.

The rarn was everything a predator should be; nimble, muscled, and elegant.

Del let out a sigh and held out his hands towards it. Slowly he could feel the Connection between them grow, letting the energy flow through him and into the rarn, gaining an understanding of its being. Del searched within and found its powerful heart, pounding a strong and thumping rhythm. He could sense it was equal parts scared and pissed off. Slowly he began to apply pressure to one of the outlets of the heart, restricting the blood from flowing through it. He could sense it as it started to become weaker and disorientated.

Then a thought occurred to him, *I can control this. I don't need to squeeze the life from the animal; I can control its life, hold it a mere hair's breadth from death without actually stealing its life.*

I can show it mercy.

"Do you trust me?" Del asked the group.

He was met with stares of distrust and a lack of surety.

"Come on, do you? Can you trust me just this once?"

"What do you need?" replied Batter as the two girls held their tongues.

"I am not going to kill it. I can hold it at bay, close to death, while you remove the tusks. I need to concentrate. If I lose my concentration, I could release its heart, and it will be madder than ever when it comes to."

Batter looked to the girls knowing their thoughts on Del's power over death. Ellie was quick to nod but didn't offer the service of getting into the pit with the temporarily subdued beast.

"I'll do it. Crea, hand me that saw from my pack."

Crea came out from behind the mound and rooted around in Batter's pack before walking over to him to hand him the saw.

"Good luck," she said with a worried smile.

Batter gave her a nod before turning back to Del, "tell me when it is clear for me to go in," then turned back to the girls, "you two may need to help me out. It is a very deep pit, and I don't want to fall on a sleeping rarn tonight."

A few more moments passed, and Del pushed a little harder on the rarn's heart until the beast was completely still, and the heart had slowed to an almost stop. He backed off slightly and maintained the pressure to keep it subdued.

"Now," Del instructed, "and please hurry. I am not sure how long I can maintain this."

Batter wasted no time jumping down into the pit. He took his damp-light torch with him, and the hole glowed from within. He placed the torch down in the corner, but before he set to work, he decided to test the slumber of the beast. He stuck the tip of the saw into the soft, meaty underside of one of its leg pits and then waited. The beast didn't move a muscle. Batter set to work on the first tusk. He sawed backwards and forwards slowly until the blade finally passed through. He threw the tusk up to the girls, and it was caught by Crea, who stuffed it into her coat pocket.

"Come on, out of there now," she called down to him, "we have what we need to get. Let's get out and go."

"Not yet," he called back, "I want the other one. All of the great Saulit warriors wore a token of their victories. Tonight is a great victory for us all."

Batter set to work on the other tusk, but the rarn was lying on it, making it difficult to get the saw to move. Batter reached over the beast and began to roll it over. Del felt fatigued after sustaining his control over the life of the rarn.

Without breaking his concentration, he called, "come on, mate, let's get a move on. I'm not sure how much longer I can hold it."

"Just a little bit longer!" came the strained reply.

Del felt his control slipping away. If he pushed too hard, his work would be for nothing, and the poor creature would slip away into death; instead, he felt himself let more and more blood flow from the heart, its heartbeat slowly picking up.

"That's it, out now. Right now!" Del said with a panicked voice, "Crea, El, get him out now!"

"Almost there!" Batter yelled as the beast slowly started to twitch back into life, "just hold it down for a few more moments. Almost done!"

A sharp sound came from behind them, an animal shriek that made Del lose his focus on the rarn's heart. Blood flow immediately returned to the beast, and it rolled over sleepily, knocking Batter to the pit's floor.

Batter scrambled back to his feet, and with the rarn on its other side, he saw that the tusk was now right there; he moved forward and kicked hard, snapping the remaining bone of the tusk. The tusk slid to a halt by the side of the pit next to the damp-light torch. Batter ran, swept up his prize and torch, and threw them over the side before making the jump himself.

By now, the rarn was regaining consciousness fast and had groggily raised itself to a kneeling position. The girls reached down and grabbed Batter's arms, pulling him up. Del was on the ground, exhausted from exerting so much will on the animal. He shook his head to push away the fuzziness and joined in. Del managed to reach down and grab the back of Batter's coat, swinging him up to the side of the pit just before the rarn jumped, clawing up at them.

Batter rolled to safety on the undergrowth, panting as he halted. He picked up the fallen tusk and handed it to Crea.

"See, it wasn't that hard now, was it?"

Crea rolled her eyes and turned away before stopping. She turned back to him and slapped him square across the face.

"What if you lost a leg? You absolute imbecile!"

Batter just smiled as though he had won some sort of game as Del slowly got to his feet.

"So, what next?" Del asked.

"Well, I can craft a quill tomorrow and make this idiot some sort of necklace from the other one," Crea answered.

"No, I mean, him down there. We can't just leave it in the hole. How do we get him out without getting eaten?"

The group all looked at each other.

"Can they climb trees?" asked Ellie.

It was almost sunrise before they had finished putting Ellie's plan into action. Throughout the night, she had grown vines to climb up four trees where they could strategically place themselves above the ground and around the pit. She and Crea also made another woven pit lid, which they planned to use as a makeshift ramp. The girls tied a couple of the vines to the woven plate, and they all climbed up their own trees.

Crea and Ellie had a vine each and were positioned to one side of the pit to pull the plate into place. Batter and Del were on the opposite side with vines to keep the plate above the ground surface and stop it from falling in. Slowly, the girls started pulling their vines evenly, and their creation began to slide. The plate was dragged across the ground before teetering on the pit's edge and toppling. The boys pulled their vines hard to keep the ramp from going all the way in.

The rarn leapt up the ramp, out of the pit, and into the darkness. The elects remained encamped high up in their respective trees for several hours, fearing a vengeful visit from the rest of the pack. Eventually, they all made their way down, collapsed the camp, and slowly began their journey back toward the mountain.

The return trip was faster than the trip out on account of them not having to track a moving animal. When they stopped to make camp for the night, Crea set to work on her primary role for the expedition. She had to craft the tusk into a writing quill for the Order-Masters.

Del sat beside her to watch her work. He understood how his powers worked and had some idea of how the Life oracles would create life, given it was the opposite of his power, but he had no idea of what to expect of a Creativity oracle. Before she set to work, she pulled several items from her pack.

She placed a metal stand on the ground; it had a clamp and a small viewing glass which distorted light. Next, she pulled a tool roll and put it on a small stump in front of her. Finally, she removed the vial of wet ash and placed it beside the tool roll.

He watched as she placed one of the tusks into the clamp and began, much like himself, to focus her energy on the object in front of her. Nothing seemed to change physically on the tusk, but she became more and more focused. Del realised that she was doing the same thing as he did within living creatures; she was reaching into the object and understanding it.

She seemed to remain entranced as she selected the first tool from the roll, setting to work carving and engraving in the bone-white ivory. After carving for a long time, she readjusted the clamp to have the base of the tusk face her and started to hollow out the centre using a precise drill while looking through the viewing glass. By the time she was finished, the tusk was as ornate as anything Del had ever seen. She had drilled a very fine hole in the narrow end of the tusk and sharpened it to a scratching point.

To test it, she pulled out a piece of blank parchment, dipped the quill into the mixture of ashes and began to write. She remained in her focused state of mind, and the tusk wrote perfectly, drawing an ornate illumination with a tremendously detailed flourish before setting it down and becoming lucid once again.

"That will do, I think," she stated matter-of-factly.

"That will more than do; that is amazing, Crea!" Del replied, marvelling at her creation.

She gave Del a shy smile and placed everything back into her pack before announcing, "now, who is for some dinner?"

17.
Lotions and Potions

Time passed by slowly for Del since returning from the hunting trip. It had been over eight span since Batter had almost had the lower half of his body removed by a rarn, and he silently wished for another opportunity to see some more danger. Each day passed the same as the one before, dry theory taught by Tom and recorded diligently in his leather-bound workbooks. His first book was almost full of diagrams and notes he had recorded since he started his lessons. It was impractical to actually get an animal and somewhat immoral to get a person to kill and dissect every day, so a textbook had to suffice.

Today Del walked into the classroom and found Tom waiting for him.

"We won't be in here today! Time to change it up a bit, I think. Let's go play with some poisonous chemicals!"

The thought of a change in curriculum piqued Del's interest, and poisonous chemicals definitely sounded interesting. He quickly followed Tom through the door of the classroom.

Tom led him through the tunnel network into another much smaller room. They entered, and Tom hit the igniter on several damp-light torches to illuminate the room. The light revealed several workstations in the centre of the room and a separate workstation to the rear with a ceiling duct situated just above table height.

The wall was lined with hundreds of vials, each labelled with an ancient, yellowing paper ticket. Del had never seen this room, not that he had bothered to explore the network of tunnels.

"This is our chemistry laboratory. From now on, we will alternate between the Living Room and the Chemistry Lab every few days."

Del nodded in excitement and moved towards the room's perimeter to inspect the contents of the vials. They seemed to be sorted into various categories based on their integral form.

He read the shelf labels aloud as he walked along, "Arcott Root, Corillia Fern, Hrenthinia husk, Malinta Palm, Urini Tree. I've never heard of any of these things."

"For each of these different plants, you can derive many different poisons, antidotes, lotions, and potions. There are hundreds of different plants and animals from which we can derive thousands of chemicals. In this class, you will learn how to identify all of those plants you named and more, as well as extract their useful ingredients and concentrate, activate or use them to make reactions."

"I was wondering when we would get to magic potions," said Del, his voice dripping with sarcasm.

Tom seemed to miss the intonation of his voice, "you know Assier-damned well that there is no such thing as magic potions. They are just figments of the imagination of the common imbecile told as fae tales. What we deal with is real science and research. We may have the power of Manipulation, but we work within the confines of physics, chemistry and biology."

Del felt as though he may have touched a bit of a nerve and thought better of continuing with any sarcastic remarks on the subject. Instead, he moved his way into the middle of the room and sat at one of the workstations.

"Do you have another book that I can use for this class? My other one is filling up, and it is probably better to keep it separate."

Tom directed him over to an old dusty bookshelf. Go and see if you can find an empty one over there.

Del made his way over to the dark wooden bookshelf and started pulling out books to check them out. He pulled out each one in turn and found that they had all been written in with other notes about various concoctions and recipes. Finally, he pulled out the last book on the shelf, flicked through it, and found that the first few hundred pages were blank with some writing in the back. Without giving it any further inspection, Del closed the book, made his way back to his desk, and set up his writing implements for the lesson.

"Today, we are going to start with some foundation notes about chemistry and chemical reactions; then, if we have time, we might make up a nice, simple formulation," Tom announced.

Del nodded and turned to the second page of his book, remembering he was still planning to get Crea to create him a title page for his other notebook.

"First things first, most of what we will work with during this class are poisons. Before you start making poisons, you should first understand the mechanisms of how they work on the body. Poisons can be ingested through food, breathed in, injected into the body or absorbed through the skin. They attack the body at the most basic level with chemical reactions to change the composition of the blood or other body parts. This can cause blood to clot or thin, the brain to swell or shrink, or prevent you from breathing. Are you with me so far?"

Del was writing furiously in his book, and Tom gave him a few moments to finish writing down the notes.

"For a lot of poisons, there are antidotes. Antidotes are the opposite of poison and work by trying to undo the chemical reaction and reverse the poison's damage. Some antidotes are also dangerous chemicals and must be administered correctly to prevent a possibly worse death than if the victim had been allowed to pass unaided."

"So, in theory, you could poison someone to make them sick and then just give them an antidote, and they will be fine?" Del questioned his Order-Master.

"In some cases, yes, but in many, no. Antidotes are rarely as effective at reversing damage as poisons are at causing it. Often victims are left with long-term damage to their organs, and more often than not, their brain or heart will suffer prolonged disease. If you poison someone, you should always intend the result to be the outcome of the poison. In general society, poison is viewed as a coward's kill, but it is not always the way. It can be an effective way for an army to incapacitate large groups of enemy soldiers by poisoning a water supply. It can also be used for hunting purposes with animals that are far too dangerous to attempt to kill through conventional means. It is not for us to decide how they will be used, only to understand how to make them, their effects and their antidotes."

"I have been meaning to ask; when we make new discoveries through research up here in the Arrats, how do we get this information out to the rest of the world?" Del asked.

"An excellent question! Have you ever heard of the great names of philosophers and scientists like Malaniana or Renecin?"

Del shook his head, and Tom groaned.

"Of course not, um, well anyway, we write parchments and send them out to libraries and universities across Azarth under various pseudonyms. These fake names carry weight in academic circles even though no one has ever met them, and they seem to have lived for more than a normal lifespan. We update the names every century or so."

"Right, so are there any scholars besides us in the world?"

"Of course there are; they are just a long way behind us in their knowledge. We tend to hang on to new discoveries for a long time until we think Azarth is ready to have more research. We hope, sometime in the future, the world will become self-sustaining in its technological progression."

"I suppose that makes sense," replied Del, "have you discovered anything yet?"

Tom looked almost happy to have been asked the question, "well, I have only been a full Order-Master for just over half a turn, but I am on the edge of a breakthrough. It is too early to tell you what yet, but it could revolutionise warfare. I will tell you this, though, The Oracle of Anew will not be happy to hear about it."

The Oracle of Malcontent followed his musing with a low chuckle, seemingly pleased about the prospect of annoying another Order-Master on an ethical level.

"Well, I look forward to hearing about it. Let me know if there is anything I can do to help you with your research."

"I will, I will. Now, back to today's lesson. Let's go through a few of the most common plants in Matraketh that can be used to produce poisons and their antidotes."

After several hours of theory, what started as a new and exciting lesson had begun to drag, and Del's eyes were becoming heavy.

"Now, with all that said, let's move on to trying to distil down a chemical component and create a bit of a fun powder. This is a little outside the normal realm of Death, but as we have already discussed, Combustion is a form of decay and disorder."

This piqued Del's interest back up instantly.

"I need you to find a jar of sap from the Elisier Flower while I set up an extraction apparatus," instructed Tom.

Del moved back to the shelf he had looked at earlier. The labels were all in alphabetical order, which made finding the correct jar a matter of simplicity. He selected the jar marked 'Elisier Flower Sap' from the shelf and placed it on the workbench at the front of the classroom where Tom had moved to.

"This desk is where you should perform any experiments where a gas might be created. The gas will get sucked out of the vent and won't poison or blow you up. Remember, immortal but not impervious to injury. Got it?"

Del nodded and looked at the apparatus that was set up. He scurried over to his table and sketched the various vials and glass tubes.

"Come back over here, and let's get started. First, you must dry the sap by removing all the water and leaving only the concentrated, dense components. To do this, deposit some sap on this plate and place it over the burner's flame."

Tom gestured toward a small candle-like object with a bright blue flame hovering above it.

"Try not to burn it; remember, we are just removing the water."

Del did precisely that; he measured a small quantity of the sap and placed it on a small silver dish. He then held it with a set of long, slender tongs and waved the sample through the flame, warming the sap and causing it to bubble. After a few long moments, the elisier flower sap had changed from a sticky liquid to a crumbling solid.

"Now, next, you need to add a few drops of Oil of Vitriol. You need to wear gloves dipped in rubber and put a good distance between your face and the vial to ensure you don't come in contact with it. If you get it on your skin, it will burn you. If you get it in your eyes, you will go blind. Do you understand me?"

Del nodded in agreement not to test Tom's list of potential outcomes.

Del moved forward and selected a dropper from the workbench, sucking up a few drops of the acid and placing them on the dry Elisier flower sap. The sap began to hiss, and tiny tendrils of smoke floated up towards the duct in the roof.

"Now give it a good stir, then leave it to dry. Do not touch it before I tell you to."

Del nodded and responded, "Okay, I promise."

At that moment, the holy bell tolled, and Tom left the room. Del picked up a small stirrer and stirred the mixture of sap and Oil of Vitriol before walking back to his workbench with his book.

Del took this opportunity to see what secrets the written-in section of the book contained. He leafed to the back pages and found that someone had started writing from the back of the book. The words and diagrams were all upside-down. Turning the book around, he found the first page. It was intricately decorated, and in the centre was written:

'Necromance and Maleficence for the Malcontented Mage'

The next page, and those that followed, did not align with anything he had been taught by the sect. These were spells like those Tom had discounted as belonging only in fae tales and potions that had supposed effects on people without direct contact or influence. It seemed as though there was possibly a difference between what was considered acceptable knowledge by the Order-Masters, and what was actually possible. For now, Del decided to keep the contents of his notebook to himself and read the details by damp-light in the security of his own quarters. As he was closing the book, the next holy bell tolled, and he left the room, heading for the Sanctum Sacellum.

He had just walked into the room to find the other Elects and Order-Masters convening for afternoon devotions when a loud bang sounded and reverberated through the tunnels.

The entire room erupted and abandoned the usual ritualistic time of silence to find the source of the explosion. Del watched as Tom looked around the room and located him. Del wasn't sure whether he was ensuring his safety or seeing if he was the direct cause of the disturbance.

Tom led the way to the chemistry laboratory, an acrid smell of smoke filling the tunnel as they approached. They arrived to find no fire but a large plume of smoke in the middle of the room and a large blackened mark above the alcove for the front workbench. It seemed as though their little experiment may have been a little more reactive than initially anticipated.

After closer inspection, Tom announced that there was no significant damage done.

"Everyone go back to the Sanctum Sacellum. Del, you stay here and help me clean this up. Missing one day of devotion won't kill you."

The elderly priest looked none too impressed at the prospect but didn't argue with the Order-Master. Everyone shuffled out of the room and left the two Death orders to their clean-up duties.

"What was it that we made, Tom?"

"Just a little touch powder. It isn't usually meant to react until it is disturbed. I had intended on us taking it outside to do that little part of the experiment."

"Well, it looks like it worked well enough," joked Del.

"A little too well," responded Tom jokingly.

18.
Necromance and Maleficence

Once safely back in his quarters for the night, Del waited for the hall outside to turn quiet before igniting his room's damp-light torch and carrying it over to the writing desk. Three books were set atop the desk; his two notebooks and the book loaned to him by Tom.

He set himself down at the desk in the chair and selected his latest book. Turning it over, he opened the back cover once again. The entries included chemical recipes, incantations and rituals that could be completed. An entry called 'Long Slumbering Night' suggested it could place someone into an eternal state of comatose. Depending on the incantation, any number of triggers could be set to end the state, but no other antidote or medicine would bring them back to reality. Another entry, 'Dead on Arrival,' would act like a sort of proximity mine whereby if an enemy came within a short distance of the subject of a ritual, they would be struck down with some terrible and almost instant death. He kept flicking through the pages; 'Undead and How to Control Them', 'Soul Interception', 'Resurrection', 'Plague and Pandemic', the list continued. He stopped at the last entry, 'I Lava Good Eruption'. He took a moment to appreciate the effort someone had made to name the title and decided to read on.

I Lava Good Eruption

How to convert a stable mountain into an erupting volcano in three easy steps.

Step 1 – Mountain Selection

Ideally, the selected mountain should be located near the Equis of Azarth. There are more free paths for molten magma to follow in this region. It is not known the reason why. You do not need an existing fault, but it helps. The mountain should be tall enough to allow the lava to explode and run down the sides; there is nothing more disappointing than watching a ground-level volcano just flood the ground with liquid rock.

Step 2 – Locate the required ingredients

You will need the following:

- A sliver of rock from the top and centre of the mountain to establish a connection with the required eruption location.

- The fruit of a Sashunian bush (found near the Equis of Azarth on Matraketh and Kesheir). Dried and imported fruit will also suffice if required, but fresh is easier to work with.
- A few drops of blood from an Initiated.
- The shell of a scuriat.

Once you have all of these items, grind them together in a mortar and pestle, then build a hot fire and let it burn down to coals. The hotter the coals, the better.

Step 3 – The ritual

Form a Connection and reach into the stone mixture to complete the ritual. Will the stone to form a volcano before emplacing the stone mixture into the coals. While holding the connection, recite the following incantation:

> Mountain of stone, on you I call
> From above, your highest peak shall fall
> Ash and rock, sulphur and smoke
> From your very depths invoked
>
> Now within you, let it flow
> Magma there shall swell and grow
> When the night grows dark and severe
> Those below shall shake with fear
>
> Create a path for what's within
> Death, I summon you now. Begin!

Important note: This ritual is best performed away from the location of the eruption for the safety of the summoner; however, the efficacy of the spell will diminish as you move farther from the site of the eruption. Experimentation may be required, but it is recommended to be at least two leagues away and upwind.

Also, it is recommended that the initiated person that you 'borrow' the blood from is not yourself.

Del sat thinking about what he had just read for a long period of time. Firstly, one thing that bothered him was the final sentence.

Was it suggesting that the blood somehow had an effect on the donor? Could it possibly be drawing power or energy from that person?

The second thought he had was about his current address. They were currently living inside a hollowed-out mountain, a seemingly perfect place for someone to create a volcano, particularly given their location not far north of the Equis of Azarth.

Had someone developed this ritual to destroy the Sanctum of the Sect along with all of its connecting tunnels, rooms and knowledge?

The thought disturbed him.

Del knew that he should probably report what he had found to Tom or one of the other Oracles.

"I will after I finish reading about them," he promised himself.

Over the course of the next few span, Del would take out the chemistry book and read over the various different entries. He made it his goal to finally understand how the spells worked using what he was being taught by Tom in class. His conclusion to date was that it was still based on creating a Connection to an object or a person and imposing your will to Manipulate that object or person. There were still parts that did not make sense to him yet, "why did a number of the rituals require a blood connection to an initiated to get them to work?", "why were there seemingly non-reactive ingredients required in the recipes?" and most importantly, "if the process centred on Manipulation through Connection, why is the incantation required?"

Del suspected he knew the answers to those questions, but they had not been confirmed. He suspected that the blood connection drew energy from the blood donor; Tom had told him several times that matter needed to be conserved through all Manipulation. He also suspected that the non-reactive ingredients and the chant were more of a farce for show. Knowing what he did now of the religion of Assier, he would not be surprised if there was some showmanship.

Notably, he decided that he would learn about this form of magic on the basis that he needed to know about it for academic purposes and would never attempt to use it himself. At least, that is what he told himself.

During classes with Tom, he would ask questions that alluded to an extension of their magic and the blood connection, making sure to never be too specific to draw attention to the fact that he may know more than he should. The book's title had 'Malcontented' in it, so he suspected that Tom had a part in its creation.

One time in class, he asked Tom, "is there anything that we can do that would require more than one of us to perform? Like one to Manipulate and one to support with their power?"

Tom had given him a strange look but answered the seemingly innocent question.

"There is nothing I will teach you during your time as an Order-Elect that will require you to draw on someone else's power. Just like when you hunted the Rarn, some tasks require you to work together or perform various jobs to achieve a single goal, but never a Connection with multiple mage's input."

Tom considered the question a little longer before adding, "why do you ask?"

Del had already prepared an answer before asking the question, just in case.

"I was just wondering whether we would have the opportunity to team up with some of the other Order-Elects for some of our practical classes."

"Hmm," responded the Order-Master, clearly trying to push away suspicion, "I am sure we can come up with some form of group practical. I will have a talk with the other Order-Masters.

Nothing had ever come of that conversation, and their individual lessons and practical sessions continued. Eventually, Del just let the book fall to the back of his mind, and it remained on his shelf except for chemistry lessons for him to write his notes.

His lessons continued as usual for several months, discussing more complex systems of the human body, like gaining a thorough understanding of the central nervous system, including the brain, or the various chemical reactions that can occur between different elements and blood. During one of these biological chemistry classes, a question, which had been at the back of his mind for a while, finally boiled to the top.

"Are we ever going to get any more experience outside of this cave?"

It had been almost half a turn since they had gone out to hunt the rarn, and so far, it had been the only time he had been required or even allowed to leave the Sanctum's underground network. The other Elects had even been on the odd supply run back to Portsworth, but for some reason, Tom had always found a reason why he was required to stay back. Del wasn't sure if it was a lack of trust or whether there was a more legitimate reason why he was being forced into the confines of the mountain. His once deeply tanned skin was starting to become ghostly pale, and he longed to breathe fresh air that wasn't cold and sharp.

"Tell me, what do you hope to learn out there that you cannot learn here?" Tom asked him.

"Well, that is just it, isn't it?" Del replied, "I don't have a farmin' clue. I have been on a completely different continent from the one I grew up on, and I have only spent a span here exploring it. Most of my time was spent walking down a road and through a forest. Surely there are things that you could show us outside the walls of this cave?"

Tom seemed to mull the question over in his mind.

"Perhaps," he said before changing the subject, "I will hear no more on this, for now, understand? I have taken what you have said under advisement, and I will discuss it with the other Order-Masters."

By now, Del knew what that meant; he was just too argument-averse to say it directly. He let the conversation die, and they went back to their lesson.

"Now," Tom continued from earlier, "can you tell me what reaction you would expect between blood and oxidanyl?"

Del thought back through his previous classes before settling on the most straightforward answer, which also happened to be the answer to almost every question the Order-Master of Death proposed. "Decomposition."

"Fine, decomposition of what?" asked Tom, clearly unhappy with the lack of detail.

"Decomposition of the oxidanyl. The blood makes it boil and bubble."

"And what effect does it have on the blood?"

Del made to answer before realising he didn't know.

"I am not sure," he admitted.

"That is good; no one actually does. But it does make you wonder, what is it that it is reacting within the blood? Experiments suggest that in small quantities, it doesn't harm the blood but may actually improve it, but if you drink it, it will kill you quickly. It is actually one of my ongoing experimental projects to find out. I have a theory that could explain a lot, and I am working with Pidge, ah sorry…" clearing his throat, "The Oracle of Anew".

Tom turned a pale shade of pink before continuing on. There was a sort of tension between the two Order-Masters that didn't simply seem to be accounted for by their differences in job position. Del suspected that the two may have been more than just work colleagues over the last few decades.

"If I am correct, we may have isolated the 'atmospheric life force' that is the whole reason why we breathe. Ground-breaking, I tell you!"

The holy bell sounded, and Del made to start packing away his things as Tom moved towards the door.

"Oh, I meant to tell you. I have a project which will need you to work with the other Elects over the next few weeks."

Del's face turned to look at Tom with curiosity. He also felt a little silly, given his earlier line of questioning.

"Assierium is just two span from today. I understand the irony, but we always throw a bit of our own celebration up here. You know, drink to our own godliness and the like. Anyway, it is going to need a little bit of organising. I need you to do the supply run with the others and do the preparation. Ole' priesty out there is a bit of a wild one with a few sips under his belt," Tom chuckled to himself.

"Of course," Del replied, "and thank you."

Tom smiled and nodded before leaving the room to complete whatever he went to do every afternoon.

19.
Assierium in the Arrats

In the lead-up to Assierium, Tom had allowed Del to leave the safety of the Sect's stone tunnels and venture back into Portsworth. The Elects had all congregated together to compile a list of the various supplies they would need for the festivities and decided that Ellie would accompany Del into town. Crea was required back at the tunnels to start preparing the plethora of decorations, and more often than not, where Crea was, you would soon find Batter lurking not too far. No rules had been set regarding relationships in the Sect. Still, considering the close quarters and the long time they would spend together in the future, Del thought it a pragmatic choice to keep his current life of abstinence.

Del didn't mind too much about being paired up with Ellie for the trip. She openly detested his discipline within the Sect, but they got along strangely well, considering.

They could have a perfectly civil and engaging conversation as long as they didn't discuss him killing things she was trying to give life. Plus, Del thought she was pretty easy on the eyes. It didn't take too much convincing to be the gentleman and allow her to walk ahead on narrow passes.

They reached Portsworth after just two days of travelling. The descent through the tunnel was much faster than his journey to the Sanctum, and he wasn't bumbling his way through a forest with a poorly drawn and encrypted mud map.

"I know of a good place to stay overnight. They know about us, or at least, they think they do," Del suggested to Ellie.

"Alright, that sounds good. So long as their food is better than up there, I'll stay anywhere!"

Del led the way to the inn where he had stayed when he arrived and was instantly met with a welcoming embrace from the barman.

"Welcome back, my son. A room for the night or just passing through for a meal?" he asked before realising Del was accompanied, "And who is this lovely young lady? I'll see you two get the best room again."

He scurried away before either of them could answer a single one of his questions. He returned, key in hand, and led them up the staircase and down through the familiar hall of the accommodation quarters.

"Please, the room is yours for the night. Free of charge for you two. Enjoy, enjoy," he said as he unlocked the door and swung it open, leaving the key in the lock and scurrying away.

The two Elects entered the room and unloaded their packs from their back. They had travelled light as they needed all the space to carry supplies back home.

Del flung himself onto the soft paddings of the sleeping pallet and sprawled like a long-legged orbite across the sheets.

"One pallet! That is a little presumptuous, don't you think!" she said with mock disgust in her voice.

"What, are you afraid you might fall in love with me or something if you sleep without a wall between us? I promise I'll keep my small clothes on and Deathly cold hands to myself," retorted Del.

"Humph!" came the reply, "you wouldn't know what to do with me anyway."

Del wasn't entirely sure what to make of the conversation but thought it to be on the safest side to change it before his previous aversions to Elect relationships were overpowered by his youthful lust. "Let's go downstairs for some real food before we go out to the markets. I am starving."

Ellie was looking out one of the room's large picture windows and nodded her reply.

After a meal of some sort of fresh, steamed, pink-fleshed ghoti with a side of crispy root vegetables, Del's stomach was well satisfied. The food came at the cost of the pandering from the barman, but it was an inconvenience Del was willing to take.

As they left the bar, Del explained the runner to Ellie, "You will see a young boy following us as we move through the port. He belongs to the barman as a messenger of sorts. He will go anywhere we go and ensure we get a fair price."

"Right," she replied, "and how does that work with keeping a low profile as we were instructed?"

"Not really well, I'll admit, but just because they believe we are somehow important to their religion doesn't mean they know who we are or where we live. We just have to ensure we aren't tailed when we leave."

Ellie agreed as they made their way from the outskirts' quiet streets and into the markets' bustling centre.

Just the same as when he arrived, there were market criers everywhere trying to spruik their wares. Various types of ghoti and shelled creatures. There were sheets of dried green paper hanging up in stalls that couldn't have been used for writing. There were also other animals that Del was familiar with for sale in the market, like onk, moog and keil. A sweet, burning smell wafted across the square from a stall with baked goods on display and many other delicacies in other booths.

They made their way to one of the meat vendors and ordered a side of onk and some prime moog cuts. Del pointed out the stealthy young boy to Ellie as he whispered to the market vendor.

"I'll even throw in a few handfuls of sliced, smoked and cured onk for you. It lasts a little longer than the raw meats outside of a cold store, but you will still want to eat it within the span," said the vendor.

When they received their meat and paid the man, Del thought the bag seemed far heavier than he had expected, given their order. When Del stuffed the wrapped packages into his pack, he found little room for anything else.

They made their way over to several more stores and were met with similar levels of generosity, either low prices or excessive stock for the price. They picked up some premium ghoti, shucked food-of-the-sea packed in salt, and were eventually drawn to the baked goods stand, where they grabbed enough crusty rolls to fill the rest of Ellie's bag to the top.

They made their way back to the bar and asked to have their packs stored overnight in the cold store before having a quick meal of roast moog and making their way up to the room.

It was dark outside by the time they were done, and it was time to sleep for the night.

Once in the room, Del was struck with a conundrum. Usually, he slept in nothing so much as a sheet and was intent on wearing his small clothes, but his small clothes had been worn all the way from the Sect and were not the sort of thing to inflict upon a fellow bedmate. He needed to change into fresh clothes.

The room was not equipped for privacy; given the single pallet, it was probably saved for those on the first night of their coupling or single travelling mages.

He was saved the first move as he watched Ellie's white shift tumble to the floor around her ankles, revealing the pale cream complexion of her body. Her long black hair sat proudly on the tops of her breasts, her nipples firm in the cool night's air. Del was stuck in a moment of shock, knowing this was the moment that a true gentleman would turn away from a lady, but he found himself unable to. His vision was drawn down her body as she extended her arms to replace the fallen shift with a clean one. She had a perfect, slender figure without being skinny, her hips forming a heart-shaped frame around her sex. Del was unsure whether she had continued to face him in an effort to tease him or whether it was simply a complete lack of modesty. He shook his head to clear it and prevent lingering thoughts of his friend's naked body.

Del turned his back before she could make eye contact with him and grabbed his fresh clothing. In a choreography of awkwardness, he stripped down and replaced his small clothes in what he had hoped would be a single fluid movement. In reality, it looked like he was imitating some kind of long-legged animal trying to stand up moments after its birth. Laughter erupted from behind him as he scrambled under the sheets to hide his embarrassment. Ellie soon followed him to the other side of the giant sleeping pallet, and there they remained for the night.

The next day they left for the Arrats, making several loops around the block to ensure they were not followed by the young boy.

After a couple of days, they reached the Sanctum of the Sect and entered the Sanctum Sacellum. They found that it had been intricately decorated by Crea and Batter. Far from the depictions of Assier and the four-pointed star of

Aiel, they found woven, colourful paper chains strung across the room. They had placed thin coloured paper over a number of the damp-light torches illuminating the room in an array of colours.

In the centre of the room sat a decorated wooden box on top of a plinth; the two recently returned Elects still wore their packs on their backs but moved in to get a closer look. The box had a large crank handle off to the side, and in the middle was a large cylinder with pins sticking out at irregular intervals. Inside the box were tens, if not hundreds, of mechanisms. Various shafts, springs, and cogs. Neither of them had seen such a contraption, but their investigation was quickly interrupted.

"Out! Both of you, get out. We aren't finished yet!"

Crea had come into the room to find them gawking at the box.

"But what is…" Ellie didn't get to finish her sentence.

"I said out; go on. Get that food out into the kitchen, and you can start cooking. It will take a while to prepare that meat, won't it?"

Ellie turned her nose and left the room. Del just shrugged and followed her towards the kitchen.

When they arrived, the heath was roaring. It would seem Batter was a bit of a pyromaniac; a fire like that would char any food cooked near it.

"Farms! Batter, what are you trying to do? Cook yourself?" Del exclaimed as he entered the kitchen.

"It is burning down to coals. I had to make a lot of coals," he explained.

"Right; what can we do about cooking now, then?" Ellie questioned him as she looked around the kitchen, "should we move some coals into the empty hearth while we use this one to burn them down?”

“That was the plan!” he said with a smile. “Now, Del, you grab that shovel and get moving while I start preparing this meat.”

Del and Ellie slung their packs onto the ground with a loud 'thud'.

“Assier Almighty, how much did you buy!? I thought you only had ten broams with you?”

“The locals are more than generous when it comes to our boy Del here, it seems,” Ellie replied, shooting Del a look.

“It's not my fault they find me charming. I don't see you complaining that we have some actual food for a while up here in the Arrats,” Del said, picking up the shovel and moving the coals around.

“Yeah, somehow I don't think that is it mate! But you are right, I'm not one to look a gift mant in the maw,” Batter replied.

With all the food preparation done in the kitchen, and the meat slowly cooking in the hearth on the coals, the three Elects moved back to their quarters for some rest before the night's festivities.

Del returned to his room and found a box in the centre of the sheets of his pallet. Instantly, Del had a feeling of guilt hit him deep inside his gut; he hadn't even considered preparing a gift for anyone here.

"Farms!" he swore quietly under his breath.

Del settled himself into the soft bedding and opened the hinged box lid, revealing a black hat. It was in the style that he had seen some of the local gentry wearing around Portsworth; in fact, if he recalled correctly, Arnult had been wearing a very similar one during his visit. It must have been worth a small fortune from a shop.

Before removing the hat, he inspected the box. Carved into the side was a hand-crafted note:

From: Crea
To: Del
Happiest of Assieriums to you

Del supposed she had probably crafted the gift and its intricate packaging during her lessons with her Order-Master. Still, it was a damn sight more than he had gotten her, or anyone else for that matter.

It is too late now! Del thought to himself.

He arose and walked to his wardrobe, selecting his charcoal grey robes. He swapped his travelling villager's clothing for them and cinched the rope at his waist before donning the hat. It felt good on his head. He wondered how she had managed to get the correct sizing, momentarily imagining her sneaking into his room at night to measure his scalp.

He made his way back into the kitchens to start serving. It was nearing nightfall, and the food would be almost ready. Crea was already there with a number of platters intricately decorated in green and red flowers. She was placing the juicy meats and ghoti onto them.

"Almost done. Could you give me a hand to carry the plates down to the Sanctum Sacellum?" she asked him before looking up. "Well, don't you look stunning? Do you like it?"

"It is amazing; thank you so much! I am so sorry I didn't get you anything," Del replied, feeling even worse than before.

"Don't you worry for a moment," replied Crea, "I wasn't expecting anything from you or the others. I just thought I would do something nice. I had seen some of the rich people down in the port wearing them and thought to myself, Del would look great in one of those!"

"Well, thank you again. I really appreciate it. Also, well done on the decorations; the place looks amazing!"

"Oh, you haven't seen anything yet; I had only just started when you two got back. Come on, let's get these plates down there."

Crea led Del down the tunnels and into the Sanctum Sacellum. It had been transformed into a sea of green and red. All the decorations seemed to be made of fine paper but resembled luftun in flight and various flowering plants.

In the corner stood a tall tree decorated with small damp-light torches, flickering with light.

"Just wait until the others get here; I have something even better."

They didn't have to wait for too long before the Elects, the Order-Masters, and Gular, the holy man, arrived.

The room was bursting with conversations about the decorations and how beautifully Crea had made the Sanctum.

"Is everyone ready?" she asked no one in particular.

Crea walked over to the centre of the room; she began to crank the handle of the box on the podium. After a few moments, she stopped winding and pressed a lever on the side. The cylinder in the centre started to turn, not just in one direction, but it seemed to be in multiple segments. Some segments turned clockwise, and some in a counter-clockwise direction. Emitting from the box was a beautiful symphony. The music was like the sound of the luftun that Del had awoken to that morning in the forest, only more organised; it was like singing but without the words.

Del had heard music played by instruments, like those at the choosing ceremony back in Strauth, but this was completely different.

Crea grabbed Batter by the hand and led him to an empty part of the room; they began to move around.

"Come on, everyone, we dance to music like this back home."

Reluctantly, everyone except the holy-man paired up to dance. Batter and Crea. Del and Ellie. Tom and The Oracle of Anew. The Oracles of Prevail and Beauty. Life with Death and Creativity with Combat.

The couplings didn't last too long. Del still felt awkward about the night he had spent with Ellie back in Portsworth, excusing himself on the basis of having two left feet.

Everyone slowly began to make for the piping hot food, which was sitting around the room's perimeter. The meat was lovely and tender, and the ghoti was fresh and crisp. As everyone started to eat, the music continued on without further winding.

All in all, Del had enjoyed Assierium for the first time in his life. Maybe he could learn to enjoy the quiet life of routine within the confines of the Arrats.

20.
Interlude: Late-Night Drinks

The Oracle of Malcontent | The Sect

The Oracle of Malcontent sat on the floor in the corner of the Sanctum Sacellum; he held a skin of liquor in his hand. One of the perks of having access to the equipment he did, and lots of time to spare, meant that he could make his own liquor. Horrible and tasteless as it was, it did the job of intoxication when it was required.

"Come on, don't hold back," called The Oracle of Anew from across the room.

"I don't know what you mean, Pidge. I'm just thirsty, is all."

"You can try that with the Elects but not me. I've known you over twenty turns now, you son of a motherless mant. You are hiding liquor in there, and I know it," she slurred.

"You have already been into your own stash by the sounds of it, woman. Nick off!"

That didn't stop her advance across the room. She sat down and laid her head against his shoulder. The Elects, along with the other Order-Masters, had all made their way back to their quarters by now.

The holy-man, as predicted by Tom, was the last man genuinely standing. Swaying to the music in his own version of a rhythm.

"Do you remember our first Assierium together?" she mused to Tom.

"Of course I do; you hated me," he chuckled. "You had been working on a project to get a moog-calf to have twins, and I thought you had brought us fresh meat for the celebration. I didn't even question it, just took the initiative to butcher it myself. You didn't talk to me for almost six span after that."

"You never did apologise for that, you know."

Tom nodded, "for what it's worth, I am sorry. Ah, the innocence of youth and the mistakes we make."

"He is just like you, you know. You would do well to remember that," Pidge noted, seeming to sober up momentarily before returning to her slouched position.

"He is Me! That is the problem! I know Me and what Me got up to when I was nineteen turns old."

"Yes, but did keeping you locked up in a cell keep you out of trouble?"

"History would suggest otherwise; what are you saying?"

"He needs to go out by himself for a while. Away from you and let him make his own stupid errors. They all do!

My elect could do with a little worldly toughening up; I've seen the way she looks at him every time he destroys a bouquet of flowers. I know we normally wait for a few more turns, but I think we let them all go on a bit of an adventure. Let them choose their own path for a while. That's what I should have done earlier."

The Oracle of Malcontent sat staring at the wall before him, thinking about what she said.

"If you let your Elect go and I don't do the same, I will have the whiniest child on Azarth in my classroom. You are pushing my hand, Pidge, and I am not sure I like it. When did you learn how to get me to do what you want?"

"Like I said before, I've known you for over twenty turns; if I didn't know by now how to manipulate you, I wouldn't be very good, would I?" she chuckled to herself.

The Oracle of Anew placed one leg over Tom and brought herself up in line with his face.

"Now, how about some more of that manipulation?" she slurred.

"Down, girl. Mister Holy is still in the room."

"What? Him? He quit caring three holy-wine skins ago. Let's go find a classroom!"

Part 3

21.

Hangover

The day following Assierium proved one thing beyond a reasonable doubt to Del, immortality does not prevent hangovers. The Elects did not have access to liquor, but it would seem that Gular and the Order-Masters were withholding a secret supply.

Lessons, and all official duties, were cancelled for the day, and none of their elders showed their faces until at least lunch time. Surprisingly, Tom was the first to find himself confronted with the bright-eyed and bushy-tailed youths standing around the kitchen.

"Urgh, how can you all be here making so much noise and standing in front of the hot hearth?" the Order-Master of Death enquired of them.

He looked almost literally green in the face and held his face in his hand as he spoke.

"I feel pretty good, actually; what about you guys?" Del asked of the room, looking around mockingly.

"Oh, shut it, or I shall think of something very uncomfortable for you to do during tomorrow's lesson. I either need to eat something or throw up. What have you got?"

"Smoked ghoti?" Crea offered from across the room.

She moved over to him, holding the platter and the smell followed in tow causing Tom to gag.

"huuh, urgh, hmmm, anything but that. Away! Away!" he recomposed himself. "Just some of that sweetbread from last night will do just fine, thank you."

Batter made his way to the dry keep and fetched a small knot of sweetbread, handing it over to the ailing Order-Master. Tom took it gingerly and slowly moved off back to his quarters.

Once he was out of earshot, the four Elects collectively let out a small chuckle, although Del secretly shared his pain, thinking back to his first few experiences with liquor aboard the Sea's Fury.

The four Elects had been sitting around the kitchen, treating it as some sort of makeshift dormitory. To be fair, it was the perfect young adult retreat; it was warm and had all the snacks you could ever need. They sat around the centre island and played Scupper, the game he had been taught by Caln while at sea, except instead of tiles, Del had made paper cut-outs with dots. He had shown them several span ago, but they had never really had a good opportunity to sit down and play undisturbed. Naturally, Del was the better player of the group at first, but Crea was slowly, but surely, beginning to win more games; Batter was not far behind. Ellie continued to struggle and hadn't won a single hand.

The game was also a good opportunity for the group to talk about the lives they left behind; besides the hunt for the rarn, they really hadn't spent much time together socially.

Crea was the first to begin reminiscing, "I've spent my whole life here on Matraketh in a seaside village called Scythe. There I was, just a young girl named Reenah. A girl who went to school every day and helped run my parent's shop by night."

"What is a school?" interrupted Del.

"It is a place where children learn how to read, write and learn numbers. How did you learn if not in a school?" she asked, seemingly genuinely curious and unphased at being rudely interrupted at the start of her story.

"Mother taught me. Most kids like me on the farm don't get an education, but she always wanted me to have a better life than that." He shook his head as though to dismiss the train of conversation. "Forget about me, please. You go."

"I guess I was always fairly creative. My parents would let me sit in the back of the shop as a young child with paints and cheap paper. I would create images of the people who walked into the shop, animals I had seen, my family and all kinds of brightly coloured flowers. As I grew up, my mother realised that I was actually good at drawing and started buying me canvases to paint on, then selling them in the shop for a price just enough to cover the cost. Most of the people who bought them did so out of pity, I am sure, but eventually, my confidence and skill level increased, and word got around. Soon I was getting commissioned to paint pictures for the local gentry. As I got older, my time came to go to school and run the shop, leaving no time for my art. You could say I was a little relieved when I arrived here and found that I was Initiated into the Order of Creativity. It seemed only natural."

"Do you miss back home?" asked Ellie before regretting the question. "Sorry, I shouldn't have asked."

"No, it's okay. Yeah, sometimes I miss my mother and father, but it already seems like it was a lifetime ago. I get to do my hobby as a job now, just without any muse for the art. I can't wait to go back outside and create by looking at nature and the people around me again. What about you, El?"

"Similar to you in many ways, I guess. My father was the village mountebank in a town just outside the capital of Cyrillia in central coastal Kesheir. I was Lillana back home and spent much of my free time working with him around his operating house. Most girls would have been forced to stay home with their mothers, but my father was a free thinker. He believed that there was no reason his daughter couldn't learn from him and help him save lives. Of course, when I got old enough, I knew that I would still be expected by the rest of Azarth to make a home for my man, but it was never to be. I was called up in the Choosing, and instead of saving lives or delivering them into the world, I ended up being the acolyte to Life. Winning, really. If you think about it, it's like a promotion to the best job in the world. It just meant giving up my identity alongside my family and friends back home." Her voice broke as she finished.

Ellie stood up and made her way over to the cold store, pardoning herself with an excuse of requiring some food and leaving a hanging discomfort in the air.

"I suppose it is my turn then," started Batter. "I think I have already told you my name was Ka back home in Saulit. I lived in the busy city of Quarn, full of people who don't know you and plenty to do to keep you occupied. My father worked hard as a ghotiman, but I never spent much time around boats. He would go out to catch his food-of-the-sea, but when he returned, he wanted nothing more than to forget about his job. While he was gone and I wasn't at school, I would spend my time with my friends in the city, up to no good. Harmless fun most of the time, but we got in the odd bit of trouble with the local enforcement priests. When my father returned from his trips, he would take me away from the city. We would travel to far-off lands in Saulit, and sometimes the trip to our destination would take a span or two. We would sleep under the stars, hunt for food and forage for snacks. He taught me all there was to know about survival and appreciating nature. My mother died in childbirth, so while he was away, I would live with the priests in a dormitory for orphans that attended my school. Sometimes it was a rough life, but I liked it."

Del shifted uncomfortably in his seat at the mention of the third father, who believed in their child and was a good role model for the family. He knew his time was coming, so instead, he continued to ask Batter for more details. "Tell me about this city; what did it look like?"

"Busy. The streets of Quarn were lined with shops two or three high. Not just people calling their wares but office buildings for officials, high-ranked priests, businessmen and the gentry. Ellie would have loved one of the blocks, a massive suite of buildings dedicated to practising mountebanks; some buildings were for expecting mothers, others for the aged and decrepit, and some which took in the bleeding and dying. Hundreds of mountebanks and assistants worked in one place; it was magnificent. I had to go there once when I broke my arm swinging from the rafters on a school recess. They set my arm back in place and glued a plaster cast around it to keep it fixed. I had never seen anything like it."

Batter turned to face Crea.

"And you, you would love the gallery downtown. I have never been inside, but I was peering through the windows one day and saw a massive building dedicated to people's art. Maybe you can create something that we could send there to be put on show; your work is brilliant, it really is."

Crea blushed slightly at being complemented by Batter.

"But enough about my home, what about yours, Del? Who were you back home?"

Del took a deep breath as Ellie returned to the table. She had recomposed herself and had a bowl of some sort of leftovers from the festivities in her hand.

"You know what, my life wasn't that interesting," Del explained hopefully.

"Nope, that is not gonna work. We all had to go; it is your turn," said Ellie through a mouthful of meat.

"Fine then. I grew up on a crop farm in the mid-north of Straulatos in a town called Strauth. I pretty much had never left my home before the priests came to my house to announce that I had to attend the Choosing. I worked the farm with Father, ploughing the fields on a mant, hand planting seed and running irrigation channels. Father was an arse. He cared only for himself and his family's reputation within the village, even though he never spent any time there."

Del could feel his previously unreleased rage build within him discussing his father. Still, he continued, "On the day before the Choosing, he told me not to embarrass the family and that Assier wouldn't choose someone as pitiful as me to join him."

A tear started to flow down his cheeks and drip to the floor, followed by many more.

"He couldn't even look back at his own son as he walked away from me at the ceremony. You may all miss your homes, but good riddance, I say."

The room was silent. After a few moments, Ellie walked over and put her arm over Del's shoulder in a light, comforting embrace. The silence continued for an indefinite amount of time before Crea spoke up.

"What about your mother?"

The thought of his mother brought a smile to his face briefly before he was once again reminded of the fact that he left her behind without a proper goodbye and no guarantee of ever seeing her again.

"My mother could have been one of the Saints of Aiel. She had all of the patience in the world with my father and never stopped trying to make my life better for me. I just wish there could have been some way that she could stand up to that cranky old bastard. I wish I could have."

"Here," offered Batter as he passed Del a kerchief. "You are here now, and we are all a family of sorts, right?"

The room nodded.

"Do you know what families do at times like these?" Batter asked.

He was met with silence.

"Raid their Order-Master's private stash of treats!"

"Just where are these treats you speak of, and why are we just hearing about them now!" demanded Ellie, play punching him in the arm.

"Well, they made me run a stocktake of the cold store and dry keep when I first arrived at the Sect. They thought I would just read the labels and not check what was inside each crate and barrel. They were wrong and greatly misjudged my ability to find hidden snacks."

"So where are they?" repeated Ellie.

"Bring a spoon."

Batter led them into the back of the cold store and cracked open the lid of a barrel labelled "Ghoti Guts Bait".

"The giveaway is that there is no way anyone in this Aiel-dammed mountain was going to be pole-catching ghoti, so why would there be bait in the cold store?"

Lifting the lid, the other three Elects peered in. There was a pale, solid substance filled almost to the top of the barrel with what looked like spoon scoops taken from it.

"Dig in everyone, and no one breathes a word of this to the Order-Masters."

Everyone nodded their firm agreement before moving in for a scoop.

"Iced moog cream, I would guess. That is amazing! I can't believe they don't share this with us!" cried Crea.

"Yeah, they must sneak in here after dark for their own late-night snacks, I'd say," suggested Del.

"Or when they need to take a break from disobedient little twerps!" grumbled a voice behind them.

They all turned to find The Oracle of Malcontent blocking their exit from the cold store.

"I think some time in here will do you all good, wouldn't you say?" asked Tom. "Now, hand over the spoons."

Tom closed the leather door and placed a chair in front of it to stand guard.

"Come on, there was no sign on it saying we can't eat it, was there?" called Ellie through the doorway.

"You live on a diet of hard cheese, hard sausage and hard bread. Did it occur to you that soft ice cream didn't quite fit the menu? Also, the longer you talk, the longer you freeze. You might want to consider shutting up."

Tom sat in front of the entry to the cold store for what seemed like an eternity before he was joined by several other voices. Del recognised them as the Life and Combat Order-Masters. The Oracle of Beauty must have been getting in all the sleep she could muster.

"Afternoon, Malcontent," came the male voice of The Oracle of Prevail.

"Have you told him yet?" came the female voice of The Oracle of Anew.

"Shut up, will ya? Why do you think I am sitting in front of the cold store? Do you think I like the cool breeze up my clacker? And no!"

"Don't tell me they are in there. How long have you locked them in for?" she questioned.

"Oh, come on, it's not like they can die. They will be fine."

"Let them out; they can still get frostbite, you know!" she demanded.

"Fine, but just so you know. They were eating your ice cream."

Tom stepped aside and moved his chair from the doorway allowing the four Elects to vacate the freezing room. As they left, Del could feel the warmth of the hearth heating his face, fingers and toes. It almost felt like he was defrosting.

"As for the ice cream and saving your fingers, you all owe me!" she scolded.

22.
Preparing for Travel

The next day when Del arrived at class, Tom was already waiting for him. Del entered the classroom and sat down in his chair. Before he could even finish placing his books in front of himself, Tom came over and sat on the edge of the desk.

"I have something that we need to discuss. I have put it off long enough, and the other Order-Masters are keen to make their own announcements." Tom cleared his throat before continuing. "A span from now, you will leave the austere comforts of the Sect and venture out into Matraketh. I personally do not think this is a good idea, nor do I think you are ready for a field test. Do not misunderstand me; this will not be a sabbatical, and you will take it seriously. Do you understand?"

"Yes," Del replied, "but what am I to do on this field test?"

"Explore, learn and collect samples. Did you ever wonder how I ended up with thousands of jars on the wall in the other classroom?"

Del had wondered exactly that but thought better of opening his mouth to agree with him.

"Your goal will be to collect a sample of everything you have so far noted in your book; I will give you vials to store everything in. You will have until Lunarian to return with all the samples, and penalties will apply for anything you don't get. I haven't decided what they are yet, so don't ask."

Lunarian was the shortest, and usually the coldest, day of the year back home in Straulatos. Given the change of seasons this side of the Equis of Azarth, Del supposed that it was the longest day of the year, about half a turn from Assierium, which here in Matraketh was cold and short of sunlight.

"While you travel around, you obviously cannot continue to call yourself Death-Elect. People tend to get a little bit funny about names like that. You can take on whatever pseudonym you want; you can continue using Del or make up a completely new persona. It is up to you."

"If it is alright with you, I would like to call myself Pthorn again?" Del asked hopefully.

His name was one of the final pieces of his childhood home that he could still own, and for the last turn, it had been taken from him by force of tradition.

Tom thought for a few moments before responding, "I would prefer you didn't, but I don't feel I am at liberty to actually stop you. Just consider this, the longer you hold that tether at arm's length, the harder it will be to finally let go."

Del nodded back to him, internally feeling the joy rise within him. He would finally be free of the cave for longer than a few days, be able to talk to other people and introduce himself as Pthorn once again.

"I still have one more lesson for you. If you are going to go out collecting things, I would hate for everything to be too easy. So far, you can trim some bark from a tree, tap some sap, or capture a slug. No, no, no, we need something truly fun."

Tom paused once more, stroking his manicured chin.

I really don't like the way this is going, thought Del.

"Yes, I think I know just the thing. There is a swamp land in the far southwest of Matraketh; actually, not too far from where the Creativity-Elect came from, I believe. The best thing about swamps is the effects of decay. It makes for very… interesting, volatile and insidious gasses. It also makes for very adaptable creatures which have slowly evolved to live, breathe and hunt in these quagmires. One such creature is the vermillion spined croaken."

Tom gestured towards the wall filled with samples, urging Del to identify and collect a jar from the collection. Given their defined alphabetical organisation, Del quickly selected a large canister from the shelf before setting it back on the table in the centre of the room.

The liquid within the jar had become dark and polluted, so it was difficult to see the creature stuffed inside. Tom briefly left the room and returned with a damp-light torch from a sconce outside the door. Using the damp-light as a focused source, Del could see through the liquid more clearly and make out the form inside.

The creature had leathery skin and was shaped much like a large river stone but with two small front legs producing from the side and two much larger hind legs tucked up into the crouching position. A row of long spines raised from the centre of its back. Notwithstanding the lifelessness of its cloudy eyes and peeling flesh, it looked set to leap at a moment's notice.

"What is the first thing you notice about the spines that might seem unusual?" Tom asked Del.

Del studied it closely and thought for a moment.

"They face forwards, not backwards like most spined creatures."

Tom nodded.

"Quite correct, and what do you think that might tell us about this creature?"

Again, it took a few moments for Del to think of a logical reason why this might set it apart from other animals

"It is aggressive and will fight rather than flee. If the spines faced towards the rear, then it would be for defence. With the spines facing towards the front, it means it will face its attacker, or prey, and fight."

"Well done, yes, you are right. Croakens, and particularly vermillion spined croakens, are known to be highly aggressive and extremely poisonous."

Del took an opportunity to write some notes about the croaken before he forgot any details but was soon interrupted by more questioning from his mentor.

"Alright, here's another tricky question. You know it is poisonous, but by what chemical mechanism does it poison?"

Del thought about its name and instantly knew he had seen something before in his previous lectures about vermillion. He stopped writing notes and vigorously flicked back through pages, upon pages, of notes from other chemistry and poison lessons.

About five or six span ago, they had discussed the dangers and mechanisms of harm associated with elements that Tom had referred to as poisonellas. A poisonella was something that, in its most basic form, without compounding with anything else, is poisonous to humans. Once compounded, many chemicals are harmless but, in elemental form, could kill; for example, it is known that if the salt-of-the-sea is converted into its elements, it forms a poisonella gas. The same could also be said of various compounds where several inert elements combine to create a deadly poison.

After turning, and un-turning of many pages, Del finally found his entry on hydrargyrum and began to read from the page.

"Hydrargyrum is a well-known and studied poisonella. It is so named as it is fluid in most normal environments and is silver in hue. Hydrargyrum is unique in that it can combine itself with other solid elements to form hybrids with unique properties, in and of themselves."

"Go on," urged Tom. "What does this have to do with our croaken over here?"

"I am getting to that." Del skipped down a few lines. "Ah, here we are. Vermillion is the ground form of its natural existence when mined from underground pits deep within the crust of Azarth."

Del turned and looked up at the Order-Master. "That is it, isn't it? It poisons with hydrargyrum."

"Top points today, Del. Yes, it does. Next time, I want an answer without you having to consult your book. You won't always be able to read about something before it tries to kill or maim you."

Tom paused for a long moment and let the lesson sink in.

"This particular croaken is capable of shooting hydrargyrum-laced spears from its spines a distance of ten to twenty paces. You will never see it coming and may not even feel it. Not until you start to feel tired and muscle-sore, or you might start seeing your vision changing on you, causing you to stumble. It will attack your brain and give you headaches and twitches. Finally, most people will succumb to organ failure within a few days. You!" he pointed accusatively. "You wouldn't be so lucky as to be killed. You would suffer for several span or even up to a halfturn until finally, it passed through you. Might I recommend not startling it when you find one? It is probably best to stop its heart before it notices you."

Del made sure to note down a few more of the necessary details before responding. "I will make sure to remember that. Thanks."

Tom absconded from the room after the croaken discussion and left Del to finalise his anatomical diagram and notes about the peculiar creature. Del had sat at his desk, holding the damp-light torch for a long time, studying the details of its body and legs. Its body wasn't smooth like he had first assumed; it had ridges running across its body, like wrinkles in a sheet. Its legs ended in five long gangly toes with bulbous suckers on the tips of each one. Its tongue protruded a little from its mouth, and he found it split trinodally with a sharp spine erupting from each node.

Del decided that given it was probably his farthest destination geographically from the Arrats, and he didn't really want to have to work out how to capture one, he would leave this particular little beast until last. He hoped secretly that he would have to return before getting a chance to try to capture it.

Del finished writing his notes and attended the devotion in the Sanctum Sacellum. When the final bell tolled for the evening, he quickly made his way over to the other Elects to discuss the morning's events.

"So, who else is keen to get out of this mountain?" Del asked.

He was met with various responses, all talking over each other.

"Yeah, man, I can't wait to get out and explore Kesheir!" said Batter excitedly.

"No way," and "Uh uh," came the responses from the two girls.

"Oh, come on, why not?" asked Del, honestly curious. Surely everyone else was sick of being holed up inside this tunnel network day in and day out.

Crea responded by herself this time, "because I have to go to Straulatos, and she has to go to Saulit. That means a ship. Do you remember what you told us about your trip over here?" She paused for a moment considering whether to say what else she was thinking, "Plus, you know."

"You won't get to make lovey eyes to your tall, dark, handsome gentleman over there?" Ellie questioned jokingly.

"Yes, as a matter of fact." Before adding, "like you are any better," under her breath.

Del wasn't exactly sure what she was referring to but had his suspicions that the girls had discussed their night together in Portsworth upon their return. The Elects started walking back down the tunnel towards the kitchens and away from the Order-Masters.

"I am sure the trip won't be as bad as mine; you all know that was the Order-Masters playing a trick on me. I doubt they would pull the same joke twice. I'm positive they will come up with other exciting ways to scare the farmin' hell out of you."

They all agreed, but it did set the thought in Del's mind. *What other tricks might they play on them while we are out travelling? How much influence did they actually have over what happens to them while they are gone?*

He pushed these questions and other thoughts of future issues from his mind and returned to the positive feeling he had before questioning everything.

"So everyone gets a new continent they haven't been to before. Crea, any recommendations for while I am travelling around your homeland?"

"Stay on the High Priests Way where you can and avoid shortcuts. Matraketh is known for its bandits, but they usually steer clear of the main road. As for tourist attractions, I wouldn't have the first idea. I lived my entire life on the southern peninsula, although I can recommend the beaches."

They arrived back in the warmth of the kitchens and sat around the centre island bench.

"Anyone up for a final game of Scupper before we all head off on our adventures?"

A span later, Del was up before the crack of dawn and packed his travel knapsack with his warm winter gear, his ship's hand outfit, and all of his spare small clothes. He even decided to bring the awful white priest outfit, although he hoped never to find himself in the situation to ever require it again.

At the top of his bag, he packed the sack of labelled glass vials, his writing implements and the two large books he had been using to record notes. Finally, he stuffed the book borrowed from Tom into the bag. Altogether it weighed far more than he would have liked, and he had not yet stopped off at the kitchens to stash some food for the road.

He donned his grey robe, cinched the black rope around his waist and capped his head with his new black hat.

Del knew that the rest of the Sect would not awaken for several more hours, especially not Tom, who was known for his particular aversion to early mornings. He snuck quietly through the tunnels, and into the kitchen, before loading up on all of the usual hard travel supplies and a water skin. Making his way back down through the tunnel, Del continued past the Sanctum Sacellum and began to follow the path through the long snaking passage of stone. Noting the advice inferred from his discussion with Batter, he kept to the well-lit tunnels and the worn path, never deviating through the warren of offtakes.

His path was the same as when he arrived on his first day and when he travelled with Ellie to get supplies. As he approached the gaping mouth of the tunnel, he dug into the bottom of his bag and pulled out the gloves, heavy boots and warm cloak, emplacing the less weather-resistant gear back into the sack. They were still close to Assierium, so he knew the cold would be biting and offensive once he exited the tunnel.

Once outside, the cold was blistering. No matter how often Del was subjected to it, it seemed that he would never get accustomed to this type of frigid weather. He fought his way out along the path that followed the mountain's edge, across the pass, and across to the abutting mountainside. This time, his fourth time crossing the pass, Del felt far more confident and quickly found himself back inside the next tunnel. He kept the heavy clothing on for several hours to warm his bones.

Eventually, he stopped for the night. He slept once again in the propped-up bedroll that had become his second home on several occasions now.

Trekking and camping was his life for the next span or so before he arrived at his first village heading west into the depths of Matraketh. Here he decided that he deserved a little of that rest and relaxation that Tom had explicitly warned him against.

23.
Flying the Coop

He stayed in the small village of Ung for four span before finally feeling a sense of duty; it instructed him to get moving on his mission and start collecting specimens. Del, or as he now introduced himself to the locals, Pthorn, had the horrible suspicion that somehow the Order-Masters would be able to scry a look at their whereabouts, and there would be consequences for too much larking about.

The villages on the High Priests Road received most of their income from the travellers who passed through, requiring hospitality, new clothing, supplies for the road, or simply entertainment. Ung seemed to have everything a traveller could need, as long as the expectation was rough-spun for clothing, hardtack for food, and puppetry for entertainment. It was a simple life, but not the life of a bored scholar as it was in the Sect; this was simplicity whilst still enjoying life.

Pthorn stayed just long enough to enjoy a few span away from the confines of his new life. He enquired about where to hire a wagon and where to purchase supplies for the journey. The procurement of the wagon had been quite lucky for Pthorn. The previous owner, known for being very spritely for his age, had suffered a very sudden ailment resulting in his demise. His family, not knowing the actual value of a wagon and desperate for a few broan, had sold it to Pthorn for little more than the value of the upholstery and included the driver free of charge. Then again, luck did seem to follow Pthorn when it came to the misfortune of others and untimely demise, especially if you were a small creature or pretty flower that had been stolen by an arrogant Order-Master.

The journey had already been nine days since they left the village at the base of the Arrat Range. The road had become increasingly rough and rutted, with a wheel suffering significant damage, requiring re-banding beside the road; this was one factor in life over which he had very little control. Pthorn started the journey lounging in the back of the wagon, enjoying the escape from the rules and regulations of the Sect but soon migrated to a more upright position on the front of the carriage with the driver. Just over a turn had passed since his induction into the Sect, and he had finally been allowed to conduct his first solo pilgrimage across the continent of Matraketh; his excitement came and went in waves.

Pthorn's quest was simple enough in theory; he must journey to the western coast, stopping along the way to collect samples for use back in the laboratory deep within the Arrat range. He also figured he would stop at all major way points and determine how best to assist those suffering using the gifts granted to him through the power of The Singular, a sort of target practice for the up-and-coming Order-Master of Death.

Pthorn figured there was a little creative licence within the definition of his mission to assist him along his way. He had sensed that the wagon owner had a blockage in one of the passages, which carried blood to his brain, completely unaware of the threat to his life; the Death-Elect had simply provided a more finite date to the end of the man's life. The process used the basic foundations of Manipulation that he had practised with the scuriat and the rarn. It was the cornerstone of the work performed by the Order of Death, expediting the inevitable to decrease long-term suffering.

Until this point, the driver had been largely silent. It was commonplace for people who kept the faith of Assierium to mourn the loss of family for seven days following death. While this man was only in the employ of the wagon's previous owner, he clearly had enough respect for the man to keep his silence. It was also apparent that the driver was not a particularly outspoken gentleman as day eight was also maintained in silence except for the required courtesies and pleasantries.

Finally, his silence broke.

"We are in for a long journey here, my brother; we'd best get to know each other. These equestra have worked hard for me for near on four turns. The black and white one on the left is Nae, and the chestnut on the right is Winnie. The name is Wal," he said as he extended his hand.

"Pthorn," the under-cover mage replied, once again feeling free in the use of the name given to him by his mother and father back in Strauth. Putting on a voice of pompous authority, he continued, "I am in training, and my employer has given me leave to travel to the farthest coast and study the, ah, fascinating botanical specimens along the way. I have been told that the climate changes drastically as we head further west."

The driver eyed him somewhat dubiously, possibly deciding whether to pursue the claim's validity.

"So that would make you a botanist-in-training then, sir? May I ask then why you chose to wear such inappropriate clothing and pack so little for such a wide variety of situations?"

Pthorn looked down at his pack, then at his grey cloak.

"That really is a great question and, I must say, a somewhat amusing answer on my part. My employer is a great believer in self-reliance. He has agreed to pay my way on the basis that I purchase only what I require as I go. I am to earn broan to cover expenses wherever I can and return with a complete ledger of outgoings. He has provided a fixed sum of money for me to use but has not, however, seen fit to provide me with the total value. I am to expect a bonus equal to the amount not spent upon my return, or if I exceed the value of the order, I must work to repay the loss. I must remain frugal at all costs and travel light to ensure the most value to myself upon my return."

The answer seemed to satisfy the driver, who returned to looking ahead with a slight nod and an affirmative hum.

Pthorn's answer had, in fact, not been entirely a lie; however, the truth was slightly different. While it was correct that he had to be frugal, this was more due to the fact that broan had no value in the caves of the Arrat range. All currency possessed by the order had been obtained from field trips or donations to Assierian priests sent to the Sect as a form of holy tithing.

Saying that he was studying botany was also hardly a solid lie, given that he was ordered to collect specimens for the laboratory. It was true that botany was of significant interest, and he did, in fact, have an enormous, heavy tome related to the subject if he ever needed to prove his guise.

Pthorn's instructions were to collect specimens for every type of plant and creature they had discussed in class which meant using the book as a checklist. Every page of the book included some sort of creature or different plant with a description of cultivation, appearance, preparation and effect on the human body.

The other part of the book was a secret that not even his Order-Master was aware of, even though he had technically given it to him. If the book were to be opened in reverse and read backwards, the book was a record of incantations for many spells and recipes for the creation of various potions, many with disclaimers of 'purely academic' and 'ethically adverse effects'. Pthorn knew, or at least strongly suspected, that these pages were a form of forbidden magic related to his work but not acceptable by its standards.

After his short discussion with Wal, Del decided that he should probably start taking some form of notice of his surroundings. The area they were travelling through was becoming denser with woodland. While the road they traversed was well worn and kept free of plants, either side of the road grew thick with hardwood trees, ten and twenty paces tall. The gigantic trees were of very little interest to Del; he was neither planning on constructing houses nor fabricating furniture. Instead, he began to survey the smaller plant life that grew within the safety of the larger trees. Of particular note were the much smaller, frond-leafed plants. The trunks of these plants stood no taller than a man and significantly broader at the base than the crown. The colouring was primarily a pale yellow but with vivid purple banding at hand-width intervals. He called for Wal to stop for a closer inspection.

Pthorn climbed down from his seat atop the front of the carriage. He removed his carry bag and book from the luggage hold, and walked over to one of the plants. He recognised the plant from the descriptions given in his book, this was clearly a Malinta Palm, and he could see its specimen jar back at the Sect in his mind's eye. Seeing the whole tree in the wild was very different, considering the specimen jar contained only bark and fruit.

He removed a well-honed flat-bladed knife and two specimen containers from his bag, which resembled small square glass vials with stoppers. From the trunk, he took several slivers of purple bark from the banding, and from underneath the shade of the palm frond, he plucked two small blue balls.

"Let's make ourselves comfortable here for a little while," Del called up to the carriage. "I want to document these as I go. As sure as Assier, I don't want to end up cataloguing a turn's worth of specimens at once."

Wal made the sign of the four-pointed star of Aiel, reminding Pthorn that he was a religious man and probably didn't take well to blasphemy and using the prophet's name in vain. He dismounted in silence before he walked forward to tend to the equestra. Each equestra had leather pannier bags on each side; they were simple and not adored with any intricate leather work. He removed a stiff brush, a bowl and a water skin.

Del removed a quill and ink pot from his bag, found a small boulder to plonk himself on within a pace of the tree and began to read his notes on the first page of the botany book, adding a reference to the specimen jar under the title.

Malinta Palm

Refer to specimens 1 (trunk band bark) and 2 (fruit).

Known for its lethal and restorative properties, the malinta palm stands ten to five-and-ten hands tall. They are natively found in densely wooded areas and grow within the protection of larger trees.

The leaves are of no significant value except for perhaps crafting purposes. The blue fruit (see specimen 2) hidden beneath the fronds have a hard casing over a soft, fleshy, pitted fruit. The flesh of this small fruit can kill a fully grown man following a delayed incubation period of up to three days; no symptoms are generally noted during this period. Death is accepted to be painless and is often mistaken for natural loss of life.

The banded trunk of yellow and purple contains the only known antidote to the toxin contained within the fruit. Once dried and powdered, the bright purple band (see specimen 1) can be administered to counteract the effect of the fruit. The quantity must be equal to that of the fruit ingested. The antidote is a poison far more dangerous than the fruit itself. No known antidote exists for the bark, and if the berries are consumed after the bark, the effects of the poison are known to become amplified and more painful. Convulsing and frothing at the mouth are believed to be the precursor to the victim's demise.

P.S. Effects are to be studied in more detail once a suitable subject is obtained; an experiment is to be conducted to administer both simultaneously. A potential antidote to specimen 1 is to be determined.

The postscript was also added while he annotated. Tom had not actually specified that he should test any of these specimens on people, only to collect them for the Sect's collection.

Del repacked his belongings back into the luggage hold, satisfied that he had at least made a start on his actual mission and retook his seat back on the carriage to await Wal, who was still in the process of brushing down Nae and straightening the equestra's mane.

After a few more moments of thought, he once again dismounted from the carriage. Walking back to the luggage hold, he retrieved the book and returned to his previous position in the back of the carriage to continue studying the reverse of the book in more detail. Before he knew it, he had fallen asleep while attempting to read. Ironically the page was left open to the method of distillation for a powerful sleeping draft that left the Connected oracle in a state of long-term insomnia and delirium.

By the time he awoke, the carriage was already moving along at its regular slow, ambling pace. They continued for a while longer before stopping at a large clearing. The clearings were situated every few leagues and were common places for travellers to stop for the night. Many led to little one-equestra towns or homesteads, but this one was hemmed in by trees and isolated.

Both Wal and Pthorn dismounted from the wagon, and Pthorn made his way over to one of the existing cook fire rings. By now, their nightly routine was well established. Wal would tend to the equestra, giving them water and feed from casks and barrels in the wagon. Pthorn would set up camp and get the fire going. Some nights there would be other travellers in the clearing, but they had the campsite all to themselves tonight.

Wal usually chose to sleep in the back of the wagon, leaving Pthorn to sleep in his bedroll, which he set up beside the wagon, keeping them both in close proximity if the need arose to make a quick getaway for any reason.

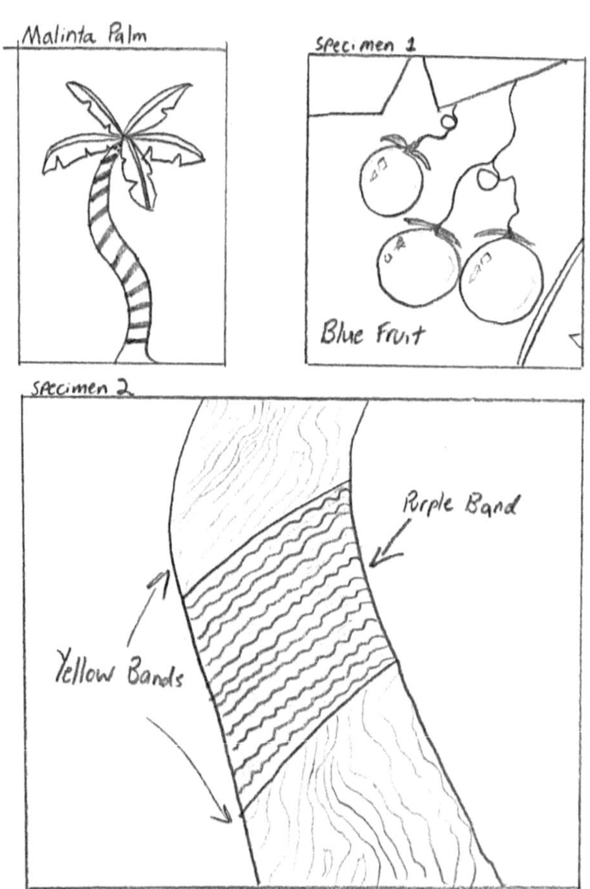

Malinta Palm
Specimen 1
Blue Fruit
Specimen 2
Purple Band
Yellow Bands

After setting up the bedroll and laying some bedding out in the back of the wagon, Pthorn unpacked an iron tripod and hung a cast kettle above the fire. Using small kindling and some larger wood found lying around the bottom of the surrounding trees, he Created a fire. Wal had never been around to witness his fire-lighting skills and hadn't questioned the fact that Pthorn had not requested a flint box.

Once Wal was finished tending to the equestra, he made his way over to warm himself by the fire. Most of the other nights, he hadn't spoken more than a few words but tonight filled his pannikin with some thin broth from the kettle, and he began to tell a story.

"Over my many turns, I have travelled this road hundreds of times," he started, staring intensely at the glowing coals. "I have spent nights around fires like this with all kinds of people. Some were rich gentry who refused to look a coachman in the eye. Others were paupers who spent half their night eyeing off the equestra and wondering how much one would fetch at the next village. I've travelled with holy men in transit off on missions, troupers who want to share their song, story and wine, and travelling families."

Wal let the silence flow into his pause as he chewed his bottom lip.

"Many turns ago, I met a young man, not much older than yourself, off on much the same journey as you. Similar poor dress sense," he said, nodding at the robes, "but didn't bother with the hat."

He gave a small chuckle under his breath.

"When I asked him where he came from, he said nowhere. When I asked him where he was going, he said somewhere. When I asked what they called him, he said, 'No one'."

Wal looked over to stare Pthorn directly in his eyes.

"And do you know the really curious thing?" He paused, not breaking his eye contact, "I could have sworn to Assier above that you were him."

Wal took his last gulp of broth from the cup, threw it into one of the equestra's saddle bags, and disappeared into the back of the wagon, leaving Pthorn wondering about the story's meaning.

The old man's mind must be going on him, Pthorn thought to himself; *as he said, he has seen many people on the road throughout all his years.*

Pthorn let the fire burn down before he crawled into his bedroll, still thinking about Wal's curious tale and let himself succumb to sleep.

24.
Fluorocor

$\mathfrak{T}$he next day started like any other. They arose with the peaking of the sun over the horizon, and no more was said about the conversation of the night before. They broke camp and set off along the road heading west in the silence to which they were now both accustomed.

Soon after leaving the clearing, the wooded area beside the road became denser and denser, blocking out the sun and enclosing them in the damp. Leaf litter covered the dirt road and clumped in a soggy mess inside the wagon tracks. Throughout the morning, the equestra had stumbled and almost lost their footing in the deep, wet grooves; it made the going slow and more tiring for all involved.

Pthorn retrieved his book and began reading through the specimens he may need to collect. He attempted to make a mental note of the type of environments and regions of Matraketh where he might find various plants or animals and plan his route across the continent.

Pthorn was flicking through the pages and naming the listed species under his breath; "Inglewood root found in southern Matraketh wildwoods, spotted arrak nut best stolen from a bushy-tailed tree squarn's nest, filamentasporianus the glowing sporio of Matraketh."

Pthorn looked up from his book to review his surroundings. The damp undergrowth would be the perfect hiding spot for sporios. After rechecking the page, he confirmed his suspicions; they were native to this area and were known to grow prolifically in woodland leaf litter.

Pthorn suggested a break to Wal on the basis that the equestra could do with a rest. He took his knife, a couple of vials and his book with him to explore, all stuffed into his knapsack.

His first foot off the carriage landed in a deep muddy puddle, soaking his boots through immediately.

"Assier's stinky scrotum!" Pthorn swore under his breath, looking up to see whether he had been overheard. "That won't dry for farmin' days!"

Wal looked down disapprovingly and shook his head wordlessly as Pthorn made his way to the edge of the road.

He began to take in his surroundings in more detail. The trees were ancient hardwood, with many being over an arm span across and some spanning several paces. Tom had once told him that trees got wider at about a thumb's width per turn. At that rate, some of these trees could be hundreds or even thousands of turns old. The bark was red and ripped, like the tree within was bursting at the seams of its exterior protection. The wood below was a deep red, like flowing blood, and the bark was as black as night.

Pthorn ran his hand along the first tree he approached and came away with a rather large splinter deeply embedded into his finger.

He slowly made his way through the trees while fussing with the side of his throbbing finger. After about fifty paces, the light was very filtered and looked like an early morning's dawn. Pthorn knelt down and brushed away some of the litter, finding nothing but moist, rich soil. Being a farmer, he wished he could have had dirt like this back on the croplands.

A little further along, he found a fallen deadwood; it looked like it had been lightning-struck. Not only was the bark black, but so was most of the wood itself. It had splintered at the base and fallen to its final resting place. In its fall, limbs must have been knocked free, forming hollows where rot had begun to set in. He noted that it must have been long dead, given the litter cover.

Pthorn noticed a dull glow emanating from one of the hollows in the trunk and made his way over to investigate closer. He brushed away the rotting litter to find six white stalks standing proud from the wood. They were capped with domes and had a bulb about halfway up the stalk. They emitted an eerie green glow, illuminating the hollow and a horde of orbites that had made this their home.

Pthorn sat down to consult his book again in more detail.

Filamentasporianus

Commonly known as The Glowing Sporio of Matraketh and found prolifically in central-eastern regions in densely wooded areas.

Its long vertical stalk has a poisonous bulb at its midsection and terminates in a narrow dome cap. The underside of the cap is ribbed with light brown gills. This species emits a dull green glow which some research suggests slightly mutates any living creatures nearby.

This sporio contains potent toxins which can shut down a fully grown human's body in a matter of hours; it attacks almost every organ in the body.

This sporio is commonly picked by inquisitive children but rarely accidentally consumed or mistaken for common edible sporios by adults.

When consumed, this sporio has a mild, meaty flavour, although you are unlikely to go back for seconds.

The symptoms start with vivid hallucinations, followed by heavy diaphoresis and panting. Finally, the heart will give up and cease beating.

Care should be taken when collecting a sample not to come into direct contact with the specimen, as this could poison the handler. It is best to retrieve the sporio as a whole; dig out the roots and stem with a small amount of dirt. The sporio will remain alive for many turns, even in a vial, and can be a valuable source of light.

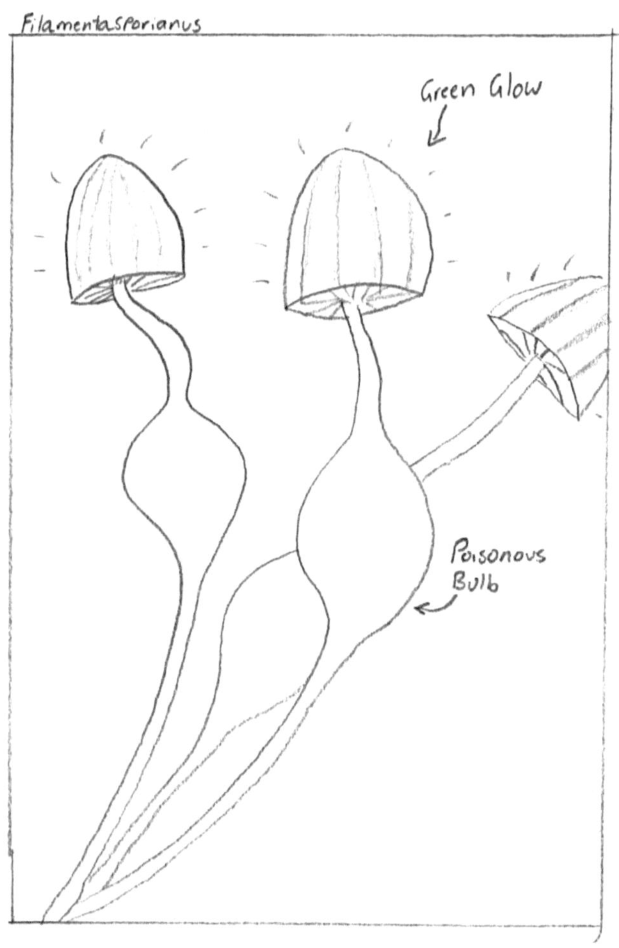
Filamentasporianus
Green Glow
Poisonous Bulb

Pthorn put down the tome and donned his gloves. Placing an unstoppered vial on the fallen tree, he reached down to pluck one of the sporios from its hollow.

As his hand entered the void, a loud screech emitted, and the dull light flickered between almost non-existent and bright green. The orbites all reared up as one and made to attack.

Pthorn fell backwards onto the wet forest floor, soaking him through almost immediately.

The orbites seemed to be guarding the sporios, but he had never seen one so aggressive, let alone a nest of them. Thinking back to the entry he had just read, it occurred to him it may be because of the filamentasporianus and whatever power they had absorbed from it.

He couldn't take any chances with the orbites; Assier only knew what effect the mutation may have had on them. While he may not be able to die exactly, an existence recovering from the effects of some unknown mutant may not exactly be favourable.

After several minutes of thinking, it occurred to Pthorn that this may be precisely what he needed to bring back to the Sect to study. Who knows, he may have just discovered a new mutant creature no one has ever seen before.

"Now, how to catch you?" he asked aloud to himself.

Pthorn had studied orbite physiology with Tom back at the Sect and knew the creatures didn't have a blood system like most beasts that can travel through veins. They were more of a 'randomly filled with goo' sort of a creature, that said there were ways of control through Manipulation. They still had a heart of sorts and something that might resemble a brain. Through trial and error in the classroom, Pthorn had discovered that if you could stop the heart from pulsating and interrupt the flow of information from its 'brain', the orbite would slow and become docile enough to pick up safely.

In the words of his ever-eloquent Order-Master, "you would have to maintain this stasis for a long period of time before death would actually become permanent for the hearty little bastards."

The second challenge for Pthorn came from the fact that there wasn't just one orbite; there were at least ten of them, all gnashing their fangs and rearing up, causing an energy disruption in their environment.

Keeping a safe distance from the spindly horde, he began to reach into one of the orbites near the end of the row. First, feeling deep for its heart, which was the easy bit, then searching deeper for its speck of a brain. Pthorn applied firm pressure until it slowly stilled and curled its legs.

Maintaining part of his focus on the first orbite, he moved on to the second and third. Finally, he reached the last orbite, almost at the end of his focal ability. The close proximity and similarity of physiology made it possible but certainly not easy.

Once he was sure that they were all finally subdued, he stuffed a couple of the orbites into a vial, making sure to keep them as much intact as possible, before relocating the remaining ten-legged creepy crawlies a far enough distance away so as not to cause him undue worry.

Once he was sure his orbite mission was complete, he relaxed his hold on them. Slowly, the two orbites inside the vial began to wake and panic about their new home inside a glass tomb.

"I'll finish you two off later," he said to the tiny black creatures before placing the well-stoppered vial into the knapsack.

He returned his efforts to the sporio. Without their guardians, the sporios had returned to being just a dull glowing stalk, almost boring compared to earlier. Pthorn removed his knife from its small scabbard and began lifting the sporio from its root structure, keeping some organic material and dirt from its base.

As he began to dig, the sporio closest to the knife started to change colour. First, it changed from a dull green to a yellow before progressing through an orange hue and finally settling on a deep red. The other sporios in its near vicinity followed suit. Pthorn made a mental note to update his very outdated notes on this species which mentioned nothing about this particular defence mechanism.

Lifting out the whole plant using his knife, he tipped it into a vial, allowing it to slide all the way to the bottom. He placed the stopper on top and lifted it to his eye level to get a closer look. It was definitely as described; however, he noted that the sporio didn't just glow. The light seemed to ripple along the stalk, around the knob and over the top cup. It seemed almost fluid, and it seemed to distort as you looked closer.

Pthorn placed the second vial into his knapsack, cleaned his knife on his cloak and set off back the way he came towards the wagon. His journey back was a little more cautious, given what he had learned about some of the creatures lurking beneath the litter.

Once he reached the wagon, Wal was waiting for him, already sitting atop the driver's seat. Pthorn threw his knapsack into the back and climbed up beside him.

"Find anything interesting?" Wal asked.

"You could say that. One thing is for certain, roasted sporio is not on the menu tonight."

Their travel for the day drew to a close in its regular fashion with the location of a clearing with a fire ring to warm themselves by. The pair stopped and began their self-assigned routines, Wal by the equestra and Pthorn by the campfire.

Pthorn made his way towards the edge of the clearing to gather some wood, wondering to himself how well this old hardwood would burn even though it was wet.

As he approached a dead-looking branch, he saw something flit in the undergrowth, followed by a couple of eyes peering out of the darkness.

Pthorn stopped in his tracks and stood very still.

The pair of eyes stalked closer to the edge of the clearing, a black leathery snout now visible protruding from beneath the wet leaves and bark.

While he couldn't yet make out the rest of the creature, he strongly suspected that he knew what it was after coming face to face with one placed in his path by the devious scraggly-haired Darn back home.

Pthorn remembered the dangers described to him by his father; he remembered the sheer look of terror on his face. A turn ago, he may have spun around and run, probably leading to him being coated in acid and eaten by the leathery devil. He had become a different man since then; his fear turned to a sense of wanting to prove himself.

A crazy idea flashed through his mind. *What if I could catch it, train it and keep it?!* he thought excitedly to himself. If he ever made it back home, he could just imagine the look on Father's face.

He also remembered how Darn said she caught it. She had said she had knocked it out with a lump of wood, which was why the beast was so angry when they stumbled upon it.

Maybe they aren't so terrifying when they haven't been given a lump on the head from a stick of lumber.

Reaching slowly into his pockets, he pulled out some of his travel snacks. Just some hardtack he kept there for emergencies. He chewed off a small corner and slowly crouched down. The cautious hydrofluor edged slowly forwards.

Pthorn threw the crumb in a slight arc to land immediately before the tiny winged acid-spitting dragon.

A long tongue leapt from its mouth. The tongue had two sets of razor-sharp teeth attached to the end, which grabbed the food from mid-air before it touched the ground, and then it swiftly retreated back into the undergrowth. There it remained, watching.

Over the course of the night, he tried to coax it back out to no avail. The small piece of hardtack had sated either its curiosity or its stomach for the night, but it stayed just out of the boundary of the clearing without moving.

As they sat around the campfire, Pthorn explained his insane idea. "I want to stay here for a couple of days. In the clearing, that is."

"And why is that?" questioned Wal.

Pthorn explained about the hydrofluor, leaving out the part about how they can kill and eat you.

"I want to earn its trust. Maybe it can accompany me."

"Hmm, okay," he agreed apprehensively. "But it had better not scare Winnie or Nae!"

That was all the agreement he needed. Tomorrow he would try harder.

The next day the hydrofluor was still exactly where he had left it. It seemed uninterested in doing anything except cautiously observing. Pthorn experimented with different types of food; a small piece of hard cheese, some crusty bread, more hardtack, and even a morsel of cured sausage.

The cured meat seemed to be the winner, not much of a surprise given the stories about these small beasts devouring people. Over the course of the day, the hydrofluor made a full-bodied appearance out into the clearing. Wal kept his distance and stayed with the equestra over the other side of the campfire.

Nearing the end of the day, the hydrofluor retreated into the safety of the under litter and returned to peering out at the two travellers as they ate their dinner.

On the third day, Pthorn thought about putting his powers to use. He couldn't physically manipulate the beast in the same way he could to steal life away, as that would be counter-productive in gaining its trust. Instead, he thought he may be able to apply it more subtly, gently slowing the hydrofluor's heart to relax it without stealing its consciousness and cognitive ability.

He held one hand out in front of him, extended toward the timid beast, and felt deep within to find its beating heart. He applied a very light pressure, almost nothing at all, and began to whisper to the beast.

"Come here, little one, that's right, everything is okay."

He held out his hand in a welcoming manner.

"That's the way, yes. I think you need a name. What do you think?"

Pthorn stopped to think for a moment.

"Ah, yes, I know, Fluorocor! Come here, Fluorocor; my name is Pthorn."

At that moment, Pthorn could not believe his eyes. It was like a bond between the two snapped into place, and an understanding was forged. From within the hydrofluor, Pthorn could sense its heartbeat increase back to a steady rhythm, not one of fear but of complacency. The small black hydrofluor splayed its wings and frill neck before it began to walk towards Pthorn. Its wing span was twice that of its body, and it gave them a flap creating a loud "crack".

"Now, I am not sure if you quite understand everything I am saying yet, but no eating Wal, Winnie or Nae! I think we might stay in the back of the wagon for a while."

Fluorocor let out a long clicking noise, which Pthorn took as acceptance of the house rules before they made their way to the carriage.

Trying his already exceptional luck, Pthorn pointed into the back of the wagon, stating, "up!"

At that, Fluorocor spread its wings and launched itself into the back of the wagon, landing with a loud "thud".

"And keep your spikey little tongue away from my vials!" Pthorn announced accusingly to his new travel companion. "Don't think I don't know you can smell the orbites!"

25.
Welcome

The next few days passed with far fewer stops than the previous days. The trees had opened up into fields of farms, and the sun had shone warmly upon them for days. Pthorn was entertained by his new leather-winged friend, and he suspected Wal was making haste to the next village to rid himself of his cargo, both living and wares.

While Pthorn had not told Wal about the particular features of a hydrofluor, Wal seemed pretty confident that it was not the sort of creature that one would usually keep as a pet. The equestra shared his sentiment deeply and would tramp the ground whenever Fluorocor passed within a few paces.

One day, as Wal walked around the carriage, he startled Fluorocor from its blind spot behind its back. The hydrofluor quickly spun around, rose high in the air in a flap of wings and opened its mouth in attack, thankfully holding fire on the acid.

As yet, no one had witnessed an acid spray event, and Pthorn was pretty grateful for that as he suspected that would be the end of his travels in a wagon immediately.

After a span on the road, they reached another sprawling village, similar in size to Ung, where their journey started. Rich farmland lined the road on either side as they rode into town. Low, dry-stacked stone walls with no mortar holding the rocks in place formed the division between each property. Large, ambling moogs made their way across the fields, tearing at tufts of green grass. As they approached the village proper, the farming allotments turned into stores and one-room cottages. Across the village centre, the land elevation began to climb, with the shops and houses being overlooked by a castle-capped hill. The structure wasn't grand, except by the measure of the surrounding village. The castle had no turrets nor castellations, but it was a stone garrison large enough to hold everyone from down below, albeit not comfortably.

The carriage rolled into the village centre.

"I know this means I find myself a driver without someone to be driven or maybe even at a loss for a carriage, but I think our time and travels together finish here, my friend." He stopped and paused for a moment. "I know you own the carriage, but you don't own me. I can find a buyer for the carriage if you like, and I will go with them. If not, I will continue my life's journey on foot."

Pthorn couldn't possibly part the man from his livelihood and income source; plus, he had a better idea.

"How about you work for me as a driver for hire. You charge people for the travel and keep a tax for me aside. Next time you see me, just pass on my share, and you keep the rest. What do you say?"

Pthorn extended his hand in offer to the man.

Wal took Pthorn's hand in his and shook.

"Deal, but what if I don't see you?"

Pthorn thought for a moment, "well, in that case, I guess you would just have to find some way of spending my share."

Finishing with a smile, Pthorn removed his hand and tipped his hat, raising his middle finger as he left as a final friendly goodbye.

As he walked away, Pthorn grabbed his loaded knapsack and slung it over his shoulder. With Fluorocor in tow, walking just behind him to his right, they walked towards the only accommodation building they could see; a single-story, stone inn with a rotted wooden timber sign hanging from the awning stating, 'Wandering Inn'.

"No animals allowed!" came the call from behind the bar, followed by a scampering man, quick to try to stop Pthorn in his tracks. Three men were sitting at the bar drinking frothy beers and quickly turned to look at what was causing the fuss.

Fluorocor raised his wings in an arc and made his clicking screech at the man, who backed off quickly.

"None of that!" Pthorn barked at his noisy friend before turning his attention back to the inn keep. "I think you will find him welcome here."

He produced a handful of broan while shielding them from the view of the room's other occupants before placing them back into his cloak pockets. "Don't you?"

"Ah yes, um, certainly, sir. You are both welcome to stay as long as you require," the innkeeper stammered.

This time Pthorn knew it was the money forcing compliance rather than faith. It was simpler that way.

The three patrons continued to stare in silence at the beast. Pthorn was sure that they would have at least heard stories of dragons and possibly hydrofluors; either way, having one as a travel companion would have been unheard of.

Pthorn broke the silence of the room, "now, while you are here, I will have whatever you have going on the pot and something rare and meaty for my friend. Oh, and a pint of mead would go down well too."

Pthorn and his awe-inducing friend sat down at one of the few tables in the inn's bistro. Fluorocor curled itself happily at Pthorn's feet; down there, the hydrofluor would draw far less attention.

The men turned their attention back to their beverages, but Pthorn could tell that conversation had turned to discussing the black reptile currently getting comfortable on the floor.

After a while, just like any conversation, the villagers returned back to the current events and rumours of their own town. By the time Pthorn had finished his fill from the pot and Fluorocor had eaten an entire Onk leg, bone and all, the drinking men were well into their cups. Their volume control had ceased, and the details of their conversations were for the entire inn to hear.

"Plague, they are calling it; Falanar is up to its balls in dead. Quidnunc said he heard it on the road; he told me they are burning them in the streets in pyres every day. He says it smells like the barbeque at the Assierium festival, but it's cooked people instead of keil," said the first man.

The man to his right shook his head, laughing, "Quidnunc has a head full of onk droppings."

"And a belly of a moog," added the one on the end of the bar as they all laughed.

"Alls I can say is what I've been told. They tell me the plague is heading this way to Maarts; who am I to tell them they ain't know, hiccup, what they is talking about."

Pthorn made a mental note about what they were talking about. Firstly, he deduced that the town he was in was Maarts, and given the distinct lack of significant villages along the way they came, Falanar was further along the High Priests Way. While in Maarts, he thought he would try to learn more about this supposed plague; it seemed like something a Death-Elect would be very interested in.

"This Quidnunc, where might I find him?" he asked the three drunken men.

"I'd check in one of the styes, behind an onk, with his clothes around his ears." He laughed raucously along with the other two.

Pthorn stood up, waking up the slumbering Fluorocor, before walking closer to the bar. "Any other ideas?" he asked, readjusting his hat and looking down at his leathery friend for backup.

The laughter petered off quickly, "ah, he, he, he is a messenger. The trading post is just the other side of the way. You will find him in there when he isn't off delivering messages. Hiccup. Don't think he is there just now, though. He was only passing through when I saw him, probably another few days." The man thought for a few seconds before adding, "The post is run by Rhet. Just leave a message with him to talk to you here, and he will send the fat lout over when he is in town."

"Thank you," Pthorn replied to the man, "a broan for your troubles."

Pthorn retrieved the note and threw it into the air, letting it float down onto the bar. The three men all clamoured for the discarded currency as he turned his attention to getting a room in the inn.

Pthorn made his way to the bistro's right-hand side, where the kitchen entrance was, and poked his head around the corner. The inn keep was inside replenishing the cook-pot with new root vegetables and broth.

"Ah yes sir, um, what should I call you?" he said when he saw Pthorn's face appear.

"Pthorn will do fine, and you? What do they call you?" he asked in return.

"Scintarnia, but Scin will do fine. What can I do for you, Pthorn?"

"A room. It looks like I am here for a little while, so something comfortable, if you will. Oh, and maybe a bowl of water and a makeshift nest for my friend here." He motioned down at his side.

Scin made an uncomfortable face. "Right away, I will get a few extra blankets we can put down on the floor for your... friend."

Scin led them back across to the other side of the bar and down a hall. There were only three doors in the hall. It would seem that there aren't that many travellers looking for accommodation in Maarts.

Scin unlocked the first door they came to and pushed the heavy wooden door open. It protested loudly on its hinges, suggesting the few rooms were seldom used at full capacity.

"This room backs onto the kitchens. The grate is on the other side of that wall, so this is the warmest room in the house. I'd have it for meself 'cept I like the cold."

Pthorn surveyed the room as they entered. It looked about as big as his room back at the Sect and about the same austerity of furnishings. There was a sleeping pallet on the wall to the left, a cheap wooden wardrobe to hang his few clothes, and a small writing desk. Like most inns, there was no private privy, but that was to be expected.

As Pthorn made his way into the room, placing his knapsack down on the bed, Scin left for a few moments before returning with a couple of hefty winter blankets, which he stacked beside the pallet on the floor. He also placed a small metal pail, filled with water to the brim, in the corner closest to the door. He then excused himself and closed the door behind him.

"What do you think, Fluorocor? Are we gonna like it here for a few days?"

The hydrofluor clicked in response before wandering over to the stack of blankets and giving them a closer inspection. After a few moments, it opened its mouth, and a clear jet of liquid sprayed out, coating the blankets.

"Really?! You sleep in leaves! Couldn't you have just not slept in them?"

Fluorocor just clicked again before flying up and landing at the foot of Pthorn's sleeping pallet and curling up happily.

"Fine! But you know Scin is going to make us pay for them, right?" he said before stripping off and climbing under the sheets at the top of the sleeping pallet. Unpacking could wait for the morning. Pthorn just wanted a good night's sleep.

The next day Pthorn awoke to find the pile of blankets was closer to being a mound of mush on the floor, almost wholly disintegrated by whatever Fluorocor had sprayed onto them. After finding the energy to climb out of his sheets and unpack his knapsack, he made his way to the trading post to see if he could locate Rhet. Given the size of the building, finding him was no issue. It was completely closed off to the outside, with access provided to speak to the proprietor through a small opening. Pthorn supposed the rest of the shop must be used to store items in transit.

As Pthorn approached the window, a plump figure appeared on the other side. He fit the broad description of the messenger given his moogish physique, but he wouldn't know him from a lump of cheese.

"I am looking for your messenger, Quidnunc; I think he is called?"

"And just what are you looking for him for? Did he lose another fortune in gambling again? I swear that kid is gonna be the death of me," the man answered.

"No, no, nothing like that. I am just travelling through and heard that he might know something about a town farther down the way that might be in a bit of trouble," Pthorn told him, hoping to put his mind at ease.

"Well, travelling with information is his job; I just wish he would keep it to the letters he is delivering and leave the gossip and fearmongering out of it."

"So, is he here? Can I talk to him?" Pthorn asked hopefully.

"Not at the moment. He will be back in a few days. He is running a job for the Baron up the hill. When he is back, I can send him your way. Why all this interest in trouble, and what sort of trouble are we talking about? Not that bloody plague again, is it?"

Pthorn stifled back a cough, "ah no, of course not, just some um." Pthorn had to think quickly of some other sort of emergency. "Sporios," he blurted.

The man, whom Pthorn assumed was Rhet, looked at him perplexed and inquisitively.

"Yeah, um, there has been some trouble with people being served poisonous sporios. I am a botanist, so I was hoping I could help identify the species and maybe prepare an antidote; that is all."

"Huh, well, like I said, I can send him over to you. I am assuming you are at the inn?"

Pthorn nodded his response and thanked him for his time. They turned to head back across the way when he heard a start from behind me.

"Good Assier's arseholes! What is that?"

Clearly, Rhet had not seen Fluorocor as they walked up to the window.

"Nothing to worry about, it's friendly... well, it is to me," Pthorn called back without turning around or missing a step.

He would have to get used to people being put off by the hydrofluor's presence.

Pthorn walked into the centre of the road and looked around at the village. Several villagers were going about their everyday work, many using moogs to pull small wayns piled high with agricultural wares or manure. To the west of the square, Pthorn could see a small village market, and given he was in no hurry to get anywhere, he decided to go for a walk.

Back home in Strauth, they could only farm arid land vegetables, many of which were in the form of roots. Here in Matraketh, the stalls had all sorts of different vegetables, many of which Pthorn had never seen. There were green, yellow and purple leafy things, grains, nuts, fresh and dried fruits, and various moog udder-products like cheese and yoghurt. The vendors at each stall stared at the weird pair; a young man in a grey cloak and black hat alongside an acid-spraying dragon.

Given his lack of breakfast, Pthorn purchased an oilcloth of yoghurt tied with a string and a small bag of crunchy nuts. Once back in his room, he would mix them together.

He also purchased a stew bone from one of the hot vendors, which he threw to Fluorocor. It was almost immediately crunched, chewed, dissolved and devoured.

26.
Raising a Little Hell

A few days passed without any word from Rhet or Quidnunc, and Pthorn was becoming reasonably well-known around town. His notoriety preceded him to the point that he would be addressed by name in the street, as people would try to get a look at the hydrofluor, from a safe distance, of course. No stranger could have possibly entered a village of this size, accompanied by a black, leathery, acid-spraying dragon, without rumours spreading faster than the supposed plague of Falanar.

Most people would have been unaware of the acid-spraying capabilities of this particular beast. Still, they would have heard stories as children of dragons swooping down and stealing disruptive children or razing entire villages to the ground in plumes of dragonfire. The mechanism of destruction didn't seem to matter; the folklore that accompanied these beasts drew the attention, particularly as it would seem that Pthorn had not only captured one but trained it.

After a few days, the attention had become too much for Pthorn, and he had retreated to the confines of his room back at the Wandering Inn. He spent his days poring over the pages of his textbooks, not just the one he was collecting specimens from but also the other books on beastiology and the one Tom had given him with lots of pictures.

Over the last year, Pthorn had read Tom's book in parts but never in detail. The book was hard leather bound with iron clasps and banding on the binding. Embossed into the cover were the words 'Fauna Almanac of Azarth', and below that, in smaller writing, was the author's name, 'Avi Brute'. Pthorn wondered if this was one of the pseudonyms used by the Oracles to distribute knowledge into the world. It had been separated into several parts; aerial, aquatic, and land, with subsets based on carapace or soft skin.

Given the scarcity of hydrofluors and their lack of documentation, the section on them in the land-based soft-skinned animals' section was minimal. It included only information Pthorn already knew. Curiously, it would seem that they weren't native to Straulatos and were extremely rare in the southern hemisphere. How the wild-haired Darn had managed to find one seemed like some sort of very unlikely event.

He read about many different types of animals he still hadn't seen in person, with most of them residing only on Saulit. Some beasts could run several times faster than a human man. He had already met a Rarn, but there were others like the sleek, spotted snoth and the pure white mauw, which was depicted in the book with a very large, furry mane and deep yellow-slitted eyes.

Some animals were the size of the cottages he had passed on the way into Maarts, and others were almost microscopic. Pthorn enjoyed reading about some of the more common beasts from back home, like the black carapace encased Mant and the various thorny reptiles which lived in the arid sands of Straulatos.

On the fifth day after his arrival, Pthorn was again reading Avi's book when a knock on his door signalled the appearance of a guest. Until now, the innkeeper, Scin, had kept to himself, avoiding any confrontation with Fluorocor that was not required, particularly after discovering the liquified slump of blankets on day three.

Pthorn made his way across the room from the writing desk to unlock the door.

As the door swung wide, a man's large, lumbering form filled the doorway.

"Allo! Ole Rhet says there is a guy by the name of Pthorn looking for me. Said summit about sporios?" the young man asked inquisitively.

"Ah yes, please come in. Take a seat."

Pthorn gestured to the chair at the writing desk and took a seat on the edge of the sleeping pallet beside the resting hydrofluor. Fluorocor wasn't much of a guard beast as it hadn't stirred at all.

Quidnunc entered the room and sat down on the chair, which complained under his weight. He eyed the sleeping hydrofluor but didn't make any attempt to ask questions;

Pthorn presumed that his boss had told him about Fluorocor. A query crossed Pthorn's mind about how a messenger could possibly reach his size and still be able to travel long distances, but he decided it was best to avoid such postulations and move on to the more pertinent ones.

"Ah yes, I may have gotten you here under false pretences to your boss. You see he, well…" Pthorn paused for a moment, "he seemed to discount your story about the plague in Falanar as just a figment of your imagination."

"I ain't lying; I told 'im that," Quidnunc replied, both offended and not seeming too surprised by his boss's reaction simultaneously. "I got some very reliable sources who have told me about it. I haven't been to Falanar m'self on account of them sending me north running errands for the Baron."

Pthorn attempted to reassure the young man, "Well, let's just say I believe you and not Rhet… what can you tell me?"

After a moment of careful consideration, Quidnunc responded, "Gherry told me he was passing through the outskirts of Falanar just two span ago, and he stopped to deliver a message to one of the small posts. Rumour has it the message was a request for divorce from a travelling merchant who decided to settle down with some lady of the night over in the far east of Matraketh. He said the poor love didn't see it coming and doted on the guy."

Pthorn sat on the end of the bed, not adding any fuel to his digression.

"Anyway, the guy at the post said he was getting heaps of these letters sent all over the country about people who had died. It seemed like some sort of disease wiping them out... young and old alike."

"Did he give you any more details about the disease? What did it do to them?" Pthorn questioned further.

"He said, supposedly, they would just start frothing from the mouth in the middle of the night, vomiting up blood, and by morning they would be loading them up on the wayns and throwing them on the pyres in the square."

"Did he say how many have died so far?"

Quidnunc sat thinking for a few more moments, "Only four or five at the time he told me. If he is right and there is a plague outbreak, then by now, half the village must be gone! He was saying that if they get any more each day, they will have to store them in the cold store because they won't be able to burn them fast enough. He said it takes ages to burn each one, and the priest has to do his last rites."

"Thank you for that, for what it's worth. I believe you; I just wish there was something I could do." Pthorn responded earnestly. He may be the Death-Elect and future Order-Master of Death, but that didn't mean he couldn't feel for these people and their grieving families.

"I know, there is just so much death around. Just this morning, I returned to the Baron's castle to find that his only daughter, Precil, passed this morning with no warning. Not even illness to show for it. They just found her dead in her pallet when the maid came to collect her for breakfast. Absolutely heartbreaking it is."

Quidnunc looked and sounded genuinely sad at the passing of the girl.

"How old was she, this Precil?" Pthorn asked.

"Just five turns old she was, pretty little thing. She was the world to the Baron and his wife. They are beside themselves, they are."

"I am very sorry to hear that... and thank you for sharing. I know it must hurt when people don't believe you." Pthorn reached out and placed a hand on Quidnunc's shoulder in support. "While I am here, let me know if you need a friend to talk to. I am pretty short on them myself. Plus, if you are nice, you might even get to give ole Fluorocor here a pat."

Quidnunc gave a broad smile, "Oh, I would like that! Imagine what everyone will say when they hear I have touched a real-life dragon. I mean, they still won't believe me, but at least I will know I ain't lying... and yeah, I might just take you up on the visit. You are right; I think we could both use a friend."

Pthorn gave him a nod and opened the door for him.

Once Quidnunc was out of the room, Pthorn sat down to think about what he had heard. He was telling the truth when he said he wanted to help. If only there was some way to do it, given his power and skills.

After a few hours of brainstorming and rereading his texts, Pthorn turned to the secret back pages of his book. His first thought was the chapter called 'Plague and

Pandemic', but it turned out it focused on creating these particular events rather than eliminating them. After reading the instructions, Pthorn determined the chance of success for reversing the effects by reversing the order of the methodology was low. Instead, he continued to look at other entries. Finally, he settled on 'Resurrection'. This chapter had the most detailed warning of all the other chapters, but he was immediately drawn to it and what it could mean for the young Baron's girl.

Resurrection

Use extreme caution! Mixed results can occur.

Bringing back the dead can have serious consequences. Remember, for what is gained, something shall be lost.

Step 1 – Prepare the corpse

Your corpse should ideally be freshly deceased. Whatever physical ailment they have will not be cured by some miracle. If they are rotted, you will end up with an undead being rather than an alive person (Refer to 'Undead and how to control them' for more details).

Step 2 – Locate the required ingredients

You will need the following:

- Blood of the corpse. Stir if separated, don't shake
- A Connected Object to a person with Life to share (hair, skin, sweat, or related object)

Place the blood of the corpse in contact with your connected object and complete the ritual below.

Step 3 – The ritual

To complete the ritual, reach into the Connected Object and feel the Connection. Once inside, funnel their life's energy into the blood. Once you start the flow, begin the chant, and the Life will syphon through the blood and into the corpse, resulting in reanimation.

The incantation is as follows:
> Once welcomed by death
> But now no more
> Once more to welcome breath
> Breathe now; I speak the lore
> Rise forth and stand unaided
> For now, you shall see no pyre
> For now, I will command it
> This life, it shall transfer!

Important note: As noted above, this will steal the life from another and transfer it to the corpse. It is recommended to find a willing participant to prevent moral dilemmas.

Pthorn couldn't help but notice the Oracle, or the person who had developed these forbidden rituals, could have done with some more literacy training. Even with his limited education, given by Mother, he could tell that the second half of this incantation didn't match the first half.

"As long as it works, hey, mate," he said quietly under his breath to his slumbering friend.

His original goal was to help with the plague, but now he thought about the smaller problem a little closer to home.

"Now, how to get a drop of Precil's blood without getting arrested by a Baron, and who would donate their Life to the cause of bringing this young girl back to life?"

These questions ran circles through his mind as he crawled into his sleeping pallet and drifted off to sleep.

Pthorn's brain must have been working overtime in his sleep because when he awoke, he did so with a well-developed plan in his mind.

The life donation would be simple. He was immortal; any division of infinity was naturally still infinite. He could use a piece of his own clothing to form the Connection. The second part of the plan was going to be more difficult. It was going to involve deception of the lowest form; flat-out lying.

Pthorn made his way down to the bistro of the inn first thing in the morning and retrieved some scraps and bones for Fluorocor before returning for his own breakfast. He decided to leave the hydrofluor alone in his room to amuse himself; it would be too difficult to disguise or explain the presence of such a beast to the Baron. Given the gossip, he was very likely aware of the beast in his village, but there was no reason to confirm Pthorn's association with such a beast while trying to develop trust.

After breaking his fast, Pthorn began his journey up the hill towards the castle. The road was slightly narrower than the High Priest's Way and looked to have recently had its wagon tracks filled in level with the rest of the road.

The dirt was well compacted, reducing the likelihood of a rolled ankle during the climb. While he was out of sight of the village and the Baron's abode, he placed his white priest's robes over grey robes and donned the red vest.

As he ascended, trees began to line the road way. They have been planted intentionally, in even spacings of about fifty paces. They were very tall, green and shaped like a spear. It was as though someone had carved them into place, and they were standing as a guard of honour on either side of the road. The castle itself began to grow as he approached. What looked from afar like just a large version of a simple cottage turned into a sprawling estate of stone and statues. As a stark juxtaposition to the state of the village down below, this particular Baron seemed to be well-financed.

The dirt of the road turned to finely crushed gravel which began to crunch below his feet as he walked. As he reached the top, the front entry of the castle came into view. It was preceded by two enormous curved stone stairways which led from the road to the door. The door itself was a deep, almost blood, red wood with gilded metal bands and knockers. The doors stood the height of four men, and Pthorn imagined it would weigh several times more than any door he had ever opened.

Pthorn climbed the left-hand flight before reaching the landing and being confronted by two very well-muscled guards. They wore tight-fitting robes with a red sash and golden waist-rope.

"State your business!" boomed the first guard.

"The Baron and his family are in mourning; it had better be a good reason," added the other.

Pthorn had been rehearsing his response during his climb up the hill but was slightly out of breath and caught off-guard by the immediate questioning.

"I am here under the directions of the High Priest of Matraketh to perform the last rites for the beloved Precil of Maarts."

The guards looked at each other, seeking confirmation from the other before one of them spoke.

"Hang on, how are you here already? We only just sent the message off just this morning. There is no way it reached any clergy, let alone the High Priest."

Pthorn had been anticipating this question too.

"Well, there you see, we have a bit of luck on our side if there were such a thing. Blessed be Assier. I was travelling through town when I intercepted your message and found myself available to complete the rites immediately. Here is my Note of Authority."

Pthorn produced a forgery, in his own hand, written on the paper from his knapsack. He knew it was unlikely the guards would even be able to read, let alone tell if the note was real or not.

The first guard 'humphed' before walking off toward the front door. At the last moment, he diverted himself through a small sally port off to the left, presumably the servant's entrance which would save opening the grand door multiple times a day.

There Pthorn, and the suspicious second guard, remained until they heard a loud clunk and the grand doors began to slowly swing open.

27.
Precil

The man stood in the centre of the doorway dressed in all black, the colour of mourning. Salt encrusted his well-kept beard from a morning spent crying over his daughter. Pthorn could see that this man would have usually had an air of power and authority about him, but today he held his head low, his shoulders drooped, and his eyes were bloodshot red. Some people hide loss deep within, and some show it on their faces; the Baron showed his loss throughout his entire body.

Pthorn bowed deeply out of respect and held his hat to his chest, making sure not to lock eyes with the grieving man.

"Please come through; she is right this way," the man stated, barely giving Pthorn half a glance before about-turning and heading back through the doors and into the grand entrance foyer.

Pthorn stood up straight and placed the hat beneath his left arm, maintaining his respect as he entered the room. Mirroring the outside of the castle, another massive set of twin stone stairs curled from the left and right to the upper levels.

Oil paintings adorned the walls of the room. Some were of his family, the Baron and his wife unsmiling with a beaming child on their knees. Others were landscapes or ancestors from the past. As grand as the castle was, it was still a family's home, now with new memories to haunt them.

The Baron led him past the stairs and down a series of dimly lit halls with traditional oil-burning sconces. The stone floor had worn smooth over centuries of people walking the halls. They finally arrived at a small room which looked to be designed for the purpose of displaying a corpse. Pthorn thought of how unusual it was to have a room such as this with a three-pace long stone plinth in the centre, although he presumed it had other uses for when there was no dead girl's corpse to display.

She was laid out on the stone wearing a light sleeping shift and simply looked peaceful like she was still sleeping. Pthorn assumed that this was as they had found her the day before.

Pthorn had no experience imitating a priest of the clergy, even though he was technically one of the leaders of their faith. He presumed they should provide comfort to the grieving.

"It is always the brightest lamp first snuffed and the most beautiful flower first plucked. So it comes to pass for beauty such as your daughter. We don't always know why the Almighty Assier chooses such people to pass into his kingdom. Have faith that Aiel himself has seen to her journey and that it was as carefree a trip as can be imagined."

Pthorn placed his hand on the grieving father in a show of comfort. He knew of the respect the gentry showed the clergy and was bargaining on this being the right move. Any common-born person from the village would have been met with severe punishments for assault by touching such a person.

"Thank you, Priest," the Baron said through fresh streaming tears, "thank you."

"Perhaps you would like to step out and be with your wife while I do this next part. There is no more you can do for her here."

The Baron didn't argue; instead, he nodded and saw himself from the room, closing the door behind him. The heavy wooden door clunked into place and the iron latch fastened behind him.

Pthorn set his hat down on the stone plinth and removed a small piece of paper from the internal banding. Before leaving his room and telling Fluorocor not to eat or dissolve anything, Pthorn had copied down the instructions from his book onto the small sheet of paper. He knew he couldn't carry the hefty tome into the room undetected and didn't want to risk having it confiscated or read. He also didn't want to rely on his memory for the incantation.

Next, he removed his knife from its scabbard tucked into his shoe, set it beside the hat, and began rereading the piece of paper.

Confident with the process, he placed the paper loosely back inside his hat and made a small incision on the inside of her arm. Somewhere he was sure he could still get fresh blood without nicking an artery and causing her to bleed out if or when she regained consciousness.

As expected, the blood did not flow willingly; Pthorn massaged her arm to get a small stream of blood to flow out onto the flat of his blade. He wiped the blade onto an inconspicuous place on the inner banding of his hat. The hat was black anyway, so he assumed it wouldn't be noticeable even on close inspection.

While planning what to do earlier in the day, the thought had also occurred to Pthorn that he would need to bind the wound. He had cut a length of bandage from his sleeping pallet sheet back at the inn. A nice, even cut that should go unnoticed by the keeper. He produced the strip from a pocket in his cloak and bound the girl's arm, covering it with the shift again.

Pthorn placed his hat upon the girl's dead body, checking the door once again for anyone looking in before picking up the paper and reading the incantation quietly aloud.

"Once welcomed by Death…."

Pthorn hoped that the walls and door were thin enough to muffle the actual words he was saying and not cause anyone to run in out of concern.

"… This life it shall transfer!" he finished.

A shimmering column of light built from the ceiling down and flowed into the hat. It swirled and ebbed inside the brim before overflowing and spilling began onto the young girl's body.

He felt absolutely no different than before. He didn't know what he expected to feel, giving away some of one's life force, but 'nothing' wasn't it. He began to feel around his body, checking his arms, legs and head, trying to see if any of his senses had changed. He was so busy checking himself that he almost didn't notice the flicker of movement from the corner of his eye.

It was simply a twitch.

The girl's little finger began to flit up and down. The movements were barely noticeable at first but then became stronger. Her hand began to curl as her skin changed from its dead, pallid grey hue to pale pink. The colour started in the arm he had pricked and began spreading across her body.

The light became stronger and stronger until finally, the flowingly ceased and the last of the light made its way into the arm of the girl.

She remained unconscious, but she was visibly breathing now. Pthorn reached out and formed a Connection with her, feeling her heart beating and growing stronger. There was something irregular; he could feel a whooshing noise accompanying her heartbeat's steady 'lub-dub'. Pthorn could tell there was something unhealthy about the girl's heart which was probably the reason she had slipped away in the night.

Pthorn felt around, searching for the cause of the abnormality. Even if he found it, he wasn't sure he would be able to fix it. He was Death; he wasn't in the business of being a surgically trained mountebank or creating life. That said, he had just brought this girl back to life.

Finally, he sensed something else. Something living inside the heart that he hadn't felt before. Some sort of microscopic life feasting on this poor girl's heart. He focused his energy directly on the tiny lifeforms inside her; they were simple, with no heart, brain, or blood. Apply enough pressure to something like that, and it will simply die. Now killing is something he can do. Tom had made him practice something similar on a rotting piece of meat, killing off the tiny lifeforms which feasted on the dead flesh. He then made him consume it, making a point that, if he'd done his job correctly, he would not be sick by dinner.

Finally, he felt the life slip from the foreign bodies. It would take time for her heart to get stronger, but knowing what he did about biology, he figured that given enough time, it should heal on its own.

Pthorn picked up his hat and wiped the inside of the brim with the hem of his cloak; he didn't want to risk smearing the girl's blood across his face.

It may make a poor impression on this little girl's grieving father.

Now was the time for the real theatrics. Pthorn flicked the latch and thrust open the heavy door.

"By the power of..." he began to orate before realising no one was actually outside the door.

"Assier's arse!" he swore much more quietly under his breath before making his way down the cold hallway.

The Baron must have heard his voice as he was making his way down the stairs; he was accompanied by his wife and one of the guards.

"What is the meaning of this shouting? What is this?" the Baron shouted back to Pthorn.

Pthorn cleared his throat and tried his proclamation again, this time with an audience.

"By the mighty power of Assier and through the guidance of his prophet Aiel, the Singular has seen fit to grant your daughter with life once more!"

Pthorn raised his hands and closed his eyes as the family rushed past him and into the room.

The guard slowed to whisper in his ear, "this had better not be some sort of parlour trick, young man, or I will put you where she lays and carve you up one piece at a time."

The emotions of anger and disbelief in his voice were unmistakable; Pthorn really hoped the girl was still breathing when they got into the room.

Pthorn followed the guard back down the hall and into the small room. The girl was still unconscious, but she was being held tightly by her two parents. Tears of joy streamed down their faces as they embraced her tiny form.

Pthorn remained standing just outside the door, giving the family space to come to terms with their loss and subsequent revival of their child. The guard stood across the other side of the hall, looking directly at him but not making any further moves to threaten or, in any other way, make conversation with him. Pthorn wasn't sure what the guard suspected, but he was confident it would be out of place to attack the man potentially responsible for reviving his master's daughter.

Eventually, the girl's mother emerged from the room. She was dressed in all black, just the same as the Baron. Pthorn hadn't noticed earlier, but she had been wearing a veil to cover her face, and now it was thrown back over her head. As she turned from the room holding her daughter, her face fell from elation to something else. He couldn't quite pick it, but it looked to Pthorn like distrust; her eyes were affixed on Pthorn as she headed back down the hall.

The Baron exited the room carrying his still unconscious daughter.

"I am not sure what happened in that room, and I am not sure I want to know. If there is anything I can do for the clergy or for you, just name it. Anything!"

Pthorn thought only for a moment before responding, "this was the work of the Almighty alone; I ask nothing of you. Please look after your girl and those below in the village. Tell everyone of the work of Assier, but perhaps leave out the part where I was there for it." He gave the Baron a smile before continuing, "I cannot promise she will be okay, that she will awaken or that it cannot happen again. These are not things I can know. But with the power of Assier and the faith you and your wife show, I hope that great things lay ahead for your daughter. Go now and be with her!"

The Baron nodded his head and left in the direction of his wife.

The guard gestured for Pthorn to follow him and Pthorn fell in tow. This time he left through the sally port of the servants; there was no display for the Baron. Pthorn didn't look back as he walked down the stone steps, into the front yard and down the sloping road back to the village.

For once, Pthorn felt good about what he had done. Instead of killing things, he had finally used his powers for good. He had given life back to a young girl, fixed her heart and gave a family hope again. He hoped the baron would repay his fortune to those he supported below.

His walk back down to the village was much faster than the walk up, the downward slope undoubtedly increased his pace, and he was lost in thought. He had successfully resurrected one girl, who had died of heart disease but was healthy in every other way. He wondered whether he could do the same thing for the village suffering from the plague. He hadn't seemed to have given up any part of himself in performing the ritual.

Perhaps the immortals aren't affected by these kinds of transfers, he thought hopefully to himself.

When he reached the village of Maarts at the base of the hill, Pthorn stripped off his priest's robes and stopped at the trading post to see Rhet or his gossiping sidekick Quidnunc; both were inside the building when he arrived.

"You might want to hold on to that message you had for the High Priest," Pthorn started.

The pair looked at him inquisitively, "what do you mean?" returned Rhet.

"It turns out that after some solemn prayer by the girl's parents, Assier has seen fit to grant Precil a new turn at living. Go see for yourself if you do not believe me… just don't tell them I told you to go. Make some excuse to deliver a message or something."

"I don't believe it," said the young Quidnunc, "I saw her myself. She was stone cold."

"What can I say? She warmed up a little."

Pthorn laughed before turning away to let the two men continue talking amongst themselves.

Pthorn had barely made it across the square before he saw they had closed the shop. Moments later, they were scurrying out the door and onto the road leading up to the castle.

The Baron would work out pretty quickly that he had told the two biggest mouths in the village his news, but he wasn't planning on hanging around too much longer to suffer any consequences.

On the way past the kitchens, he picked up another soup bone for Fluorocor and headed back to his room to pack.

28.
So Long

It was late afternoon by the time he had finished packing up his room, and he had settled his bill with Scintarnia. He ate a light meal of fresh green vegetables with a side of piping hot roasted keil but thought better of washing it down with a pint of mead; nothing is worse than travelling with a belly full of sweet, heavy drink.

He set off down the road accompanied by Fluorocor with his knapsack on his back, feeling pretty good about himself. They had to pass through the markets on their way out of town, so they stopped briefly to stock up on some fruits, cheeses and cured meats for the road.

He was relatively sure he knew where he was going but confirmed with one of the vendors, "Falanar is this way, right?"

The vendor nodded but gave him fair warning, "lots of stories coming out from that way. Might want to head along the northern road and steer clear of due west."

"Thanks for the advice!" Pthorn said, nodding his head and paying the woman two broan for the handful of sweetnuts and a loaf of hard bread.

He left the town behind, and the forest immediately began closing in on them. On the entrance to the village from the other direction, there had been acres upon acres of fields. There were no such fields in this direction. Just the darkness of a tree canopy pressing down upon them.

Now that they were on the road without the confines of a wagon or room at an inn, the hydrofluor figured it was time for him to stretch his wings.

There came a moment of panic for Pthorn as he thought his companion was abandoning him, but soon after taking to the skies, Fluorocor swooped down in a twisting dive, clearly enjoying its freedom. The beast gave another great flap and sent itself shooting high into the sky, flying across the sun and casting an enormous shadow over the world.

He seemed to hover in place for a few moments, eyeing the world below him as Pthorn continued walking along the High Priest's Way. Suddenly the hydrofluor took another great dive, swooping and snapping its jaws around a small, furry animal. It disappeared before Pthorn got a decent look at it, but he suspected it was likely a squarn or a meena based on his readings of Tom's book.

Pthorn walked well into the night with no light to guide him. He had hoped the first waystop would be close to the village, but it was several hours before the pair reached their destination for the night. Pthorn found that Fluorocor had excellent night vision; he was able to walk along the road with one hand on the hydrofluor's left wing for guidance.

Finally, they saw a dull glow in the distance. It would seem they would not be alone for their first stop on this leg of the journey.

As they approached, they found two carriages parked around the fire with a small group of people gathered together, sitting on rocks. The group didn't seem to notice the pair's approach until they were almost on top of them.

"Evening," Pthorn said, addressing the group. It was always good form to introduce yourself to others at waystops and then keep to yourself. "The name is Pthorn, and this strapping lad is Fluorocor. Don't mind us; we have no need for a fire for the night. We will just be over there."

"Well, you are welcome to it if you need to warm yourself. Just keep that," one man said, pointing at the black, leathery beast, "away from our equestra, and we will be just fine."

The group returned to their conversation as Pthorn set up his bedroll, and they both crawled in. As usual, Fluorocor nestled up, snout to tail, at his feet.

The next day when Pthorn awoke, the travellers and their wagons were gone. The fire was still smouldering slightly, with a tendril of smoke making its way up from the cooling coals into the crisp morning air.

The pair climbed out of the bedroll. Fluorocor stretched one leg at a time, followed by a full wing stretch, clicking in satisfaction as it did.

Pthorn made his way into the forest to collect some dry timber and kindling while Fluorocor made its way off to hunt for food.

By the time it returned, Pthorn had a good, intense fire going, and he was finishing off cooking the breakfast. There was something about cooking on an open fire that made him feel relaxed. Life back at the Sect could not be further from his mind. In fact, there were no species for him to collect for some distance from where he was, so there was little for him to do except travel and enjoy his freedom.

After his satisfying breakfast and watching Fluorocor maul another small furry creature, the pair set off again down the road. After several hundred paces, a thought occurred to him.

"Fluorocor?" he called to his friend, "do you think you can carry me?"

The hydrofluor cocked its head to the side, trying to understand what had just been asked. Pthorn mimed the action of throwing his leg over something and then began flapping his wings like a giant, uncoordinated luftun.

Fluorocor clicked its reply and reared its head. That was as close to an affirmative answer as Pthorn thought he would ever get.

Pthorn gently approached from the side, and Fluorocor lowered its head in a bowing motion. He lifted his leg up and over the hydrofluor's neck, just in front of its wings.

After sitting down between the wing joints on Fluorocor's back, the beast stretched its wings wide.

Pthorn scrambled for something to hold on to. He leant forward, wrapped his arms around its thick neck, and held on for dear life; the thought of being an immortal quadriplegic didn't seem very appealing.

With a mighty flap of its wings, the hydrofluor launched itself forward and up. It gained almost two paces into the air before tumbling immediately to the earthen track; Pthorn became an unwilling projectile, followed by his knapsack.

The hydrofluor shook itself, clicked apologetically, then walked over and nudged Pthorn on the face as if to say, "Sorry, but you are a little too heavy for me."

"Well, if you can't carry everything, do you think you can carry the bag?" Pthorn asked it and pointed to his knapsack.

Fluorocor clicked in response. Pthorn still couldn't tell one sound from another, but it let him approach. Pthorn tied the straps around its middle, making sure the knapsack didn't get in the way of its wings, before giving it a good smack on the hindquarters.

"Give that a try! I'm tired of lugging it around."

The hydrofluor tried to take to the skies again, this time far more successfully. The knapsack was filled with Pthorn's books and sample vials, so he hoped that future crash landings were few and far between. Pthorn wasn't sure if an excuse involving a plummeting hydrofluor would pass with Tom.

Pthorn continued walking along the High Priest's Way with a much lighter load, just his grey cloak and a black hat to weigh him down.

The walk gave him time to think of a plan for helping the village of Falanar. With a lack of people to talk to, he began to speak to himself.

"So," he began aloud, "there will be several people a day dying, more than they can complete the rites for at any time. They will have to be storing them somewhere."

Pthorn made a mental note to scout the location of a cold store or morgue.

"Once I know where they are, I will need to make some sort of plan for how to get their blood. That shouldn't be too hard if I pretend to be a priest again," he stopped in his tracks and scratched his head thoughtfully, "but if there are priests already there giving the rites, then they will know I am a fraud straight away."

Pthorn added to his mental note that he had to avoid the priests at all costs, or he would have to come up with a new ploy for access.

"I wonder if I can do more than one at a time," Pthorn considered aloud. "Hmm, worth a try."

During his conversation with himself, Pthorn was unaware that his companion had landed and was walking just behind him.

"Cliiiiick," screeched the hydrofluor, making Pthorn almost jump out of his hat.

Pthorn gave his friend a dirty look.

"Do you have to sneak up on me?!" he asked sternly.

"Cliiick," came the answer. It didn't sound much like an apology to Pthorn.

Pthorn continued running through his plan to Fluorocor as they walked down the road before finally coming to the last waystop of the day.

Just like the night before, tonight, there was already a wagon of travellers stopped at this waystop. It was clear as the pair approached that they were a family of troupers. Most traveller's camps were quiet, but Pthorn had come to learn that troupers didn't know the meaning of quiet. Their conversations were always enunciated as verbal, theatrical prose; they always spoke like they were telling a story from a faraway land to an entertained crowd. There was also always music; oftentimes, music would be played as a background to a discussion or storytelling.

Today as they approached, they found a young man fingering a stringed instrument while an older woman sang a story of a great hero to a crowd of about ten, young and old. It was a story he had heard growing up, retold by his mother, but with far less of the theatrics and music.

Pthorn and Fluorocor stood back so as not to interrupt and listened to the rest of the storytelling song.

Sir Florence, he did not know, of course
Of the beast, he was to slay
His quest was this, and this alone
We speak of it today

Jason Wylie

The fae king proclaimed to near and far
All the brave should come his way
For his daughter, she was fair but lost
And for her return, he would pay

T'was on that day, Sir Flor did swear
That he'd rescue Princess May
Yes, he'd rescue Princess May

The man playing the instrument looked up from his captive crowd and saw the two of them standing back, listening, but he didn't miss a beat, nor did he alert anyone else to their presence.

Sir Florence, he didn't waste his time
He rode off straight away
Through sand and storm and trav'led so far
And he rode all night and day

T'was aft six span
And half a day
Sir Florence, he found his princess fair
They'd kept her locked away

He stormed the castle
He had his play
Slashing his great sword
At all things in his way

The gallant young Florence
Then had to pay

The cost of the freedom
For his beautiful fae

The beast it flew
From 'cross the bay
Bellowing hellfire ahead
Lighting night to day

Sir Florence he stood
He'd not turn away
He'd face his fate
With no time to pray

So from that day forward
Until today
We sing of brave Sir Florence
Who ALMOST rescued Princess May

The crowd clapped and cheered for the rendition before the man put down his instrument and raised himself from the seat. The singing woman and the man finished with a flourish and a bow. They both stood straight before the man locked eyes with them again.

"Join us," he called to Pthorn, "and bring your friend too."

The rest of the group turned to have a look at their new visitor. Pthorn slowly approached.

"Hi, don't mind us. We are just settling down for the night."

"Nonsense, anyone staying at a trouper waystop is a trouper for the night. Come sit with us. Tell us your names," the man said, although Pthorn was not sure they all seemed as keen as him on welcoming a black dragon into their camp circle.

"I am Pthorn, and this is Fluorocor," he said by way of introduction.

"Is Fluorocor a girl or a boy?" enquired a young girl sitting on a log, not one of those showing any fear at the sight of a hydrofluor.

"Um, that is a good question. I haven't asked. Fluorocor, are you a girl or a boy?" Pthorn asked his friend jokingly.

The hydrofluor cocked its head to the side, resulting in laughter from the group.

"It either doesn't know or doesn't understand me."

Pthorn sat on the log, with his arm resting on Fluorocor, listening to various musical renditions, excerpts from plays, and children taking turns entertaining their elders long into the night. The troupers used the fire to their advantage; they used it to highlight exactly what they wanted you to see in the show and hide the things that were to remain a mystery.

Finally, Pthorn excused himself, and they set up camp for the night under the flickering glow of the flames.

The next day, the troupers were still there, and one of the older members was busy breaking his fast with a few sizzling cuts of onk. The fat in the heavy black pan was spitting and shooting fiery red arcs away from the cookfire.

The man offered a piece to Pthorn, which he gladly accepted, sharing it with Fluorocor. Pthorn had found that not sharing your food with such a beast was terrible for the return of trust.

Pthorn returned the favour by offering some of the supplies he had picked up back in Maarts.

"No, thank you," the man replied politely, pushing his hand forward. "You keep that for your travels. We are well-stocked and can survive on what we have for months. You are travelling light and need all you can get."

Pthorn thanked the man for their generosity before packing up his camp and bidding him farewell.

Pthorn slung his knapsack over Fluorocor's back, once again making sure he fastly secured it to prevent any accidents, before turning his back on the camp and beginning the day's walk.

The sun was barely halfway up into the sky and almost peering over the top of the tree canopy before Pthorn began to sense the signs of an upcoming village.

What stood out to him most wasn't the sounds, as would generally indicate civilisation, but the smell. Most villages smelt of wet and decaying feedstock, livestock manure, or salt if you were near the sea. The first smell that hit Pthorn was the smell of death. He had become used to it back in the laboratory and classroom with Tom, and he had come across plenty of dead animals working on the farm, but this was different.

This was a mixture of putrid smoke and rot.

Pthorn had arrived at Falanar, and he immediately knew it would be worse than he previously thought it would be.

29.
Plague

Pthorn continued walking into the village, dressed still in his regular grey robes; he would don his disguise if the need arose. He pulled another piece of cloth, torn from his sleeping pallet sheets, from his cloak. He secured it around his mouth and nose to try to remove some of the choking smell. It didn't do much to help; the smell was overpowering and made him gag.

As he walked through the village limits, a horrible thought suddenly occurred to him. "I really hope you aren't a scavenger," Pthorn said quietly under his breath to his companion. "No feasting!"

The hydrofluor just continued walking on in silence.

Pthorn hoped the silence was a lack of understanding rather than ignorance; he was sure he would find out soon enough.

As he entered the village, he was also met with an eerie silence not usually attributable to a town of this size. A haggard lady was walking idly down the street, coughing loudly in the acrid, smoky air. Another woman was crying over a smouldering pyre, the remains of a person outlined in the coals with white, unburned bone standing out stark against the black of the char.

The village was more built up than Maarts; many buildings were made of stone rather than wood, suggesting it was a much older settlement built before lumber became the vogue material of choice.

Smoke poured from almost every cottage chimney. It would seem that the people had taken to their homes, only venturing out when in desperate need of supplies.

Pthorn had hoped to find someone to ask about finding a morgue, but there was no one to ask. There were no priests in sight, which was a positive for his plan to pose as one again. He began to walk closer to the centre of the village. There was a community well located central to the town square, with the cottages and business radiating outwards from there. Unlike most places, built on a four-way crossroads, out of respect to Aiel, this town had an extra road pointing almost due north, with the remaining roads equidistant in other directions.

The thought briefly crossed his mind that this simple act of heresy may have been the reason for their current unfortunate situation before he dismissed it as nonsense. He knew better by now that the religion of Assier was fabricated entirely; he was part of all that was left of the Singular.

Tom had covered diseases with Pthorn during several lessons, focusing primarily on creating one rather than ones of natural origin. Although Pthorn supposed that one could probably infer the other. Pthorn understood that it was usually small animals, like squarn, meena and their smaller cousins, rodenians, that often carried a disease that caused horrible skin and blood infections.

Pthorn wasn't sure if Tom had resorted to hyperbole when describing the symptoms, but he wasn't keen to find out. Knowing what he did, he made a mental note to be cautious of any living creatures in the area lest he become infected himself.

Pthorn made his way past the pyres on the roadway to the well in the centre and began to survey the area around him. He had entered the eastern arm of the village and primarily past small houses and cottages with low stone walls for separation. Looking south at the roads, which formed a vee off, looked to be more of the same, with the houses becoming more sparse and opening up to what looked like farmland, although it was hard to see through the lingering smoke. Ahead to the west and on the road due north were the clusters of businesses. Like most villages, the village inn sat on the block between the north and western roads. A sign stating 'No Vacancies' was hung crudely across the balustrade on the entry. Pthorn assumed that no one was actually staying at the inn, but the proprietor was most likely trying to avoid contact with people.

Beyond that, the businesses were boarded up, although smoke still came from the hind-chimneys of some. It was common for business owners to live on the premises and have a small dwelling, either attached or otherwise, to the rear of the business.

With no objective basis for his decision, Pthorn decided to move north. He signalled for Fluorocor to join him at his side. The hydrofluor had slowly started edging away towards one of the cold pyres; Pthorn was worried that his suspicions would be correct, and he would have to keep his travel companion away from the smorgasbord of dead people to chew on.

The two, man and beast, started wandering down the deserted road. Pthorn still wasn't exactly sure what he was looking for, but he was sure they weren't keeping dead bodies in the residential blocks of the village. They had reached the fourth business on the road, a clothing store specialising in travel wear for the gentleman when a wayn made its way past the fountain. It was loaded high with a mountain of bodies, presumably collected from people's houses. It must have been out in the countryside as he made his way through, as he didn't recall seeing it parked anywhere.

The man sitting astride the equestra was wearing all black with a beaked hood.

Pthorn had learned during his lessons that it was common for mountebank to don these outfits with various scented flowers and salts stuffed into the beak to ward off the sickness. Pthorn knew it made no difference, but the superstition clearly still held a place in the medical community.

Pthorn moved to the side of the road and let the wayn pass. The beaked man eyed him directly as he passed.

It continued down the road for another hundred paces or so before stopping at one of the more substantial buildings in the village. Pthorn continued walking down the street with Fluorocor in tow before stopping a short distance away.

Pthorn could overhear two men talking as they unloaded the cart, their voices muffled by their horror-inspiring masks.

"Another six this afternoon. One more span like this, and I am not sure if there is going to be anyone left," the driver said as he grabbed the first body by the legs.

"That makes ten today in all," replied the second as he made his way over to assist with the other end.

Pthorn made his way across to the side of the road to sit on the stone wall, trying not to look too suspicious, although he suspected standing anywhere in the village accompanied by a hydrofluor could be counted as nothing less than peculiar. The men either didn't notice or simply didn't care about his presence as they continued unloading their corpse cargo.

"That's the last one," one of the men said as he closed the gate on the back of the wayn and latched it shut.

"Time to head home for the night, I think. Remember to lock the door!" called the other man as he began to walk towards Pthorn.

"Forget about it! Who, in the name of the Almighty Assier, would steal a plague-ridden body!" the first man returned.

Pthorn continued trying to look like he was minding his own business and sat stroking the back of Fluorocor's neck.

"You'd best keep travelling, boy," said the walking man as he passed. "Bad things are afoot here; you don't want to be caught in the middle of it. Cursed we are. Cursed!"

Pthorn looked up and acted like he had been disturbed in the middle of thought before giving the man a nod and a tip of the hat with a friendly single-finger salutation.

Pthorn continued sitting in his position for some time after the driver had left with his wayn and the sun had begun descending into the horizon. He gave Fluorocor a gentle pat on the back of the neck, and it returned with an affectionate clicking.

Pthorn led the way across the road and up to the front of the building they had loaded the bodies into. It was some sort of warehouse; Pthorn had never seen anything of the sort. They had a barn back on the farm in Strauth, but it was made of old weathered timber. This building was stone walled with a wide, flat timber roof. It was several times larger than the barn he once knew and had wide doors large enough to ride the wayn through.

Pthorn unlatched the large timber bolt on the outside and snuck inside the door with Fluorocor. Inside he found it was deathly cold; his breath turned to mist in front of his face. There was no ice for leagues from here, so it was unlikely that the room was cooled using carted blocks. Pthorn had no idea how they had achieved such a thing on a vast scale.

Slowly, his eyes became accustomed to the room's darkness and realised the horror within.

The room was almost completely filled with bodies spaced several paces apart. They were laid out on white sheets in rows, neatly arranged like the tiles in a game of Scupper.

The smell of death was less pungent in here but still infiltrated the air. It was less like foul rot and more of the natural odour of death; the smell of cold and lifelessness.

Pthorn gave one last warning to his hungry friend, "don't even think about it. Not one nibble. If I see you with a single limb in your mouth, you won't get belly scratches for a turn!"

The hydrofluor hung its head low in understanding and clicked a soft disappointed sound.

They made their way between the rows of bodies, looking at each one in turn. Those ones towards the back of the warehouse seemed to have been there longer. Even in the frigid cold of the room, rot would still eventually set in, and decay would take the structure from the flesh, turning it into a foul ooze.

Pthorn was still trying to formulate a plan when he spotted what he thought may have been the cooling source. He made his way across to the side of the building where a second small enclosed building stood, like a stone hut inset into the wall.

He poked his head inside and found something completely unexpected. The room was lined with vials, upon vials of what seemed to be blood. The mountebanks must have been collecting a sample from each victim to study, or perhaps they had a more insidious motive for the collection that didn't bear thinking about.

There was all manner of instruments also spread out on a bench in the corner of the room; they were surgical instruments, which included various sharp blades, saws, and clawed devices.

At this point, Pthorn was truly improvising, he hadn't known what would happen when he resurrected Precil, but so far, he had not seen any side-effects of his Life donation. His current theory was that these rituals would not affect immortal life.

His biggest concern at this point was the effect a few pints of blood may have on his favourite hat. He hoped that after the ritual, he could quickly wash it before the blood set in for good, ruining it with staining or foul odour.

He placed the white banded, black hat onto the bench in front of him and began unstoppering vials from the curious collection. He poured a few drops from each into the centre of the hat. Ten, twenty, thirty, he lost count after that. By the time he was done, the hat was almost half filled with thick, sticky blood.

He made his way out of the small room and into the centre of the warehouse, where he placed the hat on the dirt floor.

Almost no light was left in the room, but he had been practising the incantation in his head on the road to keep himself occupied.

"Once welcomed by Death…" His voice echoed from the cavernous walls of the warehouse, his breath turning to mist in front of his face.

As he finished the incantation, the column of light he had witnessed at Precil's resurrection returned, only this time, it was a hundred times brighter. It was no longer just a glow of flowing light; it more closely resembled a torrent. If light could be turbulent, then this is what it would look like.

The light entered the hat and splashed blood across the room, covering the ground like red paint.

The light flooded the ground and flowed across the floor and over the bodies around it, continuing to grow stronger and stronger until it was blinding. Then as quickly as it came, it receded.

At that moment, Pthorn realised that he should remove himself from the scene. He wasn't sure if the light had flowed in from outside the building, but he had his suspicions. At best, if anyone had seen it and suspected him to have been the cause, he would be tried for witchcraft and put to death, or at least they would try. At worst, he only dared to think.

The bodies on the ground began to stir slowly as he made his way towards the door, ushering Fluorocor to come faster. As he approached the door, he could hear a commotion outside. He made the split-second decision to abandon the main entrance and look for another. He scanned the dim room, finding nothing but a stone wall surrounding him. He broke into a run, and Fluorocor took flight. He ran to the opposite end of the room and located a small personal access door.

He could hear the huge doors at the other end of the warehouse clattering as people tried to gain access; the door was fastened on the inside by a second large bolt.

Pthorn threw his weight at the door to no avail; it would not budge.

"Fluorocor!" he half shouted, half whispered. "Do something! Anything!"

The hydrofluor eyed the door thoughtfully before setting his sights on the latch. The beast released a large spray of acid at the door, which immediately began to sizzle and hiss, and then it ran up and barged through the door.

The door flew open just as the villagers gained access to the room.

Pthorn slinked out of the door and closed it behind him. Hoping that no one had seen them leave and, if they had, that they wouldn't come looking for them.

When they were safely outside the door and a few hundred paces away from the warehouse, Pthorn signalled to stop. He caught his breath before tying the knapsack back on to Fluorocor.

The two set off into the darkness across a field. Pthorn had no choice but to keep his hand on his companion's back and hope they were continuing to move towards a road. It was going to be a long night, and he wouldn't feel safe until he was far from Falanar.

30.
Interlude: Breakthrough

The Oracle of Malcontent | The Sect

Back in his laboratory at the Sect, The Oracle of Malcontent was getting close to a breakthrough in his research. He had been working on his research for years, trying to isolate something which may form one of the critical building blocks of all life on Azarth.

"I'm going to need some more of that blood, Pidge," he said to his lab partner.

"This is going to start costing you, Malley," she replied.

Initially, Tom had hated her nickname for him; she had started calling him Malley back in their first year in the sect when they both hated each other. It wasn't until many turns later, when they finally gave into their physical desires for one another, that he coined the name Pidge. She had been wearing pointed dress shoes one night and was walking uncomfortably; Tom had referred to her as being pigeon-toed and almost immediately created the nickname.

The Oracle of Anew drew a blade across her wrist, letting blood flow into a large beaker on the bench before placing her hand over the fresh wound. Almost instantly, the gash sewed itself back up, leaving no trace of the laceration behind.

"I love watching you work," Tom said mockingly to her with a gentle and often hidden smile.

"You don't love anything about work," she replied. "If I recall correctly, you used to go to great lengths to avoid it unless it meant blowing something up.

Unknown to the Elects but well known to his peers, Tom had gone through a rebellious phase in his youth. Something which Pidge had never let him forget. It certainly had not helped their relationship, or even friendship, in the early days in the Sect.

Tom selected a glass stirrer from his tray of clean utensils and collected a droplet, placing it on a small glass tundish for examination. He repeated this several times until a small pool sat in the centre of the dish.

"Fetch us a candle, will you... please," Tom said as he worked, placing the dish into the ventilated alcove and onto the work bench.

The Oracle of Anew soon returned with a fat tallow candle and placed it alongside the dish in the alcove.

"So, are you going to tell me your theory or make me wait until you see if it works?" She asked him inquisitively.

"Neither!" he responded enthusiastically. "If it works, I will let you make your own conclusion to see if I am right." He laughed aloud to a less than amused audience of one.

Tom made his way across the room to his cabinet of chemicals before selecting the vial labelled 'Oxidanyl'. Del and Tom had discussed part of this experiment in class one day; Tom had secretly hoped Del might stumble across the answer to his long-awaited question.

Tom laid out all the equipment he required to complete the experiment in front of him neatly before lighting the candle. He reached into the wick, and immediately it puffed to life, darting this way and that in the draft being pulled up the flue.

"Could you please close that door, Pidge? We can't have too much draft passing by the candle." He asked, all too politely.

She eyed him curiously. "I thought you had told me before that you needed the door open whenever you used that spot. Actually, come to think of it, you yelled at me last time I closed it," she said accusatively.

"Yes, yes, yes, I know; I am sorry about that. Just trust me on this one. I don't think the gas will kill me this time," Tom replied, not sounding as apologetic as he might, given he had definitely provided her with a proper grilling not only a few span ago.

The Oracle of Anew closed the door with a loud 'thud' and latched it behind her to prevent it from swinging in with the draft forcing its way through the gaps in the jamb.

The Oracle of Malcontent turned to face his experiment as his lab partner approached and stood at his side. The candle flame stopped dancing wildly and became a thin, steady stream of pale yellow light.

He picked up the dish of blood again and held it just to the side of the flame, the light dancing on the wet surface of the blood, turning it various shades of red, orange and black.

In his other hand, he picked up another glass rod and dipped it into the open oxidanyl vial, collecting a single large drop that dangled from the tip, threatening to fall at any time.

Tom slowly moved the rod until it was hovering over the dish.

"Time for the moment of truth, Pidge," he said hopefully before tapping the rod with his index finger. The drop of clear liquid fell and splashed into the centre of the blood pool and immediately began to react.

The blood bubbled and hissed like it was boiling on a stove top.

It was then that they observed the genuine curiosity. The flame atop the candle grew brighter; as if being fed more heat. Tom knew from careful experimentation that the reaction gave off very little, if any, heat, certainly not enough to cause a flame to burn brighter.

"Ah huh, I knew it, I knew it, finally!" he squawked happily before placing the bloody dish down and turning to his fellow Order-Master. "I knew it!"

"Go on, just give me this one; what did you know?" she asked, acting like she was bored. Deep down, Tom knew she was just as curious. She had been working on these experiments with him since he began.

"Well, what did you observe?" said Tom egging her on to participate. "Come on, humour me!"

"The flame burned brighter. So what?" she said. "What exactly are you trying to prove again?"

"Do you remember the lessons we were taught all those years ago about the invention of damp-light? They spoke of a life force all around us. It is in that draft that is trying to push the door open. It is all around us in what we breathe," he explained before emphasising, "atmospherics!"

"And our little experiment proved what, exactly?" she pushed further for a proper explanation.

Tom loved this, but he didn't want to let that on.

"Urgh," he started. "Fine! We know that when you add oxidanyl to the blood, the blood isn't destroyed, so whatever comes from the reaction isn't from the blood; it must be from the oxidanyl. I am proposing that the oxidanyl is decomposing, and part of it is the same as whatever it is that they were trying to study in Atmospherics..." Tom paused for dramatic effect before raising his voice triumphantly, "I believe I have discovered what many have missed right in front of their noses. I have discovered the essence of life. I call it... Anyl."

The room was filled with a few moments of silence before the two Order-Masters realised what he had said.

Through fits of laughter, The Oracle of Anew added, "maybe take the other half of the word?" before continuing to laugh, almost doubled over.

"Fine then, be a child. I call it Oxi... Oxi... Ah, oh yes, oxygen. That sounds good to me." Tom turned to his, still almost catatonic, friend. "Oh, would you shut up!"

Tom began to pack up his equipment and wash everything down with water while Pidge recomposed herself, still muttering something about 'anal' under her breath.

After the workbench was clean, Tom pulled out his book of research notes and dipped his quill to start recording his findings.

Just as he moved to start writing, the door of the laboratory flew open, swiftly followed by the form of The Oracle of Beauty with The Oracle of Prevail just behind her.

"We need to talk," Beauty stated sternly, her eyes burning like coals. "Which one of you is doing blood magic!?"

Part 4

31.
Peace and Quiet

thorn and Fluorocor walked through the night without stopping. They kept to the farmland fields for a league before the woodland began to creep back in and became too dense to walk through. As the sun started to break through over the horizon, sending rays darting through the trees lining the road, it suddenly dawned on Pthorn that he had left something back at the village.

"Not my hat!" he exclaimed with a sigh. He threw his head back in exasperation and let out a loud groan. "Crea is going to murder me! Where am I going to find another one out here?"

Fluorocor looked up at him inquisitively.

"What? I think it suited me."

Fluorocor clicked in agreement and went back to minding its own business.

While walking along, two important things came to Pthorn's mind. Firstly, he realised that they hadn't eaten in over a day; when they arrived in Falanar, they had immediately investigated the location of the morgue, and everything had escalated from then. Secondly, he thought his eyes were playing tricks on him. His leather-skinned travel companion seemed to have shrunk overnight.

When he had strapped the knapsack to Fluorocor, it barely covered half of its back. Now it seemed to cover all the way back over the top of its hind legs and was no longer firmly strapped; it was swaying with each step. After putting two and two together, Pthorn developed a theory.

"Fluorocor? Can you shrink and grow depending on how much food you eat?" Pthorn asked hopefully.

Fluorocor clicked loudly and nodded its head.

Pthorn was learning more and more about his peculiar friend, and the hydrofluor also seemed to be learning how to communicate; this wasn't the first time Pthorn had noticed a head nod or shake that accompanied the clicking. Also, thinking back, he realised that Fluorocor's size had also changed over time, but he really hadn't paid attention, and it hadn't been this dramatic.

"Just how big can you get then?" he asked, spreading his arms wide.

Fluorocor answered by spreading his wings as far as they would go to the side.

"Well, in that case. Let's go find you a moog. Although I might carry the knapsack for a while."

They stopped briefly while Pthorn untied the bag from around Fluorocor's body, removed some of their travel rations, and fastened it on his own back. The two shared some of the hardtack they had stocked up on back in Maarts, but it only seemed to serve as a reminder of the hunger rather than filling the void.

They continued walking down the lonely road, coming across no other travellers along the way, not even a transiting messenger from a trading post. Word had clearly travelled far and wide to avoid the village of Falanar. Eventually, after travelling most of the day on foot, Pthorn's legs began to turn to a numb jelly, and they stumbled upon a waystop. It was earlier in the day than they would usually stop for the night, but Pthorn thought that if he travelled any farther, he might collapse from exhaustion.

This waystop seemed more overgrown than many they had stayed at in the past. This one didn't look like it had been frequented regularly in many span. Usually, the clearings were well pressed and trodden from animals, wagons and bedrolls. There was plenty of recent deadwood from the unpicked tree line, which Pthorn scavenged and made into a rather large bonfire, much larger than would usually be required for a cookfire.

He set up his bedroll and placed his knapsack inside. It clinked as the vials rattled together when it landed. Pthorn would eventually have to return to specimen collection, but at this moment, his head was in completely the wrong space.

As Pthorn returned to the fire, he heard a rustling deep behind the edge of the clearing, muffled by the forest trees and undergrowth.

Fluorocor raised its head curiously before Pthorn signalled for him to stand down. He slowly crept towards the noise to investigate. Not fifty paces away stood a large keil; forked and curled antlers sat proudly atop its head ending in razor-sharp tips. This was a buck that Pthorn definitely didn't want to be on the receiving end of a head-butt from.

Pthorn though back to his 'conversation' with Fluorocor earlier, where he joked that he should find him a moog to eat. It occurred to him that a keil would do just as nicely. Pthorn reached out to the beast as he had done while practising in the Sect and with the rarn. He made sure his movements were smooth and steady so as not to draw attention to himself and startle it. He created the Connection to the keil and felt around for the source of its life blood. When he found the heart, he slowly applied pressure; again trying not to do anything sudden that may startle or scare it.

Slowly but surely, the keil began to sway and feel heavy on its feet. First, it kneeled down, then placed its head on the ground before slumping to the side. Pthorn maintained his firm grasp until he was sure the animal was gone.

"Thank you for your sacrifice," he said aloud. He had been thinking about his role in the world as death. On the one hand, it felt wrong to snuff out life, particularly as majestic as the grand keil in front of him. On the other hand, he was born into the role and given the authority over death by the power of creation itself, the Singular. By way of honouring them in the name of the Singular, he had begun to offer last rites to any creature which met with an untimely demise at his hands.

Once he let go of his hold of the keil's heart and released his Connection, Pthorn turned to Fluorocor and gave the all clear.

"Go on, it's all yours… and you don't even need to save me a leg!" said Pthorn.

Fluorocor didn't bother waiting for a second permission to be granted before taking off quickly in the direction of the fallen beast.

What happened next intrigued Pthorn from a scientific perspective and somewhat horrified him from another. Between mid-afternoon and the time the sun had taken to set in the dusk, Fluorocor had alternated between acid dissolving and making sickening crunching and squelching noises while chewing. Fluorocor left nothing but the black, razor-sharp antler behind.

Pthorn had returned to warming himself by the fire after spending the first hour fixated on the process; he had even started writing a few notes about his latest observations. It would seem that hydrofluors could unlock their jaws to swallow large portions of food broken down by acid.

Eventually, after letting its meal settle for more than a few moments, Fluorocor slowly ambled back over to the cookfire, which had burned down to a far more manageable size over the afternoon. Pthorn sat eating some sausage and cheese. He could already see a noticeable difference in the beast's size.

"You know you have to sleep outside tonight, right? If I wake up to being crushed by you being bigger than a cottage, I would be most angry with you."

The hydrofluor clicked sorrowfully in response and almost seemed to shrug.

"Plus, I am certain that a hydrofluor fart after a meal like that could kill an immortal!"

That night, after letting the fire burn down to black coals, Pthorn curled up alone for the first time in many span without Fluorocor warming his feet.

The next day Pthorn awoke to the sounds of a snoring hydrofluor. He had never heard the sound before, and Fluorocor usually slept in much closer quarters. Pthorn poked his head out through the flap and found the snout of an enormous dragon firmly pressed against his own.

Pthorn immediately recoiled, realising the acid-forming potential of this particular end of his friend and scrambled up to the other end of the bedroll to exit.

Once he had made his way out, he looked over the beast curled up, facing his sleeping quarters. Fluorocor had taken on most of the size of the huge keil it had consumed the day before. Maintaining this size was clearly going to take some serious pilfering of farmer's livestock; finding a keil every few days might prove unsustainable given the few they had seen on the road. Considering Pthorn's previous life as a farming boy, he wasn't sure he really approved of this, but there seemed to be little by way of alternatives. Hopefully, they could go at least a span or so before needing to find another large animal to feast upon.

All this accelerated growing seemed to have a significant impact on the sleep requirements of his friend, which was probably not helped by the long journey the day before. The sun was high in the sky before they got moving back on the road. After about an hour, the woodland became sparser, and they came to a crossroads. The signage was simple and indicated nothing but the direction of each path rather than the destination. Pthorn had been heading west ever since he left Ung at the start of his journey and didn't really have a plan for a path. He knew that if he went north, he would likely find himself in the colder regions of the continent; given his childhood in the hot, arid lands of Straulatos, this didn't seem particularly inviting. West would likely be more of the same long roads, woodland closing in from all sides.

That left one remaining solution. Pthorn turned left and began walking down the southern road of the High Priest's Way, followed by the now lumbering form of a massive hydrofluor. The forest lining the road continued to thin before becoming dotted trees spanning across the expansive landscape. Soon the horizon was filled with tall grass waving in the wind, with small insects flitting between blades and flowers. Pthorn remembered from the map he had seen in Tom's classroom and copied down in the back of one of his books that heading south would eventually bring you to an inland sea. Finding a nice place to sink roots for a while seemed quite pleasant to Pthorn at this point. After the events in Falanar, he enjoyed the peace and quiet of the road but also missed the community of the villages like Ung and Maarts. They stopped for lunch beneath the broad canopy of a lone tree beside the road. As he sat, he decided they would stay in a seaside town for a while.

After they finished a light lunch, Pthorn thought he might give riding Fluorocor another go, given the limitation in its size last time resulted in poor outcomes for Pthorn.

"What do you say? Should we give riding another go?" Pthorn asked the hydrofluor.

Fluorocor nodded its head and screeched an affirmative click before crouching down on the ground, its belly resting firmly on the hard-packed dirt.

Pthorn still had the knapsack cinched on to his back; Fluorocor reaching the size it did, the straps would no longer pass around its midsection. Pthorn swung his leg up past Fluorocor's wings and took a seat just behind its frilly neck. If this ride was successful, he made a note to make a harness to hold on to and maybe secure the knapsack again. It would need to be well adjustable, given the variable size of the beast.

Fluorocor slowly raised itself back to its clawed feet and stretched its wings. Its wingspan was now massive, almost as wide as the road was in most places along the Way. Pthorn leaned forward and reached around its neck to hold on tightly.

With a large flap of leathery wings snapping in the air, the rider and his fantastic steed took off into the bright sky. Pthorn almost lost his grasp immediately before resettling himself and getting a good hold again.

Fluorocor rose high into the air, each flap of the wings taking them over twenty paces each time. The ground began to shrink before Pthorn's eyes until the tree they had stopped under looked as small as a squarn. Finally, they stopped ascending and began a freefall dive. Pthorn's stomach felt like he had left it at an elevation of two hundred paces as he continued to fall, the ground rushing at them faster than he had ever experienced in his life.

He was flying, and Fluorocor seemed to have minimal regard for the human body's frailty; even an immortal one could be seriously mutilated.

At the last moment, Fluorocor spread his wings back and pulled out of the dive. Pthorn could feel the forces pulling at his skin and insides, trying to force themselves away from his bones. His hands barely held on as they levelled out and began to soar a mere pace away from the ground. His heart was threatening to beat out of his chest, fear and exhilaration pumping through his body. They landed far more smoothly than he could have imagined possible and taxied in back underneath the large tree. They sat down until Pthorn had caught his breath and allowed his heart to reduce its rate to normal levels again.

After they had finished their break, Pthorn ushered Fluorocor along the roadway once again, and they set off down the southern branch from the High Priest's Way.

They passed several small, nameless villages throughout the next few days. Most comprised a few moog and onk farms, alongside some vegetable and fruit farms. None of these villages had markets to speak of, but the owners were generally friendly and quick to try to sell their wares to passers-by without the need to add vendor fees. Primarily, these villages operated as communes; each farm would supply a particular type of food or product that would be shared amongst the local villages. They were largely self-governed and only answered to the Matraketh government for the purpose of land taxes, which seemed a point of contention when questioned on the topic.

Pthorn stocked up on perishable supplies as he passed each village but allowed Fluorocor to lose a bit of his gargantuan size. Upon reaching whatever town lay at the end of the southern road, he didn't really want to enter with a hydrofluor larger than a moog. Fluorocor didn't seem to mind his diet varying in size; in fact, it seemed quite natural to consume only what it needed in order to shrink, maintain or increase in size.

Finally, after almost two span since deviating south, the two weary travellers arrived at the sprawling village of Playton-on-Sea, a ghotiman and general commerce village in southern-central Matraketh. Unlike most of the other large towns they had stayed in, this one wasn't surrounded by farmland. The vast, wide open spaces of grass and fields were replaced by a league or two of woodland before being replaced by residential cottages. The city limits were marked by an old carved archway showing the village's name and adorned with carvings of ghoti and a giant kraken in the centre. The archway was old and well-weathered but looked to be made of solid hardwood that would last centuries.

The villagers at one of the previous farms had told Pthorn about Playton-on-Sea. The housewife had sold him some leafy greens from their latest harvest and said they regularly sold their produce at the markets in town. They made the trip once every span, leaving supplies to be peddled by a local vendor while they were away. She had said that there were no local farms in the village and that all fresh produce was generally imported from neighbouring farms such as theirs. The town had a booming trade in food-of-the-sea, providing almost all the locals' income.

As they arrived, Pthorn could see what she meant. The end of the road emptied into a harbour filled with tall masts strung with rigging and sails. Lining the water was a well-established wet market. These were not the sort of vendors who wheeled out a cart or pitched a sheet of canvas every few days; these markets were built to last. Long wooden tables stood displaying the vendor's wares. An inclined roof was constructed above the market so that they could operate regardless of the weather. Pthorn continued walking with Fluorocor in tow until they reached the markets under the watchful eye of the locals. Even with the little bit of shrinking the hydrofluor had achieved, the beast was far more conspicuous than Pthorn had hoped.

32.
Reunion

Playton-on-Sea was the biggest village Pthorn had visited since he left Portsworth and certainly the highest in class as well. Most of the people in the town didn't actually live there; it was a travel hub for the traders between Kesheir and Matraketh. Silk farmers would travel from the cold north-western regions of Matraketh to meet the traders at the inland Maitke Sea's shore. The traders would then cross the Maitke to the northern ports of Kesheir or sail east to large ports like Playton-on-Sea or Portsworth for trade to the other continents. Similarly, Kesheir found their exports in commodities like minerals, metals and stone.

Being new in town, Pthorn knew there was only one reasonable course of action to get his bearings and entered the first pub he had found. It went by the name of The Ghotiman's Rod, and he sat and talked to a couple of the sailors who had stopped at the local inns for a few pints. He learned that before they had changed to notes, the global currency had been clips of metal, creatively called iron clips. The iron clips were mined in the south of Kesheir; one particular sailor was very proud of his family's heritage in minting the coins. About twenty turns ago, iron found more value in forged and worked products; the cost outweighed the value of the clips. Notes, called broan and printed on cheaper-to-produce stiff cloth, had been introduced and quickly became the primary currency.

Pthorn had made a habit of spending time at the bar of The Ghotiman's Rod and had even taken up residence during his time in Playton-on-Sea. Fluorocor had become a local attraction, and Pthorn found that he didn't need to do much to get a free meal or drink if he let people touch his friendly hydrofluor.

The Rod's innkeeper Glan, an overfed purple-faced man well into his sixtieth turn, allowed them both entry into the main bar during the day when it wasn't too busy but refused to allow such a beast to stay in the accommodation-proper. They had come to an alternative arrangement with a disused garden shed behind the inn. Over his first two span staying there, Pthorn had boarded up a few holes in the roof and made an oversized and comfortable sleeping pallet fit for the two of them. He didn't have any access to amenities after close of business, but with some prior planning, it hadn't been too much of an inconvenience yet; that said, it was on his list to discuss the procurement of a chamber pot with Glan.

In return for the accommodation, Pthorn had taken on a role working at the inn. The young man who had been filling the position previously had decided to try his luck as a ship's hand on a trading vessel and just upped and left without so much as half a day's warning. The work wasn't too onerous; the inn only had eight rooms, and the bedding was replaced once a week along with the chamber pots. He spent his afternoons helping in the kitchens while Fluorocor flew off to stretch his wings and hunt. The hydrofluor seemed to welcome this little bit of freedom while also being able to return home to the shelter of the shed. On several occasions, Pthorn found himself gifted presents, usually comprising eviscerated and partially dissolved squarns. After the second one, Pthorn had given his leather-winged friend a stern talking-to, but it didn't seem to budge the beast's resolve to provide for his friend.

Fluorocor didn't seem to be getting any bigger, so Pthorn could only assume it had stuck to hunting small game and left the moogs, keil and onk alone.

Today was much like any other day working at The Rod. Stone plates and pint glasses were being sent back for washing almost faster than he could stack them by the sink. During the peak times, Glan would get Pthorn to tend to the front of house, allowing the washing to pile up until the quieter hours of the night. The merchants, vendors and ship's hands were all out on the town, spending their day's takings on food and beer, only to go out again the next day and spend all day earning it again.

"Come on, boy!" Glan called.

The publican poked his head through the doorway into the kitchens, the night's stress accentuating the colour of the man's face.

"I need you to start running pints!"

"Right away," he called back as he threw off the washing-up apron, which landed in a crumpled heap atop the mountain of glasses.

The bar at the back of the inn was lined with four large kegs. They sat on a rail and were rolled into place from a hatch outside the building. They would decant off the keg at the end, and then when it ran out, they would move up to the next one, and so on. At the end of the span, when all but one of the kegs had beer remaining, they could just continue rolling the kegs off the end of the rail and back out the other side of the inn. Glan seemed quite proud of his ingenuity when he had described the mechanism to Pthorn. Tonight they were on the second keg in, and the orders for more beer were coming in fast.

"Four to him and six to them!" Glan called and pointed as Pthron filled and ran across the packed room.

Pthorn filled pints with two in his hand at a time. Over the past few span, he had become quite good at filling the glasses without them being almost all head. His first few pours had been a disaster, but it did result in a lot of free beer for himself.

As Pthorn moved around the bar to deliver the pints to their respective patrons, the door to the bar swung open. Through the doorway, he noted that it was pouring down rain, although he couldn't hear it over the din in the room. A person entered with an oilskin coat wrapped around them and took a seat at the last remaining booth in the bar area.

Pthorn finishing running the remaining pints over to the awaiting patrons before moving back to the bar to pour more.

Service was always performed by Glan; he wanted to be seen in the front of house and had a strong preference to shout orders rather than fill them. Glan moved across to the bistro to attend to their latest guest. As Pthorn was pouring a round of drinks, he realised that their new visitor was strangely familiar; it was not something he was used to travelling around a foreign continent.

Her hair was soaked through and clung to her face in streaks, but through the mess and tangle, he could see the same fiery brown eyes that had mocked him nearly a turn and a half ago. Pthorn felt a warmth surge through his body and became transfixed with her eyes.

Pthorn continued to stare as the pint glass in his hand overfilled and soaked the front of his clothes.

"Steady on, mate!" called one very tipsy patron. "You ain't meant to be the one drinking."

Thankfully, it seemed that neither Glan nor Darn had noticed his mess or lack of attentiveness. Pthorn quickly shut off the cask cock and scurried across the room to deliver the round.

Glan walked back to the bar to give Pthorn the next order, and such was the rest of the night. Glan yelling, Pthorn pouring drinks, and Darn sitting in the corner booth looking like a drowned squarn with her very distracting eyes.

As the night progressed into the early dark hours of the morning, patrons eventually staggered off to their rooms at the inn or back to their ships anchored in the harbour. When the crowd had died down to a manageable number, Pthorn resumed his duties in the back room on washing up duty. She was still sitting in her booth when he walked out of sight, lost in her thoughts with a pint for company. Pthorn had delivered her a couple of drinks during the night, but she hadn't even acknowledged him, and he had just left them on the table in front of her.

He was lost in his thoughts and was hoping that Darn would be the last one remaining, leaving him able to….

What? Talk to her?

Pthorn grumbled at his own mocking internal monologue.

Why does my mind have to be such a sarcastic arsehole all the time?

Pthorn wasn't sure what he thought of Darn, but there was one thing he knew for sure; approaching and talking to girls his age was not something he considered one of his strengths in life.

How would I strike up a conversation? "Hi, since we last met, I have been chosen to kill things…."

He had to consider whether he could, or even should, tell her about the Sect. He knew he wasn't meant to tell anyone about who he was. He began to try to rationalise whether there could be an exception for some people.

He couldn't very well just tell her he was a travelling botanist; she was there when he was Chosen by the High Priest.

He finished washing up before he could provide himself with any sort of realistic conclusion, or solution, to his dilemma. He passed Glan as he walked back into the main bar, letting him know he was done for the night. Some nights Glan would ask him for some extra work, like cleaning up in the front of house, but tonight he left him leave without a fight.

Pthorn was disheartened to find the bar completely devoid of patrons. Given the sun was only a couple of hours away from rising, it only made sense that she had also seen reason and found herself a pallet to sleep on.

With a glimmer of hope remaining that she had found lodging at the inn, Pthorn turned back to question Glan. "There was a young girl about my age across the bar. Is there any chance you know where she is staying tonight?"

"You randy rarn you," he said with an out-of-character chuckle. "She was the pretty sort, wasn't she?"

Pthorn waited for him to go on after amusing himself.

"No, sorry. She asked about a room at the inn, but we are full up tonight. Maybe I shoulda told her there was some extra space in your pallet out the back 'ey."

Glan continued chuckling as Pthorn made his way to the doors to leave.

"You never know; she might be back tonight for another round of Playton's finest ale… or Straulatos' smallest cock," goaded Glan as Pthorn closed the door behind him and made his way around the building to his hut.

The rain had stopped, but the ground was still sodden. It was treacherously tricky to navigate through to the shed in the pitch blackness of the night.

When he finally returned home, he found Fluorocor had already returned from its hunt and was sound asleep on the floor beside his sleeping pallet, allowing him to sneak past and crawl in under the sheets. Usually, they would share the space, but Pthorn figured his friend was just being generous.

The next day Pthorn realised that Fluorocor's sleeping arrangement was not merely an act of generosity; but more of an act of necessity. It would seem that it had found a rather large meal the night before and increased significantly in size during its rest. Given that they were attempting to keep a low profile, Pthorn made a note to himself to scold the hydrofluor when it awoke from its slumber. It was likely that it would be some time before that could occur; after a big meal, the beast liked a long sleep.

Pthorn crawled over the hindquarters of Fluorocor, who didn't flinch a muscle and made his way to the door, wondering what the stupid beast's plans were for getting out the door itself.

Once outside, Pthorn found that the sun had come back out in a dazzling fashion and was already drying the sod out from the night before. As he had always learned back home in Strauth, he upturned his shoe to check for critters. Out fell a small species of scuriat; this one was black, unlike the burnt orange ones he had seen back at the Sect and near Ung. Pthorn shooed the little creature away, and it scurried off into the grass beside the shed.

When he was finally ready to go, he made his way down the half-muddy alleyway which led through to the road, trying to stand on grassy tufts where he could to keep his footing.

Pthorn arrived at the street and turned right towards some of his regular haunts.

"Rumour has it you manned up and caught yourself a farmin' hydrofluor," called a voice from behind him.

"Assier Almighty!" Pthorn cursed as he levitated and felt his soul attempt to flee his body. He stopped dead in his tracks before slowly turning, not daring to be hopeful.

As he turned, he saw exactly what he had hoped. Her hair had sprung back to the wild snarl of brown locks, which shone through with a red glow in the late morning sun. She smiled and flashed her brown eyes at him, glinting like a chip of polished garnet.

"And you seem to have lost most of an accent!" he returned to her jokingly.

"No one could understand me this side of the Equis, so they said I had to get taught to speak proper." She laughed and moved towards him.

"How did you know I'd be back there?" Pthorn asked her, still in a state of disbelief and shock.

"Your boss in there. I saw you just after I arrived yesterday and asked your boss where you were staying. Didn't he mention I was asking after ya?" she said.

"No. No, he didn't. He just mocked me for asking after you. Remind me to set Fluorocor onto him when I see him next," he said, narrowing his gaze in mock anger.

"Yeah, he said you was staying out back there in a shack or summit because you had yourself a big leather beasty. I couldn't believe it after you damn near pissed yasself when you saw the one back home." She let a cackle escape before stifling it and acting sincere and apologetic.

"A lot has changed since I left home," he said.

"Yeah, you lost what little fashion sense you had," she said before continuing to laugh at his expense.

"And what about you then? How are you all the way over here?"

"Actually, I kinda followed you, believe it or not."

He did not believe it.

"That carriage they put you on was pretty slow, and you dressed in all ya fancy clothes; it was pretty easy to track ya at every inn. It was jus' a matter of asking the inn keep whether they had seen a couple'a idiots dressed in white sheets come by. Eventually, I arrived in Northern Port just after youse had left. Again, I just asked around and found out youse was headed for Portsworth. But that was the last I knew. I stowed away a ship headed for Matraketh. That didn't go down well with the captain, but that is another story, then arrived in Portsworth after about four span. After that, your trail went dead. No one had seen ya. I hung around for a turn or so before I jus' started wandering 'round. Now here I am."

One thing still didn't make sense to Pthorn.

"But, why follow *me*?" he asked.

"Well, I didn't really want to go home and see my Pappa again. I thought that seein' as the High Priest had such a hard time Choosing between us, there could be a chance that they could take both of us, and I could start a new life some'ere else. I didn't really think it through, to be honest. Plus, I kinda thought you were cute." She chuckled.

Pthorn felt his face turn a very bright shade of pink before turning away in the hope that she couldn't see it. All the ways he had considered trying to talk to her had completely left his mind, not that they would have helped.

Instead, he just gestured down the road, "Hungry?"

Really? That's the best I can come up with?

33.

The Little Death

arn followed Pthorn down the main street of Playton-on-Sea, past the markets selling fresh food-of-the-sea until they reached a small outdoor food vendor on the water's edge. The vendor looked like he had started with a small mobile cart before setting up a permanent shop and placing a roof over his head. At this end of the village, the deep harbour became dangerously shallow for ships to moor in and, in some areas, the shore terminated with a sandy beach. This food vendor was situated on one of these little sandy outcrops with a wood-fired skillet and a small bench for food preparation set into the original cart. Most of the travellers didn't venture up this far, and it was a well-known spot for Playton locals to sit and enjoy a meal or stare out across the inland sea. Today the area was quiet, with only a few locals out for a stroll along the water's edge. There were some small children in the small waves under the watchful eye of an adult back on the shoreline.

Darn sat down on the pale yellow sand to sun herself while Pthorn walked up to the vendor, paid his two broan and waited for the food to be ready. Pthorn looked back at the young lady on the beach; she was leaning back, staring out over the ocean, seemingly lost in the moment of the waves. Pthorn had to snap himself out of staring at her for fear of being caught ogling and returned his attention to the vendor, resorting to small talk about the weather from the previous night and its effects on sales.

The food was cheap and simple fare, but it was also one of the best things he had ever experienced. Before coming to Playton-on-Sea, Pthorn had never even seen a clucken, let alone tasted one, but he soon found that when freshly grilled with some spices from Kesheir, it was better than anything he had ever tasted. They served it chopped up on a bed of fresh vegetables and white, fluffy, steamed mifan, which added to the overall experience of the food.

When Pthorn received his order, he headed back over and joined Darn on the sand.

"Don't worry, I didn't get you mant on a stick! This is really good. Have you tried clucken?" he asked.

Darn shook her head before surveying the plate of food in front of her. She shrugged before taking a bite and responding with noises that Pthorn had never heard come from anyone else.

The blush started to rise back into his cheeks as he tried to push the thoughts aside.

"So tell me about... what did ya call it, Fluorocor? How did ya manage to catch one? Did ya take my excellent advice?" she asked through a mouthful of food.

Pthorn laughed, remembering that she had clobbered a poor hydrofluor over the head with a lump of wood and placed it onto the roadway.

"Surprisingly not, considering Fluorocor trusts me. I feel like belting it would have done the opposite."

"Then how did ya manage it?" she asked curiously.

"Well, the same as anything else I want to spend time with, I coaxed it with food." Pthorn held up his bowl of food as he replied, to which Darn laughed and snorted.

"Charmin'!" she said. "Do all the girls fall for ya offer of food in exchange fa' comp'ny?"

"Well, I am still not sure if Fluorocor is a girl or not, so I hope I am on the right track," he replied jokingly.

"Keep buying me food like this, and ya will be," she replied as she took another big bite of clucken. "We could make some serious broan if we smuggled this back home to Straulatos."

Pthorn went silent at the thought of leaving. The Sect would never let him run off to another continent for any extended period of time. As it was, he was about twelve span into his travels around Matraketh, and so far, he had very few specimens to show for it.

His silence seemed to be noticed by Darn.

"What is it?" she questioned softly.

"I am not sure how much I can tell you about why I am here. You know, after the Choosing. But I know that I have to go back. You talk like travelling the world, and smuggling back riches like cluckens, is a possibility, and for you, it is, but for me… It just can't be."

Pthorn looked down and focused on his feet, which he was digging into the sand as he spoke.

Darn put her arm on his shoulder. In the short time they had known each other, Pthorn had already determined this was not a typical act of expression for her. She was a happy-go-lucky sort who got through hard times with humour and an insult. Now she seemed to be showing genuine concern for his predicament.

"Tell ya what, I will see what I can do about helping ya with your… issue, but for now, let's just enjoy those waves, 'ey," she said, trying to put him at ease.

Pthorn agreed and leaned back on his arms, placing his hands into the sand behind him. Darn smiled and leaned over before putting her arm around his shoulder.

"Ya know, you're pretty cute when ya look concerned," she said while chuckling quietly.

Pthorn couldn't help but give her a small smile, still thinking about his future and its locked-in fate.

The awkwardness that Pthorn had predicted didn't seem to have eventuated at all. The two spent several long hours sitting on the sand until the sun started setting over in the west, throwing long purplish hues across the water. The lapping waves and ripples shone and glistened as the water touched the peaks and could not find the troughs. The end of the village they were sitting in was the quiet end, and by night, even more so. A far-off noise could be heard as the night's raucous activities started for the merchants and market traders. Thankfully Glan would not be expecting Pthorn to work tonight, although, given the lack of aught else to do some nights, Pthorn would end up working his nights off anyway. Tonight would not be one of those nights.

The two got up from their sandy seats and brushed themselves off.

Pthorn stood with his back to the sunset and turned to face Darn. As with the waves, the sun performed the same theatrics within her wild hair and flared like fire within her eyes. The two stood a bare arm span apart before they slowly closed the gap to a hand's width. They looked deeply into each other's eyes. Pthorn became transfixed by her stare as he placed his arm around her back and pulled her close.

Pthorn had no idea how he had gotten so lucky as to find Darn far away from where they had first met, nor could he explain how it was somehow so different from that night spent with Ellie back in Portsworth.

Darn offered no resistance, not even a hint of hesitation, as he began to cock his head to the side.

Their lips met in the middle with what started as a gentle and tender peck, pulling away just far enough to let the moment hang.

This type of moment wasn't just sex, passion, or love; it was the sharing of life between two people at a single point in time, with time becoming irrelevant and undefined. It was as though life paused for them. They both took a slow breath before continuing, adding a dash of passion to their shared moment of life and Darn's gentle sigh set Pthorn's body on alight with desire.

In a short moment of awkwardness, Pthorn tried to rationalise what to do about teeth and where the hell to move his tongue before giving up and just letting it happen. His arm pulled her body closer to his, closing the gap between them.

Pthorn closed his eyes, not to imagine something else, but to capture this moment and lose himself within it. Darn groaned softly as he gently nibbled her lower lip before finally pushing him away slightly.

She lifted her lips to his ear, whispering, "perhaps the public shoreline isn't the place."

Pthorn took a few moments to compose himself, for the first time self-conscious of what they were doing. It didn't look like anyone had noticed, but she was right; it certainly wasn't proper to be overly romantic in such a public setting.

The two set off holding hands, walking back into the sunset towards the inn, keeping their public displays of affection back to a minimum as they walked into the village centre.

They arrived back at the inn, and Pthorn slinked inside for a few moments to grab an oil lantern from Glan. He usually didn't bother, as Glan made him pay for oil, and he generally didn't have a need for one, but tonight he thought better of a dark shed.

When he returned, he found Darn waiting for him at the mouth of the alleyway, and he led her down, trying to stick the hard grassy places again. When they reached the end of the alley, Pthorn pulled aside the door and revealed the oversized hindquarters of a hydrofluor.

Pthorn gave the, now awake but immobile, hydrofluor a tap on the flank and began the scolding, "now what did I tell you about eating moogs and keil?! I said to stick to nothing bigger than an onklette."

Fluorocor clicked loudly in response ending in a downturn.

"Holy Assier's hairy armpits!" Darn exclaimed. "I knew ya had a hydrofluor, but I didn't know ya had one this big!"

Fluorocor attempted to turn around to get a better look at the source of the new speaker and struggled, knocking over everything in the room as it tried.

Finally, the beast faced Pthorn and gave Darn a disapproving glare.

"Now you play nice! I know for a fact she will hit you with a lump of wood if you cause any trouble."

"Cliiiick," came the response, followed by a very disapproving snort. This was not a sound that Pthorn had heard it make before, and he wasn't entirely sure that was a good thing.

"Now you need to get out of here and lose some of that size!" Said Pthorn pointing back towards the alleyway, fully expecting to get nothing more than silence from it.

Instead, the enormous beast started making its way through the doorway. Naturally, its head fit through the opening, but it was apparent the rest would not even come close.

Then a curious thing happened. It was almost like the hydrofluor could dislocate joints to get each limb through and redistribute internal organs to constrict its body. This was as close to a solid animal becoming a liquid as one could imagine.

After several moments, and a lot of noises and complaining from the converted shed, Fluorocor stood back out in the open.

"Beautiful!" exclaimed Darn, looking around it.

"Show her your wings Fluorocor," Pthorn said, gesturing with his arms. By now, Pthorn was sure he was understood, but you could never be too careful with communication with an acid-breathing dragon.

Fluorocor stretched out its broad wings, stretching the full extent of the alley's width. It was truly magnificent.

"Fluorocor even let me ride the other day. Good Assier! That almost killed me," bragged Pthorn while gently patting it on the broad neck. "I was holding on for my life… well, kind of," he shrugged, "as it dove from the clouds back down to the ground. I couldn't walk; my knees wouldn't stop shaking."

Darn laughed for a few moments before attempting to gain the trust of the hydrofluor; she held out her hand in the least aggressive way she could. Just presenting the back of her hand in front of its face.

Darn let her hand hang there for a few moments.

After nothing happened, she offered more, "my name is Darnalla, and I am from Pthorn's hometown. I bet he has told you all three things he knows about me."

Fluorocor turned to Pthorn, who just shrugged back in response before returning to look straight at Darn.

"Can we be friends?" she offered further.

The hydrofluor began to lower its head before gently edging forward and nudging her hand with its slitted nose.

Their first encounter now made even more sense to Pthorn; it wasn't until Pthorn had offered Fluorocor both a new name and his own that it had become to accept him as not a threat.

After that moment, any tension that had been hanging in the air evaporated instantly. A trusting bond was formed between them, similar to the one that Fluorocor had with Pthorn. He believed that their relationship had grown stronger, and they had begun to understand each other on a much deeper level.

"Now, how about you run off and try to burn off some of that size. You could carry both of us and a moog at this size!" said Pthorn before turning to Darn to explain further. "It turns out that hydrofluors can change size based on how much they eat. If they eat a moog, they gain the size of a moog. If they don't eat for a turn or two, they become undergrowth dwellers. Pretty awesome, huh?"

"So let me get this straight, I thought you were all big and brave after capturing a giant dragon, but in reality, you made friends with a creature not much bigger than my arm?" she questioned jokingly.

"Ha ha ha, very funny," he retorted before turning to Fluorocor for the last time. "Off you go, come on!" and gave it a good slap on the side of the neck.

Fluorocor clicked loudly before launching itself into the air and flapping its giant wings. Tonight it was going to get noticed by a large crowd of people, whether Pthorn liked it or not. He could deal with that attention tomorrow; tonight, he just wanted the attention of one lady.

Once they were alone, Pthorn led the young lady into his modest but far more private accommodation before placing the oil lamp down on the small workbench on the opposite side of the room to the sleeping pallet.

He had barely placed the lamp down before Darn approached him again, locking lips with the added passion that she could not express in front of a shoreline audience.

Pthorn felt the heat rise within his body again, like a torrent of magma looking for an exit from a volcano, radiating from his chest throughout his body.

As they reignited their moment, Darn reached up and loosened the fastening on the back of her dress, letting it cascade down her body and onto the floor. Judging by the immediate warmth experienced by the hand touching her back, he determined that she had not yet discovered under-slips.

Pthorn ran his hand down her back, drinking in the shape and curve of her body. Want was ignited deep within him, burning intensely and begging to break free from his small clothes.

Robed as he was, Pthorn could hardly just let his clothing fall to the floor. He pulled his clothing over his head while trying and failing to maintain eye contact before flinging them to the floor. Looking deep into his eyes, Darn reached down and rubbed the outside of his final piece of clothing before lowering them to the floor. She placed a gentle kiss on his tip as she raised herself up to face him.

Finally, they were as naked as their name days. Pthorn couldn't help but stare as her beauty was revealed in the dance of the dim lamplight. He leaned forward and returned the kiss on each of her nipples, feeling them harden under his touch. He continued down, guided by a gentle hand on his head, planting soft kisses down her quivering belly and finally onto her sex.

Darn tensed and shivered before laying herself down on the pallet. Desire rippled through Pthorn as his tongue pleasured her bud, and Darn arched her back, pulling him closer to her.

Her moans were the only encouragement Pthorn needed as he brought her to a climax again and again.

Finally, it seemed like she could take no more as Darn pushed him out from between her thighs and beckoned him to join her on the pallet. The tang of sweat and sex filled the air as the two embraced once more, body to body.

Passion.

Desire.

Lust.

All these emotions and more filled Pthorn as she guided him into the warmth of her sex.

Each movement, a page of a love letter written in a writhing dance of lust, building to a final crescendo within him, her moans bringing him closer to a pinnacle of passion.

Darn's back arched one last time, and Pthorn pulled her close as he spent himself with a final sigh. Her eyes danced as her lips curled into a beautiful smile, illuminated in the soft light.

That is how they slept that night, still entwined in each other's embrace as the lamp burned low.

34.
Why not Kesheir

The next day Pthorn awoke to the sound of a returning Fluorocor unsubtly making its way back into the shed. Darn was lying as naked as he was, curled up against him, underneath the white linen sheets. It was another one of the moments that Pthorn hoped he could take a mental snapshot of and store it away forever.

Darn didn't seem to have awoken entirely to the noise; instead, she stirred and snuggled up closer.

Fluorocor then did the dragon equivalent of clearing its throat by releasing a loud "Cliiiick" noise aimed directly towards the bed. Pthorn wasn't exactly sure what its end game was, but he was certain it didn't approve of the space in the bed being taken up by another person.

This much louder noise did result in Darn awakening. Instead of being a regular wild snarl, her hair had become another beast entirely. Pthorn was not sure how she was going to get that under control, even given a span of attention.

"Jealous type, aren't ya?" she said, slurring as she slowly transitioned to a more awakened state. The two pulled their legs up and made way for the slightly smaller hydrofluor to plonk itself across the end of the bed, leaving very little room.

After a few minutes, they gave up and got out of the bed. Pthorn crawled out first, picked up Darn's clothing, and gently placed it over her shoulders; regretfully watching her beautiful form disappear beneath the cloth. They then finished getting dressed for the day before leaving the slumbering beast to enjoy its limited space in the pallet.

Pthorn and Darn slipped through the door and into the fresh morning air. They moved through the alley before turning left to head north through the high-value markets lining the foreshore.

"So," Darn began while looking ahead. "Ya still haven't told me what happened after you left Northern Port. You were meant to be goin' into service with the priests, but here ya are washing dishes in a port of southern Matraketh."

Pthorn had tried to avoid the topic of his servitude to the Sect, hesitating to provide a response.

"I mean, you def'nit'ly dress weird enough to be working for 'em, but something doesn't add up," she added.

"It is a long story. I am not really sure where to start or how much I can tell you," Pthorn responded quietly.

"What? You think they might hear ya?" she said mockingly.

Pthorn didn't respond.

She quickly realised by Pthorn's silence that her response was precisely what Pthorn was concerned about. She let the question hang in the air, filling the void between them with a tension that could not be cleft by a sharpened blade.

"I can tell you about my journey to Portsworth?" he offered. "That may explain why you couldn't find me when you arrived."

Realising that she wouldn't get much more at this stage, Darn gestured for him to continue. As a comfort, she reached for his hand and held it gently.

Pthorn told her of the start of the journey, which consisted primarily of throwing up over the gunwale of the poop deck before learning nautical knots and being placed on cleaning duties. Then he told her of the calm that had befallen the sea, how that had led to rationing and tension aboard the Sea's Fury. Finally, he told her of the storm and the night of the attack from the sea monster that the crew had referred to as a kraken, how it had killed one of their crew. They were both silent as Pthorn considered whether to tell her of the moment he was to be thrown overboard and how this had marked the end of the attack and the storm.

"That explains a lot. You woulda arrived spans after I left Portsworth," she said as she slowed to look at some gleaming treasures that had distracted her and were laid out in the markets. Darn regathered her attention back to

Pthorn as they continued strolling, hand in hand, down the road.

"So I get you can't tell me anything that happened after you arrived here and what you have been doing for the last turn, but can you at least tell me how you came to be working here in Playton-on-Sea?"

Understandably the concept still baffled her, given the last time they had seen each other, he had been selected as Assier's Chosen One and sent to Matraketh to serve him as part of the clergy.

"That is also a very long story. I was given a job which involves crossing Matraketh and collecting things, mainly plants."

He looked Darn in the eyes; she looked even more curious than before he'd started explaining.

"Don't ask," he said before continuing. "As you might have guessed, I may have gotten a little sidetracked on my journey."

"So what you mean is, you didn't want to go back, so you ran away to be a kitchen hand?" she asked snidely.

"Not exactly. Let's just say that if 'They' knew about what I have been up to, I could be in a bit of trouble. I thought I would try to lay low for a while and take a break from specimen collection. I just turned left and kept walking until I got here."

"You were worried about them knowing about us talking. If ya did something so bad, wouldn't they already know?" she asked.

"That's what I am worried about. I have until four weeks after next turn's Assierium Festival to return, but I have barely started doing what I should be doing."

"Who says ya need t'go back?" she questioned. "Why not just run away. Start a life with me. We can cross the sea tomorrow, go to Kesheir, then Saulit, and travel around for the rest of our lives."

Pthorn chortled at the thought, but he couldn't tell her what the rest of his life looked like. He didn't know what happened at the end of the service of an Order-Master, but he suspected that he would not be allowed to live that long outside the Sect and would eventually be forced back into his Chosen place.

Those thoughts aside, Darn's proposition sounded like the perfect life.

"Where would we go first?" he asked, as though he had already decided to join her.

"Are you actually considering this?" she asked him hopefully. "Because I am serious. Come away with me."

Pthorn stopped and took a short time to really consider what he would do.

"Yes!" he replied. "But...."

A look of concern was painted across Darn's face as she contemplated the list of possible caveats attached to their plan.

"It may be a little difficult to convince a captain to let us on board with a hydrofluor. They would have heard stories of fire-breathing dragons spewing flames across the masts of ships and sinking them in the middle of the sea."

This time Darn was chuckling to herself, "well, that is where I come in. Ya see, not only did they teach me how to farmin' talk proper over the last turn, I have not been sitting on my arse doin' nothin'."

Pthorn was intrigued, but Darn offered no further explanation. He had no right to push her to explain herself, particularly given the little he had told her about his own exploits during the same time period.

They continued their day with no further talk of the past, only of their future and the various places they had heard of over the last turn. Due to his almost complete isolation, Pthorn had very little to add by way of landmarks and villages, but Darn had clearly spent quite some time amongst the travelling people. Recently, Pthorn had been able to talk to some of the patrons of 'The Ghotiman's Rod', and they had spoken mainly of trading routes and gossip on the road.

Darn spoke of far-off lands with caves that descended thousands of paces into the ground, with labyrinths of hidden treasures; this didn't really appeal to Pthorn, given his recent time spent inside a mountain. She also spoke of a red, hot sea of lava in central Saulit, an island with a mythical guardian beast from which no travellers return in Straulatos, and a forest in Kesheir that causes you to lose all memories once you enter. One of the less believable stories she had heard was of fae circles that could transport an unsuspecting traveller into another realm, slowing down time and trapping them.

Pthorn had some serious doubts about the last one, given what he now knew of theology; in particular, he questioned how anyone would know about it if everyone who visited became trapped and could not tell their tale.

The two had not developed much of a plan for their travels but settled on heading south across the Maitke Sea as Darn had earlier suggested. When they landed, they planned to follow the road and see where their adventure took them.

"I think it will be fun," Darn stated. "Just you, me, and an enormous acid-breathing hydrofluor on the open road."

Pthorn couldn't help but laugh.

"Well, hopefully he keeps his meals down to snacks for the next few days so we can pass him off as a pet clucken and put him in my knapsack."

"Three days," said Darn. "That is all I am giving you two, then we leave."

"And what about a ship?" Pthorn asked again. "You still haven't told me how you are getting around the issue of getting on a ship."

"I told you that is for me to know and for you to find out. Besides, why do ya think I am giving you three days? I don't exactly have one that will set sail on my command."

Pthorn thought better of joking about ways that she may have been able to influence a ship's captain and crew to take them on board. They were getting along very well, and they had shared a very intimate time the day before, but he couldn't be sure where the line between joking and insult sat.

"Anyway, I have to get back to The Rod. I don't think Glan could do without me for another day. You are welcome to come and sit in the bar," Pthorn offered.

"Maybe a little later; I have to go find me some seamen," replied Darn with a cheeky wink.

"I'm just gonna... you know," said Pthorn pointing awkwardly in the direction of the inn before cutting himself short and turning.

"I will see ya tonight," she called over to him when he had made it about ten paces away.

Pthorn waved back over his shoulder, not daring to turn and give away his blush.

Pthorn's shift at the inn came and went. It wasn't as busy as the night Darn had found her way into the corner booth. He spent the entire night working in the kitchen, cleaning used pint glasses, and prepping food for the next few days. Much like every other inn across Azarth, The Ghotiman's Rod had an Everlasting Pot on the boil, which was a thick broth with just about every type of food thrown into it, and was always kept simmering away. The flavours of the pot were a lasting remnant of meats and vegetables added many span ago. It was the cheapest meal you could buy on the road, and it was almost always served in a hollowed-out bread crust formed into a trencher.

Pthorn sliced up various root vegetables and a large hock of moog, which was all to be placed into the bubbling cauldron, along with a half-gallon of water and a few pints of beer. The smell of the Everlasting Pot was always in the kitchens, but adding the extra ingredients seemed to only make it more powerful tonight. Pthorn grabbed a trencher for himself after the raw ingredients had been simmering long enough to cook through and soften.

Once he had eaten his fill of the soup, he continued the rest of the food preparation. Slicing up the meat and vegetables in advance would save time on the nights Glan worked alone, and now that he was leaving, there would again be more work for Glan to do.

A feeling of dread entered into the pit of Pthorn's stomach; he hadn't thought about how he would break the news to his boss and landlord. Glan was used to people coming and going, but somehow it felt like he was letting him down.

As the night dragged on into the early morning hours, the dread did nothing to ease or subside. After the last few patrons had stumbled out of the front bar, either up to their accommodation at the inn or back out into the streets, Glan made his way into the kitchens.

Pthorn must have been wearing his thoughts on his robe.

"You look like you are hauling a beast on your back," the large man stated. "What is weighing you down, son?"

"Bad news… and good, I suppose," he began.

"When do you leave?" Glan asked, guessing the next part of the discussion by himself. Glan waited a few moments and leaned back on one of the wooden chopping benches. "It's okay, you know. The shed will be waiting for you if you return this way. I knew as soon as that young lass out there walked in and told me she was looking for you that it was only a matter of time."

Pthorn wasn't sure what to say and instead just settled for a simple "thank you" before excusing himself for the night.

"I will be here for a few more nights… if you still need me, that is," he said, turning back from the kitchen doorway.

"I would appreciate it," said Glan, pouring himself a trencher of the Everlasting Pot's bubbling broth.

When Pthorn returned to his cosy shed, he found that he was well accompanied. Darn was already asleep under the sheets of the sleeping pallet. Fluorocor either hadn't bothered to go out for the night or had returned early. The hydrofluor was already starting to lose some of its enormous size and was fitting more comfortably beside the sleeping pallet, curled up into a tight ball.

Pthorn stripped off his clothes and crawled in under the sheets. He shimmied over, trying not to disturb her sleep and failed.

She rolled over and manoeuvred her leg between his, pulling herself close to his body and placing her arm around him. They embraced and shared a long passionate kiss before falling asleep in each other's arms.

35.
Maitke Sea

The next three days passed quickly, and with very little preparation required, they were soon all ready to set sail across the Maitke Sea. Pthorn closed and latched the door behind them as they walked out for the last time into the warm glow of the Matraketh morning. It was almost like leaving home again after the many span he had spent working on waterproofing and making it his own refuge. He looked back, feeling almost a sense of loss, before returning to his travel party.

As he walked over to join them, Pthorn noted that Fluorocor had clearly stuck to its diet of no large beasts and minimal midnight snacks after the chastising Pthorn had given a few days past. The hydrofluor was now no taller than Pthorn's waist when standing normally. Pthorn considered this a far more acceptable size for travelling aboard a ship; hopefully, it wouldn't cause too much fear or superstition amongst the crew.

To avoid the entire issue of sea travel, Pthorn had considered trying to saddle up the beast for both himself and Darn, but they were in no hurry, and if there was a slower but safer option to get them across the sea, he would take that any day. His experimental riding of Fluorocor had been fun for the very short period it took to take off and land, but not something he wanted to rely on for long-distance travel, particularly not with two people. He wasn't even sure how two could ride astride the beast without interfering with its wings.

After a few days of sunshine, the ground down the alleyway had dried out, leaving deep ruts more treacherous than the mud that had caused them. The three walked carefully out and down to the main road before Darn led them to the more affluent markets.

"How did you manage to find a jewellery trader to take us across?" Pthorn asked, in a state of shock. He had expected entirely for them to turn right towards the ghoti markets and trawlers.

"Oh, just you wait!" she said. "You are gonna love our boat."

Darn sounded almost excited at the prospect, and Pthorn began to envisage another ship similar in size to that which carried him across the seas to Matraketh in the first place. He knew, however, that ships of that size would never trade across the inland sea. The biggest he had seen docked in Playton-on-Sea was half the size of the Sea's Fury.

"Ship," Pthorn corrected. "Don't go calling them boats to the merchant sailors!"

Darn didn't argue and continued leading them to a large vendor's stall, which was almost entirely empty; evidently, they had been packing up their wares for another supply run or to set up elsewhere. Darn approached, and from a short distance away, she stuck up her middle finger as a friendly gesture. This was almost immediately returned, followed by the richly adorned man opening his arms to her in welcome.

"Come, come, come," he said, ushering them towards the dock. "Everything is ready for you."

Pthorn could not believe his eyes. The ship was not only one of the largest anchored at the port, but it was also one of the most delicately carved. Where most ships had tarred boards on the upper levels of their hulls, this ship had stained hardwood which had been carved into the shape of various sea life and beautiful sirens. The bowsprit protruding from the front of the vessel was shaped like a naked siren riding a large leaping ghoti.

Pthorn turned to his very smug-looking travel partner and then back to the ship's merchant captain. "And just what did this young lady offer you in return for this trip?"

Both the captain and Darn laughed between themselves. Clearly, Darn had told the man not to divulge that information to keep Pthorn guessing.

Instead of answering the question, the man simply turned towards his proud ship and called loudly, "you had better get aboard if you don't want to be left behind." Before stopping for a final word of warning, "you had best stay seated in the open water; it can get a little choppy out there in the middle."

Pthorn wasn't really sure what he meant but made to follow him before he was stopped in his tracks by Darn.

"Where are you going, silly?" she asked, pointing down at the bobbing sea below.

Down below the level of the dock sat something that Pthorn had not seen until now. Tethered to the aft of the ship was a small boat, not ten paces long by three paces wide on a good day.

"You have got to be farmin' kidding me!" Pthorn exclaimed, looking around at a widely grinning Darn. "What did you agree to?"

"Well, no one was happy about having a dragon aboard their ships, and that friendly captain said he had a boat that needed towing. He said he needed a small crew to bail it out during storms, or something, so he said we could do that for 'im," Darn said excitedly, clearly enjoying herself while making Pthorn uncomfortable.

Pthorn put on his best deadpan face with a look of complete indifference. "I hate you," he said before turning back towards the tiny boat and climbing down the rungs of the rotting ladder which led to the water's edge.

"No, you don't," she called after him. "Besides, I will make it up to you when we get to Kesheir. I've got another surprise."

"Oh, Assier Almighty, no!" exclaimed an exasperated Pthorn. "If your surprises are anything like this, don't bother."

"Oh, don't be dramatic," she replied, grinning ear to ear. "Trust me, you are gonna love this one."

Once they were settled into the boat, Fluorocor spread its wings, flew over to meet them, and landed gently in the centre of the hull.

"All aboard?" came the call from the gunwale of the main ship.

"All aboard!" Pthorn and Darn replied in unison.

"Cliiiick," came the response from Fluorocor, just in case their response had somehow gone unheard.

The start of the journey was almost as pleasant as Pthorn had imagined once he knew he was going into open waters aboard a tender craft. As the ship pulled away from the ports, it tugged furiously at the rope pulling the tender behind it. Remaining seated was all they could do to stay aboard as each tug threatened to lurch them over and into the churning waters of the ship's wake.

As the port of Playton-on-Sea became a distant smudge on the horizon, they quickly realised one of the other downsides to being positioned directly below the aft of the ship, and that was the location of the poop deck.

The ship's crew members saw an opportunity for sport, namely aiming one's waste at the wandering tender's occupants. Thankfully, up to this point, the small boat seemed to be out of range of solids, but it wasn't always sea spray that washed across them, nor did that stop the smell from wafting over them.

It wasn't all bad, though; as the sun began to set over the horizon, it cast a bright orange-purple hue across the sky. Pthorn and Darn laid back in the aft of the small boat, holding each other in their arms and looking up towards the sky. The sea was relatively calm as the sun set as they looked out across the water.

Fluorocor looked out over the horizon with its head resting gently on the side of the boat before finally getting bored and began trying to stand up.

"Whoa, whoa, whoa," called out Pthorn as the boat rocked violently from one side to the other. "What exactly do you think you are doing?"

The hydrofluor screeched a loud click as it leapt, causing the boat to list violently to one side. Fluorocor spread its wings and took off, flying in large arcs around the main ship and the small boat.

There were a few calls of concern and threats thrown from the ship's deck and a few whoops of awe as it circled.

Every so often, Fluorocor would gain elevation, only to freefall dive down to the water's surface and pluck a ghoti from below. This became a sport for the black beast, who continued until well after the sun had set below the horizon. While Fluorocor feasted on unsuspecting ghoti, Pthorn and Darn nibbled at the small supply of bread and cheese they had stocked up before leaving Playton-on-Sea. They would restock at the other end, so they only packed what they needed.

Once the sun was down, the only light was cast from the lamps aboard the ship, which did little to illuminate the small boat. Instead of continuing to sit in the dark, Pthorn called Fluorocor back down to the tender, and they settled in for the night under a blanket they had found tucked under their seats.

That night sleep was hard to come by as the boat was rocked by the wake of the large ship causing water to cascade over the side.

By the time the shores of Kesheir came into view, Pthorn was feeling very weary and ready for some firm soil beneath his feet. The slapping of the water and the rocking of the waves weren't even almost the worst part of their journey across the Maitke Sea. The sun had been reflecting off the crystal clear water for days, turning his and Darn's skin a bright shade of pink. They had spent much of their days covering themselves using the sheets from the tender to keep the beating rays off their skin. They both had deep, olive skin from growing up in Straulatos, but it was no match for the wrath of the sun on the water.

They had also become a refuge for more than a few luftun who had decided that flying was too much effort. The flying pests were generally quickly shooed away upon the return of Fluorocor, who regularly went off for flights over the water to stretch its wings. That hadn't stopped the collection of droppings from accumulating over the bow of the small boat.

Speaking of bodily waste, the crew had thankfully given up on their game of aiming their own waste at their boat after the first two days. They still regularly used the poop deck, as would be expected, but they tended to at least give them the courtesy of moving to the other side of the ship and downwind.

The sun was just nearing its highest point in the sky as the merchant ship docked at the port on the northern shores of Kesheir. The crew had already cleared customs and began unloading the vessel before someone remembered that they were bobbing out to sea.

"Oi! Remember us!" Pthorn had called for what seemed like an eternity before he was finally heard.

One of the crew threw down a length of rope which Pthorn tied onto the tow rope before several of the crew pulled them ashore.

Fluorocor alighted in its usual fashion, in a flap of giant wings, while Pthorn helped Darn out of the bobbing tender and onto the rotting wooden ladder slung over the edge of the dock. The ladder was slick with lichen on the lower levels and sharp sea life shells around halfway up. Once Darn had reached the top, Pthorn threw his knapsack onto his back and made the journey up the rungs himself.

Once at the top, they both stood and surveyed the area. It was almost like looking in a mirror of Playton-on-Sea; merchant stalls were set up along the foreshore, and businesses lined the far side of the road. Pthorn caught himself looking for The Ghotiman's Rod down the road before realising that an inn was precisely what they needed.

"I think we find somewhere to stay here for a few days. At least until we stop wobbling on our feet and our skin changes colour again," Pthorn suggested.

"Agreed," said Darn nodding furiously. "I'm starting to think that captain should have paid us!"

The two laughed and started to make their way through the town.

"So what should we do with our walking leather boot over there while we stay at an inn?" Darn joked.

Fluorocor turned its head to stare at her, narrowing its slitted eyes. The hydrofluor seemed to have an excellent understanding of their conversations but wasn't particularly well-versed in humour.

Pthorn turned to comfort it. "Easy there, she is just joking," he said soothingly while patting it just behind the wing. "You really shouldn't wind Fluorocor up; you might just end up in a pool of acid."

Fluorocor added a very definite "Cliiiick" to support this argument.

"Oh, lighten up; I wouldn't turn you into a boot…" she paused for a few moments in consideration before continuing, "You would make a much better oil cloak."

The group of weary travellers decided on a shabby-looking inn called The Crusty Claw, situated on one of the back streets of the village. The inn was much smaller than The Ghotiman's Rod and had no bar or bistro attached. It was just a single-story accommodation with a few rooms for travelling merchants who were down on their luck or coin.

Pthorn began to realise the hospitality he received back in Maarts would be a unique experience. Places like this one off the main road tended to be more accepting of oddities like acid-breathing dragons, but the innkeeper still had stipulations regarding arrangements. No one else seemed to believe that Fluorocor was unable to produce great balls of fire on command, or that it was unlikely to simply gobble up all of the inn's visitors during the night. Still, at least he allowed them all to sleep in one room, even if it was an empty storeroom. At the end of the day, a roof over their head and a makeshift straw pallet were better than a night on the road or under the stars in a village.

Before they could sleep on the pallet, Pthorn had to assemble it himself. The storeroom had been used to store hay for the pallets inside The Crusty Claw as loosely tied bales. There were a few bales stacked in the corner and a number of half bales strewn across the floor. Using the string hanging from them, he knotted a dozen tufts together and laid them down on the dirt floor. There was no room for Fluorocor, but the hydrofluor didn't seem too put out about the arrangement.

As soon as their heads hit the hay, they were all lost in sleep. For the first time in over a span, the floor beneath them didn't rock from side to side, and they were completely dry.

36.
Knapsacking in Kesheir

The next morning they all awoke feeling somewhat closer to human than they had for the last span, although there was a crick in Pthorn's back that wouldn't remove itself with any level of persuasion. They all made their way out of the storeroom and into the morning air to enjoy their first day in Kesheir.

"So, did the captain mention which port he dropped us off at?" Pthorn asked Darn as he looked around for vendors who looked like they might have been cooking breakfast.

"I think 'e said it was called, Loutin or somethin'. But maybe 'e was jus' talking about what 'e was gonna do when 'e got 'ere," she laughed aloud to her own joke, reverting to her old farm tongue and accentuating her twang.

"You know you lose your refined accent when you try to make a funny," Pthorn noted.

"What? Do ya have a problem with ma farmin' accent?" She asked, really stressing the latter half of the sentence.

"Not at all," he replied, "just making an observation."

"Good, or else I might have had to give up speakin' proper like," she said, laughing at herself again before continuing. "Now, how about we find where that fried onk smell is coming from."

The three of them walked down the road until they found the source of the smell that had wafted in their direction. There was a young man with bright red hair and a very scraggly looking attempt at a beard, cooking up rashers of onk meat on a heavy cast skillet over a fire. As they approached, the smell made Pthorn's mouth water.

The man filled a bread trencher with the fried onk, and crunchy fried vegetables, for each of them, before tossing a rasher over to Fluorocor, who caught it immediately in mid-air.

Pthorn paid him the four broan he was due and threw in an extra as appreciation. This act seemed to guilt the vendor into engaging in small talk.

"So where are you all headed to?" he asked, making conversation.

"Wherever the wind blows us," Darn replied before asking, "why, do you have some suggestions for us?"

"Not really; I just thought you might have been headed to the Ayefyl Castle, you know, with him dressed like that and all," he said, pointing at Pthorn.

Darn turned and looked at the grey robes he was wearing before turning back to the man.

"And why do you think we might be interested…" she prompted.

"It is some sort of pilgrimage that priests do around here. They come in from Matraketh and visit the castle. There is something about its history with Aiel or something. Who knows, really?" he said, shrugging his shoulders.

Pthorn and Darn looked at each other to see what the other was thinking.

"Why not," Pthorn said, throwing his hands in the air indifferently. "We have no other plans. Let's go see a castle."

"Where is it?" asked Darn. "We aren't exactly from around here."

"Just follow this road south," said the young man pointing. "After about a span, you will come to a crossroads. Turn west and follow the road towards Neith for a few days; you won't miss the castle."

The couple thanked him again for the food and his advice before turning away.

Fluorocor had long since finished his breakfast, but they walked away, slowly nibbling at their crusty trenchers, enjoying the sweet and smoky flavours of the onk.

"Hey," the man called after them again. "Since when do priests travel with women and dragons, and don't they usually wear white?"

Pthorn stalled for a moment but didn't turn back around.

"Who said I was a priest?"

Before leaving the town of Loutin, Pthorn suggested that they do a pass of the markets to see if there was anything else they could get for their travels. After being on the road for a number of span, he knew the value of carrying enough food and clean water. After the first few stalls, they had already stocked up on an array of easily transported foods like hard cheese and sausage, with some hardtack in case of emergencies.

"Let's see if they have any salted nuts up further," Pthorn suggested, remembering the markets from Maarts back in Matraketh.

Fluorocor let out a loud, clicking screech.

"Fine!" said Pthorn sounding overly drawn out. "And maybe a soup bone or two for the leathery onk over here."

Darn laughed and led the way through the throng of people. Cutting your way through crowds wasn't too onerous when you were being followed by a large dragon; in fact, the streets seemed to clear themselves quite well as people kept their distance.

After a few moments, Pthorn found himself pulled towards a vendor selling high-class clothing. The stall was filled with fine suits and boots buffed to a high shine. They were stunning pieces of clothing, but they were not what caught his eye. Sitting atop a wooden mannequin, wearing a well-pressed black and white suit, was a hat. Not just any hat, but what seemed to be an almost perfectly identical replacement to the one he was forced to abandon back in Falanar.

Darn was completely oblivious to his sudden departure and had continued walking down the street.

"Found summit you like there?" came the cry from the well-dressed merchant seated against the foreshore. "That there suit would be a fine replacement for your, um... well, let's just say you would look a hundred broan."

Pthorn was initially startled but quickly regained his composure, ignoring the vendor's suggestion.

"How much for the hat?" he asked.

The merchant considered for a few moments, playing with the thin moustache which lined his upper lip.

"That there is the finest wool, what that they can get from a baahti. I couldn't let that go for any less than forty broan. They only get wool like that in the far north of Matraketh up high in them there mountains."

Pthorn remembered the advice he had received back in Portsworth from the seemingly honest Arnult, who had told him that ten broan could buy you anything you wanted.

"Ten broan or I'm walking," he replied in the most matter-of-factly voice he could muster up at a moment's notice. "Take it or leave it."

"Well, don't you drive a hard bargain?" said the merchant, whose hand had returned to its previous position atop his mouth before seeing Fluorocor standing behind Pthorn. "I see you have spent some time around us portslingers. What about a swap for your friend over there?"

This time Pthorn could not control his laughter at all. "Not only is it not for sale, but you would also be a late-night snack! Final offer of fifteen broan."

"Fine!" replied the beaten salesman. "But don't expect to get a box for it."

"Not needed," he said as he fished the notes out of his purse and handed them over.

Pthorn grabbed the hat off the top of the mannequin and flicked it into the air before topping his head with it. It felt good to have it back on his head again, like something had been missing.

Pthorn started in the direction they had been travelling to locate Darn. As he took his first step, he found his path almost immediately blocked by her form.

"Really?" she questioned in a playful, accusative manner. "You ditch me to buy yourself a hat, and just what did you get me?"

Oops, thought Pthorn to himself.

He had never believed himself to understand women, but he knew this much at least; when courting a young lady, gifts are always appreciated.

"I was just coming to find you so I could find just the thing in your size."

"Ah huh, and just what were you looking to get me then?" she asked, completely disbelieving his on-the-spot lie.

Pthorn turned and attempted to put his hand on the first lady's garment he could find in the stall. Unfortunately, what he came up with was a bright red neck scarf.

"Yes, how could you possibly not guess my size," she laughed before looking a little closer at it. "I'd love it, thank you!"

There was no going back at this point, Pthorn was well committed to his unbelievable lie, and there was nothing else for it. He returned to the merchant who had sold him the hat and paid a full twenty broan for the scarf. It was high priests way robbery and astronomically above the going rate, but he didn't want to seem too cheap. That said, he was sure that Darn would be the last person on Azarth who would truly care about the cost of gifts and clothing.

Darn picked up the scarf and wrapped it around her slender neck, letting the curls of her hair fall over the back. Pthorn reached up to help adjust a lock of hair that had become entangled. Their eyes met as his hand brushed the nape of her neck.

"Beautiful," he said as they continued to look into each other's eyes.

Their moment was ruined once again by the vocalisation of an impatient hydrofluor.

"Cliiiick!"

The two broke their gaze from one another, and instead, Pthorn took Darn's hand in his own.

"Did you find the nuts?" he enquired as they walked back the way they came.

"Yep!" she said, "and he said they were covered in the finest salt dried from the Maitke Sea."

"What makes it the finest salt?" Pthorn enquired, guessing that she was mocking the vendor.

"Well, my guess is that it has less ghoti shit in it than other salts."

They both laughed aloud as they continued to walk towards the road to exit Loutin, and Darn popped a few nuts into her mouth.

By the time the sun had begun to set, they had just made it to the first waystop. Even with the longer days closer to the Equis of Azarth, they had wasted too much of their morning in the markets. Tonight would be the first night they had all spent on the road.

Unlike most roadside stops in Matraketh, this waystop was not surrounded by a copse of trees. Instead, it was a dirt clearing surrounded by fields of crops. Across the horizon, tufts of brownish-yellow yaln swayed in the breeze. The stems stood waist tall from the ground and were topped with tiny blue florets. The sight of it brought back memories of the farm.

Pthorn first thought about how his father would have sown and reaped this year's crop without him to steer the mant and plough; he wasn't proud of it, but he secretly hoped the sad man was struggling without him. He then thought of his mother; tears began to well up in his eyes. They had passed fields upon fields of crops over the last day, but it wasn't until they stopped here that the realisation set in that he missed his mother.

Pthorn instinctively turned from Darn and made to move away to hide the shame. He hadn't cried the day he left or the days following his departure.

Why now? He thought to himself.

Pthorn made an effort to recompose himself before asking, "could you please look around for some deadwood for the fire. The drier, the better; it will smoke less."

He stopped talking before he had to sniff and set himself to work on the propped bedroll he had come to rely on during his travels.

Fluorocor padded over and nuzzled up to him.

"Thank you," Pthorn said. "Now, is there any chance you can find us some dinner... and remember, dead, not dissolved!"

Fluorocor clicked loudly in agreement before stretching its wings and taking to the air.

By the time Pthorn had finished erecting the bedroll, Darn was just returning with a bundle of sticks under one of her arms and a large log under the other. Pthorn wondered how she had managed to pick them all up without them falling into a large heap.

When she got to the fire ring nearest the bedroll, she let them tumble to the ground before releasing an exasperated sigh.

"Gave yourself the easy job didn't ya?" she called to him mockingly as he walked over.

"Alright, next time, you can set up the bedroll," he joked in return before setting to work creating the fire.

He began by placing the log into the centre and building the sticks around it. Without even thinking about his audience, Pthorn reached into the sticks and began the Combustion.

The normally quick-to-words Darn was utterly speechless as he realised his faux pas. He turned to find her mouth agape, and her hands held out in front of her in question.

ASSIER DAMMIT! He screamed internally.

"How did, I mean, what did you… umm," she stammered before finding her words in their more usual eloquent form. "What in the farmin' name of the Almighty Assier's arse was that!"

Pthorn knew at that moment there would be no more hiding himself away from her. To damnation with propriety and the sanctity of the Sect.

"You might want to sit down and get some snacks," he offered, extending his hand towards the long sitting log which sat by the fire. "It is a long story."

Once Pthorn started talking about the Sect, the Order-Masters and his fellow Elects, he could not bring himself to stop. Darn sat with her mouth agape for the entire retelling, not risking a sound to interrupt his story.

"So that makes me the apprentice to the God of Death, I suppose," Pthorn concluded his story.

Darn sat in silence for what seemed like an eternity, her mouth gaping like the imitation of a ghoti.

Finally, she spoke up, "well, now I can see why you weren't sure about leaving Matraketh. Why were you travelling anyway?"

"As part of becoming an Order-Master, we have to study all these different plants and animals. Hold on a moment…" he said as he got up and retrieved his knapsack from within the bedroll.

When he returned, he produced the few samples that he had collected during his first few span of travel.

"This one," he said, pointing to the blue balls, "can kill you with almost no way of detecting it. Whereas this one…" holding up the banded bark Malinta Palm bark, "will save you from it… just don't eat it first."

"Right," she said, still looking shell-shocked.

"This glowing sporio will give you visions before it kills you," he added before picking up the long-dead orbites. He had intended to kill the orbites peacefully but had instead forgotten about them, and they had likely died of asphyxiation within the vial.

"Mutated orbite?" he said, offering her the vial.

His offer was quickly met with a recoil of her body and a slap across his wrist. Pthorn was lucky to keep a hold of the vial, preventing it from scuttling across the ground and potentially shattering into a million pieces.

"As you can see, I didn't get too far into collecting before I got distracted by… um, other things."

Darn was still way too stunned to question what those other things may have been.

The rest of their night had been spent in silence, with Darn digesting Pthorn's story. There was no fear of him or recoil at his touch, except while holding ten-legged critters, but while he knew she believed him, he suspected that she could not bring herself to completely understand what she had heard.

Fluorocor returned briefly to deliver them some sort of small creature but took off again almost immediately. The creature may have been considered cute and fluffy prior to its evisceration at the hands, or more accurately maw, of the hydrofluor, but in its current state, it looked less appetising.

Not long after he had finished explaining everything about the Sect, leaving out the details of his wayward necromancy adventures, they had retired for the night, with the disembowelled creature remaining uneaten by the fireside.

37.
The Castle

As predicted by the vendor back in Loutin, Pthorn, Darn, and Fluorocor reached the crossroads after eight days on the road. The crossroads itself had clearly become a local icon for the travelling psychopath. It was artistic in its composition but almost without any cohesion of design; its construction had likely been a result of the hands of hundreds of passers-by. Animal bones from various species were stacked high around all four corners forming a wall demarking the road's edge. Limb bones were stacked primarily at the base, with skulls placed precariously on the top as capping. It looked like some time ago someone had put some time into the arrangement before other travellers had added to it, as the bottom almost seemed neatly arranged.

Old stone plaques were inset into the lower section of the bone arrangement indicating with an arrow the nearest towns in each direction. To the east, the plaque named a town called Sturn, south was Gnuth, and their destination to the west was Neith.

They were only a few paces down the road before Pthorn and Darn stopped in the middle of the road, distracted by a sound behind them.

They both turned to find Fluorocor treating the bone arrangement as a personal buffet.

"Hey!" called Pthorn. "Leave the bones alone!" before turning back to continue walking.

Fluorocor took minimal notice of the chastising, swallowed down the bone it was already chomping on and grabbed another for the road, crunching away loudly as it walked.

Pthorn just shook his head as they set off down the road.

A day later, they arrived in the village of Neith, with their arrival marked by the towering form of the Ayefyl Castle. To call it a village was probably giving it too much credit. It was almost entirely uninhabited for the most part. The village had positioned itself as a permanent waystop for tourists who were coming to visit the castle. There was little else except a large inn set just before the entrance of the looming castle. It was still early in the day when they arrived, so they decided not to check into the inn and instead continued to walk up to the castle itself for a look.

The road leading up to the castle wended its way around a moat which encircled the curtain wall. As they approached the front of the building, the walls rose up high in front of them, topped with castellations and turrets. The first thing Pthorn noticed was a prominent symbol carved into the stone just above the chain-lowered draw bridge.

Pthorn pointed up at it. "Do you see that symbol?" he asked Darn.

Darn nodded. "It is the four-pointed star of Aiel, isn't it? Why does it look all weird?"

"That is the same symbol that they use to represent the Sect. It is similar to the four-pointed star of Aiel, but all the angles are wrong."

Pthorn was not sure what the presence of the symbol meant for the castle and its history. One thing was for sure, he was definitely interested in discovering more.

Pthorn turned to Fluorocor, who was bringing up the rear. "You go off and find yourself something to eat. Just don't go destroying anything," he said dismissively. The last thing he needed was for Fluorocor to dissolve some piece of priceless ancient history or knock over a centuries-old vase fired by the Singular itself.

The hydrofluor stretched its wings and took off into the sky. After travelling for the last span and not hunting, it had shrunk back down to about the size that Pthorn had found it back on the road in Matraketh. Pthorn suspected that soon they would wake up again with a very large, sleepy, and slow-moving beast beside their tent following a late-night snack on a tasty moog.

As long as it does it while we are staying somewhere for a span and not travelling on the road, that is fine, Pthorn thought to himself.

Once Fluorocor had gone, they crossed the drawbridge, over the dry moat, and into the castle's central tower. It was clear that the building had not been inhabited for a very long time. While many of the heavy hardwood beams remained in place, a yawning void opened up above them. No roof remained in this section of the castle, and the floor was littered with filth and debris. Tourist traffic had gone some way to wearing a path through the worst of it, but plenty of organic rot remained.

"Urgh, that smell!" exclaimed Darn as they made their way into the centre of the main foyer. "You could have warned me," she joked.

Pthorn pulled an ugly face back at her with his tongue halfway out before continuing to investigate the room. There wasn't much to see. The floor was uneven flagstone, which was some shade of grey beneath the filth; in fact, the overwhelming grey seemed to be a key theme of the room. The walls were bare, and the stone was losing its mortar in more places than not.

Pthorn had noted from the outside that the castle was shaped as a large 'L', with the entrance they were standing in forming the short tail. He led Darn up the staircase to the left-hand side of the room and up to the first level. A dilapidated-looking handrail provided some barrier along the side of the stairs and across the balcony, which overlooked the foyer. Once they reached the top, they turned left and headed through the castle hall. Doorways stood on either side, lining the walls of the enormous hall leading to various wings and towers.

"There is still just so much more to explore here," said Darn excitedly before asking, "do you think there is anything still here to do with the Sect?"

"I dunno," Pthorn responded, shrugging. "If there is, it is likely to be well hidden...."

Pthorn trailed off as he looked through one of the doorways and noticed the ornate stained glass windows still largely unbroken. Light filtered through, casting bright colours across the grey room, illuminating the depicted forms. The colours formed part of a sunburst radiating from some celestial being, presumably the Singular itself. In the centre of the glass was something rarely seen. It looked like obsidian had been inset into the lead form to show a cloaked figure standing in silhouette to the bright array of colours. Pthorn immediately knew who the depiction was.

"Darn," he called and gestured for her to look. "Seem familiar?"

Darn walked over to join him at his side, taking in the details of the intricate artwork in the window. "Is that you?" she asked.

"Kinda," he replied. "It is someone from the Order of Death. Who knows how many years ago they stayed here. I just don't understand. Gular, the holy man, had told me they had lived in the mountains since the early days of Azarth. This castle is old, but not that old."

"And why is it only Death?" she added.

Pthorn turned to look through another room and another before coming to the same conclusion. This castle was designed for one order and one order only; Death.

Hundreds of reasons the castle could exist ran through Pthorn's mind.

Maybe he had been expelled from the order and made his own for a generation, perhaps one of the Order-Masters of Death just liked to work alone, or maybe every order has its own castle somewhere.

There were many possible reasons, each more curious than the next and no less plausible. Having already made the decision to, at the very least temporarily, leave the Sect Pthorn was under no time constraints to investigate and unravel the puzzle.

For the next few hours, the two just walked from room to room, taking in any details they could. Looking for any other signs of the Sect's presence, or more specifically, Death. They passed several other travellers who had also heard about the castle and had come to do some sightseeing. This even included a priest who eyed Pthorn's grey robes and white-banded black hat curiously but withheld comment.

After an exhaustive search, they had done nothing more than confirm their initial suspicions that this was home to a member of the Order of Death at some time in the last few centuries. Finally, the sun was beginning to set, resulting in the castle quickly becoming pitch black. They decided to make their way to check into the inn.

Upon their arrival, they immediately regretted not checking in when they arrived in Neith. A large travelling group had come just before them taking up the last of the rooms and leaving them with no choice but to continue camping in their pitched bedroll. Pthorn didn't mind too much, but he suspected Darn was missing the comforts of a warm pallet with soft, laundered sheets.

No room at the inn, thankfully, did not preclude the ability to eat dinner in the bar area. Given their rations for the last span, they were more than happy to tuck into the hot side of baahti and root vegetables served by the kitchens.

While they ate, Pthorn placed his hand over Darn's; this was as close to a romantic dinner as they'd had since the night they reunited. Pthorn gave her a smile.

"Thank you," he said.

"For what?" she asked, sounding genuinely curious.

"For this, for everything, I guess... I don't know, I am happy,"

Pthorn was still trying to work out exactly what the feelings were that he could feel inside. He had never been one for emotion, but ever since Darn had found her way into his life, it was as though something inside of him had become unlocked.

He had left his family, home, and everything familiar to him without so much as a tear. Perhaps he had thought himself cold and distant from emotion. Spending time with Darn seemed to have been proving him wrong. It wasn't just her beauty; by most people's standards, she probably still seemed like a plain farm girl. There was something else, something that he hadn't found with anyone else.

He had seen beautiful girls. One had even stripped completely naked before him and slept beside him. But none of them had made him feel like there was anything more to life than putting one foot in front of the other.

"Thank you, too," she responded, smiling and grasping his hand. "For the same."

They finished their dinner hand in hand before making their way outside to set up the bedroll in the faint glow of the inn's external lanterns. Once again, Fluorocor hadn't seen fit to arrive before they retired for the night.

The following day they awoke to the confirmation of Pthorn's prediction. Fluorocor had indeed seen this stop as a perfect excuse to devour something that was a magnitude in size greater than itself. It had barely been a few hours, and the hydrofluor had already grown over the size of the erected bedroll. Pthorn wasn't too concerned about leaving the sleeping beast to lie beside the bedroll; he knew that if anyone tried to do anything to attack or steal it, they would soon become the next victim of its gaping jaws and acid spray.

Pthorn took Darn's hand in his own as they made their way to the castle via the inn for a spot of breakfast.

They had already searched the castle as far as they could visually, but as he lay awake last night thinking about the meaning of the windows.

If I was Tom, how would I have built the castle?

Maybe it was because deep down he was more alike to Tom than he would like to admit, but soon enough, the thought came to his mind, *there has to be a dungeon or hidden room in that castle.*

He then spent most of the next few hours while Darn snuggled up to his body, thinking of ways to locate a hidden room. Again the thought came unbidden; *if you are the Order-Master of Death, you would hide it in a way that only someone from that order could find and access.* That would mean using his powers to Manipulate something for access.

His thought process had not progressed any further than that, and he still didn't know exactly where the entryway to any secret lair could be hiding; that would be today's job. That job was made more difficult by the throng of people who arrived to sightsee through the castle, the ones who had taken up all of the spaces at the inn.

As they walked down the large hall, Pthorn had an idea. He led Darn into one of the farthest rooms in the back corner of the castle, away from the bulk of the tourists.

"Could you please guard the door?" he asked her politely. "Just tell anyone that comes up this far to go away."

Darn moved her way to the door, keeping one eye for intruders and another on what Pthorn was doing.

Pthorn closed his eyes and held his arms out in front of him. Normally, he would have an object, or animal, directly in front of him to focus on and reach into; this time, he was searching.

He wasn't sure whether this would work or even what he was searching for. He felt his way through the castle, identifying the moving people throughout the castle by their strong lifeforms. He tried to filter these out in his mind and focus more below the ground level.

Within the stone beneath his feet, there was no life to speak of, nothing more than the odd fungus and micro-organism.

He needed to try something different, like when he was performing Combustion. When performing Combustion, the object is no longer alive but was alive at some point in time and capable of decomposition and decay. He relaxed his mind and began searching the depths below him for broad signals of decay.

It was then he could feel almost a pull. It wasn't physical, but he could feel the direction of a strong force of decay and death below him.

Using the pull as a guide, he held on to the loose tether and began to walk down the hall back towards the balcony, trying to feel the moment when the pull changed direction, which would indicate the source was directly below him.

Almost three-quarters of the way down the hall, the pull did just that. He knew that what he was searching for was right there.

"It is around here somewhere," he announced to Darn quietly. "Help me look. It might be a trap door or some sort of secret entrance."

They both looked around the immediate area, feeling between the stone where mortar would have once filled the gap. After searching the area of ten paces in each direction, they were about to give up hope.

"Do you reckon it might be under the stairs?" Darn asked.

"Of course," said Pthorn, and they raced out onto the balcony and down the stairs into the main foyer area.

Once again, they both set their efforts to feeling around the stone, their hopes ignited by the obviousness of the solution. Once again, they came up with no entrance that they could see. Pthorn was still holding on to the pulling tether and could feel the source was almost straight in front of him.

He let the tether fall away and allowed himself to slide to the floor, immediately regretting the decision as he landed in the rot.

Once again, it was Darn who came up with another idea. "Try your thing again on the wall. Maybe there is a latch or something only you can see," she said as she turned to lean up against the wall.

At this point, anything was worth a try.

Pthorn had barely even begun to focus his energy on the solid wall in front of him when it started to swing open under the weight of Darn's shoulders pushing on the wall. She almost fell over but managed to regain her balance.

It was dark as pitch, but Pthorn knew he had found exactly what he was looking for the moment the small amount of light washed into the corner of the room.

38.

Death's Lair

Pthorn quickly ignited one of the damp-light wall sconce torches inside the chamber before swinging the stone door shut behind them. He didn't want any unwelcome company joining them in their discovery. Once the door was shut, Pthorn made his way through the room, igniting four more damp-light torches to wash the inside of Death's Lair in cool white light.

It became immediately apparent what it was that had pulled him into the room. Glass-faced display cases entombed the mummified remains of humans long dead. The skin of the corpses was pulled tight across the skeletons and looked as dry as parchment. There were four cases in total, each with a plaque stating the region of origin; Matraketh, Saulit, Kesheir, and Straulatos.

None of the cadavers had eyes, and nothing remained of their soft identifying features; the chasms of their eye pits just stared into the wall behind him. As far as Pthorn could tell, they all looked completely identical apart from two of the bodies being notably wider in the hips; based on his recently expanded knowledge of biology, Pthorn deduced those two, from the regions of Matraketh and Kesheir, were both females. Pthorn was infinitely curious and wanted to study the bodies in more detail; back in the Sect, he had to limit his studies to diagrams in books and the biological studies of animals.

Pthorn turned to look at Darn, who was making a pretty solid impression of the mummies; her eyes wide open and mouth agape in shock. This was like nothing she had ever seen before, and Pthorn wasn't sure she wanted to see it.

Dust motes were illuminated as they floated through the stale air, swirling as Pthorn made his way through the room towards Darn whilst also taking it all in; he placed a hand on her shoulders to show some support and reassurance. The room was much like the laboratories back in the Sect; book cabinets and specimen shelves lined the left-hand wall. A writing desk was positioned next to the corpses on display, with an elevated workbench to the left of it. Old, fragile, yellowed parchments were strewn across both with no hint of organisation. A couple of old leather-bound books were also sitting on the writing desk.

Once Pthorn had calmed Darn down enough to progress further into the room, they approached the far end, which was bathed in shadows. It slowly came into view as Pthorn ignited more damp-light torches. Darn continued to follow him in a state of shell-shocked silence.

Towards the rear of the castle's floorplan, they found living quarters with a mouldy sleeping pallet and straw, which had rotted away to almost nothing. Further on still was a small kitchenette consisting primarily of a range ducted through the ceiling and a stone food preparation bench. There was no cold store or any store at all, for that matter. Pthorn wondered what the previous occupants had done to keep food in the past; perhaps the upstairs castle had a working kitchen at the time, and they would send food down regularly.

Pthorn was inspecting the inside of the range's grate when Darn finally found her voice. "Do ya think there is more? Maybe there's a dungeon or something," she postulated. Once again, Pthorn wasn't sure she actually wanted to know the answer to her own question.

Pthorn nodded and continued his search for any other hidden surprises. It was possible that the person responsible for this lair had created another level of secrecy in case the first was discovered. Pthorn knew that it wasn't uncommon for castles such as this to have dungeons. He had heard about them in the stories his mother had told him as a child of gallant heroes who had chosen the wrong side to fight for and become the losers of wartime, becoming locked away until they were either put to death or died of exposure.

Pthorn noted to himself that any further extensions to the castle would have to be directly through the floor rather than in a wall, as the lower level they were in was wide enough to take in the entire floor width of the level. Pthorn surveyed the room for several moments, pushing on the limited number of furnishings in the room before a thought came to him.

"Help me move the sleeping pallet, will you?" he asked of Darn as she watched him think in silence.

She made her way over, and they began to feel around the solid timber pallet. Firstly they tried pushing it, but it seemed to be fixed in place. This gave Pthorn hope that they were on to something. After trying several ways to get it out of the way, they both walked to the foot and lifted.

It was as though it was somehow counterweighted; the sleeping pallet lifted up on an angle with minimal effort and revealed a stone stairway into the dark. Pthorn looked towards Darn before turning his attention back towards the hole in the floor.

More stale air rushed from the abyss into the living quarters, causing them both to cough for a few moments.

Pthorn made his way to the wall of the room and removed one of the damp-light torches from its sconce before he started to make his way down the stairs. The damp-light cast dancing shadows across the stone walls and the steps below.

Pthorn had no idea what he was expecting to find when he started his decent but quickly, the familiar scent of old parchment and ink surrounded him. The walls were lined with texts, and shelves protruded from the walls like spines. It was the most densely packed library of books he had ever seen, not that he had many libraries to draw a comparison of, just the small collections of books back at the Sect.

"Don't worry," he called up to Darn. "No more dead bodies down here, I promise."

"There will be if ya jump out and scare me down there, I promise ya!" she warned.

Darn soon joined him at his side, and they began walking through the vast subterranean library. The wall opposing the stairway had 'Athenaeum' carved into the stone in neat, bold lettering. Pthorn suspected that, while this place was clearly occupied by the Order of Death, someone from the Order of Creativity may have had a hand in some of the design elements. The room had an echo that accentuated the sound of his feet shuffling on the hard, stone floor and made his voice reverberate.

Aside from the interesting acoustics, another thing caught his attention almost immediately. Pthorn thought back to those stories his mother had told of the people locked up inside the dungeons, and in nearly all of them, they were almost always up to their heels in water seeping through the walls. This one seemed well sealed; perhaps the walls were lined with clay, or the room was carved into impervious stone. Either way, the air felt dry and crisp, and the books seemed undamaged by lichen or damp. While the moat outside was dry, he knew that even then, he would have expected to see some groundwater ingress.

Pthorn continued perusing the room. As he walked through the stacks of books, Pthorn could not help but run his hands along the spines, feeling the hard leather on his fingertips. Growing up, his family never had so much as a few scraps of paper, and knowledge was held only in their minds. Within this room were thousands of tomes, each with thousands of words. Pthorn tried to comprehend how much knowledge was contained within the confines of this one room but could not even begin to grasp it. There was simply nothing equivalent to something of this magnitude that he had experienced before.

Darn had also returned to her look of shell shock, although it seemed to be for a far less morbid reason and the same as that which stunned Pthorn; the books.

"I wonder if the current Order-Masters know about this place or whether it has just been lost to time," Pthorn thought aloud.

"Assier only knows!" exclaimed Darn as she followed closely behind him. "I can't even begin to imagine how old this place is."

There were no wall sconces down here, so Pthorn was happy that he had brought a damp-light down with him.

The athenaeum was separated into various topics down each spine of shelving. In the first half of the room, there were sections on agriculture, mining minerals and metals, biology, chemistry, and physics; each marked neatly by more stone engraving on the walls opposing them. As they made their way further into the depths of the room, they found the texts turned to theology and religion, rows upon rows.

"It would take a lifetime and more to make it halfway through these," Pthorn noted as he selected one book randomly from the shelf in front of him.

Pthorn passed his damp-light to Darn, who seemed very intrigued by the light itself. Pthorn quickly realised that she had probably never seen one and had to introduce her to the concept.

"They are just like an ordinary lantern, but they produce almost no smoke or heat; that is why we can use them inside like this and around the dry books. If you brought a tallow candle in here, you would never make it out alive, one way or another."

Once he had finished his description, he directed her to shine the light over the book as he opened it. It was entitled 'Initiation for the uninitiated' and wrapped in a hard leather binding with iron bands. The penmanship on the pages was exceptionally neat, as though written by a professional scribe, but it was intricate and swirled, making it very hard to read on the thin, fragile pages.

Gently filing through, he found pages of preamble before he came across the description of the ceremony he had been at the centre of. Detailed illustrations showed the various Order-Masters wearing nothing but the skin on their backs. The incantation was also included, bringing back vivid memories of the night he had believed was a dream.

He placed the book back on the shelf and continued perusing the athenaeum.

Finally, right at the back, tucked into the corner, was a final section entitled, 'The Fae'. This was particularly curious to Pthorn. Nothing about the fae had ever been mentioned back in the Sect, and it had always been the stuff of travellers' tales of people whisked away into a far-off realm where time and space seemed not to be of any substance.

This hardly seems to be the place for a collection of ancient fiction and fae tales.

He selected a book at random from the shelf. The leather had been dyed a bright purple and embossed with a small, green, winged creature. Painted highlights were added to show the definition of the strange creature. As Pthorn made to turn the page, he could have sworn he saw the wings flutter before very quickly dismissing it as a trick of the mind and eyes. He had clearly been inhaling too much of the old dust from the room.

Perhaps the old ink is slightly hallucinogenic.

Pthorn had just begun to flit through the pages, looking at the descriptions of what it noted as four races of mythical fae creatures, when his train of thought was disturbed.

"I am sure it is getting late; we should get out of here before nightfall. If we are seen walking around with this," pointing to the damp-light torch, "whatever it was called outside, people are going to get suspicious."

Pthorn agreed, placing the purple tome back into its place on the fae section shelf, and made their way back up the stairs and into the living quarters again. Once they had reset the sleeping pallet back to its correct position, Pthorn extinguished the damp-light torches in succession. They made their way back through the lair, past the corpses and to the hidden door.

Pthorn reached in and tripped the invisible latch once more before slowly inching the door open. He slowly stuck his head through the opening and surveyed the room, realising how stupid he was and that he could have done the same thing as he did to locate the cadavers on the living people. Once he was sure there was no one outside, he ushered Darn through the doorway and into the foyer.

The air was very refreshing, even in the foyer, which they thought had smelled so terrible when they first arrived. Pthorn breathed in a deep breath of the cool afternoon air before exhaling with a loud "ah".

They made their way out through the front entrance to the castle and over the drawbridge. Just as Darn had predicted, the sun was just above the horizon and quickly descending into night.

When they returned to the pitched bedroll, they found the enormous form of Fluorocor waiting for them, along with a small crowd. Most of them seemed to be from the large group travelling together, standing at what they all probably thought was a safe distance. It would seem they had all found the second tourist attraction in Neith.

39.
Bad News Travels Fast

Pthorn led the way past the crowd towards their campsite. He could hear some of the conversations as he passed.

"My great-great-grandfather slayed one over a hundred turns ago," bragged one man to his wife, who had probably heard the story that many times.

"Good thing the ruins are stone, so it can't burn them down," said another.

Pthorn just shook his head and approached Fluorocor before gently placing his hand just in front of its wing joint. This time he had to reach up quite high, but Fluorocor lowered itself slightly to assist, probably hoping for a back scratch.

Pthorn turned to address the shocked crowd. "For anyone thinking you can do the same, I would strongly suggest against it. It trusts me, and I it. Also, if you think you can kill my large friend here, keep in mind that you will be dissolved into a puddle and eaten before you get within twenty paces."

The man who had been gloating about his ancestor shuffled a few steps back, realising he was well within this range. Pthorn suspected he had been thinking about replicating the heroics for himself.

"I'll tell ya what. If you all go inside and leave my friend here alone, Pthorn here will buy you all a pint. Sound fair?" Darn offered loudly on Pthorn's behalf.

No one was going to pass up on the offer of a free beer, so they slowly shuffled back towards to inn and into the bar area. Tankards were passed around, and Pthorn opened his purse to the innkeeper before going back outside to check on the hydrofluor.

Pthorn found Fluorocor looking far more relaxed than a few moments earlier, curling up around the bedroll entrance.

"Thank you for not eating the tourists," said Pthorn, half-jokingly. "To be fair, you did go off and eat at least one moog and become the same size as a room at the inn! It's not like you weren't going to draw attention."

Fluorocor clicked loudly in its defence. Pthorn wasn't really sure what that defence consisted of, but the hydrofluor seemed to believe it validated its actions.

Once Pthorn was satisfied no one was going to be dissolved or gobbled up and eaten, he re-joined Darn back inside. She had taken up a spot in a booth and ordered them both a trencher of Everlasting Soup, which Pthorn quickly devoured, realising they hadn't eaten all day inside the bowels of the castle.

Once they had finished stuffing their faces, the pair started discussing their discoveries of the day while keeping their voices to a minimum, not wanting to be overheard by any other patrons.

"I think we should stay here a while," stated Pthorn between sips of beer. "I know I said I wanted out of the Sect to travel, but I think I just want to understand more about it." He paused for a moment. "And I want you to help."

Darn thought for a couple of moments before replying, "I thought you would say something like that. I will make you a deal. We can stay here as long as ya like, as long as you read the books out loud. Of course, I will help."

At that moment, Pthorn thought himself to be the dumbest man alive. Of course, she couldn't read. She had been raised on a farm just like him, but with an angry, drunkard of a dad who hadn't taken the time to teach her like his mother had done for him.

Pthorn let his head fall. "Sorry, I wasn't thinking. I just...."

Darn raised her hand and placed it on his shoulders.

"It's okay, you know. Most people can't read or write; I don't care. Hasn't stopped me ever!"

Pthorn let his eyes do the talking. He loved the way that she didn't take offence to his everyday moments of placing his foot, well and truly, into his mouth. They had enough in common that the things they didn't have in common just didn't seem to drive a wedge.

Pthorn and Darn sat at the table, smiling like idiots at each other, almost entirely oblivious to the ever-increasing rowdiness of the bar as people's intoxication levels slowly climbed.

Their bubble suddenly burst when a new traveller entered the door, announcing his arrival with a crier's bell.

Almost immediately, the buzzing atmosphere of the room turned to a deathly silence.

The man was lean and dressed in well-worn and dusty riding gear. He was a town-to-town messenger who would deliver news that the clergy considered important enough to disseminate broadly.

Even though Pthorn was reasonably confident that, just like Darn, he too could not read, the man held a scroll in front of his face as he orated.

"Hear ye, hear ye, from this day forth, and until notified otherwise, all travel from Kesheir to Matraketh is banned, and no ships shall cross the Maitke Sea."

The man paused for effect before continuing.

"While the exact details are unknown at this time, it is believed that a plague outbreak has become very serious and needs to be contained."

The man lowered his scroll and made his way to the bar. With his work done for the day, he seemed intent on wetting his whistle with a pint.

Before he reached his destination, the questions began piling on from all sides, and he did his best to answer them with candor.

"Where is the plague?" one man shouted from the far side of the bar.

"I believe it started in Falanar and hasn't travelled far yet," he answered.

"Why lock down the whole land for one town? Plagues happen all the time?" called another much closer to him.

"I only know rumours. They say the dead have started rising. The priests didn't want the word getting out. They started burning their dead, but when they couldn't keep up, they stored them all in a cold store. One night they all just started waking up and killing the living."

"Moogshit!" yelled one.

"o'course, the priests dun want you saying nuthin," called another, "next you will be tellin' us dem fae rings down south is real."

"Believe what you want," answered the messenger. "I'm just tellin' you what I've been told, officially and unofficially." The barman handed over his pint, and the messenger held it in the air. "Either way, you ain't getting into Matraketh any time soon."

Pthorn had been sitting wide-eyed through the entire announcement and had begun sweating profusely as he thought more about the news.

Pthorn gestured quietly for Darn to follow him outside, and they walked out towards their bedroll. Fluorocor had disembarked for the night, probably to eat something to maintain its size for a few days.

Once there, Pthorn decided it was time to tell the rest of his story.

"There is something you should know. Remember when I told you I was collecting specimens and got distracted by something…."

Darn nodded, remembering the conversation and ushered him on to continue.

"Well, the thing is, well... I might have done the opposite of what I was meant to do. You know how I belong to the Order of Death...."

Pthorn let the allusion hang in the air and let Darn draw the conclusion.

"Are you tellin' me you brought them back to life?" she asked very accusingly, almost yelling under her breath.

"I thought I could help!" said Pthorn in his defence. "I managed to help someone in another town, and nothing went wrong. Now a little girl gets to see her next nameday. Then I tried it in Falanar... and I may have made a mistake."

"What did you do?" she asked.

"Well, now I think back, it is more what I didn't do. You see, when I saved the little girl, I helped heal the heart that killed her. When I brought the town back to life, I didn't get a chance to fix anything... They all still have the plague, but they are alive! But also dead."

"Oh, Assier Almighty!" she cursed. "You farmin' idiot. Even I know that was a bad idea. Do they even teach you anything back in that accursed mountain?"

Pthorn remained silent with his head turned towards the ground.

Slowly the realisation set in for Darn. "They don't teach you that at all, do they?" she asked.

"No"

"Now I know why it was so easy for me to convince you to join me!" she yelled, raising her voice a little too much for Pthorn's liking.

"Shh," he said, trying not to attract any attention to themselves. "And no, it wasn't just that. I, um, well... I don't know what it was, but there was something the day

I met you back home in Strauth. Something I didn't realise at the time, but couldn't ignore when I saw you again. It was why I ignored the first girl to get naked in front of me... I didn't know at the time, but now I do. It was always going to be you. I love you, Darn."

His proclamation was met swiftly with a slap across the face.

"Really? Now? This is the time ya want to pull that one out. The farmin' Singular's schlong slap me!" she cursed.

She calmed herself down as Pthorn massaged his reddening cheek. "Fine, well, what are you gonna do about it," she said, pointing accusatively.

"To the Athen-ae-um!" he said, slowly annunciating the word as best he could and pointing to the castle.

"To the what?" she asked.

"Don't ask me; it was written on the wall in that underground library," he answered, shrugging.

Pthorn grabbed his knapsack from within the pitched bedroll before he and Darn slowly made their way across the way and into the even deeper darkness of the castle.

At least this guarantees no one is snooping around, thought Pthorn to himself, still trying not to make too much noise on the off chance his voice carried out of the echoing chamber of the foyer.

Pthorn Manipulated the invisible mechanism within the wall, once again noting that he would love to investigate how it actually works before feeling his way for the damp-light sconce. He immediately regretted not leaving one ignited while they were gone as he knocked various items off the writing desk and onto the floor. A shattered inkpot came into view as the damp-light sputtered to life; the ink was long dried, so there was little to no mess on the floor from the ink, just shards of ceramic coated in black dust scatted far and wide.

Once the room began to take form in front of them, Darn closed the door, and they made their way through to the living quarters again, lighting sconces as they passed. Once there, they lifted the levered sleeping pallet and revealed the hidden staircase cloaked in darkness below.

Pthorn wasn't sure what he was searching for within the vast collection of volumes, and he wasn't even sure there would be what he needed. The type of text he required was likely to be considered blasphemous to the Assierian priests and the Sect alike.

A feeling of anxiety knotted deep within the pit of his stomach as he started inspecting the spines of the tomes lining the shelves of the 'Theology' section. He silently cursed his predecessor for not having the forethought to create an 'Undo idiotic and illegal spells' section.

Most of the books didn't have a labelled spine or cover inscribed. Pthorn had to open each one in turn and flick through the pages surveying the topics covered within that particular volume. Most books covered pure theological teachings about the Singular, Assier and the Prophet Aiel; specifically, they were about what the priests should teach the masses, not about the theology as taught in the Sect. Grouped together on the top shelf was a section focusing specifically on this 'True Theology' as the books referred to it and the process by which the knowledge and power of the Singular's divinity was passed on to the Chosen Four. Pthorn didn't spend much time digesting the information but noted that it was affirming to see texts which agreed with the teachings of the Sect and that it wasn't just verbal hearsay passed down through the generations.

Darn was holding the damp-light torch as Pthorn flicked through.

"What do they say?" she asked as he picked up the next book. "Anything about whatever it is you did?"

"Nothing yet," he said. "There is a long way to go; these are all about religion. Nothing even about standard Manipulation, let alone Blood Magic."

"Blood Magic?" she repeated. "What do you mean Blood Magic?"

Pthorn cringed, realising just how badly he had messed up.

"I kinda had to transfer some life into them using their blood as some sort of a conduit?" he said. "It's okay; it didn't seem to affect me at all."

Darn just shook her head, liking the situation less and less as she learned more about what he had done. Given that she hadn't just up and left when he told her gave him a small amount of confidence that she would support him through fixing his mistakes, but the more she found out, the less confident he grew that she wouldn't simply walk away when it became too much.

"I think we need to try another shelf," Pthorn said as he moved to the next finger of shelves down the room.

It was well into the morning before he located the first book, which discussed any mention of Manipulation. This gave him the first hope that he was now looking in the right area of the library. He continued opening books and reading the sections he opened aloud to Darn.

Pthorn noted that some of the books had some techniques that he hadn't yet tried, and he made a mental note to return to the shelf at some point and read more in-depth. One book, in particular, looked so good that he stuffed it into his knapsack, lying at the entrance near the 'Athenaeum' engraving.

Finally, he came to a set of five black books, all bound exactly the same to match. Pthorn opened the first one, and a large illumination was presented on the first page with the words 'Necromance and Maleficence for the Malcontented Mage; the Collection' inscribed in a swirling cursive.

Pthorn knew instantly that this was the source of the information which had been copied into the back of his writing book.

Pthorn passed two of the heavy books to Darn and collected the remaining three himself before he led her up the stairs and out to the upper room's writing desk, dropping the books onto the desk with a loud thud.

If the solution to his problem wasn't within these five books, Pthorn knew there was little hope of reversing the spells. In an effort of pointless futility, Pthorn said a short prayer to Assier before he reopened the cover of the first volume and set to work reading each line looking for an answer within or between the lines.

40.
Interlude: Not My Problem

The Oracle of Malcontent | The Sect

Four span and a day had passed since he had been accused of partaking in forbidden magic; again. The Oracle of Beauty had been ropable.

And rightfully so, he thought to himself in hindsight.

The use of the forbidden magic had been banned within the Sect's ranks for hundreds of turns, since the Cold Blood War, when the Four had agreed never again to fight one another using such methods. These methods of Manipulation were more potent than traditional forms as they tended to transfer power, in the form of living energy, to achieve their purposes, usually at the expense of someone's life.

In this particular case, Beauty had been most upset as her own Elect had been the victim of the theft of life;

rather than a member of the general public. While the Elects were meant to be travelling alone to different continents, Beauty and Prevail had allowed their Elects to travel together for the first part of the journey.

The Combat-Elect had first raised the alarm that something was not quite right with the girl he called Crea, the Creativity-Elect. They had written to the Sect via the trading post at Portsworth to say that one day they were sitting down and talking when suddenly Crea had become silent and started, in his opinion, glowing.

Beauty had dismissed this event as nothing more than a trick of the mind and had not thought much of it. A few days later, a second gram was received, saying another event had occurred. As he described it, they had been asleep when the room had burst into light, and it flowed up into the sky as a great column. The event had only continued for a few moments, but after that, Crea had not awoken. She was still breathing but seemed to have fallen into a deep sleep or coma.

The Combat-Elect had told them where they were staying and remained there until they could transport Crea back to the Sect, where she now remained in the coma.

Since the event, Tom's name had been mud. Even though he, himself, had pleaded ignorance to knowing of anyone performing any type of forbidden magic, the Order-Masters had instantly blamed him for either instigating or providing Del with the means.

Tom still had no idea how Del had come to learn of the forbidden magic nor how he had managed to use it to such an extent as to debilitate a fellow Elect. For the most part,

Tom believed the transfer of life from an Elect was typically safe; although what he knew of these arts was simply from knowledge passed down to him from his Order-Master in the latter part of his training. Whatever Del had done must have been on a grand scale to cause an extended loss of consciousness such as this.

Contrary to what they let their Elects believe, the Order-Masters do not possess the power to see or track people across Azarth. The only widespread use of their power is to 'Broadcast' or 'Focus' particular Manipulations across a great distance.

Broadcasting was what the Order-Master of Death would do every evening in his efforts to provide balance, offsetting Life's influence on Azarth. This would typically involve a more general, blanket form of Manipulation in no specific direction and without focusing on any particular individual or object.

Focus was what they used to play the prank on Del when he had been setting sail for Matraketh. Given they knew his approximate location, they could focus on various Manipulations of sea creatures and weather patterns. This actually took a tremendous amount of energy and the cooperation of all four Order-Masters to achieve. It was hardly a good use of their energies or powers, but it hadn't stopped them from having a little fun at the expense of an uninitiated Elect. The hard part was knowing when to stop; when acting as a combined force, there was an intangible knowledge of the outcome of their actions without actually seeing the event. For example, Tom found out later that the ship's crew had been about to throw Del overboard when they stopped. Back at the

Sect, they could sense that the joke had gone too far but didn't actually know how close they came to getting their newest Elect fed to a kraken. In hindsight, it was probably too close this time.

It wasn't often that the mages combined their powers to perform Synchronised Manipulation. Alone their abilities could only influence that which was related to their particular order; when combined, it blurred the boundaries of influence. Together they could instigate and control various Acts of Assier, as the commoners would refer to them, things like earthquakes, floods, and eruptions without relying on a transfer of life energy. The Sect saved this sort of Manipulation for special occasions, so to speak.

Once Tom had finally convinced the others that there was no way he was performing such magic, particularly at the expense of an Elect, and that he was quote-unquote "deeply offended that they had believed otherwise", he considered what he should do about both the situation and his rogue Elect.

On the one hand, Del could be out there continuing to perform forbidden magic at the expense of the Creativity-Elect and potentially other members of the Sect or the public. On the other hand, Tom had expressly told the others that the entire field exercise was a bad idea and that Del was not ready to be given unbridled access to the world.

I told you so, came to Tom's mind.

While he continued contemplating how much this was his problem, he penned a letter to the local trading post in an attempt to garner some idea of the scale of the mess that Del had been creating. In the letter, he asked for details of any rumours of ill-tidings or large-scale disasters. His answer came by way of the clergy's decree that any travel through Matraketh would be limited, and outside was completely off limits due to a worsening plague. Various other rumours were included with the formal message, which indicated that Del may have been involved in making the situation far worse than it already had been.

Trust Del to ruin a perfectly good plague, thought Tom as he read the stack of letters and reports when he received them.

Tom had left almost immediately following the news and set off towards Falanar. With the wealth of the Sect behind him, he had travelled first to Portsworth and acquired a Gentleman's Caravan, an equestra drawn wagon with the comforts of living quarters far exceeding his own in the Sect.

Almost two span had passed since he left, and The Oracle of Malcontent had made good time across the continent. The wagon had just stopped moving for the day, and Tom climbed down the enclosed quarters and stretched his aching limbs.

"Where are we now?" he enquired of the driver as he looked around the village.

"Maarts, oh holy one," replied the overly pious driver, bowing low as he spoke. Tom had first considered telling him to stop with the ridiculous show but thought better of it; after all, he was wearing the holy vestments for a good reason. The more he was respected as a member of the clergy, the more influence he may have if the need arose. For now, he maintained an air of courtesy.

As he walked away from the wagon, Tom spotted the trading post across the square and started to make his way over to see if there was any more news coming out of Falanar. He was still a good few paces off the window when a voice called out from the depths.

"You wouldn't happen to be related to Pthorn, would you?" the voice said.

"What makes you think that," he asked as he got a little closer

"Spitting image, I tell ya. Plus, you seem to share the same fashion sense; 'cept he had a nice hat. Do all botanists dress like they work for Assier?" The man laughed, and Tom could see his jowls jiggling grotesquely.

"Right," he started ignoring the question and returning with his own, "well, what can you tell me about our common acquaintance? Is he around here somewhere?"

"He and that big, black beast of his left a few span ago he did; he was asking lots of questions about Falanar," the large man answered.

"What do you mean, black beast?" Tom asked, narrowing his eyes curiously.

"He was travelling with a pet dragon or somethin', never seen anything like it. Seemed the friendly sort it did. Though I wasn't going to get too close to finding out." The man chuckled to himself.

This was news to Tom. Either the man was seeing things, or Del had taken to collecting specimens a little too well.

"Thank you for your help," said Tom, excusing himself before turning to cross the road towards the wagon.

As he walked away, he was interrupted again by the man in the trading post window. "Where are you heading anyway?"

"Business to attend to in the west," he replied.

"Well, probably best to head north first. Terrible what's happening in Falanar at the moment. The plague started off bad, but the stories I have heard. Makes you shudder," he said, imitating the shudder.

"What sort of stories are you talking about?"

"They say the dead are walking again, and they ain't just getting up to smell the flowers. They say they are killing just as many as the plague did," he answered, sounding genuinely concerned before adding, "thankfully, they seem to be staying put. We haven't seen anyone, dead or alive, walk in from Falanar in weeks."

Tom thanked the trading post attendant and bid him farewell before crossing the road towards the wagon. The driver had just finished tending to the equestra and was heading into the bar for dinner. Tom walked inside to join him but sat separately by himself as he had done every other day.

After he finished dining and enjoying a pint of beer, Tom returned to the wagon. Unfortunately, his duties as an Order-Master could not be neglected just because he wasn't back inside the Arrat Range. He closed the door to the Gentleman's Carriage and began his evening ritual.

Just like every other day, he retrieved the wax from his cloak pockets and inserted it into his ears; there was very little noise here, but it was part of the routine. He closed his eyes, held his arms out in front of him, and pushed. Unlike local Focus Manipulation, where you 'feel' around inside of an object, Broadcasting Manipulation was more of a trance state, which was why he needed to block out sound up in the windy mountains. There was no need to receive any local or distant feedback on the effects of his Manipulation. The general intent, repeated day in and day out, was enough to achieve the balance.

Without the holy bell to signal the end of his routine, Tom had recruited his driver to gently tap him on the shoulder an hour after he started.

Once he was done, he settled in for the night and fell asleep. Tomorrow they would leave for Falanar and find out just how much damage that stupid boy had caused.

Part 5

41.

Back in Town

It had taken all night to scour the pages of the five volumes, sitting at the writing desk in Death's lair and scrawling notes. Most of the other books in the athenaeum were well presented and neatly scribed, with many colourful illuminations. These volumes looked like they had been written, rewritten and annotated, all within the same pages. There were notes and diagrams in the margins and between lines. Crude depictions of anatomy with callouts indicating the various organs being dissected.

The volumes of Necromance and Maleficence for the Malcontented Mage were a far cry from the neatly scribed version in the back of his book, but they also contained much more. The spells and enchantments were tenfold darker than those he had already seen; many focused on ensuring suffering and torment, while others spoke of forbidden deeds like raising the dead and soul transference.

One of the options he focused on was entitled 'Undead and How to Control Them'; he had already seen this entry in his own book and had previously dismissed it, but he was slowly beginning to entertain the idea as a backup plan.

"You are not creating your own undead army," scolded Darn when he had mentioned it aloud. "You have enough issues controlling the one beast you already have."

She was, of course, correct, but that didn't stop him from considering it.

After many hours he stumbled across some words squeezed between an unrelated paragraph.

If thou result, should not suit thyne intent, then reverse ye chant before one turn's time.

Was it really that simple? Thought Pthorn as he sat reading and re-reading the scrawled handwriting again. As he read, more questions continued to plague his mind.

Do you read each sentence but starting from the bottom of the stanza?

Do you just read the words in reverse order?

Or even worse, he thought, *Do you need to pronounce everything backwards?*

Pthorn suspected the latter, and Darn sleepily agreed with him on the basis that it was likely to be the most difficult. She had made herself a makeshift pallet on the floor of the lair out of some very old and dusty blankets. She was dozing in and out as Pthorn worked. He had only left one damp-light torch ignited as he read to help keep the room dim for her.

In a sudden moment of clarity, Pthorn had made up his mind. "We need to go to Falanar now," he announced as Darn stirred.

Darn let out a less-than-impressed groan before rolling off the sheets and joining him by the writing desk. Pthorn picked up three volumes, and Darn collected the remaining ones as they made their way back downstairs into the athenaeum below. Once they returned upstairs, they lowered the sleeping pallet to its normal position, guttered the damp-light torch, and made their way into the crisp early morning air.

The sun was just peaking over the horizon as they walked to the pitched bedroll. There they found Fluorocor curled up but awake. The hydrofluor arose to its feet as they arrived in welcome before happily receiving a back scratch from Pthorn.

"I have a favour to ask," stated Pthorn without missing a beat in the back scratch. "We need to get back to Falanar immediately. Do you think you can get us both there?"

Pthorn waited a few moments before adding the stipulation, "alive…."

The hydrofluor hesitated, looking down at its own body as if to be completing a calculation of how much load it could carry, before proceeding with a nod and a screeching click.

Darn left Pthorn to pack up the campsite while she went inside the inn to collect some supplies. Soon the bedroll was rolled, and their small collection of belongings was packed into the knapsack. Darn returned with an armful of hard, travelling foods and a couple of lengths of rope.

Pthorn stuffed these into the top of the bag and then secured it to the hindquarters of Fluorocor using the rope that Darn had procured; the hydrofluor was now way too large for the straps to be tied together around its girth.

Once the knapsack was sorted, Pthorn created a makeshift bridle that fit around its neck and shoulders. With Fluorocor's recent gain in size, it was now almost too large to place your legs on either side, with its back being almost flat; this meant there was nothing to hold on to. Pthorn gave it a tug and convinced himself that it would not come free, even with his limited knowledge of knots learned aboard the Sea's Fury almost a turn and a half ago.

Pthorn gave the hydrofluor a friendly pat on the shoulders. "It is time," he said.

Fluorocor bowed its head, and Darn mounted first, sideling up to the front of its neck. Then Pthorn joined her, pulling himself up and holding the rope reigns either side of her.

With no warning, Fluorocor launched himself skyward with a loud crack of its enormous wings, causing Pthorn to curse loudly, "Farrrrrmmmmmm...."

It wasn't long before they were comfortably soaring through the air, with the ground disappearing below them intermittently behind sheets of clouds. The air was frigidly cold, and the fast-moving air stung Pthorn's eyes. They had set off in the morning and started the journey with very little sleep. There were a few moments where Pthorn felt himself begin to doze off before quickly jolting himself back into consciousness. The last thing he needed was to fall asleep a league above the surface of Azarth and plummet to the ground. He wasn't sure what that would mean for his immortality, but he knew with certainty it would not be a pleasant recovery and definitely wouldn't end well for Darn if she fell too.

As they flew over the countryside, Darn pointed out various beasts. Anything smaller than a baahti would have gone entirely unnoticed if not pointed out directly. Great moogs and keil resembled nothing but tiny scuriats making their way across the green pastures.

From their vantage point, they could see the road heading north they had followed to arrive at the Ayefyl Castle. It was as though Fluorocor had read his mind, and they seemed to be following it to assist with navigation.

They didn't stop for lunch; instead, they continued to fly directly to the outskirts of Loutin, where they landed and made camp for the night in a grassy clearing beside a farm.

"I want everyone to be fresh for tomorrow's journey across the Maitke Sea. Fluorocor, just a quick hunt to keep up for size tonight, then straight back here; nothing too big, okay. We don't need your napping mid-flight; maybe steal a baahti or something."

The hydrofluor clicked loudly and took off searching for dinner while Darn and Pthorn made camp. Fluorocor returned before sunset, and they all settled in for the night. Pthorn didn't even bother setting a fire.

The next morning they arose early.

"Perhaps we should put on our cold weather clothes," Darn suggested, "it may be warm now, but if we fly through the night, it is going to get freezing, and we are not going to be able to get changed up there."

Pthorn agreed and dug out the woollen gear he had purchased back in Portsworth. Darn had a similar coat and boots; Pthorn wondered why she had bothered to buy such things but decided not to press her for details.

Once again, they packed up their gear, placing plenty of food and a waterskin each into their warm coats before mounting the great lumbering beast for their long-haul flight over the sea. This time they were both ready for their violent ascent into the skies, and much less screaming and swearing was required.

While flying, Darn and Pthorn had tried to have a conversation to pass the time but found that it was impossible to hear each other over the buffeting of the wind.

At one point, she had either said, "I really love flying!" or "the lute was lying." He figured one was far more likely than the other, but either way, it confirmed that no dialogue would happen while they were travelling by hydrofluor.

As daylight began to fade, the sea below them turned from a deep green-blue to inky black. The cold started to infiltrate through his heavy coat, causing him to shiver;

just the odd quiver at first, but after an hour, it became almost constant.

Pthorn put his arms around Darn and pulled her in close. She leaned back to press herself against him. After a while, either their body heat had been shared enough, or the cold had just made them both numb, but they ceased shivering altogether.

Pthorn looked out over the horizon, staring off into the blackness. He stayed like this for hours until he could see the fight signs of the sunrise to his right. He was so distracted by the beauty of it that he completely missed the shores of Matraketh coming into view. By the time he turned around, they had crossed the shoreline and were starting to head across the vast fields. They must have passed either east or west of Playton-on-Sea as he could see no sign of the village.

Fluorocor continued flying north in the direction of Falanar. Pthorn was sure that it was no optical illusion that Fluorocor seemed to be smaller than when they left. The giant beast had been flying non-stop for a full day without any rest or food. The knapsack behind him started sliding from side to side with each flap of its wings.

Pthorn had seen the familiar village of Falanar in the distance, but once again, without being told, Fluorocor had seemed to sense that the best place to set down would be some distance away from the trouble. After many gruelling hours of flying, they landed and rested in a large grassy field. Fluorocor practically collapsed from fatigue and looked physically smaller in size. Here they could recuperate and go in fresher; without fear of attack by the awakened villagers.

They didn't even bother to set up the bedroll; they just changed into their regular travelling clothes and laid down for a rest in the soft, waving grass. There they stayed for a few hours until the worst of their sleep deprivation faded.

The final walk into town took another half hour or so, by Pthorn's estimate. He wasn't sure what to expect when they arrived. In the best-case scenario, the whole fiasco was already fixed by the practising Pthorn had done of the backwards incantation. Given what he had come to learn about the forbidden magics, this seemed highly unlikely; all of the spells required either a direct connection to the subject or, at the very least, a close proximity.

In one last-ditch effort of hope, Pthorn chanted the spell in reverse as he walked into the village.

> "Refsnrat llahs ti, efil siht
> Ti dnammoc lliw I won rof
> Eryp on ees llahs uoy won rof
> Dedianu dnats dna htrof esir
> Erol eht kaeps I won ehtaerb
> Htaerb emoclew ot erom ecno
> Erom on won tub
> Htaed yb democlew ecno"

He finished the incantation while trying to force the energy into the village en mass. As he completed the last line, two things became immediately evident; firstly, it had not worked at all, meaning that his entire plan to subdue them was wholly foiled, and secondly, which was arguably more important, they were in trouble.

The village had become a sea of the walking dead, with rotting flesh beginning to slough through festering wounds. Many moved sluggishly, seemingly limited by the dystrophy of their muscles. Others seemed to be less affected by their ailments and approached swiftly.

They began their retreat from the village centre back towards the way they had entered. As Pthorn turned to leave, a body fell from a rooftop, knocking him to the ground.

The flailing body's face hung loosely from the bone, its eye sockets deep and blank. Its mouth was gnashing at him as its arms struggled to pull him to the ground.

Pthorn tried to push off but found it difficult to get a purchase on the grotesque man. Each kick glanced off him, spreading gore over the ground as he did.

This had all happened in a matter of swift moments; instantly, Fluorocor swung into action. The beast locked its mouth around the rotting corpse and threw it across the ground, dismembering it in the process. The man's head rolled several paces along the hard-packed dirt road before coming to rest at the foot of another walking corpse.

Pthorn scampered to his feet with the aid of Darn.

"Are you okay?" she asked worriedly.

"Yes, for now, but might I suggest we run. Now!" He retorted before they all made haste for the exit.

Once again, they found their way blocked by more rotting bodies. While Pthorn had been tussling with his attacker, the undead had managed to strategise and encircle the group.

"We need to get out of here," Pthorn said, deeply concerned, particularly for Darn. "I don't think they can turn us into one of them, but they are all infected with the plague. We are as good as dead if that gets into our blood."

"What about Fluorocor?" Darn asked, "Didn't it just bite one of them?"

"Good point," he said, turning to the hydrofluor. "Don't swallow. Now, do you think you can get us out of here?"

The large beast responded with a loud "cliiiick" before slowly lowering its head. In one sudden movement, Darn and Pthorn both took a running jump onto the beast's back as it kicked off and took to the air. Darn had managed to get her leg over its neck, but Pthorn was lying face down across its back, struggling to grip its leathery hide.

The beast flew a short way away; Pthorn supposed it was probably about the same distance as where they had stopped to rest earlier, except there was a small running stream just a few paces away.

Pthorn cleaned himself of all the gore, washed his grey robes, and double-checked himself for any puncture wounds. After a few moments, he was sure he had come out of it with just a few minor scrapes and grazes. Darn had thankfully not been attacked, and Fluorocor seemed to be trying to wash its mouth out with water for about the tenth time.

"Taste that bad, huh?" Pthorn asked as he removed himself from the stream and dressed himself in his small clothes.

"Cliiiick," came the disgusted response.

"Are you okay?" Pthorn asked Darn as he approached and placed his arms around her. She pulled him closer into a tight embrace. Pthorn hadn't noticed before, but tears cascaded down her cheeks, and she sobbed into his shoulder.

"I thought... I thought..." she stammered in between cries.

"It's okay," he reassured her. "I'm still here, and I'm not going anywhere. We will come up with another plan before we go running in there again. Trust me. And I am sorry, I should have asked you to hang back."

She nodded silently in between the sobs.

"I wouldn't have done it anyway, ya know," she said.

They stayed in that position for some time, gently swaying soothingly back and forth. When they finally decoupled themselves from each other, her tears had dried, and salt encrusted her cheeks.

She chuckled to herself, and Pthorn raised an eyebrow.

"You should have seen your big dumb face when he jumped on you," before she began to mock his flailing arms. It seemed she was trying to make light of the situation lest it becomes real and downright terrifying.

42.

Stronghold

The next day they were no closer to having a working plan than they were the day before, and even though Pthorn had an abysmal night's sleep, he was far better rested than he had been the day before. They packed up their camp and strapped the knapsack to Fluorocor again, who was now noticeably smaller once again. Pthorn noted that if they had any requirement for an evacuation today, it would be considerably more difficult.

The three walked back towards the village, Pthorn wishing he could leave Darn somewhere safe, but he knew any protest was simply a waste of breath. Once the village was in sight, they kept at that distance while they circumnavigated it. For the most part, it just looked like the same town as it had the day they had arrived the first time; to the south, it was a medley of low unmortared stone walls dotted with cottages lining the radiating streets. As they walked around to the east, Pthorn remembered the peculiarity regarding the roads; Falanar was built on a five-way intersection rather than a four-way crossroads. They had camped south of the village between the two southern roads; their first attempt at entry had been on the more western route.

They now crossed over the eastern route and began to head north, continuing to skirt widely. Their path led them from the fields into the cover of the trees to the east.

"We will have to be careful in here," Pthorn said as he made his way into the copse of trees. "We may be able to hide in here, but so can they."

Darn nodded and started to follow. After a few paces, they both noticed a problem; there was no way that Fluorocor was going to be able to walk through this forest at its current size.

"Meet us on the other side," said Pthorn pointing towards the northern road. While the forest continued all the way from this point over to the west, at least they could regroup on the northern roadway and formulate a plan if required.

Fluorocor took off and flew wide around the village, leaving the two alone to trek through the trees.

For much of the time, it was impossible to see anything in the village, which made it necessary to approach closer than made him comfortable. The twigs in the undergrowth snapped loudly as they walked; if anyone was nearby, their less-than-stealthy advance would be easily overheard.

As they continued to walk, Pthorn noticed for the first time that the smoke he had seen the first time he had entered the village was no longer coming from each cottage. This meant one of two things; either the entire town was dead, or they were all holed up somewhere together. Pthorn hoped for the latter, not wanting to be responsible for the deaths of the entire village.

They walked through the trees for a few hundred more paces before Pthorn noticed a welcome sight.

"Can you see the smoke in the distance?" Pthorn observed aloud but softly.

Darn replied with a nod.

"That is the business district; no one alive is left on this side of the village. We need to keep going."

That is exactly what they did. They trooped through the thick forest, eventually crossing the eastern roadway and continuing towards the north. When they finally reached the northern road, they found Fluorocor hiding just off to the side.

From where they stood, Pthorn could see the large cold store warehouse where he had started the problem. Further along on the same side of the road, Pthorn could see the source of the smoke. Barricading had been erected using whatever had been left lying around to wall off a building a few places down from the warehouse. There were a number of rotting bodies strewn across the roadway, many with what seemed to be arrows protruding from them like some sort of spiny animal.

The old plague wagon sat abandoned on the street, its equestra still hitched and rotting. They, too, had been feathered, presumably as a mercy.

The undead seemed to wander aimlessly about the street but still stayed close to the village centre for some reason; they didn't seem interested in venturing beyond the limits. Pthorn knew that even if half of the dead he raised were still walking around, they would meet a lot of resistance. Their first welcome party had only been a small number compared to what he knew to be in the village.

Pthorn and Darn crouched down under the cover of the trees to develop a plan.

"I have a plan, but I am not sure you are going to like it," Pthorn said earnestly and pointed at the stronghold down the road. "Do you see that compound?"

Darn nodded.

"I am not sure how to kill these things, seeing as the spell doesn't seem to be working, but maybe if we can find some of the villagers, we can learn more about them. Find out what they want and what makes them stay in this village."

Darn agreed silently before saying, "So, what is your plan for getting in there?"

"I have been thinking about that; when I escaped, I ran out the back door of that warehouse," he said, pointing in its direction. "There is a field behind there which could give us good access to it. Hopefully, those things are focused on being inside the village, and we can approach from the rear safely."

"You don't sound very confident," said Darn jokingly, trying to make light of the situation.

"There might be a good reason for that," he retorted.

Another hour passed as they trekked through the remaining forest, which lay northwest of the village. Here the trees thinned a little and could easily accommodate Fluorocor, meaning it didn't need to fly around. Once they arrived in the field behind the buildings, Pthorn surveyed the area again.

He hadn't been able to take everything in last time as he was running for his life figuratively at least, and the sun had set. In the glow of the early afternoon sun, they had a good view of the area. The rear of most of the buildings was used for storage; there were old wagons, crates, hay bales, and just about anything else you could imagine strewn around in various forms of organisation. There were also a few small wooden sheds, presumably used for the storage of things that they didn't want to be subjected to the weather. The pathway to the stronghold was not going to be completely straightforward; in fact, one of those sheds blocked most of their view of the building.

Over towards the south, an expensive-looking carriage was parked on the roadway; it could not have been parked there long as the equestra were not only still attached but alive. It seemed that the undead weren't particularly interested in devouring or attacking quadrupeds. They ruffled their leathery wings as they stood patiently for no one to return to them; they were clearly well-trained.

One final thought struck Pthorn as he made his final plan for the approach, "Fluorocor, you are going to have to wait for us out here. I will signal you when I can for you to join us, but if you come charging in there, they will attack you and probably us as well."

Fluorocor clicked sadly, but Pthorn suspected it not only agreed but already knew it couldn't join them immediately.

With that sorted, Pthorn and Darn left the safety of the tree line and began their trek across the open field towards to village once again. They both looked around anxiously as they walked slowly. There was no point in running and drawing attention to themselves while this far away. Pthorn had never felt so exposed, and his skin prickled with nervousness.

As they slowly closed the gap on the fortification, the forms of two sentries came into view. They had been situated atop the roof of the building, and they seemed to be alerting the others about the couple's presence.

Pthorn pointed them out to Darn. "Hopefully, this means that we have a chance of getting in."

"Or it means they are getting ready to kill us when we get into range," she returned less optimistically.

They continued their advance with still no undead to be seen

It almost seems too easy, thought Pthorn, daring not to voice that thought aloud lest some unknown force in the universe hear it and make it unso.

They were still fifty paces off the wall when a voice rang out. "Who goes there?"

"This is Darnalla, and I am Pthorn. We have come to help," Pthorn replied before begging, "please let us in," a little bit too desperately.

"How can you help us?" the man asked as they continued trying to close the gap.

"Can we discuss that when we don't have dead people trying to kill us?" questioned Darn.

"Who sent you?" came the reply, still not committing to granting them access.

"Special division of the Clergy of Assierium; we deal with matters of, um, the unique," said Pthorn trying to think quickly on his feet.

As his voice rang out, their situation turned instantly more dire. It must have been heard by the undead locals who had remained unseen up until now. At that moment, a horrible thought, or more of a realisation, occurred to Pthorn. *The living may be in this stronghold, but the undead are in the warehouse.*

It instantly made sense; where else would they feel more at home than the place where they were created.

The issue for Pthorn and Darn was that the warehouse was only a few buildings up the road and had a rear door that had been busted open by Fluorocor during their escape.

The undead poured out en mass coming straight for them.

"Let us in now," came the cry from Darn, far more desperately.

"There is no gate; you will have to climb!" came the reply.

Pthorn cursed loudly as they broke into a run. Their increase in pace could not have come at a better time as more of them burst forth from the storage shed and began their attack from behind. There were at least three or four off to their right and a horde of almost half a hundred filing through the door. Each exited to investigate the voices before breaking out into whatever version of a run they could manage upon seeing them approach the stronghold.

The people behind the walls of the stronghold had begun to line the top of the barricading wielding a wide range of arsenal. Some had short-range weapons consisting of nothing more than clubs and bats, while others who had probably enjoyed hunting in the past wielded crossbows or bows knocked with feathered arrows.

Those with the longer-range weapons began loosing their arrows at the nearest of the attackers. They were clearly concerned about their supply of arrows, as they only fired when they deemed it necessary to prevent a direct attack on the pair.

A couple of the villagers had begun to lean over the barricading, offering an arm to pull them up and over.

"Thrum, thrum," came the noise as arrows were notched and loosed in turn; the rate increased as they became more surrounded. By the time Pthorn reached the barricade, he was almost wholly penned in. He had lost sight of Darn, even though she had only just been a pace beside him a moment ago, and there was no time to look around. A hand shot down; he grabbed it without delay and began pulling himself up. More hands joined in to lift him as he felt the undead clawing at his boots and the bottom of his robes.

Once at the top, he rolled onto his back, staring at the sky, the uneven splintered wood below him digging into him painfully. He pushed himself up off the ground and accepted another hand from one of the villagers who had saved him.

"Phew, we did it," he called aloud before turning around to meet the downturned faces that met him.

Horror immediately dawned on him as he read the villager's faces.

"Where is Darn? WHERE IS SHE?!"

When he was met with silence, he knew. He forced himself to look over the top of the barricade at the limp form lying on the ground under the swathe of the undead.

He felt the bile rise up within him, and his head spun. He could feel the blackness closing in from all around, but there was one thing he knew he didn't imagine.

One image that he knew would stay with him forever.

The arrow sticking from one of her big, beautiful brown eyes and the blood streaming down and matting her hair.

"Fuck you!" he cursed before the world went black.

Pthorn never felt the crack as he fell backwards, and his head met the rough timber floor again.

43.
Planning

Pthorn had no idea how long he had been out for. He remembered brief moments of lucidity dotted throughout a long period of blackness. Voices faded in and out, but he was unsure what was a dream and what was real.

Eventually, the room filtered into view, and he managed to cling to the consciousness. He began to sit up to survey the room before the feelings began to well up within him. He sobbed loudly before collapsing into the pallet and pulling the sheets over his head.

"I see our saviour is awake," came a disembodied female voice from across the room.

Pthorn pulled the covers up further and hugged them tightly to his body, letting his tears soak into them.

"I know it won't mean much, but for what it is worth, we are sorry about what happened to your partner." The female voice paused for a moment before continuing to explain, "no one is sure how it happened or whose arrow it was. They all swear they were firing well away from both of you, but somehow she made her way into the cross fire."

The room reverted to silence for a few moments while she made her way across to the pallet.

"I want you to know that there was nothing you or anyone else could have done." She tried to reassure him.

"Yes, there was!" he replied harshly through the intermittent sobs that happen when you have cried yourself dry. "I should never have asked her to come; this wasn't her problem to fix. I should have insisted she stay somewhere safe."

"That was her choice, dear; it doesn't sound like you forced her to do anything she didn't want to do. She knew the risks and accepted them."

Pthorn didn't want to hear it, instead rolling over and facing the wall clenching his eyes shut as though it might make some difference to his situation. He just lay there wishing this was all a bad dream and that he would hear Darn's sweet voice joking with him.

"We will talk soon," said the woman as she started to walk back towards the door. "We will not wait for you to feel better about yourself. You have until tomorrow to tell us why you are here and how you think you are going to help us. Otherwise, you are going to wish it was you that we had accidentally feathered and fed to them."

Pthorn already wished it was him that had been hit; he didn't need the threat to make him want it.

The rest of the day and night rolled around without the offer of food.

Pthorn was in no mood to eat, and given the scarcity of such items in a stronghold surrounded by the walking dead, Pthorn figured they would be hesitant to feed the intruder.

The following morning the woman appeared by his bedside once again.

Pthorn was entirely out of tears, but a bottomless pit had established itself within his gut. A part of him had been stripped away and was missing like an organ pulled from his living body. The pain was almost physical.

"I said we would talk soon. Now is soon. Sit up, boy," the woman ordered.

Pthorn slowly forced himself to rise, sitting up with his back to the wall and making eye contact with the woman for the first time.

She was almost unnaturally tall, and her skin hung from her almost as loosely as it did from the undead outside. Pthorn observed that she had clearly been well-fed before the plague and probably in a position of authority in the village; now, malnutrition had set in with the shortage of food and water.

"Now, it is time for some answers," she continued. "I am Lowta, and I was the wife to the mayor of Falanar. He was sadly lost to the plague and burned at the pyre before they began turning."

"I am sorry to hear that, Lowta," said Pthorn sympathetically. "My name is Pthorn, and my friend is, or was, Darnalla. Darn for short."

Pthorn could feel the emotion start to well up inside him, and the sick feeling in the pit of his stomach continued to grow.

"You will find everyone in this building has lost at least one person they held dear. For some, it was their wife or husband. For others, it was their son or daughter. We have lost friends. Every person here will understand your pain of loss; I suggest you talk to them; I find it helps."

Pthorn nodded, not sure that he would actually heed the advice. The last thing he wanted to do was think about it, let alone talk about it. A single tear had already begun forming in the corner of his eye, and he wiped it away quickly.

"That said, I think the best thing for you is to think about what you came here to do. It may be for selfish reasons that I want you to focus on that, but I also think it will help you grieve," she said, placing her bony hand on his shoulder.

"I am here on behalf of the clergy of Assierium because I believe I can help. I have already tried what I thought would work, which has clearly failed. I was hoping by coming in here that I might learn more about what they are doing and what they want so that I can make a plan for how we can end this."

"Do you have any ideas for how we can get more supplies in the meantime?" she asked hopefully.

Pthorn thought for a few moments before remembering Fluorocor was still outside with his knapsack.

"Actually, I might," he answered, returning with what might pass as a vague smile.

At first, Lowta had naturally been resistant to the idea of letting a dragon into her compound, but after a lot of explanation and assurance that he hadn't seen Fluorocor eat anyone yet, she agreed to the plan. She called a meeting in the main common area. Pthorn assumed there would still be others on guard duty or sleeping in preparation for the night shift.

"Good morning, everyone," she began, and the murmuring din of noise calmed down to silence. "By now, you should all be aware of our latest guest. This is Pthorn, and he will be staying with us. He says he may be able to help us with our undead problem, but for now, he may have a solution to our other problem."

"He's not really my type, but I'll make it work!" heckled a man from the back of the room. His comment was met with raucous laughter from the room. Pthorn guessed that humour had become the coping mechanism for many.

"As sad as the loss of the only brothel for fifty leagues may be for you, Greff, that isn't what he can do for us. Plus, Sabelle is still here; you just have to find a way to pay her!"

The laughter continued for a few moments before Lowta continued talking. "Pthorn has access to a flying beast which he can ride to collect supplies for us. What he can carry will be limited; as such, we will only be stocking up on the essentials."

The noise in the room began to increase again as people started talking amongst themselves, creating wish lists of everything they could want.

"If anyone wants to evacuate, we can also arrange for that. Given that there is nowhere else for most of us to go, I don't see that as being an option for many. Now, when the beast approaches, do not attack. It is friendly as long as you do not engage it; if you do, be it on your own head," she warned.

"When you say beast, what exactly do you mean?" one man asked.

"The beast is called a hydrofluor, a type of dragon, but it is as loyal as a moog to Pthorn here," she answered, trying to downplay the perceived risk to the group. "Now go and tell the guards what I have told you, and fill in anyone not here today. We don't need any accidents."

The room began to clear out at her word, and Pthorn made his way up to the same place as he had climbed the wall when he arrived. Just the sight of the location hurt him, and he dared not look down lest he sees what might remain of the girl he loved.

Instead, he put his mind to getting the attention of Fluorocor. The hydrofluor would be hiding in the forest, but he had told it to await his signal. That wasn't to say that it wasn't away hunting or sleeping.

Pthorn raised his hands in a wide-arcing wave for a few moments and then stared out at the edge of the forest.

Nothing moved.

He tried again and again with the same result before concluding that it simply wasn't there or watching at the moment, and he would try again later.

While he waited, he thought about what he could do about the undead situation. The backwards incantation had not worked, even when he was nearby. Something told him it was the correct solution, but it just wasn't complete; something was missing from the process.

He looked around the room to see if he could find someone to talk to about the situation before realising he hadn't actually taken in the space around him. With the room now cleared out of people, Pthorn realised that this was actually a hospital. They had all gathered in the waiting room earlier, and the bedrooms were likely the mountebank's consultation rooms or surgeries. Before the plague struck, Falanar must have been a bustling hub to have needed such a large hospital; it probably helped to have that brothel to draw in the crowds, he supposed.

After looking around the room, he noticed one man sitting by himself, seemly daydreaming or just generally keeping to himself. He must have been about forty turns old, with grey streaking his jet-black hair.

"Excuse me," Pthorn said, by way of engagement, "Do you mind if I talk to you?"

"Not at all," he said, "any conversation beats staring at the floor."

"Aren't there jobs you can do to keep busy?" Pthorn asked, not wanting to pry too much.

"There are some I can do, but most of the time, I just find myself sitting on account of the lack of legs," he said, pointing at what Pthorn could now see were limp, dangling trouser legs.

"I am so sorry, I hadn't noticed. Do you mind me asking how it happened?" Pthorn asked.

"Not at all; it was a farming accident. When I was a little boy, I was helping my father plough the fields behind a moog. The tynes had become jammed on a large rock, and I went to investigate. I should have unhitched the moog because as I got the plough free, it became startled. It knocked me down and lamed my legs. The mountebanks managed to save me, but not my kickers."

"I am sorry to hear that," said Pthorn beginning to sound like he would be repeating that phrase regularly around here.

"I can't be too sorry. I believe it was all part of Assier's plan to save my life a few span ago, and probably many other times too. I still need the odd surgery or injure myself regularly by falling. That was why I was in this hospital the night of the undead's turning. I just hunkered down here while the others fortified the building," said the man, who seemed genuinely happy just to be alive.

"Do you hear much about what is happening outside the walls?" asked Pthorn, hoping that he hadn't picked the one person who knew the least.

"Oh yes," he said. "A lot of people stop for a chat, just like you. I think I have become the trading post of gossip around the compound."

"That's good then; I was hoping to learn more about the undead. You see, I think I can help, but I just need to understand more about them," said Pthorn positively.

"Unfortunately, I am not sure how much there is to tell. They don't really do much. Most of them just stay in the cold store warehouse a few buildings up," he said, pointing in the direction of the scene of Pthorn's ill-fated ritual. "A few have taken up residence back in their houses, but not many. They leave the buildings just to wander around aimlessly, mainly during the day; there is something to be said about a person's habits given they seem to continue to do them even after they are dead."

"Why do you think they are drawn to the warehouse?" probed Pthorn.

"Not sure exactly; maybe it helps preserve their bodies, although I am not sure they would be able to think about that. I had heard that they kept the bodies there when they arose; maybe that is just where they feel most at home," postulated the man.

"Or maybe there is something in there that connects them all," said Pthorn under his breath.

"What was that?" asked the man, leaning in to hear better.

"Oh, nothing, I was just thinking out loud," answered Pthorn quickly.

That had to be it, thought Pthorn to himself.

The hat.

He had left the hat behind filled with their blood. They were drawn to the connection of the blood. That had to be the missing part of the spell to rid the village of the walking dead.

Now he just needed a plan to get them to leave the warehouse so he could enter uninterrupted.

Pthorn excused himself from the conversation with the legless man and went up to the outer wall again to try to signal for Fluorocor again. Once again, his thoughts immediately turned to 'Undead and How to Control Them' from the *Necromance and Maleficence for the Malcontented Mage*, but he quickly dismissed it as the last resort option.

He would need a diversion over the other side of the village while he worked. Now he just had to work out what would cause the undead to investigate.

Pthorn had barely reached the barricading when he spotted a large black figure off into the distance; it was clear that another moog had succumbed to the hydrofluor as it was back the size of when they had left the Ayefyl Castle.

Pthorn waved to the beast, and it took off in a flap of wings, heading for the hospital compound.

"Do not fire!" announced Pthorn to reiterate Lowta's message earlier. "It will not harm you."

Fluorocor passed the barricade and landed on the open area behind Pthorn, lowering its head for the neck and back scratch it knew was coming.

As Pthorn obliged, Fluorocor placed its head on Pthorn's shoulder comfortingly.

44.

Supply Run

Fluorocor had barely been in the compound for an hour before Lowta thrust a scrawled, handwritten note into Pthorn's hand, along with a small wad of broan notes. He had been sitting outside, beside the napping hydrofluor, with his head buried into his hands. He was desperately trying to come to terms with the loss of Darn, but his friend by his side provided him with some small amount of support.

The arrival and direct approach of the late mayor's wife shook him out of his mind and into the daylight.

"I'm not sure how much this will buy," she said without any preamble, "but see what you can get from the list with what we have there."

Pthorn pocketed the stack of broan without counting them before holding up the note to read it. Even without counting the money, he could tell there would be nowhere near enough to cover the cost of the supplies. He made a mental note to dig into his own purse from the Sect funds; it would be the least he could do for the village's people.

"I will see what I can manage," he said as he placed the note into his pocket alongside the broan. "In the meantime, I want you to take this."

Pthorn reached into his knapsack, which he had untied from Fluorocor and was sitting beside him, then pulled out his remaining food supplies from their journey to Falanar.

"Thank you," she said, taking the hardtack, cheese and sausage. They both knew the food would not go far, but any supplies would be better than no supplies.

Pthorn cinched up the knapsack again, placing it by his side before he reclined up against Fluorocor's bulging underbelly.

"So tell me, how is it that you manage to come by a pet dragon?" she asked inquisitively. "Particularly being part of the clergy."

Pthorn thought for a few moments, trying to work out a way of maintaining his cover story without creating any new lies.

"I met Fluorocor while travelling here from Portsworth. At first, it was just a challenge to see if I could capture a hydrofluor for myself, you know, as a pet. But almost instantly, I realised that it was more than that. When you earn the trust of a hydrofluor, you create a bond. It was kinda like..." Pthorn trailed off as he realised what he was about to say; it was like the love between a couple.

Pthorn returned to his previous position of placing his head into his hands and hiding his face from the people around him.

Lowta placed her hand on his shoulder in solidarity. He wasn't sure if she had finished the sentence herself, but she knew when to leave him to his thoughts.

"It is too late in the day now to leave, but first thing tomorrow, you can go and be back by dark. There is a market in Maarts."

Pthorn made no move to confirm that he understood what she had said. Lowta gave him a couple of empathic pats on the shoulder before moving off.

Pthorn could feel the eyes of the surviving villagers staring at him and his slumbering friend, but he simply couldn't bring himself to care.

True to his word, as little as he had felt like it when he rolled out of the sleeping pallet, Pthorn mounted Fluorocor with his near-empty knapsack tied to its hindquarters. Fluorocor bowed its head as Pthorn threw his leg over its back, and he held on tightly to the rope reigns as they launched into the sky.

Pthorn looked down and surveyed the town as they soared higher into the sky. The five roads that intersected the village's centre looked like an orbite's web. There were a few undead wandering around aimlessly or just standing there staring blankly into the faelands; they looked like tiny insects stuck in the orbite's trap.

He could see the guards stationed on all sides of the hospital stronghold compound, keeping watch as they flew east towards Maarts.

They followed the road that they had entered the town on the first time, only this time half a league above the ground. The farmland turned into forest as the dense tree canopy spanned below them almost as far as the eye could see in all directions except the south.

He could pick out the waystops along the road by the tree clearings, although there seemed to be no travellers on the road between Falanar and Maarts, which was not surprising given the unfolding events. There hadn't been any on his first journey either.

The sun was almost directly overhead as the village of Maarts came into view. He first spotted the sizable market on the western end and the castle atop the hill to the north. Pthorn made a note to find out about the girl, Precil, whom he had raised. A cold chill surged through his body as he considered the consequences which may have occurred through her resurrection. He tried to set his mind at ease, telling himself that he had fixed her heart condition, and rot had not set in. It did little to comfort him.

Pthorn usually gave minimal direction to Fluorocor, but today he gave a slight tug to the right on the rope reins to direct them towards the southern road before they got close enough to be spotted. The hydrofluor banked right and they circled around in a wide arc, past the trees and over the edge of the broad fields. They didn't need any rumours spreading around the village that they had come from Falanar.

They came to land on the southern road and walked the rest of the way into the village centre, past the inn where they had stayed during their first visit.

Pthorn was about to turn left towards the markets when a familiar voice rang out from inside the trading post.

"Pthorn!" the voice called. "Hey, come over here!"

Pthorn stopped in his tracks before crossing the square to the trading post window.

Quidnunc was nowhere to be seen, but Rhet's colossal form was standing there, filling the void of the store.

"Good Assier, that thing has gotten huge!" he exclaimed. "How have your travels been recently? What brings you back to Maarts?" He asked as Pthorn approached the window.

Pthorn rathered not answer the first part of the question at the moment, instead focussing on the latter.

"One of the perks of being a mythical beast, I suppose. I am just filling up on supplies as I am passing through. It takes a lot to feed a hungry hydrofluor, you know." Pthorn was trying his best to politely return the conversation without actively engaging him further.

"We haven't seen her yet, but supposedly the mayor's girl made a miraculous recovery, just as you said. The village still can't believe it! I bet that bloody Quidnunc just made up the whole story to start a rumour. Then again, he was right about that plague over there in

Falanar," the large man said, gesticulating with his arms as his jowls flapped under his chin.

"You know what they say, sometimes miracles just happen," Pthorn answered non-committally and ignored the comments about the plague before continuing, "anyway, we had best be off. We want to make it to the first waystop before dark tonight."

"It is good to see you again, young man," Rhet said as Pthorn began to turn away. "Feel free to call in any time on your next travels."

Pthorn gave him a friendly one-fingered salute over his shoulder as he walked away with Fluorocor by his side.

The two walked the few hundred paces, past the low cottages and businesses, into the permanent markets that lined the western roadway. Just before the first stall, Pthorn removed the list from his cloak.

List of Supplies, in order of priority:
1. Finely milled flour
2. Water skins – 3 or 4 large volume
3. Root vegetables – Get a variety if possible
4. Hard cheese
5. Salt meats
6. *Chewing and smoking tobacco for Greff*

The final line of the list was in distinctively different handwriting. Pthorn suspected that Greff had somehow intercepted the note and added his own personal requirements.

Pthorn set off through the markets under the intently watchful eyes of the vendors, who would have clearly remembered his travel companion from their previous visit.

The first stand he stopped at sold a variety of ground nuts, germs and meals. He asked them to fill a small hessian bag with flour. He knew that this was going to fill half of the knapsack and weigh them down significantly, but he also knew that flour could be used as a base for almost all cooking within the compound. While he hoped he could find a solution to their undead problem quickly, there was no guarantee that he would achieve that goal.

Pthorn handed over almost the entire stack of broan he had received from Lowta to the vendor to pay for the flour. He knew for sure that he was going to be using his own funds for the rest of the list.

A vendor was selling hardened onk-bladder water skins, which he promptly purchased four of and tied to the side of the knapsack. The skins clunked together as he walked.

He purchased various root vegetables, some of which he had never seen before. Some were smooth and orange, while others were rough and purple or pink. Pthorn had no idea what they would taste like, but it didn't stop him from getting them to throw a few extras in.

He purchased the hard cheese and salt meats from the same vendor who offered him tastings of everything in the stall and even threw in a free soup bone for Fluorocor, who promptly devoured it before their eyes.

Lastly, Pthorn found a small vendor who was selling various grades, and types, of tobacco. The vendor claimed that some of the varieties would cause different intoxicating effects on the body; some would cause you to relax almost to the point of sleep, and others would have the opposite effect, meaning that you could stay awake for days. Pthorn opted for just the plain old smoking tobacco, which also happened to be the cheapest option at two broan for a pouch and papers.

Pthorn continued walking to the end of the markets and found a felled tree to set himself down on, placing the knapsack at his feet. He remembered seeing Tom smoking a pipe back inside the caves of the Sect and had smelt the harsh smoky smell on his robes, but he had never tried it himself. At that moment, curiosity got the better of him. He removed the pouch of tobacco he had placed into the bag and the tin of papers.

He took a small pinch of the brown, chopped-up leaf and placed it in the centre of the paper. Having never seen anyone roll one before, it was clumsy work. After several attempts at rolling, he was left with a reasonably crumpled, albeit almost cylindrical, tobacco tube.

He immediately realised that most people usually carry flint boxes to light their smokes. Without it, he would need to rely on his Manipulated Combustion. He covered his hand movements with the knapsack as he ignited one end of the tube. The paper which overhung the filling flared up and burnt down quickly before slowing down at the brown packing.

He raised the tobacco tube to his lips and tried inhaling.

Thick, acrid smoke immediately filled his lungs and set him to coughing. This seemed to bring almost as much attention to him as the gigantic hydrofluor had. He tried excusing himself through the coughs but instead opted to dismissively wave that he was okay.

Once he composed himself, he sat for a few moments before trying again. This time seemed far less harsh, although he still wondered why anyone would bother subjecting themselves to such discomfort. The tube had barely started to burn down before he disposed of it on the ground, crushing it with his boot. When he stood up, his head spun, and he immediately found reason to sit back down again.

He wasn't sure if the vendor had slipped him some of the 'special product' as he had called it or whether this was just the effect of the regular stuff. Either way, he sat there for far longer than he had intended before getting back up and leading Fluorocor back through the markets and into the square.

Pthorn was hoping that Rhet would have packed up the shop by then, but instead, he was still standing in his window watching as he walked by. If they left by the same road, the man would be suspicious about their destination; no one enters and leaves from the same direction. They continued walking in the opposite direction to Falanar and began down the eastern road towards Ung.

Heading in this direction, they came across several travellers on wagons pulled by equestra, as well as a small group travelling on foot. They had to travel for almost an hour before they were sure they were out of sight of the village and other travellers. By then, Pthorn could see the sun beginning to lower in the sky. If the sun set completely before they made it back to the stronghold, he would be relying completely on Fluorocor's nighttime vision to get them back. There would be nothing he could do to correct their course or observe dangers.

They took off into the sky and headed north; there would be more tree cover and less risk of them being seen flying back towards Falanar.

They circled in a wide arc while keeping the village, and mayor's castle, in view at all times. Pthorn wondered what sort of house Lowta, and her late husband, had lived in, being the mayor of Falanar. He had not seen any grand residence or castle in the village, but he also didn't want to pry into their recently destroyed private lives.

As they travelled further west, the air became colder once again, and Falanar flew closer to the ground; they were hidden by the trees, and very few people would dare to head west, so they didn't need elevation at this point to hide. The sun also dipped lower and lower, brightly beaming directly into their eyes. Pthorn had to hold on with one arm while he shielded his face from the wind and sun simultaneously.

Finally, they were met with a reprieve from the discomfort. Just as the sun was about to finish its descent beyond the horizon, the village of Falanar came into view. Pthorn blinked the blindness out of his eyes as he tried to focus on the buildings. Curiously, he noted that the fancy black wagon that he had noticed upon their arrival to the stronghold was still parked in the village;

however, he saw that it seemed to be facing the other direction. The equestra also seemed to be completely unaccosted by the undead.

Pthorn tried to get a better look, but the wagon fell from view as they came in to land within the barricades of the hospital's compound.

Pthorn made a mental note to ask around the hospital to see if anyone knew who might have been travelling in the wagon; although he couldn't seem to see it from within the compound, he wondered if anyone else even knew it was there.

45.
The Distraction

The moment Pthorn landed inside the compound, he was immediately set upon by the local villages. He had the horrible, gut-wrenching thought for a moment that somehow they had either become or been replaced by the walking dead from outside. Instead, they were just hungry and malnourished villages who wanted to get the first takings of the supplies.

Thankfully they were quickly dispersed by Lowta, who slapped a moog leather belt on the hospital's wall, creating a surprisingly loud, 'crack' noise to be emitted.

The sound echoed off the buildings in the area as the villagers all scurried away.

"Follow me," she said as Pthorn untied the knapsack from Fluorocor, "we needn't unpack where this lot can see us."

Pthorn finished untying the last strap and gave the hydrofluor a quick scratch on the back of the neck before falling in tow behind the mayor's wife.

She led him into the hospital's kitchen. It was down a flight of stone stairs in the basement of the building. It was pretty large, as it had been used to cater for quite a number of people, both sick and working in the hospital.

Pthorn placed the bag on the preparation bench and unloaded the goods. He put them in turn onto the counter as a look of surprise spread across the woman's face.

Pthorn stopped short of removing the tobacco but was met with a disbelieving look and a beckoning hand.

"Come on, I can read it on your face. What aren't you handing over? Are you keeping something for yourself?" she asked accusingly.

"No!" he said all too quickly and defensively. "It's not that. I didn't think you knew about the last thing on the list."

Pthorn removed the tobacco and papers before handing them over alongside the note for her to see the final request.

"That little bastard!" she exclaimed, although she didn't seem to sound that surprised or disappointed. "Well, if there is one thing for sure, he is going to share the puff around... and he goes last!"

Pthorn stood awaiting his dismissal, which came shortly thereafter in the form of a backhanded wave as Lowta stacked the supplies into a cupboard and locked it behind her. Pthorn noted the key was placed into her pocket as he left the room.

It was several more days before Pthorn felt confident enough that he had developed a plan for distracting the undead, allowing him to enter the cold store unhindered. Over that time, he had asked several of the villagers and, in particular, the guards whether they had noticed the carriage. One said they had seen the carriage on the day he arrived but not since; he suspected it had moved along shortly after, probably after discovering the village was missing its friendly portion of villagers. Pthorn knew it had lingered longer after seeing it as he flew back from the supply run, but it must have remained out of sight of the compound.

While Pthorn didn't get any form of confirmation about who it was or why it was lurking, he concluded that the undead didn't seem bothered about attacking animals. The seemly unprotected equestra were unharmed on both occasions that he had witnessed the carriage loitering.

This was insightful, but if anything it was counterproductive to his plan. It meant that any live bait to lure the undead away from the cold store could not be of the beastly variety; instead, it would need to be human. That would require brave volunteers, something they were desperately in short supply. Pthorn hardly could blame them for not wanting to get torn about by rotting corpses wielding rudimentary weapons.

His plan was going to be simple.

He would be the one to distract them.

It was early on the fourth day after he had gone on the supply run, and food stocks were again dwindling; the root vegetable soup had simply become a ration of water and unleavened bread. Lowta had gathered everyone not currently on guard duty to listen to Pthorn's plan and allow volunteers to assist. Besides needing time to devise the plan, he also required the villagers to feel desperate enough to want to help with the dangerous task.

The room was awash with noise. The cacophony was beginning to hurt his ears as he stood patiently waiting for Lowta to call the meeting to order.

She didn't.

Instead, he realised that it was his show to run.

Firstly he tried loudly clearing his throat, which was about as ineffectively as stopping a sea's wave with his foot. Next, he tried yelling "oi", which was also swept away in the din.

His struggles with calling the room to attention were quickly noticed by the legless man that he had met a few days passed. *I must ask him his name,* thought Pthorn to himself as the man placed two fingers into his mouth and blew a loud, ear-piercing whistle.

The room quickly drew to a calm murmur as everyone about-turned to see where the noise had come from.

Pthorn cleared his throat again.

"Ahem, I have asked everyone to be here tonight because I cannot do what I plan to do alone."

Before he could say any more, the heckling began.

"He wants us to be the bait."

"Suicide. It's bloody suicide, I tell ya."

It took all of Pthorn's willpower not to use his powers to reach into the various heckler's chests and slow their hearts down until they collapsed. Pthorn calmed himself and held his hand up to silence them.

"I am not asking any of you to be the bait. That is my job," he said before awaiting the change in mood and gasping to dissipate. "All I ask is for four volunteers. I will need two to close the front door of the cold store and two to close the back door. You will need to find some way of wedging or securing the door. That will be up to you."

"… and just what will you be doing?" responded one of the men who had started the heckling moments before.

"I will be doing two jobs. Firstly, Fluorocor there," he said, pointing outside, "will fly me out into the village centre, causing all of the walkers to try to attack me. It won't take long if it is anything like the welcome party I got on the way here. While I do that, you guys will shut and secure the doors to the cold store."

Pthorn waited for the heckler to continue, but they seemed to have given up trying to goad him.

"Once you give me the signal that the cold store is secure, Fluorocor will fly me up to the roof. During a flyover yesterday, I noticed an access hatch I can use. From then on, just hope and pray that I know what I am doing."

The room now remained in a state of silence, a stark contrast to the raging noise at the start of the meeting.

"So, who wants to volunteer?" Pthorn asked.

The silence continued and became deafening until finally, the last person Pthorn expected to volunteer did just that.

"Fine, you can sign Greff here up. But only as long as I get to take the backdoor… hey Sabelle." The greasy and overgrown-faced man, who had just been heckling Pthorn throughout his speech, chuckled at his own joke and made eyes towards the woman sitting on the other side of the room. She rolled her eyes at him as though it was the hundredth time he had made the same creepy joke.

Slowly others, spurred on by Greff's bravery, began to volunteer. Shortly Pthorn had his four volunteers and several others who offered to assist in other ways, such as creating a jamming device for the doors.

Eventually, the room filled with noise again as everyone discussed the plan and all the ways they believed it could go wrong. Not least of which was the discussion of what Pthorn planned to do once he was inside the building.

Even that question was on the tip of Pthorn's own tongue as he left the room to gather his thoughts and be alone for a few more hours.

He wasn't quite sure what made him do it, but as he sat on the end of his sleeping pallet, he closed his eyes and read his plan quietly to Darn. Pthorn knew she wasn't there, but somehow talking to her calmed him and gave him the confidence that it might just work.

When he was finished, he found himself crying softly to himself before laying down and curling up for the night; once again wishing that she would be by his side in the morning's light.

Once again, his wish was not granted, and he woke up alone, by himself, in the cold sleeping pallet. Pthorn forced himself to get out of bed before heading outside towards Fluorocor. The hydrofluor was to be their meeting point for the start of the mission; it wasn't long before the volunteers, and a large number of villagers showed up.

"So everyone knows what they are doing?" Pthorn confirmed with the teams. "Greff and Salla, you are both on the back door. It is a single door and should be fairly easy to secure, although I am led to believe the latch has been badly damaged... somehow. Thomat and Hun, you are on the front door. It is a double door and is fairly easily swung open. How are you securing it?"

The two large men standing at the front of the ground held up an arsenal of nails, hammers and wooden planks.

"Good!" said Pthorn, surveying their tools and supplies. "I suppose we are lucky we even had that much. Now, who do I signal?"

A shout came from the roof of the hospital. "Aye, that would be me. We have a bell up here. One ring, and it means you have them distracted. Two rings, and it means it is clear for you to return... and if I ring it like this...." He rang the bell furiously. "It means you are fucked."

The man laughed to himself and was joined by a select few in the crowd.

"Thank you, I think," said Pthorn as he redirected his attention to the volunteers. "May Assier look fondly upon you this day. Praise be to Assier!" he said, expecting an echoed response.

The response didn't come; given the circumstances, it would seem that the village had lost faith in the Almighty. Pthorn couldn't blame them, even if it was he who they were losing their faith in. Pthorn wasn't entirely sure he had faith in himself either. In that moment, Pthorn remembered his first lesson in Creating fire; he had to truly believe that he could do it before it would work.

The thought spurred him into action. Pthorn mounted Fluorocor and took off into the air, but they didn't fly high into the sky this time. This time they stayed low and hovered for a few moments before heading north towards the cold store. Fluorocor set itself down in front of the large double door. Pthorn surveyed the road and beyond, finding that there were no undead within sight. He knew that once alerted, they could become completely engulfed in a matter of moments.

After last night's meeting, Pthorn had spoken to the legless man; whom he now knew was named Semma. He had asked him how to make the whistle with his hand. After being shown and trying in vain for half the night, he finally managed to make the correct shape with his tongue to whistle.

Now was the moment.

He placed his thumb and mid-finger into his mouth, pushing back his tongue and blew. A perfect whistle emitted from his mouth.

Pthorn didn't have long to celebrate, the undead were immediately on the offensive, and the doors flew open. They stayed on the ground long enough to ensure the walkers took the bait before Fluorocor kicked off and started hovering again. This time they were just out of reach for the tallest of them. Slowly they led the group, which was still filing through the doors, down the road and into the village centre. Fluorocor gained altitude as the undead began to push each other over and stand on the fallen, writhing bodies.

By this time, the flow of bodies from the cold store had gone from a torrent to a steady stream to a trickle, with just the last few stragglers coming through now. The last ones exiting had been the most affected by the rot, with many looking like it would not be long before they completely succumbed to it.

Pthorn noted below that many of the bodies had mortal wounds, like deep gashes and the odd arrow protruding from an eye socket. He thought about how difficult it must have been to overpower them and get everyone they could into the hospital.

Another thought also came unbidden to his mind. *What happened to the plague? Wasn't everyone dying from the disease in the first place before all of this started?*

These questions were shaken from his mind as he heard the first bell ring. That would mean someone had scouted in through the back door to confirm that he had completed the first phase of his plan and distracted them. He had no idea how long it would last; eventually, they would tire of trying to reach him, just as they had given up trying to penetrate the walls of the hospital stronghold.

Pthorn tried not to look in the direction of the cold store lest he give away their position.

The pile of undead continued to grow and fall as they all clambered over each other.

After a few long moments, some of the latecomers simply about turned and started heading back towards the ice-cold comforts of the cold store. Pthorn dared a glance finding Thomat and Hun still working feverishly to secure the doors.

Pthorn immediately knew they were out of time, as did the guard atop the hospital, who started ringing the bell as fast as he could.

The two-man front door security team went into double time, not caring how much noise they made to mount the planks of wood across the door. There was no guarantee for how long it would hold, but by the time they broke off into a run, three planks crossed the wooden doors and a wedge below each hammered into place.

The two sprinted as the slow undead howled the alarm, alerting the others to the deception occurring below their noses. Some remained intent on trying to bring down Fluorocor; the ones who got too close received a healthy spray of acid, which began bubbling their already grotesque skin, but didn't completely stop them. Most of the others made for the two on the ground.

Pthorn had distracted for as long as he could, he gave Fluorocor a pat on the back of the neck, and they shot off into the air and back in the direction of the cold store.

They alighted the roof in a matter of moments, unable to spare any time to help those on the ground; they had no way of knowing how, or if, the doors would hold and for how long.

Pthorn turned to his friend. "Thank you," he said. "Now, you go see if the others need help."

Fluorocor took to the air once more as Pthorn turned his attention to the hatch.

46.
Neutralisation

Pthorn pulled hard on the iron handle attached to the weather-worn timber hatch. Naively, he had expected it to come away freely, but when he pulled, all he achieved was throwing himself off balance. He repositioned himself above the hatch again, placing his feet on either side and bending his knees. He grasped the handle with both hands and pulled as hard as he could. Once again, the hatch didn't budge.

Pthorn was mentally kicking himself for not landing on the roof yesterday and ensuring that the hatch could move.

He looked around frantically, placing both hands on his head to think. The roof was completely barren, with no tools or planks in sight. Pthorn walked to the edge of the roof, back towards the direction of the hospital. At ground level, he could see several villagers leaning over the edge of the barricade, trying to grab flailing hands. Pthorn couldn't tell who was still outside the compound or whether any of the four security volunteers had yet been saved.

Checking in on the progress of the others was doing nothing to improve his own predicament. He continued looking around for anything he could use to pry the hatch open or break the hinges.

"How is there nothing here?" Pthorn cried aloud. "Who doesn't store shit on their roof to help people break in?" he continued sarcastically.

Pthorn sat on the ground and closed his eyes to think; surely he could use his powers to get himself out of this mess. After a few long moments, one thought sprang to mind.

He cursed himself for not thinking of it sooner. He stood back and held out his arms at full extension towards the hatch. Just as he usually did with kindling for a fire, he Manipulated the old wood to Combust. Usually, he would just cut off the connection once he saw a flame, but today would be an exception. He didn't just want to ignite the wood; he wanted to burn it away. He hoped that the rest of the structure wouldn't follow suit and become engulfed as well.

Pthorn burned enough of the wood away that he could see through a gap and into the cold store below. He reached back down and grabbed the handle again; the edge of the wood would be too hot to handle. This time when he pulled, the hatch creaked open on its rusty hinges.

Pthorn looked down through the hole to assess what lay below. There was no ladder nor staircase for him to safely descend. There was nothing except hard stone.

At this point, Pthorn was entirely out of options, and he knew he was also running out of time. He could hear the double front doors banging and creaking on their hinges through the hole. Pthorn hoped that once the security team was safely back behind the barricades, Fluorocor would start clearing off the undead from the entrance.

Pthorn sat down on the edge of the roof, the hatch was still smouldering, but without the constant Manipulation, it wasn't able to sustain the flame. As his feet passed into the void, he felt the ice-cold air rushing up below his robes; it wasn't entirely a pleasant feeling.

Pthorn collected himself and let his body fall to the floor. He was in freefall for several moments before he felt his legs crumple underneath the weight of his body. His knees came up, and pushed one of his teeth through his lip.

Assier farmin' Almighty!

He felt around, coming up with a red hand, but there seemed to be no broken or missing teeth to be found.

He collected himself from the ground and rose to his feet. The pounding at the door was getting more incessant and had also moved to the rear door. For now, everything seemed to be holding.

As he started taking in his surroundings, everything turned upside down again. The attack had come from his right, and he never saw the assailant coming towards him in the dark. His head hit the stone floor with a deafening and sickening 'crack,' causing his vision to darken further and fae-wisps to dance in front of his eyes.

Thankfully his wits didn't altogether leave him, and he rolled defensively to his side, kicking off the attacker as he went. He felt the body fly in the opposite direction and heard the 'thunk' as it contacted the wall or floor.

Pthorn staggered to his feet, still unable to see properly in the dim light. He immediately regretted not arming himself with anything, even as little as a small knife. He once again cursed himself for not using his abilities to look for lifeforms before entering.

One day I might finally learn!

Pthorn tried to focus in the low light, looking for movement rather than bodies. He tried to pick outlines in the dark or light dancing off anything that shouldn't move. He didn't have time now to use his power.

For a few moments, there was nothing, and then came the grunting and gnashing of teeth. When the form was only two or three paces from himself, he finally saw the outline of the aggressive undead.

It wasn't really the moment for critical thinking, but it crossed his mind that this must have been one of the least rotted corpses with some level of brain power remaining. It had the forethought not to run off and follow the others, fearing a trap. Pthorn hadn't previously given the idea of them being able to strategize any credence, but now he was second-guessing that assumption.

The crafty undead launched itself at Pthorn again, but this time he was ready. Pthorn quickly sprinted across the room, desperately searching the floor to make sure he didn't trip over.

He was also searching for a weapon, anything which could be used to slow down his attacker. He knew it was unlikely that he would be able to completely incapacitate it, short of removing its head or legs.

Fearing no alternative, Pthorn attempted to reach into the undead's body and control its heart. Unfortunately for Pthorn, this yielded abysmal results. Besides being able to focus on its body, which at least allowed him to locate and track it, there was nothing he could do to exploit its weaknesses. He found the heart was still; there was clearly some sort of external force allowing its muscles to contract in lieu of blood flow. He searched deeper within and found the microscopic lifeforms which constituted the plague were still alive and thriving within the deceased body; this confirmed his suspicions that an attack from one of them could transfer the disease to your own body.

Pthorn zoomed his senses out to focus on the human-sized lifeforms in the room. There was his direct attacker, clearly trying to stalk him in the dark room, and there were also several very faint shadows of life strewn across the floor. They didn't seem to be a source of immediate danger, so Pthorn returned his attention to the one zeroing in on him.

The undead launched itself again at him, and Pthorn dodged, using his power to his advantage to almost predict each attack. The undead didn't seem to be armed with any form of weapon, which was something at least, but Pthorn needed to find something to give himself the upper hand.

Pthorn circled back around the room, trying not to put his back to his attacker. He started going back towards the front entrance, trying to ignore the noises coming from that direction, when he tripped over again. His shoulder hit the ground hard, but the hard shape under his leg gave him reason to pause.

His hand shot down towards his feet, and he felt the ice-cold iron bar. His fingers curled around it, pain immediately filling his hand from the cold.

He pushed himself up from the floor and waited.

The figure he was focusing on very slowly crept towards him, and he raised his arm over his shoulder. He gripped the bar with two hands, shaking from the anticipation.

One step.

Two steps.

Three steps.

Finally, the form was in range. Pthorn lashed out as hard as he could, swinging the bar at the undead's head. The sound resembled a combined 'crack' and wet 'squelch' as the bar collapsed the side of its head. It wasn't quite the decapitation that Pthorn was hoping for, but it seemed to do the job.

The undead form staggered for a moment before falling to the ground in a crumpled heap.

Finally, Pthorn could breathe the cold frigid air and take in the room without imminent fear of attack, besides those outside the door pounding to get in. He looked around the dim room; the only light passing in was through the hatch he had left open above his head. Throughout the attack, he hadn't been able to focus on anything. Now everything was still again; his eyes soon adjusted, and what he found was certainly not what he expected.

A few bodies were lying on the floor, wholly immobile but seemingly still animated. He had seen them while searching for the attacker's form but hadn't realised what they were. They groaned almost silently with nothing moving but their lips, like a gasping ghoti.

But it wasn't the almost dead undead that surprised him; it was the shrine that had been built within the small broken-off room. There were all sorts of personal effects like clothes, boots, and the odd piece of jewellery, and sitting proudly atop the lot was his white banded, black hat.

The undead must have been able to either sense the power of it, or it had simply been the only thing in the room when they awoke. Either way, it seemed very curious to Pthorn.

He made his way over to the improvised shrine and removed the hat, peering inside as he did. It was far heavier than he had expected. The undead had clearly been careful when moving it to ensure the blood contained within it did not spill; either that or they had waited for the blood to dry before they attempted its relocation.

The hat was still half full with a solid, black mass.

Pthorn remembered that the instructions for the resurrection had specified that you must stir the blood if it had separated, so he hoped that this would still work.

Pthorn heard one of the planks on the door splinter as he placed the hat in the centre of the room, about the same location as when he had first performed the ritual.

Standing back, he completed the chant backwards, just as he had practised.

He watched and waited.

Nothing happened.

The banging continued outside on the door, "What am I missing?" Thought Pthorn aloud to himself.

He paced around the room, cursing as he walked.

He was so distracted by trying to work out what to do that he almost missed the first sign that it was working.

When he performed the resurrection, the light entered the hat and then flowed out into the room, touching each plague victim. This time the light was travelling in reverse. It flowed into the room through the door and solid stone wall.

The light collected and coalesced in the middle of the hat before shooting into the sky through the roof. When the light had entered during the first ritual, it had been cold; now, it felt like a furnace had taken its place. The space around the hat rippled in waves of heat as the column of light became a column of fire.

What started as cool white light had become a fierce red fire, burning away the blood which had been used to focus the life into the beings in the first place, and along with it, the hat, which had acted as a channel of life from his own supply.

As the light flared, it poured into the room, illuminating the mangled bodies strewn across the floor. The banging on the doors finally began to slow, and the heat from the column of light-turned-fire began to cool within the cold store once more.

Silence and icy cold returned once more.

Pthorn hadn't realised just how loud the sound of the undead outside the door had been until it stopped. It was like suddenly becoming deaf; only he could hear his own heart beating violently, trying to escape from his chest.

Pthorn couldn't believe what his senses were telling him. Had he really done it? Had he achieved what he and Darn had set out to do?

The thought of Darn at that moment was the final straw in the well of emotion that had been building within him. He fell to his knees, placed his head on the ice-cold stone floor, and wept.

Pthorn had no concept of how long he stayed in that position on the floor. By the time he raised his head, both the front and back doors had been jimmied open, and natural light flooded the gruesome scene.

Directly in front of him sat a small pile of ash, no evidence left of the hat, or the blood, that he had used for the resurrection ritual. It was for the best; if the locals had recognised the hat as being the same as the one he was currently wearing, then questions were sure to be asked, and he was confident he didn't want to try to come up with an explanation.

Pthorn wasn't sure how the villages would react coming face to face with their attackers, but it wasn't what he witnessed. He watched on as villager after villager sat down beside a corpse and wept over it.

It occurred to Pthorn that these weren't just killer undead beings out for vengeance that he had slain; these were family members who had died tragically. They were mothers, fathers, sons, daughters, and various other relatives.

What he expected to see was relief. What he saw was love and grief.

It was now time for the villagers to mourn their loss, just as he needed to find a way to mourn the loss of Darn.

It was Lowta who first came over to approach him. She had no one in the room to mourn; she had already lost her husband to the plague and watched him burn in a pyre.

She didn't offer any words of gratitude, nor did she offer words of comfort. She simply stood beside him and placed her hand on his shoulder before offering the other to him.

For a good few moments, he let her hand hover in the void in front of his face. She didn't wave her hand nor force it upon him.

Finally, he reached out his hand and took hers in his, allowing her to pull him to his feet.

He didn't know what, or how, to feel at this time. This moment was the culmination of one of the worst mistakes of his life, combined with the most tremendous loss, coupled with the greatest success. What the following days, span or turns held for him, he wasn't sure.

He had made plans to leave the Sect, either temporarily or permanently, and travel the world with Darn; those plans have come crashing down.

He knew how he was meant to feel; it was a victory, and he should feel elated. Pthorn felt this victory was anything but elating.

He allowed Lowta to pull him to his feet and followed her into the evening air. Comparatively to the room, it was warm and mild.

"Thank you," she finally said, offering the gratitude that would have been deserved had he not been the cause in the first place. "We are in your debt. There is no need to cash in now, but should you ever need anything, Falanar will be here for you."

She patted him on the shoulder and moved on to comfort her peers.

Pthorn looked around at the carnage which lay strewn across the road and verge. Rotting corpses lined the street, as did the mourners who clutched them with overwhelming grief.

47.

Got to Go

That night the pyres started to burn brightly once more. Where they had previously waited before to have the rites read for each of the dead, tonight they were given no such ritual or individual ceremony. It had come as an unspoken general consensus that the bodies of those who were undead should be burned to prevent any further reoccurrence of reanimation.

The pyres started as being neatly laid out, almost in a grid, in the centre of the village. By the time all the bodies had been collected, the gaps in between had been filled, and it became one huge bonfire. The wood had primarily been sourced from the barricading used as protection around the hospital to keep the very people they were burning out.

In lieu of the usual proceedings, Lowta insisted that Pthorn himself should lead them all on a short prayer and combined eulogy; given that he was there as a representative of the clergy, it only made sense that he should be able to deliver something.

The fires had not yet been lit when Pthorn started his address. The remaining villagers-in-mourning stood on the northern road as he stood beside Lowta just in front of the great pyre.

"People of Falanar. Today will always be looked back upon as both a day of great sadness and of great victory. Sadness over those loved ones who have been lost, not only once to disease but twice to strange, unholy events. The victory was won in coming together as a village and overcoming those events."

Pthorn let his words wash over the crowd.

"You will all have questions; these will linger long after those who witnessed them today are gone. I am sure you will pass these questions, as stories, on to your children, who will, in turn, pass them on to their children. Today will be spoken of in legend as though they are fae tales. Know this as truth; those whom we bid a final farewell today will be welcomed by Assier Almighty into the Kingdom of the Singularity. Now we say goodbye."

Pthorn turned to watch as Lowta used flint to ignite a torch, which she then used to start the flames dancing through the kindling on the base of the pyre.

Pthorn subtly focused on the slowly combusting wood and helped it along with some Manipulation. Within moments, the fire spread across the vast timber structure, forcing the locals to move back. Sections of the structure hissed and spat as the oils dripped from the wood. It was clear that at least some of the wood had not been aged long and sent a large plume of smoke high into the air, drifting off silently into the night.

As everyone looked on, Pthorn slipped away back towards the hospital where Fluorocor was patiently awaiting his return. Looking on as the fire burned away the bodies of all those that had been located just made the pain worse for Pthorn; there would be no further closure for the loss of Darn. She would never have her rites, pyre or public eulogy. Only one person was mourning her loss, and he couldn't give her anything of the ceremony she deserved.

Guilt began to eat him from inside once again, and the bile started to rise as he walked. He held it down until he reached the front door to the hospital before he could feel it find his throat. Pthorn turned to the bushes to the right of the entrance and violently upended his lunch. It did little to stop the feeling inside him, which continued to burn far worse than any stomach acid could.

Pthorn passed through the front door, wiping the vomit from his face onto his sleeve, before making his way upstairs to pick up his knapsack from his sleeping quarters. All he could think of now was putting as much distance as possible between himself and this village. He had almost finished filling the bag with his vials and books when he suddenly became aware that he was not the only person to have left the burning early.

Pthorn turned and found his exit blocked by the late mayor's wife.

"I assume you plan to leave now?" she asked him, full-well knowing the answer to her own question.

"My job here is done," Pthorn replied, not offering any more by way of response.

"I know you can't tell me what happened in there," she said, pointing at the wall in the direction of the warehouse. "But I just want to reiterate to you that this village will forever be in your debt."

Pthorn lowered his eyes to the floor, unable to meet her gaze for fear of her finding out the cause of the problem in the first place. He tried to push his thoughts of Darn aside and think of some way to leave without the perception of debt. He remembered all of the questions that he had meant to ask.

"A debt is the last thing Assier, the clergy, or I want. If you can answer my questions, I will consider the debt to be paid, agreed?" Pthorn offered, hopefully.

"Ask me anything, and if I know the answer, it is yours for the taking," she replied.

"What happened to the plague?" he asked of her. "Wasn't there a plague causing everyone to die in the first place?"

Lowta gave a half chortle under her breath. "I have asked myself that same question. I don't know for certain, but I can give you my opinion."

Pthorn gestured for her to continue.

"I believe the resurrection of the undead actually saved this town from the plague," she said, almost sounding like she didn't quite believe her own theory. "When they began to rise, we all shut ourselves in the hospital, which also happens to be one of the cleanest places in the village. No dirt floors and no rodent infestations. We lost a few in the first couple of days, but after that, the disease ended. Who knows how many others could have perished if the disease had not been stopped."

Pthorn considered her theory for a few moments before accepting that he had no better theory or rebuttal.

"My second question is purely for personal interest. When I was in the warehouse, it was frigidly cold. How does that work with no ice for leagues?"

"A man who can't help but question how everything works. You were just like my husband; the cold store was one of the town's highlights that he couldn't wait to explain to every gentleman and noble who came by. You must be aware of the existence of volcanos?" she asked.

Pthorn had heard of them, but most recently, in the book of Necromance and Maleficence for the Malcontented Mage, which gave instructions for causing a regular mountain to erupt. Pthorn nodded his head, thinking better of getting into more detail.

"Well, fire and molten rock isn't the only thing Azarth hides below its crusty exterior. Deep within the rock is a storage of some sort of gas. We cannot see or smell it, and it doesn't seem to ignite with flame, but it passes up constantly through a fissure in the rock below the cold store. Generations ago, our village discovered this gas, which was ice cold. They built the store around the fissure and allowed the gas to pass inside the double stone walls," she explained, proud on behalf of her village and late husband.

"Thank you," Pthorn replied honestly. He hated not knowing the answer to a question, and he had told himself to discover the answer to these ones.

"You may consider the debt settled, but if you ever need anything, Falanar will be here for you. All you need to do is ask." Lowta began to turn to leave the room but stopped short of walking down the hallway, "I meant what I said just after you arrived, you need to keep focusing on achieving the things you want, and need, to achieve, but you also need to grieve. Everything you do, do it to keep the memory of Darn alive, and most importantly, you need to learn how to forgive yourself."

Pthorn continued to stare at the floor as Lowta left down the hallway. He was going to be a long way off forgiving himself for a lot of things.

Pthorn found Fluorocor standing out in the field behind the hospital. Once they acknowledged each other's presence, they closed the gap between themselves, meeting in the middle.

"I am not sure what happens after we leave here," said Pthorn as he reached up to scratch the back of the hydrofluor's neck. "But I think I have to go back."

Fluorocor let out a long, drawn-out clicking screech, lowering its head further in disappointment.

"Come with me, at least for now. I am unsure how, but we will make it work," Pthorn promised hopefully. "But first, we need to stop off back at Maarts. There is something I think I need to do."

The giant beast perked up at the thought of another adventure, clicking happily again. Pthorn tied his knapsack on to Fluorocor and mounted it with the rope reins in hand. Fluorocor kicked off the ground and flapped its wings, sending them into a wide arc around the field. They looped around to the north, avoiding the large plume of smoke from the burning wood and bodies below. Pthorn noted that there was no sign of the black equestra-drawn carriage that had been parked in the village for the last few days. Pthorn kicked himself for not asking Lowta if she had known anything about it but given the rest of the villagers had no idea, he didn't hold high hopes anyway.

Once again, not wanting to draw any attention to themselves, they stayed low over the northern forest and began their journey east. This time he wanted as few people as possible to be aware of his trip to Maarts; if his fears were correct, then there would still be one more person left to deal with. He only had the basic outline of a plan in his head; while he did have a new hat, he no longer had any of the girl's blood, so he wasn't even sure he had a way to reverse the resurrection. When he had drawn the blood from her arm, she had recently died; if the rot had set in, it was unlikely he would be able to get a sample from her.

Either way, he decided that arriving in the middle of the night would not achieve any desirable results. Instead, he pointed Fluorocor in the direction of a waystop, and they set down for the night.

48.

One Last One

The next day they set off once more into the sky, heading east towards Maarts. Pthorn felt like a cauldron of emotion; the loss of Darn, nervous about what he might find with Precil, and terrified of what would happen if Tom found out what had transpired.

He had already decided that he would not tell Tom any details, only that he was returning to the Sect because he was not ready to enter the world as Death. He hoped that he could bury himself back into study to help forgive himself and forget.

Today, his focus needed to be on one thing: finding out whether Precil was a happy and healthy child again or a monster locked away in the castle by her still grieving parents who had been fed false hope. The thought that he had caused this type of grief for a family ate at him from within.

No matter how often he had told himself that it was somehow different for her, it didn't make any difference to the ball of concern that had swelled inside his gut.

As they flew, Fluorocor tried its best to raise his spirits. It performed a swooping dive to pluck a small squarn from the ground as the rodent stuck its head from the exit of its warren. It flew up and down, banking left and right. The aerial acrobatics went some way to distract him, and he felt a small smile begin to radiate across his face before the worry started to set back in.

After several hours the mayor's castle came into view, and they veered their path towards the north. They passed over the dense forest before coming to a rest within the sprawling grounds of the estate. Pthorn thought it best for them to enter via the road; it was always a better option to limit the number of things that might increase the unease of your hosts at any given time. He was already travelling with a black dragon and had brought their daughter back from the dead so just appearing in the mayor's courtyard seemed to be a step too far.

Pthorn led Fluorocor up the road towards the manor. The last time he had been here, the grounds were bare of people; he assumed that all servants, aside from the personal guards, had been temporarily dismissed on the grounds of mourning. Now the grounds seemed like a veritable hive of activity. At least ten gardeners spread across the estate that he could see tending to grass, flowers and various other forms of foliage. They were all dressed in white robes, not dissimilar to those he had been given back in Strauth before heading overseas. Most nobles would have provided nothing more than rough spun, like his clothes back home on the farm. This mayor clearly treated his workers well or, at the very least, wished to appear that way.

The workers all stopped in the middle of what they were doing to turn and watch the pair pass by. Perhaps it was that Pthorn's description matched that of the man who had brought either further pain, or relief, to the family, or it could just be the enormous hydrofluor accompanying a strange man in grey robes.

Pthorn was used to inquisitive eyes by now, but somehow his guilty conscience made him second-guess his mission for the day. There was nothing more that he could do now except face the mayor and hope for the best-case scenario; that she had regained her consciousness, her heart had healed and that he would simply see her chasing flying insects over the manicured lawns.

So far, there was no such sign of the girl, although he hoped that the return of the gardeners wasn't simply a matter that a period of grief had passed. Rhet had said that he believed the girl to be in good health but that no one had seen her since. The way rumours went with Rhet and Quidnunc, Pthorn simply didn't know what to believe.

One of the guards must have spotted them on the approach as the large double doors began to open just as they arrived at the base of the stairs. Fluorocor hung back as Pthorn gave him a scratch and continued towards the entrance.

Before Pthorn had even reached the top of the stone staircase, he found the doorway darkened by the forms of the mayor and his wife. They were no longer in the robe of mourning that they had donned last time, and they seemed to be out of tears.

They also seemed to be short of words.

Pthorn was offered nothing by way of greeting, or dismissal for that matter. Instead, the two turned and led Pthorn silently through the main foyer of the manor and down the long hall. Pthorn also realised that he was dressed as a priest the last time he was here; if they asked, he would need to make up some excuse like these were his travelling robes or something.

They were heading towards the makeshift mortuary that had been set up towards the rear of the building. Concern began to rise once more within Pthorn.

He looked back over his shoulder towards the front door, trying to make a mental note of an escape route should the need arise. He found the guards had already closed the door behind him, leaving him no easy choice. When he turned back, he found himself falling a few steps behind and half-jogged to catch back up again.

His heartbeat reached a crescendo as the couple reached the room with the stone bench and passed right by without given the room a second thought or glance. As Pthorn passed, he peered inside and caught a glimpse of the room piled high with boxes and miscellaneous items. He gathered that it had once again returned to its previous use as a storage room.

Just past the storage room was the end of the hall, which terminated in a large, heavy, iron-banded door. The mayor fingered the latch and pulled it open, revealing a private garden. The garden was centred with a huge, pure white form of two intertwined bodies with crystal clear water cascading down their bodies. A large font encircled the statues, which collected the water. Pthorn looked around for the source of the water and found a raised tank off to the side of the manor. A lone servant was turning a wheel that sent a bucketing mechanism from the font's drain to the top of the tower.

Surely his arm must be killing him? Was Pthorn's first thought as he continued to take in the surrounds.

At first, he could see nothing more than the curious fountain mechanism and the surrounding bushes, which were in full flower with purple and white blossoms.

As he looked further into the gardens, down a path framed by an arbour, he saw the girl standing still.

Pthorn looked to the stoic parents, who simply responded with "go" and gestured in her direction. Their faces continued to remain unemotional and unreadable. Whatever the outcome was, they wanted him to find out for himself.

Pthorn proceeded to walk through the arbour. The flowers smelled sweet in the morning air, and the fresh smell of grass wafted across the field to either side of them. The girl remained completely oblivious to his approach.

Her parents followed him down the path, remaining a few paces behind.

Once he was almost within reaching distance, Pthorn tried coughing to announce himself and followed it up with her name.

"Precil."

Pthorn's worst fear became realised. He had woken the body but not the brain. Mended her heart but not her mind.

Pthorn felt his knees start to fall out from beneath him, and he tried to clutch on to anything near him for support. Unlike the undead in Falanar, who had become violent and insane from the pain and rot, Precil was simply there but not there.

His head began to follow his knees as he swayed before he was quickly brought back by a hand on his shoulder.

"Announcing yourself from behind won't do you any good, son," said her father as he moved to stand in front of the girl. "Didn't anyone tell you that our darling Precil is completely deaf?"

Pthorn immediately felt a rush of relief, almost as powerful as the feeling of dread and regret that he had just felt.

The young girl finally stirred when her father moved into view. The man used his hands, making various gestures, as he spoke aloud to the girl. "The man who saved your life is here to check on you."

Precil turned on the spot and, without sparing a moment, wrapped her arms around him tightly. She only came up to his midsection, but Pthorn could hear her sobbing. Pthorn returned the embrace, feeling his own emotions well up and flow to the surface. He wasn't sure what the complete recipe was, but he was confident it was a mixture of loss, grief, and more than a little bit of relief.

As he moved closer and closer to the girl, he had become more certain that he would have to end one more life that he had doomed.

After a few long moments, the girl moved back, and with her hands allowed to move freely, she made several gestures towards her father.

"She wanted me to tell you how thankful she is. I don't think she knows all of the words yet, but I know she knows she owes her life to you."

"Tell her she owes me nothing except to be careful with that life and enjoy it. When you speak to her of this story, please tell her that her life was returned to her by the Almighty Assier; I was just the witness to the miracle," said Pthorn. He once again wanted to avoid owing anyone anything or gaining any level of infamy.

For the first time and only for a fleeting moment, her father's face betrayed him; it was a brief look of derision and disbelief, but he still relayed Pthorn's message again using the hand gestures. The mayor likely suspected that what happened in that room was not simply a matter of holy prayer.

The little girl nodded and hugged Pthorn again, this time for a much shorter time.

"Would you care for some tea?" offered the mother, "it truly is the least we can do."

"Of course," replied Pthorn, and they all turned back towards the manor. They stopped once again in the private courtyard near the fountain while the mother went inside to fetch the tea.

She returned moments later, and Pthorn realised that by fetching tea, she was more likely bringing a servant. The mayor gestured for them all to sit on the stone benches surrounding the courtyard.

"I don't think we ever introduced ourselves to you, given everything that was going on. My name is Lei, and as I am sure you know, my husband is Mayor Alarn," she said by way of a belated introduction.

"My name is Pthorn," he responded. "I am just a servant of the Almighty who just happened to be passing by, but I am delighted to see Precil in good health."

Mayor Alarn and Lei clearly didn't look like they were buying his story, but they didn't want to challenge it.

A few moments later, one of the white-robed servants arrived with a tray carrying an ornate teapot with three cups and saucers. The servant placed the tray on a small table and poured the tea, carefully distributing the cups in the correct order; it showed a lot about the family that the help would serve the guests first and the mayor last.

"Sweetroot?" The young servant offered, her voice sounding almost as sweet as her offer.

"Please," said Pthorn as he held his cup out. The girl used a spoon to empty a small scoop of pinkish-white powder into the tea and stir it in.

The tea was delicious and unlike anything else he had ever tried. The tea was a mix of strong tartness and almost overpowering sweetness. It left an interesting mouthfeel, almost rough, like a swill of strongwine.

Two observations became clear to Pthorn at that moment; firstly, he was the only one taking sweetroot in his tea, and secondly, what had been a nice mild day seemed to have become uncomfortably warm all of a sudden.

The colours of the world began to become more vivid, twisting and whirling together as his vision moved across the landscape.

Those ungrateful pricks are trying to kill me.

All formality was lost in that moment as he barged his way past the girl and flung open the door. He tried to run, but the turbulent-looking world around him forced his body to ricochet off the hallway walls.

The guards were clearly not expecting his presence, as the front door stood unprotected but closed. Remembering the servants' access, he staggered across the foyer and pulled open the sallyport to make his way into the open air.

The mayor and his wife clearly weren't concerned that he would get far with the poison, as they weren't offering anything in the way of resistance as he made his way across to the stone staircase. They did, however, name him such things as "demon", "blasphemer", and "unholy brigand".

Ungrateful pricks!

The world tumbled as he lost his footing; the sky was replaced by stone, which was in turn replaced by sky once more. Finally, he felt his body come to rest at the foot of the stairs, even if his vision was continuing the fall.

Almost as soon as he came to a stop, he felt something clamp around his ankle and throw him into the air. All he could see was the sky's blue swirling like water through a drain.

Flying, he thought to himself, *I'm flying.*

And then he promptly passed out.

Pthorn was brought back to consciousness as he felt himself become immersed in ice-cold water. Fluorocor had clearly thought it might just be the shock he needed, and it had been right. The world had stopped spinning as violently, but he felt gravely ill. Any mortal person would have likely succumbed to whatever poison had been slipped to him in the tea, but they didn't know he was immortal and didn't count on him being saved by his own personal hydrofluor.

Pthorn fought the muddiness of his thoughts and tried to devise a plan.

"Think, think!" he forced himself. "Had Tom taught him anything that could help?"

"Sporios," he said aloud. "That will be why they mixed it with the sweetroot to cover the flavour."

He knew that with something so potent and taken in such a small volume that any common methods, such as consuming coals to soak up the poison, would not be effective as there was very little toxin that had not already entered his system.

Without a proper antidote, which he neither knew of nor had access to, his body would continue trying to shut down. There was only one option that came to him besides simply laying down in the icy river; he would need to hasten his journey back to the Sect.

49.

Returning to the Sect

Pthorn, fearing that he may end up in an everlasting coma, pulled his toxin-laced body from the stream and threw his leg over the crouching form of Fluorocor.

"Hold on a moment," he said as he grabbed for the reigns. Pthorn leaned forwards and tied himself to the back of the beast. He knew there was a good chance his current state of lucidity may once again pass, and he would find himself unconscious a league above the surface of Azarth.

"Head into the peaks of the Arrats, find the Sect. If I can, I will show you; if not…." Pthorn let himself trail off. He knew there was almost no chance that Fluorocor would be able to find the hidden entrances to the Sect without his help. He would also likely freeze to death if he didn't get changed before they arrived.

Once Pthorn was settled and tied on, Fluorocor took to the air heading east for the Arrats. Thankfully Pthorn, besides passing in and out of consciousness, was managing to maintain enough lucidity to give gentle nudges and directions.

It was a good day's flying before Pthorn recognised the intersection just west of Portsworth that denoted the track to the entrance of the tunnels. Pthorn signalled for them to turn left at the crossroads and pointed toward the hidden path towards the mountain range.

The two made their way towards the mountains.

"It is right there," said Pthorn pointing towards the clearly visible gaping hole in the side of the mountain.

The two alighted the rocky outcrop, which radiated out from the mountain's base just next to the entrance.

The hydrofluor slowly approached the apparently solid wall and stuck its nose against it. Surprisingly to the beast, its head passed effortlessly through the illusion, which startled it a little, causing the hydrofluor to jump backwards.

"Just go!" exclaimed Pthorn as he gave Fluorocor a whack on the side for encouragement, "I am trying not to die here."

Fluorocor seemed to remember the seriousness of their situation and started back into the tunnel in earnest. The tunnels were dark without damp-light torches to guide them, but Pthorn knew the beast's eyesight was almost perfect in near pitch black.

They walked through the seemingly endless tunnels as Pthorn passed back into unconsciousness.

By the time he came too again, the air was freezing; it was the frigid cold that seemed to have awoken him. He had no concept of how long they had been travelling without stopping, but he knew they were approaching the pass.

Fluorocor had come to a stop to allow him to get changed into his warmer clothes. Pthorn just pulled them on over the top of his grey robes before tying himself back onto the beast.

They travelled out into the swirling whiteness of the pass and across the narrow bridge before Pthorn directed Fluorocor into the next entrance. The rest of the tunnel would now be lit by damp-light, and they continued on until they finally reached the Sanctum Sacellum.

Pthorn was unspeakably weak by the time they arrived in the room, and he was met with a very shocked-looking Gular.

Pthorn was just in the process of losing consciousness once more as he choked out the words, "Sporio... poison... farmin' mayor."

Once again, he succumbed to the blackness.

Pthorn opened his eyes and immediately felt the world spin. His stomach immediately followed suit, causing him to heave and vomit. He felt a pail thrust underneath his chin just in time and found the Oracle of Prevail sitting by his bedside.

His head felt like someone had stuffed it with whatever clouds were made of, making it difficult to make sense of his surroundings.

"What hap, urgh..." he said as he followed through with another round of retching.

"Don't speak. Be still," said the Order-Master of Combat. "You were lucky you got here when you did and that Tom was not far behind."

"Not far behind?" he managed to ask without vomiting but cut off any further questioning to keep his mouth closed. He let the rest of the remainder hang unspoken. "Why would Tom be behind?"

Prevail had either not realised the rest of the question or chose to ignore it.

"Tom managed to isolate a partial antidote to the poison. It was enough to keep you out of a coma while it passes through your body. He also gave you a heavy sleeping tonic, which is why you can't keep your eyes open." The mage dabbed Pthorn's forehead to mop up sweat as he spoke.

"I need to see Tom," he said, still unsure what he would say when he eventually saw him.

"Not yet, for now, you rest," he instructed. "I expect you will want to be feeling a whole lot better before you have to explain yourself to your Master."

The Oracle of Prevail was not wrong. Pthorn was going to be in no state to explain, nor defend, his actions or the events that had taken place over the last few span.

"Fluorocor? The dragon?" he asked hopefully.

"Given the finest quarters it could imagine within a mountain," he reassured him. "Although I am certain Tom will also have some words to you about the company you have decided to keep on the road."

Assured that no ill fate had befallen his friend, Pthorn placed his head back down on the sleeping pallet and closed his eyes, wishing the world would stop spinning beneath his eyelids.

After a few long moments, hoping that sleep would take him before the urge to vomit overcame him again, blackness once again enveloped him.

This time when he awoke, the world was still once more, although the blackness persisted through open eyes. He had awoken in the middle of the night, or at least he hoped that was the reason for his blindness.

He swung his legs over the edge of the bed, feeling the cold stone beneath his bare feet. He made his way over to his writing desk and fumbled with a damp-light torch, igniting it and flooding the room with a rising, cool white glow.

He was alone in the room. There was a three-legged stool by his bedside with a cup of water; he wasn't sure how he had avoided kicking it on the way past, but he was grateful for the absence of a throbbing toe.

As he stood in the silence of his room, Pthorn realised that now the nausea had passed; he was feeling more than a little hungry. Famished, in fact.

He didn't know how much time had passed since he had visited the traitorous mayor but was positive that he hadn't eaten anything in days.

Pthorn made his way through the dark corridor until he found the kitchen before raiding the dry store for some plain, dry bread. He knew he could not stomach anything richer in flavour without revisiting the events of earlier in the day.

At first, the food made his stomach feel uneasy before the feeling passed, and it began to settle and relieve the hunger pangs.

Pthorn thought about trying to find Fluorocor but quickly realised that not only could it be anywhere, but any noise he made would also echo within the tunnels and would soon wake everyone up. Once he had eaten enough of the plain bread, he quietly returned to his quarters.

As he pushed the leather door cloth out of the way to enter the room, he realised something he had not seen when he had first awoken. His knapsack lay limp on the floor across the room; it had been relieved of its contents before being placed there.

The vials were nowhere to be seen, but the books he had been carrying were on the writing desk.

One of them was open.

Even without investigating closer, Pthorn knew what was being displayed.

Tom knew what he had done. He was completely certain of it.

His stomach knotted up, not with sickness, but with guilt and worry. He knew that he would not be lying out of this situation.

As he made his way into the room, he set the damp-light torch into its sconce and looked down at the open book. It was as he feared; it was open specifically to the page entitled 'Resurrection'.

Worse still, he found a dry quill lying across the book, its nib clearly pointing towards a single line of text.

Important note: As noted above, this will steal the life from another and transfer it to the corpse. It is recommended to find a willing participant to prevent moral dilemmas.

This Pthorn found the fact it was pointing here to be odd.

Why would he point out this particular line? He thought to himself. He had used his own life force to create the undead, and he had been left entirely unscathed.

He was expecting to receive a grilling over the note about the creation of undead beings if the deceased person was rotting and not fresh. Tom couldn't possibly have known about his successful resurrection of Precil, only the unintentional creation of undead which had overrun the town of Falanar and had become the topic of a continent-wide travel ban.

A horrible thought occurred to him. *Perhaps the situation was even worse than I had imagined.*

He thought back to both of the resurrection rituals that he had performed and even the fiery reversal. The light that he had seen penetrate the room each time had not flowed from him, but from the sky, before flowing into the corpses.

The realisation set in; he had not transferred his own life force. It had been donated by an unwilling participant in the ritual.

But how? he thought to himself, the feeling of guilt and regret causing his hands to shake. He had used his own clothing as a conduit; it was his hat.

A hat which had been a gift, said a voice deep within his subconscious.

Pthorn threw caution to the wind and didn't care whom he woke up. He grabbed the damp-light once more and took off into the tunnel.

He raced down the stone hallway; the thudding sound of his bare feet slapping on the hard stone almost seemed deafening in the silence.

Almost fifty paces along, he located the doorway to Crea's room and pulled the leather door to the side. The space within was dark as pitch, lit only by the damp-light he held within his hand.

She lay peacefully on her sleeping pallet, and Batter sat slumped over at her side.

He stirred as Pthorn entered the room, but Crea remained perfectly still.

"Is she...?" Pthorn asked as Batter's eyes flicked open and tried to adjust to the light at his side.

"Del?" asked Batter. "Is that you?"

Pthorn, remembering who he was here again, lowered the torch by his side to reveal his face. "Is Crea okay?" he repeated hopefully, "I need to know."

"I don't know; no one does. No one can even explain what happened," he said sadly, reaching out to hold her hand. "She just won't wake up."

At least he knew he hadn't killed her…. Yet. That was some small comfort.

Before he could open his mouth to say anything else, Batter asked, "how did you know?"

Del had to think quickly. "Someone left me a note saying she had fallen ill. I just had to see for myself."

Batter seemed satisfied with this answer as he just nodded and returned his attention to the comatose girl.

Del gave him a weak smile and a nod before turning to leave. Crea's room was cast once more into darkness as he made his way back into the hall towards his room.

Sleep did not come easily to him for the remainder of the night. The sheets itched, and the straw within the pallet felt hard and lumpy. He tossed and turned, unable to rid himself of the unease that had recently taken hold of his body.

50.
Facing the Music

el awoke to find that he was not alone in his room. Tom's form loomed over his bed, looking less than impressed.

"What in the name of The Singular were you thinking?" chastised Tom. "Huh? How was it when I told you to collect specimens from across the continent, you think, oh, here's a great idea, let's go and RAISE THE FUCKING DEAD!"

Del opened his mouth to defend himself, but the words just would not come.

The Order-Master of Death turned on his heels to pace across the room and picked up the forbidden tome from Del's writing desk.

"Let's start with this then; where did you get it?" he asked more calmly.

"It was in your classroom; I thought it was a blank book," Del answered honestly. "I found the writing in the back after I picked it up to use it for notes."

"And you didn't think to tell me about it?"

Del shook his head but lowered his gaze to the floor, unable to meet his master's eyes.

"I suppose you are now aware of what you have done to the Creativity-Elect?" Tom asked; Del could see that he was still waving the book around from the corner of his eye.

Del didn't lift his head but nodded silently. He already felt ashamed enough about what he had done without Tom reminding him of every detail.

"You will be lucky if she ever wakes up. Even one blood magic ritual can be enough to kill a normal person; who knows how much life force you drained from her."

"Has anyone ever done anything like this before? Do you know how to help her?" Del asked, finally bringing himself to raise his head to meet Tom's piercing eyes.

"Not for generations, and I can so far find no record of how to bring her out of her coma. We going to keep researching to find out a way."

"We?" Del questioned.

"Oh, I'm sorry, I must have misspoken. You! You will continue researching. I'm not the one who tried killing my friend." Tom wasn't pulling his punches, and if he felt any empathy for Del's situation, he certainly didn't show it.

"I wasn't trying to kill anyone!" Del yelled angrily, no longer willing to be talked down to as a naughty child. "I was trying to save people! I thought it was my life force! I thought…" Del trailed off, unsure of how he was even planning on finishing that sentence.

What had I thought?

Tom let the silence hang between them for several long moments before breaking it with the sound of tearing paper. He scrunched the pages containing the forbidden magic between his hands and then held the ball in front of him.

As Del watched, he saw the paper ball combust; a large puff of flame and smoke rose up through the roof vent while the ash fell to the floor like a gentle flurry of black snow.

"It doesn't matter what you were trying to do, what you thought you were doing, or the fact you thought you had fixed it. In the end, you would have known that magic was forbidden and chose to perform it anyway."

Del thought for a few moments, thinking over what Tom had just said.

"Where were you the day I arrived back in the Sect?" Del asked. "When I woke up the first time, The Order-Master of Combat said that you had arrived *back* shortly after me; where were you?

"I don't think you are in any position to ask about my comings and goings!" said the Order-Master sternly.

"TELL ME!" Del yelled, feeling the heat begin to rise in his face.

He was starting to put the events of the last few span together, and something just wasn't adding up. "Tell me where you have been."

"Travelling, and that is all you need to know," Tom said, dismissing Del altogether.

This did nothing to allay Del's thoughts and suspicions that were starting to knit themselves together.

"I bet that you hire the most comfortable carriage you can find when you travel. Have you done any 'travelling' to Falanar recently? Huh?" Del was done insinuating; now he was moving to flat-out accuse his master.

Tom's few moments of silence were all of the confirmation that Del needed to know exactly who had been sitting in the carriage. What he didn't know was why or what he had been doing there.

"Come on, you can stand there and accuse me. If you are going to dish it, you can take it. What were you doing in Falanar?"

"Observing," he said simply, choosing to continue not to engage in the accusation against him.

"Moogshit!" Del yelled again. "If you were just there to watch me clean up my mess, you wouldn't be avoiding the question. They all said their arrows should have missed her. It was you! You fucking killed her? Did you even know her name?"

Del got to his feet and closed the space between himself and Tom.

"Huh, did you? Her name was Darnalla. I hope you remember that for the rest of your miserable life."

"Del," was all the Order-Master managed to say before he was shoved across the room and into the writing table.

"Now there's a name you can forget. It's Pthorn, and I'll be Assier damned if you think I am going to have any part of this," he shouted as he picked up his knapsack, threw his spare clothes into it, pushed open the leather door flap, and stormed out into the hall; grabbing his hat from the writing table as he passed.

A few days ago, he had seen vibrant swirling colours, yesterday, all he had seen was black, and now all he could see was red. His anger boiled to the surface; he didn't even hang around to find out why. The questions circled around in his head.

Why would Tom kill Darn? What could have possibly been his motivation?

The question remained unanswered, but for now, the only thing he could do was get as far away from the Arrats as possible. First, he would have to find Fluorocor; he hoped that nothing had happened to it. The Order-Masters wouldn't have put it anywhere near the living or teaching quarters if the beast was inside the mountain. Pthorn knew that there were hundreds, if not thousands, of rooms hollowed out within the network of tunnels.

Pthorn ran down the hall and into the Sanctum, turning left and heading towards the teaching rooms. He kept running, pausing only to snatch a damp-light torch from one of the wall sconces.

"Fluorocor!" he yelled as he turned right and kept running. Unexpectedly, he found himself standing outside in the cold and dark. He called out the name of his friend and waited for a few moments before turning and heading back into the tunnels. He tried several tunnels finding either disused rooms or dead ends. He found the main hall again and continued further into the mountain's depths. The light soon came to an end, and he ignited the torch he had stolen earlier to light his way.

Pthorn continued calling out for Fluorocor before he heard a distant noise down, echoing up from the next hallway.

Pthorn redoubled his pace as he ran, finally coming to a heavy door sitting ajar. The latch was still steaming as parts of it dripped and fell to the ground. The room was clearly never made to hold such a beast, and the only reason it was still in the room was that it wanted to be. Fluorocor was waiting for Pthorn to retrieve them.

The Order-Masters hadn't tried to remove the ropes which were fastened around Fluorocor's neck and hind quarters, although now they hung loose. Pthorn retied the ropes quickly and secured his knapsack before leading the way back down through the halls and towards the plateau he had discovered while searching for Fluorocor.

In the centre of the plateau stood The Oracle of Malcontent, his grey robes snapping violently in the wind.

"You just have to believe me that everything I did was for your own good and for the good of the Sect. I was protecting your future." Tom pleaded his case over the wind while trying to block Pthorn's path of escape.

"How could killing her possibly be for the good of the Sect? Just give me one reason!" Pthorn fired back.

Once again, Tom remained unable to provide any tangible reason for his actions.

Pthorn had heard enough; this was not a man to be trusted. He swung his leg over the neck of Fluorocor and held on tight as the hydrofluor kicked off into the ice-cold air of the night.

They set off into the sky before circling back around. They swooped low as Tom began to walk back into the tunnel before the hydrofluor released a stream of acid across the mouth of the opening.

Tom must have seen them coming and tried diving out of the way. Pthorn didn't get a good look, but it didn't look like he had made it away wholly unscathed.

He hadn't explicitly directed Fluorocor to attack. Still, somehow the hydrofluor had sensed his hatred and intent in that moment and carried out the exact actions he had been thinking about.

Pthorn had not been prepared for his flight through the Arrat Range at night and was almost frozen through by the time they reached ground level. They continued flying low until they found a clearing surrounded by dense woodland. It would have to do for shelter until they could set off in earnest the next day.

As they flew, Pthorn tried to develop a plan of what to do next. He couldn't return to the Sect; he was done with that place and Tom in particular.

He thought about all the places in Azarth he could go to. He thought about the Ayefyl Castle back in Kesheir; it was a place he felt drawing him back, but somehow it felt like the wrong time.

The more he thought about what the future held, the more it led him to think about the past. Finally, he decided that his next destination would be his home back in Strauth. He couldn't guess how long he would stay for, he couldn't guess, but Pthorn needed to find something familiar to hold onto.

No love was lost between him and his father when they parted ways; that had been nothing new in his life, but he missed his caring mother. What he would do to be held by her one more time.

With his next destination decided, he returned to letting the feelings driving his departure repeat in his mind.

Betrayal.

Loss.

Anger.

Hate.

Over and over, he let those feelings crash like ocean waves throughout his body before one final concept came to rest firmly in his mind, unable to be shifted.

Revenge.

Epilogue

The Oracle of Beauty | The Sect

He didn't know what he was doing!" That was the excuse she was being fed by that miserable Order-Master.

So why did you let him go through with it? She thought angrily.

She knew that there was more that he wasn't telling her. She could hear the two arguing several doors down the hall but couldn't make out the words.

She knew that it would have been him who equipped the idiotic young man with the knowledge of performing blood magic.

Where else could he have possibly learned how to do it?

The Oracle of Beauty looked down over the still body of her Elect. Her chest rose and fell gently with each breath as though she was sleeping.

She wasn't sleeping, though; her life force had been stolen from her and used in forbidden magic practices.

The young Combat-Elect had brought her back to the Sect in a hired carriage, carrying her all the way from the Portsworth crossroads and into the mountains.

Now that is an Elect to be proud of, she thought.

He had sat by his friend's bedside for an entire span before being told that there was nothing else he could do but continue his travels or study.

His immediate answer was that he should remain by her side, but with that eliminated, he chose to immerse himself in study.

By day he studied and trained with his Master. By night he would sit by her bed and fall asleep with his back against the wall, wishing and hoping for a miracle.

The Order-Masters had all agreed that the source of her attack should remain amongst them for now; Tom had argued that no good would come from creating bad blood between the Elects.

Beauty couldn't have agreed less; she considered the Death-Elect's actions to be heinous and deserved the direst consequences. Ridicule and hatred by his friends were the least of which on the list of these.

It had been several span since her Elect had fallen into the coma, and the Order-Master of Death still claimed that he was no closer to uncovering any sort of antidote or reversal of her loss of life force.

When he returned from his travels, he had immediately set himself to work curing his own Elect, but he was clearly in no rush to help anyone else.

Poisoning was too good for that boy, she thought sourly as she ran her fingers through her Elect's hair; *if only that bloody dragon of his wasn't there to save his sorry arse.*

They had all had a vote on what to do about his little pet too.

She had argued it was far too dangerous, Prevail had asserted that it had a military advantage to keep it around, and Tom had commented about his policy of no pets. It had clearly developed an understanding of the common tongue of Azarth because, at the suggestion of eviction, the beast had taken to spraying some sort of acid at a stack of books, reducing them to a bubbling river of slime.

The beast knew what Tom was capable of but showed no fear, resulting in a stand-off between the two and Tom agreeing to keep it temporarily. At least until his elect regained consciousness and he could convince him to set it free.

The Oracle of Beauty shook her head to clear it of thoughts of anger and disgust at the actions of the Order of Death. Instead, she returned her attention to the young girl lying helpless on the sleeping pallet beside her and began to sing a soft lullaby with the earnest hope that she could hear it and take comfort that people cared.

Fauna Almanac of Azarth (Abridged Pocket Book)

By Avi Brute

<u>Aerial (Ability to Fly)</u>

Luftun

Luftun are flying creatures of various species, which are found all on the inhabited continents of Azarth. Their bodies are covered in fur, including their wings and present in all colours, shapes and sizes. Black, grey and brown luftun are more common on Straulatos and Saulit, with more vibrant colours in Matraketh and Kesheir.

Kesheirian Dragon

The Kesheirian Dragon, as the name suggests, is a native of Kesheir. It is also the dragon of folklore known for being responsible for the death of many brave knights. The Kesheirian Dragon, Common Dragon, or Fire-Breathing Dragon, is capable of producing a very hot jet of flame between two and five-and-twenty paces long. They are competent fliers but don't have much speed on land.

Hydrofluor

The Hydrofluor is a type of size-changing dragon which can spit acid and is native to Matraketh and Kesheir. Their size is dependent on the amount of food they consume. They can unlock their jaws to swallow large portions of food that has been broken down by acid. They have wings, can fly, and are fast runners when required. Their tongue has two sets of razor-sharp teeth attached to the end, which can grab food.

Aquatic
Croaken

Croaken are small amphibious creatures with leathery skin. They are shaped like a large river stone but have two small front legs protruding from the side and two much larger hind legs tucked into the crouching position. Some species also have spines and may be poisonous, venomous or both. Croaken are found in many swampy marshes across Azarth but far less common in Straulatos. This guidebook recommends neither approaching nor consuming a croaken, no matter how hungry you are.

Kraken

Kraken are enormous, tentacled creatures that are known to attack ships and sink them. They have one eye and a massive slimy, black, bulbous head. Those who have seen them and survived report that they smell absolutely terrible, although this is likely not their worst characteristic.

Ghoti

Ghoti is a general term given to the large number of aquatic species which live in the sea. Most are covered in oily fur, and their hides make excellent gloves and cloaks.

<u>Land</u>

With Carapace

Mants

Mants are strong, large, shelled creatures with a hard, black shell that overlaps and moves with the animal. It has a longish neck with a bulbous shelled head and eyes which protrude from the end of black stalks. It has six long spindly legs protruding up from its body and back down to the ground like an oversized insect. Mants are native only to Straulatos.

With Soft Hide

Rarn

Rarn are slender beasts with large two tusks and a long tail. They are just over a pace long and half a pace tall. They are bright orange with a pattern of black lines crisscrossing their entire body. Rarn are known to live primarily in the sub-alpine regions of Matraketh and Saulit.

Kiel

Keil are large, hoofed, four-legged animals that are fast running and wild. They are sometimes hunted for food by good hunters; bad hunters tend to become hungry. They are ordinarily grey in colour but may vary on location. Bucks have black, forked and curled antlers sitting proudly atop their head, ending in razor-sharp tips; in this case, bad hunters tend to become dead.

Onk

Onk are small, slow, brown animals with short fur and hoofed feet. They are common across all continents of Azarth. They are often hunted for food and, in some places, farmed.

Moog

Moog are common farm animals across Azarth. They are large, hoofed, four-legged animals that are very slow. They spend most of their day eating grass and getting fat.

Equestra

Equestra are large, muscley animals with long thick necks and flowing manes. They have long, pointed snouts and massive wings which protrude from their flanks. Equestra are flightless, and their wings often have several colours in their under-wing plumage. Equestra are not native, nor commonly found, on Straulatos.

Baahti

A large, hoofed, four-legged animal that is very slow and covered in thick wool. These animals natively live in the cold, mountainous regions of the neighbouring continent Matraketh but have also been exported as domesticated livestock across the four inhabited continents.

Munkley

Munkleys are cheeky animals that live in the forests of Kesheir and Saulit. Six arms and two tails provide them with all the limbs necessary to swing fluidly between the boughs of a tree canopy. They are also well known for being intelligent, crafty and manipulative.

Squarn/Meena/Rodenians

A Squarn and Meena are small, hand-sized rodents that live in both trees and in underground warrens, depending on the climate and the inclination of the animal. It is difficult to differentiate between these two animals, with the key variation being their snout; squarn have a square snout, and the meena has a pointed snout.

Rodenian refers to a large family of smaller rodents resembling the Squarn and the Meena.

Snoths

A Snoth is a medium-sized, sleek-figured beast with octagonal spots covering its hide. Snoths are most commonly found on Saulit but have been imported and set free around both Matraketh and Kesheir.

Mauw

A Mauw is a very large, furry-maned beast with deep yellow-slitted eyes. Mauw are most commonly found on Saulit but, similar to the Snoth, have been imported and set free around both Matraketh and Kesheir.

Clucken

Aside from being another flightless, winged animal on Azarth, the most important thing to note about the Clucken is that they are exceedingly delicious and easy to farm in cool climates. Like many similarly featured Luften, the Clucken has a short-fur hide, but they are almost as wide as they are tall, resembling a clucking, brown ball.

Insect and Orbitellite

Barg

A Barg is a small, blood-sucking creature which, once it hatches from its shell, attaches itself to the nearest living creature and starts draining it. Its entire life is spent draining its host of life before reproducing. They have two offspring, which grow over a year before hatching. The Barg is a native of Saulit.

Scuriat

A small hard-shelled creature, usually burnt orange or black in colour, depending on the region. They have dark, stalked eyes and have two cardiovascular and nervous systems; left and right. Scuriats are predominantly found in Matraketh but can be located anywhere north of the Equis of Azarth.

Orbite

A small ten-legged creature that builds, and lives in, webs. Found all across Azarth.

Acknowledgements

The first person I would like to acknowledge is you, the reader of this book. You have personally contributed to supporting an indie author by buying or borrowing this book. If you are looking for any other ways to contribute, please leave a review (quick or detailed) on Goodreads, Amazon or any other site. I would also love for you to give me a shout-out on Instagram @athenaeum_of_assierium.

Next, thank you to everyone in my family and friends who have read and provided feedback to me. This is not an exhaustive list but includes my wife, Abbi Wylie, brother Matthew Wylie and his partner Riss Gibson, my father, Chris Wylie and my good mate, Luke Kearney. Additionally, this minor revision also has input from the eagle-eyed Cameron Ryan and Caleb Simmich.

Also, thank you to Deborah Murrell for the feedback on my development edit and for pointing me in the right direction for my self-led copy edit. My sincere apologies if I haven't done it justice and there are still too many wayward commas or semi-colons.

About the Author

Jason Wylie

Jason Wylie is an Australian author who lives in the semi-rural town of Dayboro in Queensland, Australia. Jason is a qualified process and project engineer whose hobbies include writing, reading, fabrication and working on cars in the shed.

Jason has a beautiful wife, Abbi, and two gorgeous children named Aria and Noah.

www.ingramcontent.com/pod-product-compliance
Lightning Source LLC
Chambersburg PA
CBHW030835190726